THE NEW FIVE

Also by Ralph Dennis

The Broken Fixer
Dust in the Heart
The Spy In a Box
A Talent for Killing
Tales of a Sad Fat Wordman
The War Heist

The Hardman Series

Atlanta Deathwatch
The Charleston Knife is Back in Town
The Golden Girl And All
Pimp For The Dead
Down Among The Jocks
Murder Is Not An Odd Job
Working For The Man
The Deadly Cotton Heart
The One Dollar Rip-Off
Hump's First Case
The Last Of The Armageddon Wars
The Buy Back Blues
All Kinds of Ugly

THE NEW FIVE

RALPH DENNIS

CUTTING EDGE

ISBN-13: 978-1-952138-71-3

Published by
Cutting Edge Books
PO Box 8212
Calabasas, CA 91372
www.cuttingedgebooks.com

PUBLISHER'S NOTE

Author Ralph Dennis is best known for his ground-breaking *Hardman* series, thirteen crime novels set in Atlanta in the 1970s. He died in 1988, leaving behind several unpublished manuscripts. *The New Five* is one of those manuscripts.

PART ONE

SEASONS 1978-1979 TO 1981-1982

CHAPTER ONE

Sandersville was a quiet little college town in the mountains of North Carolina. Main Street was four short blocks of mom-and-pop businesses in century-old brick buildings along the northern boundary of Hunt Morgan University. It was not a town where dreams were made, fortunes were won, and legends were born. It was, however, the perfect place to hunker down after failing in those pursuits, which was why Timothy McCarren ended up there.

Growing up in Philadelphia, he'd spent some summers in Sandersville at a cabin that his late grandparents had owned at Loon Lake, a few miles outside of town. Those months of fishing and reading were always a welcome time-out from the real world and gave him a fresh perspective on life.

McCarren definitely needed that now. And he was certain that the man sitting across from him, University President Frank Edwards, was well aware of that.

"Do you always invite strangers that you see walking across the campus into your office for a cup of coffee?" McCarren asked. It was fine coffee, the best he'd had in years. They were sitting in a huge, wood-paneled office with rich, leather furniture and a warm fire burning in the stone fireplace. He'd happily sit here all day.

"It's a snowy morning and you looked cold. I also saw you at the Mountaineers' game last night," Edwards said. He was a portly, gray-haired man in his fifties who proudly wore his weight as if it was a status symbol of wealth and power. On him, it probably was. "I've been seeing you at a lot of our games."

"I like basketball."

"It's more than that, Mr. McCarren. I checked you out," Edwards sat down behind his massive, ornate desk, set aside his coffee mug, and opened a file. McCarren's instincts about Edwards were right. "You played for five years in the NBA with the Royals, then you quit to become an assistant coach with the 76'ers, rising to head coach. After a few years there, you became head coach with the Ironmen, the cocky little expansion team in Pittsburgh. You had a four year contract at $100,000-a-year. But after your first and only season, an impressive one that earned your center Abdul Markham rookie-of-the-year, here you are in Sandersville. I'm curious. What happened?"

"Abdul and I didn't get along." McCarren wasn't going to tell anyone the full story. Abdul had a nose for cocaine. He only wanted to play fifteen minutes a game and make his eighteen or twenty points in that time. That's not how McCarren did things. "I told the owners it was him or me. They chose him. I can't blame them. You can always hire another coach, but you can't find another Abdul Markham."

Even so, the Ironmen were contractually obligated to pay McCarren for three more years. So, he left Pittsburgh, leased a house in Sandersville, and decided to sit out life for a while, or at least until his contract ran out. But it was hard to shut basketball out of his life. So he ended up in the audience at a few Mountaineer basketball games at Hunt Morgan. What he saw was an outmanned team without a conference affiliation. A school that played an independent schedule without the quality players to compete with a South Carolina, a DePaul or a Notre Dame.

"You're pragmatic," Edwards said. "I respect that. I couldn't help noticing how closely you've been watching the play at our games. What do you think of the coaching?"

McCarren wouldn't undercut another basketball coach. It was a part of the ethics of coaching. You spoke no evil of the man in the center chair. Besides, he liked what he'd seen. Coach Jack Turner got the best effort, night after night, from the players he had. The team might not have potential, but Turner did.

"Jack Turner is a fine young coach. You're lucky to have him here."

"His contract expires at the end of the season."

"I hope you renew it."

Edwards waited. The coffee cooled in front of him. It seemed that minutes passed. McCarren looked out the window at the gently falling snow. He had nowhere to go and nothing to do. But Edwards did and gave in first.

"What is said in here should not go beyond that door." Edwards nodded at the closed door that led to the reception room. "To be honest, Mr. McCarren, I have asked you here for your candid, professional advice. If you like, I can put in a voucher and make you a paid advisor."

"That's not necessary. The Ironmen pay me quite well to stay away from Pittsburgh, but I'm sure you already know that."

Edwards nodded. "The trustees have already decided that only a miracle can save Jack Turner's job."

McCarren sipped his coffee and considered his reply. "Have you ever witnessed a race between mules and thoroughbreds?"

Edwards shook his head.

"Yes, you have. Last week's game against DePaul and to a degree, last night's game against Furman. Your mules against their horses. You don't win with mules. You can stay close now and then and if you're lucky you can steal a game. But you don't have a great season with mules."

"I think I understand your image."

"I thought you might," McCarren said.

"How do you change mules into racehorses?"

5

"You don't," McCarren said. "You clean the stable and put the mules to pasture and recruit racehorses."

"How do you do that?"

"Carter gym."

"What about it?"

"I've seen better courts where junior high teams play their games."

Edwards nodded. "It's old."

"And out of date. No blue chip player would consider playing at a school with a gym like Carter."

"And . . .?"

"A dedicated athletic dorm. A place that's first rate all the way. Comfortable rooms. A dining hall. A swimming pool. A game room. All of the perks. It would improve recruitment in all of your sports."

President Edwards buzzed the reception room. The plain secretary returned and refilled their cups.

"And you've got to get your first two or three blue chip basketball players." McCarren waited until the door closed behind the secretary. "You have to have those before you can attract the other blue chippers you need to complete the team."

"How does one recruit a blue chipper?"

"With difficulty. Cheat if you have to."

"Cheat?"

"Buy players on the hoof. So much a pound."

"Could that be done?" President Edwards sipped his coffee and then pursed his mouth in thought.

"It's done all the time."

"But there are rules, aren't there?"

"And ways around the rules," McCarren said.

"Safe ways?"

"Ninety-eight percent safe. A two percent risk is not a bad one."

"Could you build such a program?"

"If I had assurances." McCarren listed them for Edwards. "I'd have to know that I'd have the new gym. A gym that has to seat at least fifteen thousand. A top drawer place all the way. From the dressing rooms to the weight rooms. The athletic dorm. A sizeable recruiting budget." McCarren hesitated for a moment. "And a war chest."

"What's a war chest?"

"Money that would not have to be accounted for in any way."

"I see."

"And the big one. I'd expect to be Athletic Director."

President Edwards shook his head. "We have a tradition. . ."

"I know. That the football coach is the athletic director. But I couldn't build a program with table scraps left over from the football program. Does your football team make money?"

"Usually, they lose.."

"In two years, I could have the Mountaineers in one of the holiday tournaments. Maybe the Cable Car Classic. Or the Sugar Bowl tournament that comes before the game on New Years. That's expenses and a good pay off and, more than that, a way of letting people see how our program is doing. In three years, perhaps a bid to the N.I.T. and the minimal prestige that comes with it."

"I'm not sure I could convince the trustees to make the basketball coach the Athletic Director. We have years of tradition."

"Show them the figures. How much it takes to outfit a single football player. Pads, shoes, helmets, practice uniforms and game uniforms. The scholarship costs. Room and board and multiply that by eighty of ninety. And show them how little profit there is in that. Especially when that team struggles to break even over the season. Compare that to a basketball program. The same scholarship, room and board costs. The cost of basketball uniforms and shoes. And multiply that by fifteen. And tell them that I ought to be able to return a hundred thousand a year to the athletic treasury. More on a good year."

"I'll talk to two or three of the more influential members of the board."

McCarren stood. "I'm not saying that I'd take the job. But no coach worth having would take over a losing program under other circumstances."

President Edwards put out his hand. "I will call you in a day or two."

McCarren nodded. "Thanks for the fine cup of coffee. If nothing else, I hope I've been helpful."

Three days later, McCarren and Frank Edwards stood beside the President's car on the north side, the undeveloped part, of the campus. The single building there was a freak, a yellow brick eyesore. It was narrow and straight up and had at the top, on the third floor, what might be considered a turret, a tower.

Edwards pointed to his right. "There. The new coliseum will be built there." He turned and his arm swept past the single yellow brick building. "The new athletic dorm there."

"Is that a promise?"

"Fund raising had already begun."

McCarren nodded. He lifted a gloved hand and indicated the single building. "And that?"

"Ipsom Hall. A relic. The oldest building on the campus. It's been everything from the administration building to a classroom building. At the moment, it's not being used. It's not old enough to qualify as a national landmark. It'll be demolished and the space used for a parking lot."

"No," McCarren said. "I want it."

"Do you have some purpose in mind?"

McCarren laughed. "Don't you know every Irishman wants his own castle?"

❧ ❧ ❧

The announcement was not to be made for another week. Somehow the rumor first surfaced in the *News and Observer*. After that, there was a phone call from the sports editor of the *Morning Herald* and the *Winston-Salem Journal*. He told each caller that he had no comment. He directed them to President Edwards' office. Later that day Edwards' secretary called to say that the President had invited the press to a conference the next morning and a luncheon to follow.

McCarren drove through the snow-mush streets and parked in visitor parking beside old Carter gym. He tracked snow and water into Coach Turner's office and gave his name to the attractive dark-hair secretary in the outer office. The woman, when she heard his name, did a double take that belonged in an old silent film. She hurried away to find Jack Turner.

Turner rushed in moments later. He wore his sweats, a whistle on a lanyard around his neck and a thin coat of perspiration on his face. He turned in the doorway and waited for the secretary, Ellen Fletcher, to catch up with him.

"Ellen, could you please get us some coffee?" Turner looked at McCarren. "Coffee all right with you?" When McCarren nodded, Turner put out his hand, almost as an afterthought, "Good to see you, Tim. Let's go in here."

The office was a reflection of Jack Turner. Rumpled and messy, with a kind of orderly disorder, as if Jack knew where everything was and didn't want anything moved or dusted. Turner circled his desk and sat down.

"Is it true, Tim?"

"Some of it," McCarren said.

Turner reached into one of the desk drawers and brought out a wadded hand towel. He rubbed it across his face. "I can't say I didn't expect it. The last year of a contract, it can give a man ulcers."

"You've done the best you could under the circumstances."

"What I don't understand is why you'd take the program on. You know as well as I do what our limitations are."

"It'll be different. The new man gets what he wants."

"That's what I thought," Turner said.

"I've told them what I need. I don't get it, that's when I move on."

"I can have my things out of here in a day or two."

McCarren thought about what he knew of Jack Turner. Good small forward at Duke. A straight arrow who married his high school sweetheart. Cheated on her once, the word was, and had the bad luck to be caught at it. Big in the Christian Athletes. Lived like a monk now.

"I don't want you to leave," McCarren said.

"You mean you want me to finish the season?"

"More than that."

"You've lost me, Tim."

"What are you're making now?"

"Twenty-seven," Turner said.

"How'd you like to make fifty thousand a year?"

"You've got to be kidding." Turner shook his head. "Where would that money come from?"

"Your share of the basketball camp."

Turner's mouth dropped open. "What camp?"

"The one we'll start after we've got the new Coliseum to work in."

"Jesus, Tim."

The secretary, Ellen, entered. She placed coffee on the desk. McCarren saw that her eyes were red. He knew she believed that Turner was fired and she probably expected to get the boot as well. McCarren stood.

"Miss," he said to her, "it's not what you think. Don't file for unemployment yet."

There was a wondering look on Ellen's face as she backed out of the office and closed the door behind her.

"What is it you want from me, Tim?"

"You stay on and coach this year. You finish the season while I look around for some blue chippers. Next year I take over as head coach. You stay on as assistant coach." McCarren hesitated. "That damage your ego?"

Turner shook his head. "I'm not against learning under you, Tim."

"You'll take a cut. Five thousand or so."

Turner started to shake his head.

"It's a paper cut. Not a real one. We'll cover it from the war chest. And later from some work you do with me on the television show."

"We don't have a weekly highlights show."

McCarren grinned. "We will."

"What else?"

"You handle the detail work for the basketball camp after we get it started. We undercut the price... say fifty or seventy-five dollars below Carolina or N.C. State. We throw in hiking and paddling a canoe, mountain air and all those healthy things. You handle the business side, registration, setting up the housing. I bring in the guest players and we share the instruction. You share in the profits, say thirty percent of the net."

"You're talking about...?"

"At the start, starting small, we clear maybe fifty thousand. With some luck, if we work our tails off, maybe we rival Carolina. Say right up to a hundred thousand. And don't forget, these camps give us a head start on recruiting. We see the kids when they're fourteen or fifteen. We discover them and love them first. How do you think Dean gets some of his blue chippers?"

Turner wadded the hand towel and tossed it in the air. "You sure of all this?"

"I've got Edwards by the hair on his balls. He's tired of having a loser."

"I'm with you." Turner stood. "I've got a practice going on. I got to tell you that the kids are upset. I might lose a couple. They might transfer."

"Which ones?"

"Wilkins and Cash."

"Can't let it happen this year. We need them. If they want to drop off after the season's over I'll help them pack and buy their bus tickets myself."

"The rest of the year … you'll be helping out?"

"Only if you need me." McCarren stood. "You been to New York and Washington lately?"

"No."

"We ought to go up there so I can introduce you around. Maybe over Christmas. You like the idea?"

"Good with me."

CHAPTER TWO

When school broke for Christmas that year, Coach Turner had led the team to a five-and-five record. There was no Christmas tournament for Hunt Morgan University that year and the players packed their bags and left for home.

The day after classes ended, Timothy McCarren and Jack Turner took a flight from Raleigh-Durham and landed at Kennedy in a drifting snowstorm. They checked in at the Sheraton New Yorker. While Turner unpacked his two-suiter, McCarren got on the phone and called the first body broker on his list. Abe Stein. Good old Abe. The man who knew all the players and the warm bodies in the length and breadth of New York City. They arranged to meet at the Two Dudes Bar and Grill in forty minutes.

It was a shabby bar, a crusty place. Smoked and greased-over framed photos of old, almost forgotten sports figures lined the walls. Old men sat at the bar and looked over their shoulders at Abe Stein and McCarren as they ran together and embraced in the aisle. McCarren backed away from Abe and cocked a finger at Turner. "He's my second, in case this turns into a duel." Then he made the introductions.

Abe led them to a table in the back of the bar. McCarren ordered scotch on the rocks and Turner settled for a mug of draft beer.

Sleepy talk, tired talk. Turner almost dozed in the warmth of the bar, after the time in the cold and wind outside. The old times talk rambled on for what seemed like an hour. How is this guy doing? That one gets over his heart attack? Is Billy still running a book in that candy store in Brooklyn?

Turner shook himself awake when Abe said, "You didn't come all this way to talk about beat-up old men." Abe was huge and round – faced with a belly that hardly fitted under the table. There was a bush of gray hairs in his ears like wire brushes.

"You know about Hunt Morgan? I need a hammer, a big man."

Abe nodded. "I heard you'd got senile." He waved a hand and the bartender brought the cognac bottle and poured at the table.

"And a shooter. At least those two. I'll take a whole team if you've got one hidden away."

"We've got four scholarship places open for next year," Turner said.

"The limit's fifteen." McCarren smiled. "Jack keeps me honest."

"You busy tomorrow afternoon?"

"You got the bodies?"

"I didn't say that. I asked if you were free tomorrow afternoon."

"I'll keep my schedule open," McCarren said.

Abe leaned across the table. "There's a gym in the Bronx. Cardinal Murphy High."

"I know it."

"Be there at four," Abe said.

Another drink. No more talk about players or bodies. McCarren lifted the whole tab. Abe wanted to protest and did until McCarren said, "It's expense account."

Abe said, "Now that's the way to live."

The next day, McCarren and Turned met Edgar Rosato, the other body broker, in the hotel dining room for lunch.

He was tall and thin as a whisper. His face was cratered with the scars of old acne. His suit was bargain basement, off the rack, and his shoes were two hundred dollars at the least.

He slurped as he drank his soup. "I understand that you are looking for a forward, Tim."

"Where'd you hear that, Edgar?"

"I have one hidden away that no one knows about."

"The measurement, Edgar?"

"Six-six and two hundred and ten."

McCarren buttered the end of a breadstick and crunched it. "When can I see him strut?"

"Later this afternoon?"

McCarren shook his head. "Busy."

"Tomorrow morning?"

"Where?"

"The playground on the Avenue, across from the Delux."

McCarren knew the territory. The fenced-in playground across the Avenue from the Delux Deli. "In this weather?"

"The way these kids play they don't even get snowflakes on them."

"Time, Edgar?"

"You'll buy the coffee and the Danish later?"

McCarren nodded.

"Ten in the morning."

McCarren agreed to it. Edgar Rosato pushed his empty soup plate away and waited eagerly for the waitress to bring him his $5.00 deluxe burger. Paid for by McCarren, of course.

It was a dark, cramped high school gym.

"A rat's ass of a gym," McCarren mumbled from their seats on the dirty benches high above the court. It was cold and it smelled of fermented socks and jock straps. Sweat had splattered and dried on the walls like bloodstains.

Abe Stein, in the same rumpled sweater and baggy trousers he'd worn the night before, stood courtside next to a tall black kid with close-cropped hair. The young black man wore a set of sweats that was ragged and faded. His basketball shoes were, however, new and in good shape.

While Abe talked to him, the black turned and looked past him into the stands. His eyes cut here and there until they settled on McCarren. There was the tap-tap of basketballs at the other end of the court where nine other young men, all black but one, warmed up for the game of Ten.

The black youth nodded and stripped the sweat top over his head and tossed it on a floor level bleacher seat. Then he sat down and tugged the elastic ends of the sweat suit bottom over his shoes. He dropped the sweat pants beside the top and stood. He wore a t-shirt top and a pair of gray shorts with a red band down the sides.

"Weight?" McCarren said.

"Two ten," Turner said. "At the most two fifteen. Less than what Abe said. "

"Height?"

"How tall is Abe?"

"Five-eleven."

"The kid's six-eight or nine," Turner said.

"Well-muscled. Room for him to fill out, add another twenty or thirty pounds."

Turner agreed. His arms seemed overlong for his body. With those arms his reach might be equal to that of a six-ten or six-eleven man.

The game of Ten began. First team to score ten goals won, but the team had to win by two. It was really almost a half-court game, until the shooting team missed and the team on defense rebounded and wanted to fast break. A "made" shot and the team that went on offense moved to mid-court and started from there.

In game one of the Tens, the kid they were watching hardly touched the ball at all on offense. He rebounded well and he blocked the shot of one of the guards who tried to drive on him. He screened and fed the guards and the forwards.

His team won.

"What do you think, Jack?"

"Mixed. He hasn't put up anything."

"That's Abe Stein for you. He orchestrates it. This game we'll see what the kid has. Last game was to let us know he can live with team ball."

A short break ended. The second game began. The first time down the court on offense, Abe Stein's kid took a pass on his extended fingertips along the right baseline. He put the ball down on the floor and faked toward the baseline, as if he intended to drive in that direction. Instead, he turned away from the baseline, to his right. A couple of dribbles and he was in the lane. The other center was taller but slower. The ball was in the kid's left hand now as he turned and moved toward the basket. High, up, off his feet, he released the basketball in a soft finger roll.

In.

The next time down, moving without the ball, the tall kid took a step toward the lane and backed away. The pass from the guard was crisp. One bounce and into his hands and it was at almost the right height for the shot. He was twenty feet from the basket when he put up the jump shot.

In.

The third time down on offense, the guard put up a shot from twenty-five feet. It missed. The tall kid moved across the lane at the basket rim level. He timed it right. The moment the ball moved out of the cone, he touched it with his hand, a gentle nudge, and it dropped through the net.

"You impressed, Jack?"

Turner nodded.

"He could be the sledgehammer we need. But we'd have to put some weight and some strength on him."

"He could carry the weight."

At the other end of the court now. On defense. The small forward missed a shot from beyond the foul circle. The big kid took it just below the rim and whipped the basketball to the outlet man. In the fast break, he filled the middle lane. The outlet man's pass went to the forward on the left. The forward made his move toward the basket, drawing the single defender toward him. At the last moment, really an instant too late, the forward one-handed the basketball to the big kid. The big kid caught the ball and handled it. He was past the backboard when he reached back with his right hand and slammed the ball through the rim.

There was a roar from the small crowd at that end of the court. Abe Stein lifted his head toward McCarren and Turner and smiled.

"This a setup?"

"No way," McCarren said, "Not the people playing the kid on defense anyway. Too much macho for that. Wouldn't lay back and let somebody do that to them. But it's a showcase. The boys on the team with him are letting him have his shots this time. He'd do the same for them if a coach was down here scouting one of the other guys on his team." McCarren stood and picked up his topcoat. He wrapped his scarf around his neck. "How does coffee and a danish sound to you?"

"You've seen enough?"

"For now. We need some answers. If the kid is for real why haven't we heard of him? Why's he been hiding away?"

They left the gym and walked down the street, braced against the December wind. They entered a cafe. They'd finished their danish and were on a second cup of coffee when Abe Stein waddled in. He waved at McCarren and stopped at the counter for a coffee and a warm prune danish.

McCarren gestured to the counterman. "That's on my check."

Stein unwrapped himself from a scarf, an overcoat and a tweed cap. He sat down and carefully spread two pats of butter on the surface of the danish. When he lifted his eyes to McCarren, there was a question on his face.

"What's the kid's problem?" McCarren said. "He turn into a werewolf once a month at the full of the moon?"

"Nothing like that. He's a good kid. He's never been in trouble in his life."

"Say I believe that. What gives me the feeling he's being avoided because of some problem or other? Drugs?"

Stein shook his head. "The kid is a basketball junky. Daylight to midnight. He ain't got the time to do anything else."

"Then why don't I see Thompson or Davis here smiling at him? Why am I doing all the smiling?"

"He didn't finish school."

"How close?"

"He dropped out the middle of his junior year." Stein said.

"When was that?"

"Two years ago." Stein cut a wedge of the danish with his fork. He spread it and lifted it toward his mouth. Butter dripped onto his chin.

"Shit," McCarren said. "I knew he was too good to be true."

"You heard of those tests? The ones you can take and get the same as a high school degree?"

"Yeah."

"He could pass one," Stein said.

"You sure?"

"Well, he wouldn't exactly be the one taking the test."

"Very risky." McCarren carried his cup to the counter and had it refilled. When he returned he said, "It might blow up in somebody's face."

Stein chewed for a moment. He shook his head. "I got this college graduate. Same size as Hinson. Looks like his twin brother. He takes the test and who'd know?"

"That's the kid's name? Hinson?"

Stein lowered his eyelids. He didn't answer.

"If he passed that," Jack Turner said, "he'd still have to take the S.A.T.'s."

"That would be in your end of the court," Stein said. "I don't know anything about any S.A.T.'s."

"How much?"

Stein looked shocked. He cut his eyes toward Jack Turner. "In front of him?"

"He's my man. Next year you might be dealing with him."

"Two grand for me."

McCarren nodded.

"Two and a half for the guy takes the test for Hinson."

"All right."

"Say three thousand for the kid. He can't come to no college with his butt peeking out of his jeans."

"The whole nut is fifty-two and five?"

Stein said it was. "Hell, you know me. I'd do the scouting for nothing, especially for a guy like you. But I got expenses. You know what a tank of gas goes for? You know how many miles I log a year? How long it takes to locate a guy like this one? And once I find him I got to keep him in change and basketball shoes. I got to buy him meals. I got to see that ..."

McCarren held up his open palm like a traffic cop. "How long I've known you, Abe? Better than twenty years? You think I need to hear this from you? You know damned well I don't."

"Sometimes I forget," Stein said. "You interested?"

"I'll need to talk to the kid. But, before that, I need to check some of his reflexes. You got some sweats and shoes that'll fit Jack here?"

Stein studied Turner. "He play?"

"Duke six years ago."

"That Jack Turner. I saw you in the Garden."

"Must have been against St. John's."

"Six years is a long time. Hinson'll make him look foolish."

"No harm done," McCarren said.

Jack and Abe left. McCarren remained behind to settle the check. A few minutes later, he passed Abe and Jack rummaging about in the trunk of Abe's old Buick. McCarren entered the gym, this time at the court level. He could see, at the other end of the court, Hinson toweling off his chest with a dirty t-shirt while he talked with a small black kid. McCarren headed in Hinson's direction. The small black kid saw McCarren first. He saw something down the court that interested him and trotted away.

"McCarren." He held out his hand. Hinson looked at the hand for a long time before he gave the hand a slight touch and dropped it. His hand was large enough to make two of McCarren's.

"I remember when you coached pros," Hinson said.

"It wasn't that long ago."

"I was talking about the Six-ers. Not the Ironmen. I never liked that team."

McCarren smiled. "I didn't care much for them either. "

"Had some problem with Abdul?"

"He was making too much money and I wasn't making enough."

"It ain't in my mind to imagine too much money," Hinson said.

"Keep that positive thought." McCarren turned and saw Jack and Abe enter the gym. They stopped at mid-court. There were no women or girls in the place. Jack undressed to his shorts and t-shirts and pulled on the bottom of his sweats. Then he sat on a bleacher seat and put on white cotton socks and a new pair of basketball shoes.

"Who's that?"

"Coach Turner. Works with me. Used to be a pretty fair small forward at Duke. You want to show me some one-on-one? You too tired?"

"I never get tired," Hinson said.

Hinson stood along the baseline, about ten feet from the basket, his back to it. He tap-tapped the ball, dribbling, eyes down, waiting. McCarren had planted himself firmly on the free throw line. He leaned forward and put a hand on Jack's shoulder. Turner was breathing hard, beads of sweat bubbled on Jack's forehead. Strings ran down his nose and chin.

"This time try to force him to the baseline and pin him there. Block him. Deny him the baseline."

"That's easy for you to say." Turner grinned.

"Tired?"

"I was tired yesterday. Today I need a nap." Turner trotted the short distance and placed himself between Hinson and the basket.

"You can't win if you don't put it in there," McCarren said to Hinson.

"Ready?" Hinson looked at McCarren, dribbling.

"Ready," Turner said.

Still dribbling, Hinson backed toward Jack Turner. Turner tried to reach around. He clawed at the ball. At the same time, Turner overplayed him, forcing him toward the end line. Trying to force him there and hold him there with a hip and a knee. There was the bump, bump of flesh. The slow slap-slap of the ball. Turner snaked an arm and tried to hook the ball. Hinson moved it away. Turner pinned Hinson there, denying him the move that would free him for a drive across the lane toward the basket. Seconds passed. There was the hard slap of flesh. Turner grunted. Slowly, slowly, almost inch by inch Hinson edged away from the baseline.

Now, now was the time, McCarren thought. Now he would make the wide, looping turn toward where McCarren stood and move across the lane toward the basket. A move to his right, a movement of Hinson's head and shoulders and Turner went with him, trying to block that path.

Instead, calmly, with all the ease in the world, Hinson wheeled away, toward the baseline again. He drove past Turner, picked up his dribble, and slammed the basketball through the net with a stiff armed stuff.

Turner stood with his hands on his hips. He shook his head. He slouched toward McCarren. As he came he rubbed a place high on the right side of his ribs. "You seen enough?"

"You?"

"On top of that, I think I've got a floating rib or two."

Hinson stood under the basket. Ball on his hip.

"Good move," McCarren said to Hinson. He turned and walked toward Abe Stein. Turner followed him and undressed and put on his street clothes.

"What do you think?"

"It's a deal, Abe, if the kid can pass that high school degree exam."

Stein put out his hand. McCarren took it. Then McCarren waited while Hinson walked the ball down the court toward him.

"We'll be in touch," McCarren said.

Hinson's expression didn't change. "I never heard of that school of yours."

"National champions your senior year."

"The shit you say."

"Final four at least. My word on it. And play the way I tell you and you'll he a high round draft choice by the pros."

Hinson shook his head and looked at the floor.

❖ ❖ ❖

Half of the playground court had been cleared, scraped and dried. That and some space on the other side of the basket.

McCarren stood beside the court, his coat collar up. He stamped his feet and slapped his gloved hands together. They were watching the tall, skinny kid in the blue jogging suit.

Edgar Rosato stood on the far side of the court. He'd waved at McCarren and Turner when they arrived and since then he'd ignored them and put all his attention on his boy.

"Size?" McCarren said.

"Six-four or five."

The kid, on the far side of the court, away from them, put up a flat shot that wished through without hitting any part of the rim.

"Reminds me a little of Albert King."

McCarren pursed his lips. "Notice anything odd?"

"Huh?"

"The kid doesn't move much."

It was true. In the time the two of them at been at the playground, the kid had kept his position fairly well on the far side of the court. It was half court play. After one team scored the other team brought it back to mid-court or if there was a defensive rebound the rebounding team dribbled back to mid-court before they took it back toward the basket. The kid hadn't brought the ball to center court, he hadn't rebounded and he didn't seem to be playing defense.

"Doesn't drive much either," McCarren said.

Also true. All the kid did was put on a shooting clinic. From the corner, from fifteen feet, from twelve feet. Turner realized he'd been so mesmerized by the shots that he hadn't paid any attention to the lack of movement on the kid's part.

"I've seen enough." McCarren pulled his hat down over his eyes. He headed for the gate that led to the street.

Turner followed. "What about Rosato?"

"He knows where we'll be."

A cold wind blew down the street and stirred a cloud of dirt and old newsprint. The Delux Deli was directly across the street. From the distance, the windows looked steamed over. Closer, it was obvious the windows had been soaped as a snow Christmas decoration.

McCarren ordered a poached egg on whole wheat toast and a glass of milk. Turner settled for a mug of steaming coffee. McCarren had finished his egg and was cleaning the plate with a final crust of toast when Edgar Rosato rushed in and got himself a coffee and joined them. He sat across from McCarren and waited. There was a scared smell of sweat about him.

McCarren pushed his plate away. He lifted the half glass of milk that remained and gulped it. "What the fuck do you think you're doing, Edgar? You think I'm some potato eater right off the boat?"

McCarren's harshness stunned Turner. He looked from McCarren to Rosato. The little color that had been in Edgar's face drained away.

"The boy's got a shot. You got to admit that."

"It's a ninety-five foot game. How's he going to get up and down the court? In a wheelchair? You think we're playing wheelchair ball down there?"

"The ankle's not that bad," Rosato said. "It's getting better every day."

The smell of sweat on Rosato was overpowering now. Turner leaned away so that he could breathe. "What's wrong with his ankle?"

"Broke it this summer. Fast break and he made a cut. Ankle couldn't take the weight."

McCarren left them and went to the counter. He stood there while the counterman filled a cup with coffee.

"How was it treated?"

"What do you mean … treated?"

"Did an orthopedic surgeon operate on it? Pins and screws put in?"

Edgar shook his head. "Kid didn't have money for that. A cast and that was all."

McCarren returned to the table. "Why'd you showcase him for me?"

"I thought …" Edgar cut his eyes toward Turner, pleading. "I thought you might like what you saw and take the kid south with you and have one of those … those special doctors work on the ankle and fix it."

McCarren sat down and placed the coffee in front of him. He leaned forward and allowed the steam from the coffee to float over his face. "Not this year. What I take this year has got to pay off right away. Maybe five years from now I could risk it. After I've got the program humming and I have a throwaway."

"It was a thought," Rosato said.

"You wasted my time."

"I've got another for you to look at. His name's Jorge Morgan."

"Jorge?" McCarren pronounced it the way Edgar did. Hor-gay. "What kind of name is that?"

"Cuban mama, American daddy."

"White daddy?"

Edgar nodded.

"Tell me about him."

"Six-two. Big. Might go to two hundred in a year or two with good food."

Turner stood. "Back in a minute." He grabbed his coat and put it on and buttoned it as he left the table.

"Quick?" McCarren asked.

"Lightning in a bottle," Edgar said.

Jack Turner stepped outside and stood on the sidewalk. He backed into the doorway and avoided the wind. Across the street the game had broken up on the open court. The kid in the blue jogging suit was alone in the cleared half of the court. He was shooting baskets by himself. When he moved to retrieve the ball the limp showed. Right ankle, Turner thought, lost about seventy percent mobility. But, God, that shot. It was silk. And now it was wasted. All lost.

Turner returned to the deli. McCarren was at the cash register, settling the bill. Edgar was beside him, laughing now, all buddy-buddy and relaxed. McCarren put his valet away and said, "Let's see if I can still flag a cab."

Turner fell in beside Edgar and followed McCarren outside. On the playground court the kid in the blue jogging suit turned and looked in their direction. He stood there, dribbling the ball slowly in front of him.

"You going to talk to him?" Turner said.

Rosato shook his head. "He knows. It happened before."

McCarren wagged an arm at a passing cab. It swerved and bumped against the curb.

"Get in." McCarren said, "before we freeze."

Turner was last in the cab. Before he ducked his head and stepped in, he saw that the kid was leaning over, rubbing his right ankle.

That summer, a couple of days before the first summer session at Hunt Morgan, Robert Hinson and Jorge Morgan flew in together on the same flight for New York. They registered for basic classes and worked out in old Carter gym with leftovers from Turner's team. Hinson was awesome. Jorge improved as the summer went on. Now and then, passing through the gym, McCarren smiled to himself. Yes, oh, yes. This coming season was the beginning of it.

CHAPTER THREE

When Frank Edwards made a promise he kept it. By late spring, by the time McCarren had signed Robert Hinson and Jorge Morgan to their national letters of intent, Edwards had collected fifteen million dollars for the Coliseum. Seven million of that fifteen was a grant from the Hudson Biddle Foundation of New York City. Hudson Biddle, now in his nineties, had been a three letter man at Princeton before he took over the family fortune and moved the operation to Wall Street. He was a shrewd, cold man. He set up the Hudson Biddle foundation when it became clear to him that he was making more money than he could spend or hide in foreign banks. Each year, even years when the grant proposals were worthless, he gave away at least five million dollars.

The spring President Edwards approached the Foundation, the grants were running far behind expectations. It appealed to the foundation's board that President Edwards wanted to name the new Coliseum after old man Biddle. However, it did not seem dignified to name a gym after a man of such substance. It was suggested by President Edwards that the structure could be named the Hudson Biddle Convocation Center. It had a fine sound, the board agreed.

The other eight million was raised from influential and wealthy supporters of the University. With fifteen million in hand and pledges President Edwards carried his campaign to the North Carolina Trust Company of Charlotte. A sweetheart loan was arranged at sixty percent of prime for another ten million.

Groundbreaking on the Biddle began that June. From his window in the turret, McCarren watched the bulldozers scrape the land. He saw the foundations poured. He peered down at the intricate steel work. All summer, the Ipsom Building shook and vibrated with the noises of construction.

McCarren could not demand that his players attend summer school. Still, the word got out and by the second summer session all the scholarship boys in his program were in town and registered for classes. The team played pickup ball in old Carter gym in the late afternoon, after classes were over and after the gym was emptied of the physical education classes that met there all day.

McCarren worried about the grades of his two new recruits, Robert Hinson and Jorge Morgan. He needn't have worried about Jorge. The Morgan family, in the way of the poor, had a fetish about magazines and books and the value of education and Jorge had an excellent preparation for college. He collected three B's and a C that summer and that, McCarren knew, was with an exhausting social life and only minimal time over the books.

Robert Hinson was his real worry. He or his double had passed the high school equivalency test. Hinson himself had taken the S.A.T.'s and, wonder of wonders, he'd been projected as a C or a C – student. Hinson had a tutor provided by the athletic department. Jorge spent all summer rolling Hinson out of bed and getting him to breakfast and his first class. The first summer session, Hinson received a C and a C-. The second session, two C-'s. Gifts, Jack Turner told McCarren, that were the result of matching the courses and the profs and instructors. On every faculty there were those sports fans Jack called "jock-sniffers." These were teachers who wanted the sports program at Hunt Morgan to succeed. They were capable of bending a grade so that a D became a C without feeling a pang about it. At the other end of the scale were professors like Dr. Raymond Talbert. He relished his belief that all athletes were some form of subhuman life and his treatment of athletes in his classes and his harsh grading of papers and exams were part of a legend on campus. In the time Jack Turner had been at Hunt Morgan, no basketball player had registered for a Talbert class.

The summer passed.

From his turret office, McCarren continued to watch the slow progress on the Coliseum. Completion of the Biddle was still more than a year away. Even uncompleted, the Coliseum was a selling point for the recruiting that McCarren would begin that fill and winter.

Once, passing the window, McCarren looked down and saw two young men standing a short distance from the hull of the Coliseum. It took him a brief time to recognize Jorge Morgan and Robert Hinson. Then he was amazed to see the two young men go into a pantomime of dribbling and shooting, all the shots directed toward the Coliseum.

It warmed him in some odd way, McCarren admitted. It was an insight. He realized that Jorge and Robert looked forward to playing in the new facility.

McCarren considered himself a patient man. He told himself that waiting didn't bother him. High in his turret, he kept a clipboard on his desk. There was a thick sheaf of pages clipped to the board, on each page the printed outline of a basketball court. All day, in his free time, he played a kind of chess game on the court in his mind.

Jorge and Hinson. Jorge at point guard and Hinson at center. That much was set and he would have to live and die with them. He had to give them the experience, temper them, if he lost every game this coming year. He wanted them to know his system for the following year when he brought in another blue chipper or two. Or, failing that, a blue chipper and a junior college transfer.

The rest of the team. Wilkins, the senior captain now, at strong forward. He gave away a lot in weight and strength. He'd have to make it up in hustle.

Pierce, slim and quick and a couple of inches too short for a true small forward. But a shooter and a leaper. Have to go with him until he found a small forward in the six-five or six-six range. A senior. His last year anyway.

Simpson, another point guard. A junior. He was listed at six feet but he was hardly that when he stood on his tiptoes. That was one of the problems. Two point guards. No shooting guard. Might have to make do with Jorge this year as a shooting guard. Damned either way. It would hurt the team not to have Jorge at the point. But he needed outside shooting. And Jorge was a better than adequate shot.

McCarren tried all the combinations on paper. Was Pierce, the small forward, a good enough ball handler to roll him to guard now and then and move Jorge in at small forward? Could Jorge make the transition? From looking for the assist to looking for the shot?

And, after a year of looking for the shot, could Jorge adjust to being the point guard again when McCarren had his shooting guard?

Questions. Lines made with the board strokes of a pen on the outline of the basketball court. A stack of variations. Offense and defense. Drawn and stacked and never looked at again because Timothy McCarren never forgot anything.

The fall semester began. September turned into October, and he hardly noticed the blazing colors of the leaf changes, the golds and the reds. The last week in October he stopped by the old gym to see Jack Turner.

"Pass the word. Jack. Tell the boys I expect them to be in shape. Opening day of practice, I want a mile run at the outdoor track. They do an eight minute mile or they run it until they do. Nobody practices or plays until he complete the mile in eight minutes or less."

When opening day of practice arrived, it was a chill gray afternoon. The team, fourteen young men, met at three-thirty at the track that circled the football field. "Warm up," McCarren said. "I don't want muscle pulls or hamstrings."

After a short time of jogging and stretching the players, dressed in everything from sweat suits to shorts grouped at the starting line.

"Ready?" McCarren looked at Jack Turner. Turner waved the stop watch at him.

"Go."

Jorge Morgan finished the mile first, thick shoulders rolling and slightly bowed legs churning to maintain a distance of about five yards between him and Robert Hinson.

"Time?" McCarren looked at Turner.

"Seven minutes and four seconds."

Eleven more of the players straggled over the finish line. In ones and twos and threes. Until there was only one player left on the track. It was one of the seniors, a small forward named Eddy Dilmore. One of the pretty boys, McCarren told himself. Probably had it out of his fly more than it was zipped in. Black curly hair and the kind of bony face the girls seemed to like. Even after the last of the other runners finished Dilmore was still two hundred yards from the finish line. He wobbled from side to side, hardly making any progress at all.

Jack Turner put the stop watch in front of McCarren. It had already gone past the eight minute mark. "Want me to stop Dilmore?"

McCarren shook his head. Two strides and he was on the track. Dilmore saw him. He staggered forward fifty yards and then another fifty yards. Painful yard after yard until he was about twenty-five yards from the finish line. Dilmore stopped then. He gulped air and swayed from side to side.

"Finish it," McCarren shouted at him.

Dilmore's head snapped up. He stepped forward two steps and almost fell on his face.

"Finish it, you cunt."

A few more steps. Dilmore staggered and fell to his hands and knees.

"Finish it if you've got to crawl," McCarren shouted. "I won't have any quitters on this team."

Dilmore groaned. He got to his feet and wobbled toward the finish line. It seemed to take him a full minute to cover the last twenty yards. He passed McCarren and swayed there until two players caught him under the arms and dragged him from the track to the grass inner field which was where football was played. Dilmore doubled over, dry heaving.

McCarren said, "The rest of you to the gym. Practice in half an hour."

The players who'd finished the run within the time limit left. McCarren nodded at Turner and they walked over and stood in front of Eddy Dilmore.

"Seven in the morning all right with you?" McCarren said.

"Huh?" Dilmore lifted his head. His eyes were almost glazed over.

"You got to run it or you don't practice."

Turner put the stop watch in his pocket. "Seven o'clock?"

"All right, Coach."

Dilmore waited until McCarren and Turner left the field before he fell face forward onto the grass.

The players who'd completed the mile within time sat in a narrow block of seats near mid court of the gym. The student manager had been waiting for him but he said he had been given orders not to bring the ball cart onto court until Coach McCarren told him to. Why, Jorge wanted to know. The student manager could only shake his head.

McCarren walked in, followed by Turner, and stopped at center court. "One thing I insist on and that's conditioning. No player who plays for me ever runs out of gas in the last five minutes and quits. The man who quits lets the team down and I won't have that." McCarren pointed toward the end of the court on his left. "Line up for wind sprints."

When the players were in a line, McCarren walked to the side of the court. "Down running forward and return backing up." He lifted his whistle and blew. The line broke and the faster men jumped ahead. A ragged, bent line reached the baseline at the other end of the court. Then the players retreated, ran backing up until they reached the original starting point. There they stopped, got their breath and waited for the slow men.

McCarren turned it over to Coach Turner. He blew the whistle. Twenty times down forward, twenty times returning backwards. The gym was full of the sound of the slap and squeak of basketball shoes and the groans, the sucking of air.

The twenty each way done. Turner looked at McCarren. "Five more," McCarren said.

Coach Turner blew his whistle. The line of players charged down the court. McCarren walked over and said something to the student manager. The manager left and returned about the time the players had completed the five wind sprints each way. He pushed the ball cart ahead of him.

"Five more," McCarren said.

There were groans from a couple of players. Coach Turner blew the whistle. The young men, yelling, shouting and cursing, charged down the court. McCarren stepped to the ball cart and selected a basketball. He tapped it in a slow dribble while the players completed the five sprints each way.

McCarren looked at the thirteen of them, bent over, pulling their socks up, gulping air. "Didn't think you had those in you, did you?"

Nods. Wheezing for air.

"Who can do five more?"

Jorge Morgan drew in a rasping breath and charged down the court. Robert Hinson mumbled, "Shit, man," and ran after him. Others, unwilling, hating McCarren, joined in.

One player remained on the line, bent over. That was Simpson, the other point guard. "Laps around the court," McCarren said, "until I tell you to stop."

Simpson lifted his head. He pretended he hadn't heard McCarren. He pushed himself down the court after the other players. He barely made the final five wind sprints.

McCarren dribbled slowly into the half court where the players were bunched. "Anybody still want to play basketball?"

"That's why I'm here," Jorge said.

McCarren threw him a hard chest pass. Jorge caught it and laid it over his head into the basket behind him.

Practice continued.

Eddy Dilmore, shamed and crest fallen, completed the mile the following morning in seven and a half minutes. He joined practice that afternoon.

Wind sprints opened and closed every practice session. Coach Turner pitted the players at the same positions against each other. The centers against each other, the guards, the forwards.

When the conditioning wasn't painful, it became a lark. The players outdoing each other.

McCarren moved from the half court, where they'd been working on offensive patterns and defenses, to full court scrimmages. That was good for the wind too, he knew. Players got so involved in the back and forth, the game-like situation, that they didn't seem to realize how hard they were working.

Time was short. They were heading for their opening game against Citadel. A home game for Hunt Morgan. Citadel had no real size but it had some quickness and a couple of shooters. And it was a disciplined team, an outgrowth of the fact the Citadel was a military school.

McCarren wasn't really worried about the Cadets. Not really. But he wanted to make a good showing for his team. He knew he needed to make a good showing.

A few days before the opening game, McCarren heard coughing in the stands. Usually, at his request, observers weren't allowed in Carter gym. Later, after the season was underway, he'd consider relaxing the rule.

He turned and looked into the stands. He saw President Edwards, with a handkerchief pressed to his mouth, seat up high at center court. No wonder security hadn't stopped him. The President went where he wanted to.

McCarren turned practice of over to Turner and walked up the aisle to join President Edwards.

"I hope you don't mind," Edwards said.

"I'm glad you're interested." McCarren sat in the seat to the left of Edwards. On the court level, Coach Turner was working on the mid court trap and jump switching, the first team on defense and the second team on offense. "How do they look?"

"Maybe you'd better tell me," Edwards said.

"We'll compete," McCarren said. "We'll probably split the season. We might have a winning edge by the end of it. I've got two of the players I need."

"Which ones?"

McCarren pointed. "The big one there, under the basket." Even as he spoke, the second string center got the ball in low and tried to power it over Hinson. Hinson went straight up and pushed the shot away. "That's Robert Hinson."

Jorge caught the rejected shot in stride and started the fast break. "And the one with the ball now, Jorge Morgan."

Just past center court, Jorge passed the ball to Simpson and filled the center lane. Just behind them, covering huge lengths of court with his stride, was Hinson. At the lane Simpson tap passed to Morgan. Morgan went up, faking the shot, and slicked the ball over his shoulder to Hinson in the right lane. Hinson slammed the ball through with a force that shook the backboards.

President Edwards nodded. "And next year?"

"I need a power forward, a shooting small forward and a shooting guard."

Edwards lowered his voice. "You haven't mentioned the war chest."

"I'll need twenty-five thousand."

"When?"

"Before Christmas break," McCarren said.

"I'll start collecting it now."

McCarren nodded. He stood.

"I was thinking," Edwards said, "The big schools, Duke and State and Carolina, have squad games to introduce the players to the students. You like that idea?"

"Next year," McCarren said. "There's not much to show the students this year."

Edwards laughed.

McCarren returned to court and took over control of practice again. When he looked into the stands a few minutes later, President Edwards was gone.

❖ ❖ ❖

The pre-game meal before the Citadel game was at five, three hours before tipoff. It consisted of rare or medium rare steak, toast and tea. While the players ate, McCarren and Turner studied the brochure one of the Citadel coaches had furnished them. It was a time for nerves, the way it usually was, and McCarren was amazed at how cool Jorge and Hinson were. The rest of the team, Turner whispered, was sweating birdshot.

In most ways, the Hunt Morgan Mountaineers matched up well with Citadel. In size and weight anyway. Jorge had a two inch advantage over the guard matched against him. Other matchup differences were minimal until they reached the center position. Hinson had three inches and twenty pounds on the Cadets center and with his long arms it might even be a five inch advantage, McCarren thought. Got the work the post. That is where the money is hidden.

It turned out, when the game started, that the Citadel center was tough and more experienced than Hinson was. He'd been an enlisted man for two years and he'd played service ball and he was in his junior year at military school now. That was at least four years of experience that Robert Hinson didn't have.

He banged bodies, his used his hips and shoulders, and he kept Robert Hinson off balance the whole first half of the game. What should have been a Mountaineer plus was wiped away by the Citadel center's aggressive play. That left it to Jorge and the power forward, Wilkins, and they did most of the scoring. At the half the teams left the court with Hunt Morgan up by four points, 44-40.

It was subdued in the Mountaineer dressing room. Robert Hinson stood at the cooler and poured himself a Gatorade and drank it back in one swallow. Jorge, who knew what was going on, chewed on half an orange and shook his head at McCarren.

What Jorge was saying was that it wasn't going right, the game plan was being messed over.

"Coach Turner is going to talk about why they're getting second shots on us," McCarren said. He turned and tapped Robert Hinson on the shoulder. "Let's go take a piss together."

Hinson said, "Coach, I don't have to…" He broke off and followed McCarren into the bathroom.

McCarren went down the row of urinals, flushing each of them. When he turned Robert Hinson was leaning against one of the John stalls. "You nervous tonight, Robert?"

"I was at first. I got over it."

"The Citadel center…"

"His name's Bradford, Coach."

"You introduce yourself?" McCarren's sarcasm was strong and bitter. "You think this is a fucking tea party out there?"

"He's a tough kid," Hinson said.

"What does that make you?"

"Tough ain't my game. Coach."

"It don't matter what you think your game is," McCarren shouted. "Bradford is playing with your balls. He's making you look like you don't even have any balls. And he's making me look stupid because I picked you to build this team around. You get what I'm saying? You understand me?"

"What you want me to do, Coach?" Hinson sounded resigned, hurt.

"I don't want you to do anything. It's what you want to do that matters. But I'll tell you this. Over four years of college you play around a hundred and twenty games. If you don't do something tonight you're going to carry a bad rap. The word'll go around from coach to coach, player to player. They'll say, the Hinson kid is a big one but he doesn't like it when it gets rough. He can be made to back away."

"What do you want me to do, Coach?"

"I'll give you the first five minutes of the second half. If you don't have your balls back by then, if you haven't drawn blood or come close to it, I'll bench you and play Jason the rest of the game,"

Jason was a joke, six-ten and one-ninety and shaped like a toothpick.

McCarren left the toilet area without looking back. He entered the dressing room. Turner had finished his chalk talk. "Rest a bit," McCarren told the team. "Back on the court in ten." He nodded at the student manager. "You keep the time, Buster."

He and Turner left the dressing room. Before the door closed behind them, McCarren saw Hinson standing over Jorge, saying something. Jorge's eyes cut toward the closing door.

Turner stopped at the head of the ramp. "What was that about?"

"What?"

"You know,"

"I told Robert that Citadel center was pissing in his hip pocket."

"How'd he take it?"

"We'll see. I told him I'd give him five minutes. If it doesn't get better I'll bench him."

"You're hard on him his first college game," Turner said.

"During warm-ups, before the second half, you take Jason aside and go over what we expect from him if we have to replace Robert."

"That won't look good."

"It'll look exactly the way I want it to. Like I'm ready to keep my promise to Robert."

"All right." Turner looked away.

The first time the Mountaineers were on offense, the first time down the court, the Citadel center planted himself behind Hinson and tried to deny him a lane toward the basket. The pass from Jorge to Hinson was a bounce pass past the Citadel small forward. Hinson took the pass, dribbled the ball a couple of times and made his move toward the basket. Bradford, the Citadel center, tried to use his hip to block Hinson's path. Hinson banged into him at the same time he looped the ball toward the basket. The ball bounced on the rim for a long moment and then was swatted away by the Citadel big forward. Robert Hinson didn't see what happened to the ball after he shot. As soon as he released the ball, he crashed into the Citadel center. The force of his weight knocked Bradford down. Hinson fell on top of him and one elbow, as if by accident, struck Bradford in the mouth. His right knee moved upward, as if searching for the Citadel center's groin. Bradford said, "What the fuck…?" and pushed at Hinson. Hinson rolled away in time to see the official call the basket good, a goaltending against the Citadel big forward. The trailing official called out, "Number four two, blocking."

Forty-two was Bradford. Hinson went to the free throw line. While he waited for the ball, he looked at Bradford. The Citadel center rubbed at his puffy lower lip. It was split and bleeding.

Hinson made the free throw. He turned and trotted down the court. He Waited for Bradford to set up and then took a position behind him. That was a change. He'd been fronting Bradford the first half. The Citadel point guard saw the change and swung to his right. The pass to Brad ford came in high and Hinson reached over his shoulder and batted the ball away. Wilkins jumped high and touched the ball and diverted it toward Jorge. Jorge was off and running.

The Citadel center swung an arm back, trying to slow Hinson. Hinson whacked the arm away and sprinted down the court after Jorge. Even as he ran, he knew the other center was behind him. One step or one and half steps. He might have pulled away. He didn't. Jorge pushed the ball down the left lane. Pierce, the small forward, was in the center lane of the break. Hinson curled away and took the right lane. Jorge was three steps from the basket when he looked toward Pierce and, beyond him, at Hinson.

Hinson nodded. Jorge picked up his dribble and faked a pass to Pierce. The ball went past him to Hinson. The slam dunk was there for Hinson. He didn't take it. He knew Bradford was that step behind him. Hinson faked going up for the shot and came down. Bradford went for the fake and soared high. Only Hinson wasn't there. He was bent over and Bradford, trying to block the shot, hit his feet on Hinson's back and tumbled head over heels into the front two rows of baseline seating.

"Four two, on his back," the official yelled.

He hadn't got the shot off before the foul call. He stood at the foul line and watched Bradford. Bradford was limping now. And he looked angry.

Hinson made both free throws. As he trotted toward the defensive end of the court he passed the Hunt Morgan bench. The Coach, McCarren, was smiling. <u>Screw you, white man</u>. But he did feel better. If it was true the white boy was trying to make him look like a pussy. If that was true …

The next two or three encounters there was only pushing and shoving. The officials moved around them. "Watch those elbows, men. Watch those elbows."

And then the big one. Hinson was still playing Bradford from the back. He was letting the pass in if he couldn't reach over the Citadel center and swat it away. This time he let Bradford take the pass and turn toward the basket. Hinson pretended to stumble and Bradford got around him and took the step that would free him for the layup. Hinson touched the floor with his hands and seemed to recover. He lunged after Bradford. Bradford was in the air, putting the ball up, when Hinson hammered him. He hit ball and arms and head and shoulders. The ball bounced loose and. Bradford hit the floor with a loud thud.

"Five two, five two," the official said.

Hinson backed away and look his rebounding position beneath the basket. Bradford got to his hands and knees and shook his head from side to side, as if clearing it. He got to his feet and stood there. He was still until he spotted Hinson. Then he shouted. "You black son of a bitch ..." and lunged at Hinson. Hinson ducked a wild swing by Bradford. Then the official was there, helped by the Citadel players. They pulled Bradford away.

The other official blew his whistle shrilly. He let the whistle pop from his mouth. "Official time out."

Hinson moved toward Bradford. He held out his hand. "No hard feeling, huh?"

Bradford looked at the hand and turned away. The crowd, seeing this, hooted and booed.

One official stood at the scorer's table while the other official summoned the two head coaches to a meeting with him. McCarren took his time walking the sidelines. When he reached the scorer's table, he heard the Citadel coach say, "... control that game out there? That black ape is a killer. He's trying to hurt my center." The Citadel coach lifted his head and saw McCarren. "Where'd you get that center, Tim? Out of Attica Prison? Either you do something ..."

McCarren looked away from the Citadel coach. "You want to see me?" he said to the official.

"It's getting out of hand, Tim." the official said.

"You let his man bang on mine in the first half and nobody complained." McCarren looked at the Citadel coach. "I didn't hear you complaining when your center was knocking mine around, Bill."

"I won't have it," the official said. "Not if I have to throw both of them out of the game. You understand?"

The rest of the game was played under control. Bradford seemed tentative and, for the last fifteen minutes, Hinson moved over and around him for scores. By the final buzzer, the Mountaineers were up by twenty and McCarren had played his bench the last four minutes.

The write up in the next afternoon's local paper, The Daily Register, quoted the angry Citadel coach. He complained about cheap shots and rough play.

"That Hinson is a killer," the coach said. "You mark my word. If they let him play the way they did tonight he's going to hurt somebody."

At Thursday's practice, the day after the opening game with Citadel, Jorge came in smiling. He carried the ragged tear from the sports page of the Register. He handed the article to Hinson and said, "Read about yourself, Killer."

The name stuck. Half in fun at first and then for real as Robert Hinson patrolled the baseline and staked his territory around the basket.

The first year under the coaching of Timothy McCarren the Hunt Morgan Mountaineers had a record of 18 and 10. Under other circumstances, if Hunt Morgan had been a well-known basketball school, that record would have been good enough for a trip to the National Invitation Tournament.

McCarren didn't lobby for an invitation. He knew that he didn't have the talent to compete with the established programs yet. If and when he went to the N.I.T., he wanted more from it than an opening round loss.

That Christmas, as they'd done the year before, McCarren and Jack Turner tried New York again to recruit players.

McCarren couldn't find the overpowering big forward he wanted there so they took the shuttle to Washington. He took a long look at a big white forward named Ames Ashley. He wasn't the true blue chipper McCarren wanted but he was better than anyone else he'd seen. It turned out Ames liked skiing and that helped with the recruiting. Ames signed his national letter of intent and attended summer school. That same year, to replace graduating seniors, McCarren recruited Billy Stoddard from Monck's Corners, South Carolina and Tom Alley from Raleigh. It wasn't the good year McCarren had wanted but the program was on the upswing.

CHAPTER FOUR

Early that November, the year Robert Hinson and Jorge Morgan were juniors, whole truckloads of workers swarmed over the Biddle Coliseum and Student Convocation Center. It was time for the finishing touches.

This was Timothy McCarren's third year as head coach and he was smiling to himself. This was the first time he thought he had a team capable of winning big for him.

The Killer was no longer a well-kept secret. *Sports Illustrated* had called and there was talk about some mention of him in the upcoming College Basketball issue. And *Sport* had already written and asked for some action photographs for a college roundup section in the December issue. The Sports Information office had sent *Sport* enough material to write a whole book on Robert Hinson.

The freshmen from a year ago were sophomores now. Stoddard and Ashley and Alley had a year's experience under their basketball shoes.

The new class of freshmen had been on campus all summer, playing the games of Ten with the upperclassmen.

Bo Regis looked like he could be some help at center or big forward and Harold Case, at big forward, would be some help as soon as he recovered fully from a stress fracture of his right foot.

The surprise of the summer was Walter Turk, the shooting guard, McCarren had picked up as an afterthought on the recommendation of a friend who coached in Richmond. Walter Turk was being passed up by most schools because of a knee operation he'd had his senior year in high school. McCarren's old friend, Wilkie, said the knee was ninety percent and, without further injury, it would be a hundred percent by the time the season began in November.

Trusting Wilkie, McCarren drove to Richmond and watched Turk in an all-star game. He was all Wilkie said he was but he was even a better shooter. Now, with the program going, this was the time to take a risk. He talked it over with Jack Turner and they decided to offer the boy a scholarship.

That was the team. Those and the three seniors that were left-overs from the last year when Turner had coached the team by himself. That poor recruiting year.

The practices were hard from day one. Nobody missed the cutoff time on the mile run. All the players reported in better than average shape. McCarren wanted them in even better condition. There were wind sprints before and after practice. And there were full length fast break drills that worked as well as the wind sprints but threw in the intricate patterns that lessened the drudgery.

After two weeks of practice, they held the second annual Green and White game. McCarren split the team as evenly as he could. He coached the team with the Killer on it and Jack Turner got Jorge. The first year they'd charged one dollar admission to the game. This year they charged two. The game was held in old Carter gym. Biddle wouldn't be used until it was dedicated the middle of November.

Seven thousand students, faculty and townspeople showed up for the Green and White game. The way McCarren and Turner coached the game it didn't matter which team won. When the Green team, the Killer's team, took a ten point lead McCarren replaced the Killer with Harold Case. He allowed Bo Regis, the other center, to bring the game within two points before he inserted the Killer again. In the stretch drive the Killer scored two baskets to one for Regis and the Green team won.

The crowd stood and cheered. The players were happy. Everybody had scored, even the seniors.

The next day, McCarren and Turner began to plan the ambush. To gain credibility for his basketball program, McCarren knew that he had to score a major upset over an established power. He began his search for that team as soon as the groundbreaking began on the Biddle. Carolina would have been the natural choice. It was a team that had been ranked in the top ten for years, a team that won twenty-odd games a year for years, a team with an established program and a quality coach. But he couldn't get a game with Carolina. Not this soon anyway. Perhaps in a few years. But, he knew, by then he wouldn't have the element of surprise on his side.

He considered Duke, but Duke was rebuilding and it wouldn't be any great upset if Hunt Morgan defeated them. Wake Forest was considered, but Wake wasn't sure that much a game would be to their advantage. Perhaps in a year or two a game at the Greensboro Coliseum.

That left North Carolina State. State was a risk-taker and McCarren was able to make the guarantee more than generous. As Athletic Director, with President Edward's approval, he offered State sixty percent of the gross of what a full Biddle Coliseum would take in.

"Great of you to help us out," McCarren told the Athletic Director at State. "It won't be something we forget."

Later, after he broke the connection, he added, "And if I have my way you won't forget it for a long time, either."

Part of the summer and all fall, he and Jack Turner studied the game films he'd taped the year before from the ACC Game of the Week telecasts. The won games in one batch, and the lost games in the other, each time looking to see what went wrong and what went right. Weaknesses and strengths. How the opposing teams exploited the weakness or handled the strengths or failed to handle them.

After the Green and White game, McCarren worked with Turner to set up a game plan. For the next week they prepared the team for N.C. State.

Most of team was back so there weren't that many player changes to worry about. State's front line was set. State's center was a junior, six-ten or eleven and he thought of himself as a finesses player. He wasn't a banger like the Killer was. All week the paper wrote about that matchup. The smooth grace against the brute strength.

"A surprise for them there," McCarren said.

State's big scorer was the power forward, a six-seven white kid from Virginia. He had a good shooting touch but he was slow. And he wasn't especially physical.

The small forward was six-five. A shooter but he didn't have the range he liked to think he had. Deadly from twelve to fifteen feet. Beyond that, forget about it and rebound. And he could, McCarren decided, be tempted to shoot beyond his effective range.

The guards were the usual State types. Black and quick and usually from one of the Washington High schools that prided themselves on turning out ballplayers. Most of the time, both guards were recruited as shooters and one of them found his Role changed to that of a point guard. With the background as shooters the guards could be tempted into a long range game of shootout, especially if the big men, the center and the forwards, were shut down.

That was how McCarren approached the game. Man to man. Instead of the Killer matching up with the State center, Bo Regis would. The Killer would move out and cover the big forward, the leading scorer. Jorge would play the point on offense but, on defense, he would move in and play the small forward. Jorge gave up three or four inches to his man. That was dangerous. But Jorge was tough and played sticky and it might work.

That was the key, McCarren and Turner decided. They had to shut down the front line. Give them nothing inside. Make them beat us from twenty feet. Beat us there or don't beat us at all.

McCarren listed his options. If the State center had a good night or a decent night against Bo Regis he would move the Killer on him in the second half and put Bo on the power forward. After letting the State center show his finesse in the first half let him get banged by the Killer a few times and see how much stomach he had for it.

Risks. A handful of risks.

The Biddle Coliseum seated 16,650. A week before the N.C. State game all seats were sold and there were requests for press box seating from most of the major papers in the state and Virginia.

The night of the game, there were sandwiches, soft drinks and coffee for the newspapermen in the press box. From the television platform high above the floor two TV stations filmed parts of the game for the late night news. On the other side of the court, at the preferred level, Hampton Withers filmed the game so there would be highlights for the McCarren Sunday show over WAII, Winston-Salem. The network was expanding this year and the highlight show would be seen in the Durham and Raleigh area on a delayed, nighttime basis.

McCarren had surprised the team with new uniforms. The tops had the V-neck that the Carolina team had made popular. For home, the colors were white with green trim. There were also new warm-ups with hoods. Cheerleaders danced on the sidelines.

After the ribbon-cutting at mid court to dedicate the Biddle, the crowd seemed caught in some kind of mass hysteria. All McCarren hoped was that the team wouldn't lose their cool before the game began.

⚜   ⚜   ⚜

Hub Wilson, the Mountaineer radio network play-by-play announcer, said. "The State center, Byrd, stole the tap."

"He did just that," Ted Eastman, the color man said. "He got up about half a count early."

"Ball's to the State point guard, Stillman. He circles to his right and whips the ball to the big forward, Roster. Foster takes a couple of dribbles and stops."

"You see what I see. Hub?" Eastman said.

"The Killer, Hinson, is on him. It must be only for this time down the court, the result of …"

"I don't think so, Hub. I think we're seeing the first chess move of the game."

"The ball's back to Stillman. He moves to his left. He finds the small forward, Billings. Jorge Morgan's on Billings like a wet postage stamp."

"Jorge looks like a windmill down there," Eastman said.

"Stillman can't get the ball into Billings. He whips the ball across court to Foster. Foster takes the ball at seventeen feet. He goes into his shooting motion. Listen to the crowd. That tells you the Killer blocked the shot."

"That's the strategy, Hub. A bigger and taller and quicker man against their leading scorer. You make my word. If this move works here it is going to be a long year for Foster. Every team State plays will …"

"Stillman recovered the ball. He looks at Foster. The Killer's got a blanket on him. Stillman moves in two steps and shoots. It's off the front rim. Byrd and Regis battle for it. Regis taps it to Jorge Morgan."

"Not a good shot," Eastman said. "Not a patient shot."

The Mountaineers set up at the offensive end of the court. The Killer moved into the low post, the center spot, and Bo Regis moved to big forward. State is in a two-three zone. Two men along the foul circle and three men, the big men along the baseline.

"Morgan passes it to Regis on the left. Regis tap-passes it to Hinson near the basket. Hinson taps it out to Jorge."

"They're setting up a triangle," Eastman said. "They're passing around the left side of the zone until one of the three men in the triangle gets a good shot."

"Morgan into Hinson. Hinson to Regis. The man on Regis, Foster, backed off and fronted Hinson. Regis is free. In two steps and he fires. In. Two points."

"That's one way to break the zone," Eastman said. "This time down let's see if State tries to go at the kid, Regis'."

"You called it, Ted. That's what Coach McCarren gave up when he switched the Killer on Foster. The experience and size of Byrd against the kid, Regis. Stillman to Butters. Butters into Byrd. Byrd wants to do his turn around hook. He puts the ball on the floor. Tom Alley reaches in, helping out, and rakes the ball free. Alley to Jorge. State's back, in that two-three zone again. The Mountaineers set up the triangle on the other side. Jorge to Stoddard. Stoddard to Hinson. Back to Jorge Morgan. One more time. Morgan to Hinson. Hinson to Stoddard. Stoddard turns toward Morgan. Yes, it's a fake. He drops the ball in to Hinson. Hinson's up. A finger roll from about three feet. Two."

At the ten minute mark of the first half, the Mountaineers led 24 to 10. State's big forward, Foster, had two frustration fouls on him, times when he'd pushed and shoved the Killer for position and to give himself a chance for a clear shot.

During each timeout McCarren cautioned the Killer, "Don't shove back. Let him do the fouling." McCarren leaned closer so that only the Killer could hear him. "The last five minutes his ass belongs to you."

The Killer nodded.

On the other side of the scorer's table the State Coach, Jim Rosewall, must have been asking himself what had influenced him and the Athletic Director to accept this game with Hunt Morgan University in the first place. It was the opening game for the Wolf pack and it looked very much like they'd have a record of 0 and 1 when they left and headed back to Raleigh.

At the half, the big forward for State, Foster, had his third foul and was on the bench. The Killer and Bo Regis roamed the lane uncontested. The Killer had 16 points and Regis 10 and the Mountaineers led 45 to 31.

State took a timeout with 5:34 remaining in the game. The Killer wiped his face with a towel. He sipped Gatorade. He had run his point total to 22. Bo Regis had 16. The lead over State was ten points, 74 to 64.

McCarren moved down the bench and leaned over Hinson. "Just for the hell of it, let's run it up to fourteen points. Then he's yours."

"He's got a bad mouth on him," the Killer said. "For what he's been calling me, I think I owe him a lump or two."

"Fourteen points," McCarren reminded him.

On the inbounds play, Jorge moved in front of Butters and slapped the ball away, high and hard toward the Mountaineer offensive end of the court. The Killer was on it in two long strides. Three dribbles and he straight-arm slam ducked the ball.

"Twelve," the Killer said.

When Stillman inbounded the ball, Jorge and Alley trapped Butters against the end of the court, almost in the corner. The ten second time count was going, the time the Wolfpack had to get the ball over mid court. The official's arm moved as he counted it. In desperation, Butters tried to pass the ball over his head toward Stillman. Regis stepped away from his man at center court and tapped the ball toward the Killer. The Killer caught the ball and stood there. He yelled at Bo Regis. Bo loped the few extra steps toward the basket. The Killer grinned and tossed the ball high toward the basket. Bo Regis powered it through the net, just like during the tip drills.

"Fourteen," the Killer said.

On his way down the court to set up on defense, Hinson looked toward the Mountaineer bench. McCarren looked up at the clock. Then he grinned and nodded.

"A really regrettable accident," Hub Wilson said. "No, Jim, we'll stay here another minute or two." Hub was talking to his engineer who wanted to break for commercials.

"I could hear the bone break all the way up here," Eastman said.

"I've got the say something, Ted. This is the third year of the Mountaineer basketball network. All that time we've watched Robert Hinson. He's developed from an awkward kid to a polished player. He's had that nickname the Killer since his first college game Some people might misunderstand it. All it really means is that Robert wants to win and he fights hard to win."

"That's the crowd applauding young Foster as he's helped from the court," Eastman said.

"The new defensive wrinkled Coach McCarren used on the young man overmatched him. But he's a game kid and we wish him the best."

"That's right," Eastman said. "One hundred percent, Hub."

"How do you think it happened, Ted?"

"Maybe we ought to wait for the films, Hub. But what I think the films will show is that Hinson was making his move toward the basket. He got a step on the State center, Byrd. Foster came over to help out. I don't even think Hinson knew the kid was there when he turned. The Killer was going up, putting up that left handed finger roll of his when his right elbow caught Foster on the right cheekbone. From the way Foster and the doctors are treating it, I'd say it's shattered into a hundred pieces."

"Part of the game," Hub said. "Now, Jim, we'll take sixty seconds while the teams go to the benches for a timeout."

The final score was the Mountaineers 94 and the Wolf pack 70.

The Hudson Biddle Coliseum was dedicated and the team, the coaches and most of the Athletic Department administration moved from old Carter gym into new quarters. Coach McCarren remained apart, in his castle at Ipsom Hall.

Foster was operated on the following morning at Memorial Hospital in Chapel Hill. The shattered cheekbone was reconstructed. He never really came back that year. Because he'd only played in one game, the game when he was injured, and the limit was six games before he used up a year of eligibility, he was "reshirted" by N.C. State and returned the following year.

Coach McCarren waited until two days after the operation before he tried to place a call to young Foster. Foster would not accept a call from him.

CHAPTER FIVE

The Mountaineers were 10 and 0 when they flew across country to San Francisco after Christmas. They were 11 and 0 after the opening round win against Santa Clara, the host team.

The second night, in the championship game, Kansas doubled on the Killer, put a man in front of him and behind him, and dared Alley and Stoddard and Regis and Morgan to shoot from twenty feet. The shots didn't fall. After a horrible first half of shooting, the Mountaineers were behind 37 to 30. The score at the final buzzer was 68 to 59 and the mountaineers had lost their first game of the season.

It was a solemn, down team that flew back from San Francisco the next afternoon. The second place trophy was packed away in the student manager's luggage and wasn't on display.

Almost half the season was gone.

McCarren told himself that he wasn't about to let up on his team. He gave them three days to make up for the Christmas vacation they'd missed during the Cable Car Classic. At the first practice after returning, McCarren drove them without mercy and without rest breaks. He and Turner pushed them from the moment they touched the court. Wind sprints at the beginning until they could hardly stagger from baseline to baseline.

"We're not losers," McCarren shouted at them from one side of the court. "You just didn't want to embarrass those pig farmers."

The players saved their breath. There was only the sound of grunting, the slap and squeak of basketball shoes.

Across the court from McCarren, Turner shouted, "You're losers. You're all losers."

"Shut up, Jack," McCarren yelled. "What do you know about it?"

"I know losers when I see them," Turner answered. "I know a bunch of cunts when I see them play."

"'Come on, Jack. Can't you see the boys have their feelings hurt?"

"Dumb, useless losers," Jack shouted. "Screw their feelings. They made us look bad in Frisco."

"That all you're worrying about? How you feel? Think how these poor boys feel. They're the ones got themselves beat."

"Pig farmers with two left feet beat them," Turner said. "Losers. They're all losers."

The ragged line of sprinting players was halfway down the court, near the center jump circle,

"Dumb losers."

At center court, Robert Hinson turned and stopped. He faced Jack Turner.

"I ain't no loser," he bellowed. "I'll kill anybody says I'm a loser." He staggered and righted himself. One arm back, the hand balled into a fist, he ran straight for Coach Turner.

One look at Hinson and Turner wanted to run. He knew he couldn't.

"Do it if you can," he shouted.

"I'll kill you, white ass." Hinson lunged for Turner.

Jack Turner held his ground. He knew he was going to take a hard lick.

"Killer, don't do it." Jorge Morgan grabbed at Hinson's arm and missed it. He was three steps behind the Killer when the rest of the team ran to join him. Jorge put his head down and tackled Hinson when he was barely more than a swing away from Coach Turner. The Killer went down hard and tried to roll away from Jorge. A mass of the players piled on Hinson. It was a writhing, cursing pileup. Ames Ashley, big at six-eight and two hundred and ten pounds, flew out of the pile and landed several feet away. He sat there, dazed, blood running down his chin from a broken nose.

The bodies rocked and moved. Then it was still. Robert Hinson was pinned to the floor. In other circumstances, at other times, it might have taken longer. On this day, he was tired from the wind sprints. As the players got up, only Jorge and Bo Regis held Hinson's arms. The Killer was crying out of anger and frustration. His face was contorted with shame.

McCarren stood over them. "Let him go." There was concern stamped on his flat Irish face. Then he smiled. It was an odd smile, the smile of a priest blessing a child. He leaned forward and held his hand toward Robert Hinson. Hinson used his right hand to wipe the tears away from his face. Then he took Coach McCarren's hand and staggered to his feet. McCarren put an arm around him and turned him, half leading him, toward the ramp that led to the dressing room. "You take a long shower," McCarren said to Hinson.

Head down, still wobbling, Hinson headed for the ramp.

McCarren raised his head toward the roof of the Coliseum. "You see that man? I said <u>man.</u> I'd take him over any five of you cunts."

Hinson walked out of sight, up the ramp. He didn't look back.

"Wind sprints," McCarren yelled.

He ran them until they couldn't walk, until they fell down. Then he left them to Jack Turner and went looking for the Killer.

Robert Hinson had showered and dressed. He saw in the chair in the hallway outside Coach Turner's orifice. He looked at

McCarren with a sheepish smile. "I got this bad temper, Coach. I got to quit the team or apologize to Coach Turner."

"Do that tomorrow," McCarren said evenly. "Just say you're sorry. Nothing fancy. He'll accept it."

McCarren walked away. Hinson got to his feet and followed him. They left the hall and entered the third tier of the Coliseum. The court below them was empty, the lights dimmed. They walked down the steps to the staff entrance away that faced the Ipsom Building. There was a chill to the late afternoon wind.

"Want a beer, Robert?"

"I'm dry."

They climbed the steps to the turret office. His secretary, Ellen, had left for the day. McCarren led Robert through the reception room and into his office. He opened the low refrigerator behind his desk and took out two bottles of Harp. He pried the caps away and passed a bottle to Hinson. He waved him toward a chair.

"What if I told you you were going to make second team All-America this year?"

Hinson grinned. "Am I?"

"That's what you'd say."

"No. Am I?"

"We show well the rest of the year. We make the N.C.A.A's you'll make some honorable mentions and you might make second team on two or three of the lists."

Hinson gulped his beer. "Depends on that, huh?"

McCarren nodded. "And you're going to start making the pro coaches and pro scout's lists of future pro prospects."

"Any coaches I know?"

McCarren smiled. "Some I know."

"This is our year?"

"Maybe, but I don't think so. With luck, with a good draw, we can make a good showing. Next year is our year."

"Why?" Hinson tipped back the bottle and let the last of the foam trickle down his throat.

McCarren reached behind him and got out another bottle of Harp for Hinson. The cap flew high. He passed the Harp to the Killer. "Theold Brown. You know about him?"

"The kid from Society Hill?"

"We get him and one or two more. Then it's our year."

"You sure you've got Brown?"

McCarren nodded. "Unless somebody steals him."

Hinson closed his eyes. "That over at the gym …?"

"Yeah?"

"That an act?"

"I wanted to see if we still had a team and I wanted to see if you were leading it."

"Do we?"

"Yes."

"Am I leading it?"

McCarren nodded and grinned.

The piece on Robert Hinson didn't make *Sports Illustrated* in the basketball issue. The emphasis, instead, was on speedy guards of the year.

The only mention of the Hunt Morgan Mountaineers was in a roundup article on the independents. "The Mountaineers are coached by Timothy McCarren, the gray Irish fox. Could make a breakthrough this year if help is found for Jorge Morgan and Robert (the Killer) Hinson. Worth watching."

By the middle of January, the Mountaineers had a five point win over South Carolina at Columbia and a one point win over Rutgers at Madison Square Garden. The game with Rutgers had been arranged by Frank McGuire as a favor. Frank was an old friend who was now with the Garden. The game was won, with the Mountaineers down one point, on a long inbounds pass from Jorge to the Killer. The Killer slapped it on the glass and through the net as the buzzer sounded.

There was a four point loss to DePaul at the Horizon, a six point win over Yale at New Haven, a two point loss to Clemson at Little john, a ten point victory over Georgia Tech at Atlanta and a twelve point win over Georgia Southern.

McCarren had stacked his schedule so that the last eight games were home games, played at the Hudson Biddle. They were all played in the month of February. Win those eight games, McCarren told himself, and he would have a lock on an at large berth in the N.CA.A's. Lose one and there was still a chance. Lose two and he knew he could forget it until the next year.

The first week of February, there was a two page article on the Killer and the Mountaineers in Sport's Illustrated. It was the lead-in article, placed before the roundup of the previous week's basketball scores.

There was a photo of Robert Hinson making the one-handed tap against Rutgers in the Garden and another of him walking around the Hunt Morgan campus with the snow-covered mountains above him.

It was a hoked-up article. The poor black kid from the north comes south and doesn't know what to expect. The shy kid is drawn out of his shell by Timothy McCarren. The streetwise kid learns to love chitterlings, salt-cured ham and collards. There was a long paragraph on Hinson's running mate, Jorge. The quotes from Jorge, McCarren said, made him sound like the Cisco Kid.

The article also covered the naming of Hinson as the Killer by the Citadel coach. It cited his statistics, almost twenty points a game and over ten rebounds.

The final part of the article was an interview with Timothy McCarren. He talked about the challenge of building a program. In an aside, he credited the former coach, now his co-coach, Jack Turner, with having established a strong foundation. Now, all the program needed was the one or two blue chippers a year to keep the team improving.

And, yes, there was hope for an at-large berth in the N.C.A.A. field in March. "We've played and beaten some of the best of them. N.C. State, Santa Clara, South Carolina, Rutgers…"

Billy's Newsstand downtown sold out their usual allotment of *Sports Illustrated*, the twenty-five copies, in an hour. N.C. News brought in another hundred copies and those lasted less than a day. Basketball was finally big news at Hunt Morgan.

The Mountaineers won seven of their last games on the home stand at the Biddle. The record was 23 and 4 that Sunday morning, that whole day, when McCarren and Turner camped out in Ipsom Hall and waited for the call from the N.C.A.A. selection committee.

In the final polls, out the Tuesday before, the Mountaineers were 19th in the UPI and 20th in the AP.

Without being asked to, Ellen came in that Sunday and manned the outside office. When McCarren looked in the refrigerator, he found foil-wrapped dishes and plastic bowls that turned out to be baked ham and potato salad and coleslaw that she'd prepared the day before. Lunch so they wouldn't have to send out if the waiting took all afternoon.

There was a color TV in the closet of the office. McCarren and Turner watched one of the last of the regular season games broadcast. At halftime, while they had Ellen's picnic lunch, they watched while the first of the N.C.A.A. selections were announced. The top seeds in the four regions and the automatic bids that went with the conference championships. Twenty-eight bids gone and only twenty left.

The phone in the outside office rang at ten after three. Jack Turner leaned forward and turned down the sound on the TV set. McCarren looked at the phone beside his elbow and waited for Ellen to answer it in the outside office.

"It's Harley Williams," Ellen said from the doorway.

"What the hell does…?" Then McCarren remembered that Williams, Commissioner of the Sunbelt Conference, was a member of the selection committee. He lifted the phone. "Hello, Harley."

"A quick question, Tim. How do you feel about a trip to the N.C.A.A.'s this month?"

"You know the answer to that, Harley. We accept."

"We need an official answer from the Athletic Director."

"You're talking to him," McCarren said.

"I forgot," Harley William said. "We're putting you in the Mideast."

"Are we seeded?"

"Not this year. You've got to play an opening round game in Tuscaloosa."

"What trap did you set for me, Harley?"

"Just a second." There was a pause. "St. John's."

"Our little boys against their big boys?"

"Don't try to fool me, Tim. I know better."

"Before I turn you over to my secretary to get the details, how about setting up a game or two with your Sunbelt schools for next year?"

"Talk to me year after next, after that Hinson kid leaves." Williams laughed.

McCarren looked at Ellen. "He'll put on somebody to give you the details. Date and time of the game, where we'll stay in Tuscaloosa."

Ellen glided away from the doorway. McCarren held the phone until he heard her come on the line. Then he replaced the receiver and held out his hand to Jack Turner. "We're in."

"Hot damn."

"We're got three or four days. Got to find out everything we can about St. John's. I'll make a couple of calls as soon as Ellen's off the line."

Turner struggled into his topcoat. "I'll be in my office."

"Practice in an hour," McCarren said.

"Huh?"

McCarren nodded. "Got to get their minds ready." He stepped around Jack Turner. Ellen had finished with the selection people. "Call the second floor. Basketball practice in an hour. Use the campus police to find anybody who's not at the dorm."

"Yes, boss." Ellen began dialing.

"And then find President Edwards for me."

Jack Turner adjusted his scarf. On the way from the office he said, "You're the only one could have done it this fast, Tim."

McCarren patted him on the back and returned to his office. He sat behind his desk and waited. After a couple of minutes, Ellen stopped in the doorway and nodded. "Mrs. Edwards on the line."

"It's a Presidential tea for the seniors," Mrs. Edwards said. "I'm not sure I should…"

"Well," McCarren said, "it's big news and I think he'd rather hear it from me than someone else."

After a minute, President Edwards came on the line. McCarren told him the news.

"Is it certain?"

"The bid's been offered and I've accepted it," McCarren said.

"Hold the phone a minute, Tim."

McCarren had the strong scent of Ellen's perfume in his nostrils as she moved around him and opened the refrigerator. He couldn't hear what President Edwards said but he heard loud cheering and shouting.

"That's the reaction of the seniors here. They're proud as punch, Tim."

"I'm proud too, sir."

Ellen moved around the desk again. She carried a bottle of champagne and two tulip glasses. She placed a couple of paper towels around the bottle and began unwrapping the wire from the cork.

"Can we win, Tim?"

"Yes, sir."

"Any help you need from me?"

"I'd like the pep band there. We won't have many fans in Tuscaloosa and…"

"Done," President Edwards said.

"One other matter. Any of my players at your tea?"

"I think one or two are."

"Tell them practice in an hour," McCarren said.

Ellen removed the wire and tossed it in the trash can. She waited one hand on the cork.

"I'll be going with the team," Edwards said.

"We'd expect that, sir."

"I'll invite a group of our boosters."

"It'll help," McCarren said.

The call ended. Ellen passed the bottle to McCarren and he worked the cork slowly from the heck and placed it aside. He poured two glasses. "Thank you, Ellen."

"If you paid me better, it would have been a better brand," she said.

"Remind me when the season's over."

"I will."

They drank. McCarren didn't like champagne but he approved of the use of it to celebrate a moment like this one. "You want to travel to Tuscaloosa with us?"

There was a lone moment. Finally, Ellen shook her head. "It would be misunderstood."

"How?"

"Too many people think I'm your mistress already, Tim."

McCarren refilled their glasses. "You worried about what people think?"

"Yes." She walked to the doorway and stopped there. "I'll be leaving in a few minutes. Are there any calls you want placed?"

"Do you still have a number for Steve Wold at Worldwide Cable?"

"I think so."

Wold wasn't at the cable network. She found him at his apartment in Philadelphia.

"Steve, you heard the news? Look, I need all the footage I can find on St. John's. Whole games. Two or three at least." He heard the front door close and looked up. Ellen had left.

McCarren sipped the last of the champagne while Steve checked with the sports department to see what was available on St. John's.

Behind him, through the window, he could see a light, snowy mist falling.

CHAPTER SIX

When McCarren entered the Coliseum fifty minutes later, he found the team assembled there. It was a loud celebration, clowning and fun and games. Jack Turner sat in a front row seat with a folder in one hand. He was watching the antics on the court but not reacting to them.

McCarren eased into a chair next to him. "You order this?"

Turner shook his head.

"You could have stopped it."

"I'm still learning," Turner said. "I wanted to see how you'd use this."

McCarren looked at the folder Turner held. "What's that?"

"Early facts on St. John's."

"Run through it for me."

"Not a bad matchup. This center is six-ten ..."

"Six-eleven," McCarren said. "In fact, he's closer to being a true seven footer."

On court, there was a wild yell as Jorge drove the length of the lane and did a three-sixty spin before he dunked the ball.

"Others?"

Turner ran through them, heights, quick or slow, point average and rebounds a game. "Record?"

"Twenty and six. Split with Georgetown. Beat Rutgers by six. Five more than we beat them by. Beat Southern Cal at the Far West Classic."

McCarren stood. "That's enough." McCarren nodded at Turner and waited until Jack blew three shrill blasts on his whistle. He walked to center court and stood there. "You guys enjoying yourselves?"

"Yeah, Coach." There was a chorus of voices.

"I'm glad for you. Savor it now because by next Friday morning you're going to feel as low as snake shit."

The smiles faded. There was complete silence.

"You think I'm kidding you? You remember Rutgers? Remember how proud you were when you beat Rutgers on a shot at the buzzer that the Killer couldn't make ten times out of a hundred? St. John's beat them by ten, going away, no trouble. That bother you? Let me tell you about their center. He's a true seven footer. Two hundred and sixty pounds. Seventeen points a game and over eleven rebounds a game. You want me to run down the rest of the team? Sure, they've got more losses than you have. But they play in the Big East. The Big East might be a notch better than the ACC this year. If you don't believe me, why don't you take off the rest of the week? You can party and celebrate and all the girls can tell you how great you are. We'll meet in Tuscaloosa Thursday night and play the game. That sounds good to you?"

Robert Hinson stepped forward. His hands were down by his sides, in fists. "What do you want, Coach?"

"I want what you want, Robert. Tell me what you want?" There was a bite of sarcasm in McCarren's voice.

"I want to win."

"You do?" McCarren lifted his head and stared at the roof as if he had trouble believing that.

"Yes, Coach."

McCarren waved a hand at the baseline to his left. "Line up. Wind sprints until I tell you to stop. I want to see what you had for lunch."

"Bluefish and a bagel," Hinson said.

"Don't tell me. Show me."

The Killer laughed and set off down the court at a loose, easy lope. Down forward and then returning backwards.

"Steak and eggs," Jorge yelled. He set out after Hinson.

"Show me," McCarren yelled.

"Tuna fish on rye and a beer." Billy Stoddard followed Jorge down the court.

One after another the players shouted out what they'd had for lunch and started their wind sprints. McCarren walked to the side of the court and joined Turner. "Let me have your whistle."

Turner placed the lanyard over McCarren's neck. "You want me to handle this, Tim?"

McCarren shook his head. "Unless you want to help me inspect some half-digested food, I need you over at the Winston-Salem airport. Worldwide Cable, Steve Wold there, is sending me some tapes of St. John's games."

"When do they get there?"

"That's the problem. First available flight."

"That might be half the night," Turner said.

"That's coaching for you."

"I wasn't complaining," Turner said.

"Make it easy for yourself. Check in at the motel at the airport. Have air freight contact you when the tapes arrive."

"That's the idea." Turner nodded. "I'll preview the tapes tonight. You'll sit with me in the morning?"

"Pick a time."

"Eleven."

McCarren nodded. "I might bring Hinson and Jorge with me."

Turner left for the drive to Winston-Salem. McCarren turned and faced the players. "Move it. Move it. What do you think this is, a tea party at the President's house?"

The student manager was at courtside. McCarren waved a hand at him. "Get a couple of mops and a mop bucket with a squeezer on it."

The manager seemed puzzled.

"You heard me, son."

Jorge lost his lunch first. He had the presence of mind to run off the court and vomit on the border between the court and the first row of seats. Jorge leaned there, head down, until the manager arrived with the mops and the bucket.

"See how purified you feel?" McCarren said. "Clean up after yourself."

Jorge smiled and got a mop and went to work on the mess at his feet.

Stoddard was next. Then the Killer.

In the end, all the players, except two, threw up. Those two admitted that they'd slept late and hadn't eaten lunch at all. By the time the cleanup was completed, the student manager was green-faced and sick. At McCarren's order, he took the mop water away and replaced it with fresh water. He mopped the second time those places where the players had been sick.

McCarren sat the players down at one end of the court. "You men serious now?"

Nods. Serious faces.

"Good."

"Get a shower. Back to the training table. No junk food. Practice tomorrow at four."

The players filed from the seats and walked up the ramp to the dressing room.

"Robert. Jorge."

The Killer and Jorge returned and stood in front of McCarren. "We've got some film coming in on St. John today. Coach Turner will pick it apart for us. I want you two to sit in with us at eleven in the morning."

Hinson and Jorge nodded.

"We going to win?"

"I ain't going all that way to lose," Hinson said.

Jorge laughed. "Hear the man."

❧   ❧   ❧

They flew into Tuscaloosa airport on a charter the following Wednesday. A bus carried them to their rooms at the Ramada Inn. Along with the players and coaches, there was a group from the athletic department and the sports information staff. President Edwards and his wife were on the flight, with several members of the board of trustees of the University. Ten remaining seats were made available to important boosters who wanted to attend.

The pep band, enlarged for the game, rode a bus that left the college that morning and would arrive later that night. Spare seats on the charter bus were sold to students.

After he saw that his team was settled in their rooms and he'd arranged for meals, McCarren called the tournament office and scheduled an hour on the court floor that night and another hour the next morning.

The scheduled evening hour was from nine to ten. The St. John's team was leaving the court when Coach Turner led his players, trotting behind him, onto the floor. From a seat high above courtside, McCarren watched the Killer seek out the opposing St. John's center and introduce himself. McCarren smiled as he watched Hinson measure himself against Scarpetti.

The team began warmups. There was nothing to work on. It was mainly a matter of letting the players loosen up muscles after the flight and some shooting drills to see if the lights would be any problem. Light in most gyms across the country seemed to differ to some degree.

He was relaxed, whistling between his teeth, when the writer from the *Times Picayune* eased into a seat next to him. "Bill Meredith," the writer said. "I remember you from the time you were with the Ironmen."

"I didn't know I was there long enough to make an impression."

Meredith grinned. "How do you feel?"

"Like any little backwoods college that brings his little team in to play a powerhouse like the Redmen."

"You going to sit up here?"

"Jack Turner's my co-coach. He knows what I expect."

Meredith lifted the cover on his steno pad. "Casual of you."

"What's been done to get us ready has already been done. It's too late to change anything. You go with what got you this far."

They were running a weave, making layups. Robert Hinson did a stiff armed slam dunk.

"He as tough as they say?"

"Who?"

"The Killer," Meredith said.

"Him?" McCarren laughed. "Look, I want to get the record straight on that. All four of those men he killed attacked him first and he only ate the heart of one of them."

"You're kidding." Meredith's pen scribbled across the steno pad page.

"Of course, I am. Robert Hinson … that's his real name … is as nice a kid as you'd ever want to meet. That's as long as you don't get between the basket and him and you don't try to camp in the lane when he's playing defense."

"I read the article in *Sports Illustrated* …"

"They've got a right to try to hype things and sell magazines. I've know the kid for better than three years. He's had no trouble off the court. He's a fine person and a model student."

Meredith made a few notes. "Your other senior …"

"Jorge. Now, he's the mean one. I caught him pulling wings off flies and made him glue them back on. It took him almost a whole day."

"Tell me how you're going to play the Redmen."

"To tell the truth, I'm worried. This morning I went to our athletic dorm and watched some of my kids pack for the trip. You know what I found? Most of the kids only packed one spare set of underwear. It's like they know they're going to lose tomorrow and go straight home."

Meredith grinned. He wrote it all down. "What did you do about it?"

"Nothing. I figure, if we're lucky and win a game, we can always drop by J.C. Penney's and buy a few shorts and undershirts."

They had their game meal at five the next afternoon, two hours before the tap off. The players were loose, passing around copies of the article that Meredith had done about the team and the interview with McCarren.

"Slick," Jorge said.

"Sheeeeet." Hinson put back his head and hooted.

McCarren sat in the chair to the Killer's right. "I saw you talking to Scarpetti."

Hinson lowered his right eye in a lazy wink. "I begged that big man not to embarrass us in front of the whole world."

"What did he say?"

"He was too busy swallowing the hook and laughing his head off to say anything."

The meal was steak and soft eggs and dry toast and hot tea.

Five minutes into the game, Scarpetti, with the game tied at ten to ten, tried to roll around Robert Hinson. He took the pass, flipped it back to his guard, and then started his roll around the Killer. His hand was up, he was expecting the return pass, when he ran into the muscular inner part of Robert Hinson's right forearm. It struck him on the Adam's apple and he went down like he'd been running across a dark backyard and hit clothesline.

Before the whistle was blown for an injury timeout, the Redman guard put up a shot. The Killer blocked it to midcourt where Jorge took it and drove the lane for an uncontested dunk.

The whistle blew. Scarpetti, gasping for breath and clutching his throat, was helped from the court and into the dressing room. His replacement, a freshman named Art Higgins, wasn't big enough or tough enough to stay with Hinson. At half-time, the Mountaineers led by fifteen points.

Scarpetti returned for the second half. He tried to move back into the mainstream of the game but he was gun-shy. The Killer blocked his shots and out-rebounded him at both ends of the court. During the last five minutes, McCarren cleared the bench and sat down his starters. The victory margin was twelve points.

At the buzzer, McCarren walked past the scorer's table to shake hands with the Redman coach. He was a man McCarren had known for years and they'd coached against each other many times.

The Redman coach hardly touched McCarren's hand. He seemed to push the hand away.

"What happened to my center, Scarpetti…"

"An accident," McCarren said.

"Shit, you say," the Redman coach hissed at him.

What McCarren saw stopped him. One of the big boosters, Frank Sellers, was walking around the dressing room. He was passing out letter-sized envelopes. McCarren saw the open envelope Jorge held. The end of a hundred dollar bill stuck out of it. McCarren turned and faced Turner. "I'll be back in five minutes. I don't want to see any envelopes or money in here when I get back."

When McCarren returned ten minutes later, there was no sign of Sellers, and the only envelope he saw was wadded and stuffed in the trash can. But there were cat grins, from player to player, and he knew that the money had passed hands.

"How many of you want to stay for the second game?"

The vote was for staying. McCarren set a curfew for half past midnight. The student manager passed around supper meal money.

McCarren watched the players file from the dressing room. There was a sick feeling in his stomach. A coach cheated some and he had to know he had control. If he lost control, the whole house of cards could fall down.

Jack Turner stopped beside him. "The damage was done by the time we got here."

"That bastard Sellers. I'd like to break his fat neck."

Passing them, the Killer grinned. "Now, that's what I call a good night."

⚜   ⚜   ⚜

McCarren had his run-in with Frank Sellers the following Thursday in Louisville. Sellers had the bad taste to stage it in the lobby of the hotel where the Mountaineer team was staying for the Mideast Regionals.

McCarren had just left a meeting with Jack Turner and the student manager. He had the schedule set, meal times and workout times, and he was crossing the lobby on the way to a meeting with an old friend, who was on the Mideast Regionals staff. That was when Frank Sellers, big and heavy and with the red face of a man who liked his booze too much, sprang out of an easy chair in the corner of the lobby and stormed toward him.

"I understand that I am not welcome in your dressing room anymore," Sellers said.

"I didn't say that." McCarren looked around the room. He didn't see anyone he knew. The desk clerk was, however, watching them from a distance.

"President Edwards as much as said…"

"Look, Frank." McCarren took his arm and turned him. He lowered his voice. "It's just that I don't want you to pass around money in public …"

Sellers jerked his arm free. "Don't act so lily pure with me, Coach. I know what has been—"

McCarren interrupted him. "This isn't the time or the place to have this kind of talk." McCarren took a deep breath to steady himself. He swallowed some anger and kept his voice at a whisper. "I can't have anybody passing cash in public. If a newspaper writer had seen it …"

"What I did is nothing compared to the way you …"

McCarren realized that being reasonable wasn't meant to work with Sellers. "Call me tonight, Frank, after the workout, and we'll have a drink. We'll talk then." He turned his back on Sellers and headed for the lounge entrance.

A huge hand caught his arm and whirled him around. "Don't turn your back on me, you son of a bitch."

McCarren pushed Sellers hand away, "Call me. That's my final offer."

Sellers drew back his right arm and swung at McCarren with his open hand. McCarren caught the hand and squeezed the fingers together. His grip was hard and he saw the pain on the man's face and the beginning of a few drops of perspiration on his forehead. "Call me." He released Seller's crushed hand and stepped away.

He entered the hotel lounge. His friend, Grant Swartz, hadn't arrived yet. He got change at the bar and used the phone in the pay booth to call President Edwards room. Edwards listened to McCarren's account of the incident in the hotel lobby.

"I'll handle it, Timothy."

"I'd appreciate it. I've got enough to worry about with San Jose State tomorrow night. I can't worry about Sellers too."

"I'll talk to him this afternoon."

"See you at the workout?"

"I wouldn't miss it," President Edwards said.

He stayed with the workout the way he'd handled it before the St. John's game. He sat in the stands and let Jack Turner put the team through the drills. He was alone. There wasn't a newspaperman in the stands. The press conference had been held after a dinner earlier that evening so the sports writers could make the morning deadlines with no trouble and have time left for serious drinking and partying,

"Mind if we join you, Timothy?" It was President Edward's voice.

McCarren looked over his shoulder. Sellers was with President Edwards. "Sit down."

"I want to settle this," Edwards said. "Frank understands now what your concern is."

"Sure." Sellers gave him a sheepish smile. "I don't want to do anything to hurt Mountaineer basketball. Hell, I love basketball."

"I'm glad you're backing us." McCarren put out his hand and Sellers took it. His eyes looked into the big man's face and he realized there was a residue of anger left in Sellers, a hard edge that hadn't been softened by all the persuasion that President Edwards could muster.

"See how easy it is to work this out?" Edwards said.

"If I want to make gifts …"

McCarren looked from Sellers to Edwards. "It's better to funnel any giving through the President here. Look, we know the N.C.A.A. rules are unrealistic. If a kid comes to school on an academic scholarship he's got all expenses and spending money, walking-around money. The N.C.A.A. rules say an athlete isn't supposed to have two dollars to rub together in his pocket. That's dumb. But that's the regulation and we've got to seem to comply with it."

There was a loud shout on the court. The Killer, in the layup drill, did a behind his back, over his head two-handed dunk. Edwards and Sellers laughed and applauded.

"What I don't want is an investigation. The program can't stand it at this point in time. If any cash is handed around, it's got to be done with care."

"I think Frank understands now," President Edwards said.

"One hundred percent." Sellers nodded.

Edwards stood. Sellers got to his feet and weaved slightly. McCarren thought he could smell booze oozing from Sellers' pores. "Well," Edwards said, "we'll leave you to your work. We going to win tomorrow?"

"Bank on it," McCarren said.

Edwards and Sellers left. McCarren stared down at the court. There was, he thought, always one turd in the free soup.

CHAPTER SEVEN

Until three days before the game, San Jose State seemed the worst possible draw the Mountaineers could have encountered. Or, at least, the second worst draw behind the number one seeded team in the Mideast Regionals, Louisville. San Jose State had been given the second seed and hadn't been forced to play an opening round game the way the Mountaineers were.

San Jose State had a power forward that McCarren knew his team couldn't match up with. He and Turner had talked about switching the Killer as they'd done earlier in the season against N.C. State. It had worked then. McCarren wasn't sure he'd get the same result against Henderson, the San Jose State power forward. Sure, he believed that Hinson could play Henderson to a standstill, at least a draw. The problem was the San Jose center. If McCarren put Hinson on Henderson, then it left Bo Regis on the San Jose center, Templeton. Templeton was just too quick and too big for Regis.

Three days before the game between San Jose and the Mountaineers, the power forward, Henderson, during a workout, came down on the side of his foot and sprained his ankle. It was a bad sprain, the kind that didn't heal for weeks. Sometimes, it took months for the damage to be repaired. Henderson, according to his coach, still intended to play but the coach had doubts about how effective he would be.

It was all McCarren could do not to break into a grin at the press conference. "Of course, I'm sorry Henderson is not at full strength," McCarren said. "When you play a good team like San Jose State, you want to play them at their best."

The San Jose coach agreed. "Why, it would be like us playing them without the Killer being available." The San Jose coach gave McCarren a wry grin. "How is the Killer's ankle anyway, Coach?"

"One hundred percent," McCarren said, "and he's locked away in a Brink's truck until game time."

It brought down the house. Laughter swirled around McCarren like a strong wind.

McCarren sat on the bench and watched Henderson, all six-eight and two hundred and thirty pounds of him, limp around during the warmups before the game. He didn't seem to want to put weight on that right ankle. He moved with caution. But it wasn't until the game began that McCarren knew that he could discount Henderson altogether.

Two minutes into the game Jorge led a fast break that took the ball down the gut of the lane. The Killer filled the three man pattern on the right side. Hinson took the pass from Jorge and went up for the basket. Henderson was directly in the Killer's path and he was in position to take the charge. Instead, Henderson fell away, beyond the baseline, and let the Killer have the basket. During the next timeout, the San Jose coach removed Henderson and replaced him with a small forward.

McCarren could almost see Ames Ashley lick his lips when he saw the small forward. The next three times down the court on offense, Jorge fed Ames Ashley and he took the ball straight at the small forward who'd replaced Henderson. At halftime, Ashley had ten points and the replacement had three fouls on him. The San Jose coach tried to shift his defense to help out with Ashley and Jorge directed the ball toward the Killer. By the final buzzer, the Killer had eighteen points, five blocked shots and ten rebounds. The Mountaineers had won by twenty-two points.

McCarren met the San Jose coach in front of the scorer's table for the obligatory handshake. The San Jose coach put an arm around McCarren and walked a few steps with him. "Jesus, Tim, where have you been hiding this team?"

"In the mountains," McCarren said.

While the team showered and dressed, McCarren washed his face and changed his undershirt and shirt. He returned to the court where he was met by the television production assistant. On court, the two teams that would play to see which team met the Mountaineers on Sunday were warming up. McCarren hadn't seen either team, the University of New Orleans or the at-large team from the Midwest, Creighton, and he was impatient to join Turner so they could scout the teams during the game. But, first, there was the interview to do.

While a commercial ran, McCarren was fitted with a lapel mike and placed in front of a banner that proclaimed the Mideast Regionals.

When the floor director wagged a finger at the interviewer, and the red light flashed on, the color man asked McCarren about his game with San Jose State.

"It wasn't pretty," McCarren admitted. "It was butcher's work. Without Henderson, they just couldn't match up with us at big forward."

"A lot of the talk around Louisville during the last day or two has been about your center, Robert Hinson. He has a reputation as a rough player. Would you say that reputation is deserved, Coach?"

"Absolutely not. I challenge anybody to look at the game films tonight and show me one rough play that Robert Hinson instigated."

"The Redman coach, last week…"

McCarren interrupted him. "We all say things in the heat of the moment that we wouldn't want to repeat the next day. For the record, I want to say that it hurts a nice kid like Robert to read junk like that about him. Robert plays hard. He wants to win and that's all it is to it."

Even as he talked, McCarren saw Jack Turner lead his players to the seats that were reserved for them. The Mountaineers were dressed in their travel clothes, the dark green blazers and the pale tan trousers. They looked like choir boys.

"How do you see the second game, Coach?"

McCarren smiled. "Well, that's why I'm here rather than being back in the hotel. My co-coach, Jack Turner, and I want to see which of these powerhouses our poor little country team has to play on Sunday."

The color man wished him luck on Sunday.

"We'll need it," McCarren said.

McCarren sat between Jorge and Robert Hinson. As the game moved into the second half, it became obvious that the University of New Orleans would win.

McCarren leaned toward the Killer. "Take a minute and watch the New Orleans center. Tell me what you see."

It was three times down the court on offense before Robert answered him. "He's one-handed. He wants to move across the lane with that dipshit half hook of his. He's got no move along the baseline."

McCarren nodded. "How do we play him?"

"Jam him down the baseline and give him the shot he doesn't want."

McCarren patted the Killer on the shoulder. "Good man." He grinned. "While you were showering, I had me an interview on national television."

"Is that right?"

"From what the man said, you're getting a bad reputation, Robert. I told the whole world that you're a choir boy."

"Yes, indeed," the Killer said.

Something funny happened on the way to the finals of the Mideast Regionals. Louisville won its first game and then ran into a Western Arkansas Wildcat team that clawed at them from the opening buzzer to the final buzzer and beat them by one point on a shot from thirty feet out.

The Mountaineers, with Robert Hinson ramming and jamming and shoving the New Orleans center out of his game and his rhythm, won their semi-final game by eight points.

It set up what was billed, in the newspapers, as the battle of the unknowns. It was also called "the upset regionals." That was because in the West, the Midwest and the East the games and the results went pretty well as predicted.

My fault, my fault, McCarren would mumble to himself over the next few months. He'd been thinking ahead, thinking of the finals the allowing weekend in Los Angeles. He knew he had the better team and that nobody on the Western Arkansas team could match up with the Killer and Jorge.

The game began and he suddenly noticed something he hadn't seen before. The speed, the sheer speed of the Western Arkansas team, was astounding. The Wildcat guards and forwards seemed to glide about the court on afterburners while his players appeared caught in some kind of strange slow motion.

If he'd been fair to himself, he might have found plausible excuses for the lapse in his planning. After all, the difference in team speed between Western Arkansas and Louisville hadn't been apparent. That meant he'd misjudged Louisville's speed and quickness as well.

It was a testament to the Mountaineer desire that they stayed with the Wildcats most of the way. They were only down by three points at the half. With eleven minutes to go and the Western Arkansas team spurting to a margin of ten, the Mountaineers cut it to six with six minutes to go. Then four on a breakaway slam by the Killer. That slam dunk by the Killer was the last shout before the whimper. Western Arkansas ran it back to ten points.

At the final buzzer, he knew he'd lost and he didn't bother to look at the clock over the court. He ducked his head and led the team from the court into the dressing room. He locked the door and moved from player to player, soft-voiced, telling them they had nothing to be ashamed of, that they were to hold their heads high and proud. The Killer and Jorge sat side by side on a bench. Both of them looked like they wanted to cry but damned if they would.

There was pounding at the door. The N.C.A.A. officials warned McCarren that he had already exceeded the specified time and that he was expected at the post-game interview.

"One more minute," McCarren yelled. Then he turned and put his back to the door. "Nobody gave us a show flake's chance in hell of getting this far. Screw what anybody else thinks."

He unlocked the door and went to face the press.

"The wheels came off the Red Flyer," he said in answer to the first question.

"What happened to the wheels?" This question was from the same sports writer, a man from one of the Arkansas papers who wanted a good quote from the losing coach.

"Western Arkansas has the fastest wheels I've ever seen." McCarren blinked into the harsh lights and slowly shook his head. "It was like jets racing against prop planes."

"What hurt your team the most?"

"The small forward, Fitch, and the shooting guard, Ballard. We didn't have the speed to stay with them."

"Tell us about the centers."

"I thought you saw the game." McCarren gave him his Irish smile to soften the remark. "Mine was more physical. Their man, Shippers, might have had half, a step on the Killer in quickness. Call it a draw." The interview ended a few questions later.

McCarren stood back in the darkness, away from the lights, and watched the Western Arkansas coach run through his tricks and jumps. Near the end, he had nice things to say about the Killer and Jorge Morgan. That was as it should have been and McCarren nodded to himself.

That night at the hotel, Hinson and Jorge and Coach Turner had their meeting. Later, they invited the other players they could find on the floor. It wasn't sad, there were no tears, and they swore they'd be back at the tournament the following year.

Back at Hunt Morgan the next afternoon, during a light snow storm, the bus dropped the players at the front steps of the Biddle. Fifteen thousand students and faculty and townspeople waited there for them. It was a hero's welcome. McCarren said his few words. He praised the team for their desire and dedication and then he left for his office in Ipsom Hall. It was, he believed, a moment that belonged to the players and he didn't want to remain there and upstage them.

McCarren watched from the turret window. A microphone had been prepared and each of the players had his few words to say. McCarren got a Harp from the refrigerator behind his desk and sipped it and watched the snow fall and caught a few words and phrases and nodded to himself. It was a beginning. He was ahead of the schedule he'd prepared deep inside him. That was the comfort. His only comfort.

He clicked on the lamp over his desk. It was then he saw the pad on the blotter.

Call me.
Ellen

"I wasn't sure you'd want to talk to a loser," he said.

"Don't be foolish." Her voice was even and steady.

"Am I being foolish?"

"Yes."

"Then I'll stop." He tore the top sheet from the pad and folded it and placed it in the center desk drawer and locked it there. "I thought you might want to have dinner with me tonight."

"I would."

"Not here in town," McCarren said. "Perhaps in Winston-Salem."

"Why not here in town?"

"I feel like Floyd Patterson always felt after he got beaten in the ring: I want to put on a wig and a mustache and become someone else."

There was a hesitation. He thought he could hear the soft rush of her breath. "I could fix dinner here, Tim."

"I like that."

"What?"

"That you called me Tim."

"Eight o'clock?"

He said that eight was fine.

He stood beside the window in her kitchen while she filled the dishwasher and switched it on. There was a glass of a soft Muscadet in his hand and he watched the snow fall beyond the panes and he studied her movements as she stored away the left-overs from the dinner. Broiled lobster tails, a rice dish with a faint hint of curry to it, a tossed salad and sourdough bread she'd baked fresh from a starter crock in her refrigerator. Click, click, click. The plastic covers of the storage dishes snapping into place.

Ellen brought the bottle of wine to him and he filled her empty glass and topped his. There were dark shadows in her hair and he lifted his hand and dropped it to his side. The urge was in him to touch her hair but he put it aside.

"Are you really down tonight, Tim?"

"I don't know. I was. I'm not sure now."

"You know how to say all the right things."

"It's truth," he said.

"I have clean sheets on the bed, Tim."

He almost dropped the wine glass. She walked away from him and stopped beside the light switch on the wall beside the door that led to the living room. "Bring the wine."

In the week that followed the loss to Western Arkansas, McCarren intensified his recruiting for the next year.

He visited Theold Brown and his mother in Society Hill. Theold was no longer a well-kept secret. After his showing at one of the five-star summer camps the year before the hounds were after him. A misstep, McCarren knew, and he could lose Theold before the official date for signing the letter of intent.

When he was satisfied that Theold was in the catch bag, that his mother would keep him there, McCarren moved north to play the sly Irish fox with Paul Gilson.

He'd dogged Gilson all through his senior year at Cardinal Mathews High in the Bronx. The first of April, McCarren flew to New York for a last talk with Gilson and his family. Gilson knew who he was now. That was one advantage of making a good showing in the Mideast Regionals. That and the fact he knew about the Killer and Jorge Morgan. He'd never played against them but they were playground legends the length and breadth of New York City.

Gilson's mother served McCarren iced tea in the soiled and rent-controlled housing development where they lived. In a timid voice that still had traces of its southern flavor she told him about her childhood in the south. It might have been, those roots, a plus in his recruiting, but he was aware that the son, Paul, was impatient with his mother and with her childhood memories of a south that probably didn't exist anymore and probably never had.

At the proper moment, alone with Paul, McCarren said, "We'd certainly like you to come down and play with us."

"That depends on what my Uncle thinks," Paul said.

"You saw what happened to us in the Regionals, didn't you?" McCarren was taking his time, trying to decide what Paul's Uncle had to do with the boy's decision.

"You got your tails kicked, Coach."

"We were out-quicked," McCarren said.

Gilson considered that for a long moment and nodded.

"I've got Theold Brown coming in."

"Who's he?"

"A kid from Society Hill in South Carolina."

"Never heard of him," Gilson said.

"He leaps like a young David Thompson. And he's the best pure shooter I've seen in twenty years."

"Quick?"

"Maybe as quick as you are."

Gilson nodded. "You got to talk to my Uncle, Mama's brother. He's making the decision for me."

"No car." That was McCarren's first gambit in the bargaining with Paul's Uncle, George Marks. "A car's a dead giveaway. It starts the sports writers talking. And that gets the N.C.A.A. investigation cranking away."

It was late evening, the same day. McCarren had offered to meet Marks at his law office or his home. Marks had suggested that the discussion take place in McCarren's room at the New York Sheraton.

"After a couple of years, Paul can have a car that's four or five years old. Whatever he can afford himself. When he leaves the University in four years, he can drive away in anything he wants to."

"The car is not important." Marks was tall and lean and well-dressed, though he dressed more as a bookie or a pimp than a lawyer with a downtown firm. He wore a dark velvet jacket, designer jeans and half-boots that probably cost better than two hundred dollars.

"An athletic scholarship covers tuition, books, fees, housing and food."

"How about spending money?"

McCarren shook his head. "No such thing, according to the rules."

"Paul'll need some clothing. Two thousand out front." Marks said. McCarren nodded. "After he enrolls at your University, he'll receive from me each month a check for four hundred dollars walking-around money. Somehow, Coach McCarren, that money will be mailed to me from you from some untraceable source. I'll write Paul a nice, talky letter and enclose the check. I'll tell him I don't want him to feel poor among all those rich kids. The check from your source will be for five hundred each month. My fee, for handling it, will be one hundred-a-month."

"I can arrange that," McCarren said.

"If you can, we have a deal," Marks said.

They left the room and went downstairs to the bar and sealed the bargain over a couple of drinks.

The next day, McCarren arranged for the two thousand in cash. He didn't hand over the money to Marks until the letter of intent was signed. Back in North Carolina, President Edwards arranged with a banker in Charlotte, a graduate of Hunt Morgan, for a check to be mailed to George Marks at his law office the first of each month, starting that June.

Later, by accident, McCarren discovered that only two hundred a month was being sent to Paul Gilson. The other two hundred, it turned out, was being sent to Gilson's mother to help her with her living expenses.

It gave McCarren a warm feeling for the boy. The Irish, he told himself, have always been a sucker for people who love and took care of their mothers.

CHAPTER EIGHT

Now, at the beginning of his fourth year as full time coach, he still kept his offices in the Ipsom Building. The outside remained as it had been. The interior had been renovated with Athletic Foundation money. A new heating and cooling system. Wall-to-wall carpets. New office equipment, desks and chairs. Prints on the outer office walls. On the walls of McCarren's office, photographs of McCarren with the famous and the near famous. On the window ledge behind the desk in the inner office, there was the second place trophy from the Cable Car Classic the year before. It was dusted from time to time but otherwise ignored.

Ellen sat at the desk in the outer office. She'd made the move from old Carter gym to Ipsom.

It was his castle now and he'd worked hard for it. Only he and Jack Turner and Ellen knew how hard.

"Are they here yet?" he asked Ellen. He was referring to the five freshman expected on campus for the first summer session

"They've all arrived but the Gilson boy."

It was his real prime crop, the best recruiting year he'd ever had. He thought of the players by the functions he'd recruited them for Paul Gilson was "the speed." Of the five freshmen McCarren brought in that summer, only Paul Gilson had really been bought and paid for.

"Where are the others?"

"Coach Turner has them at the dorm."

"Stay by the phone." McCarren got a white summer jacket from the closet and folded it over his arm. "If you hear from Gilson, call me at the dorm."

"Yes, boss."

A smile. When he passed her he could smell the subtle claws of her perfume..

The perfume trailed him across campus.

Four of what McCarren like to think of as the New Five were in the rec room on the second floor of the athletic dorm. There was a basketball motif to the rec room. There were old team pictures and pen and ink drawings of the players who'd been with the team for the last three years, since McCarren took over as coach. There were a couple of card tables, a large color TV and a pool table. Jack Turner sat on the sofa near the card tables. "The moose," Mitchell Winters and "the throw-in," Houston Tarr flanked him.

Mitchell Winters was six-ten and two hundred and Forty pounds and still growing. Strong as an ox and he would be stronger yet after a year with the weight program. He had sun-bleached blond hair and the start of a tan.

Houston Tarr was a late addition, a giveaway scholarship, signed after another player McCarren wanted decided to go to Notre Dame instead. A team needed enough bodies for practice and Tarr was a body. He was about five-ten and a hundred and sixty with a couple of pounds of water in his hair. He didn't have all the talent in the world but he had a good attitude. He was black with a fine boned face and long blunt fingers.

"The natural," Theold Brown, was at the pool table with Jimmy Stefano. Stefano was "the role player", the all-purpose man. When McCarren entered the room, he saw that Stefano had been teaching Brown to shoot pool. McCarren stopped in the doorway and watched. In a matter of minutes, with his reflexes and his eye and hand coordination. Brown had already learned enough to make himself dangerous in a game.

"You sure you never played this before?" Stefano didn't appear convinced.

"Pool halls wasn't allowed in Society Hill. Some man got cut to death in one during World War Two and the town outlawed them."

That was what being a natural meant. After a natural picked his game, he could be as good as he wanted to be. Some games a natural mastered right away and they bored him. Pool would be that way with Theold. Easy, too easy, not enough challenge.

Theold Brown was midnight black, six-six and it didn't matter what he weighed. Likely one hundred and eighty would be his playing weight. He was two handed, with a new shot for every new situation. He was a scoring machine who would have to be taught to play defense. McCarren wasn't worried about Brown and his defense. It would be a new challenge, if it was put to Brown in the right way, and naturals never backed away from hard work.

Jimmy Stefano looked up and saw McCarren in the doorway. "Coach is here," he said.

Stefano was "the role player." That meant he would do whatever was asked of him, whatever it took to win. He'd play defense like a tiger if he needed to guard a man who was having a hot shooting streak. He'd play chest to chest with that man until he lost his touch or tired. He'd rebound and feed the fast break. In the half-court game he'd feed the big men inside, the crisp unexpected passes that caught the defense flat footed. And if he had to score he would. The high looping shot from the corners or from the open slots in the zone. And if he had to take a roll on the court after a ball or deliver a hard foul he'd do that as well.

Stefano was an Italian-American street kid from Philly. His family ran a small mom and pop deli in Little Italy on Camac

Street. "The best corned beef in Philly" it bragged in the menu and McCarren thought it was probably true. He'd eaten it on one of his recruiting trips.

"Good to see you, gentlemen," McCarren said. He went around the room, from player to player, shaking hands, calling them by name and asking how the trip had been. He never showed more regard for one boy than another one. A fair chance was all that a player asked for and he knew he'd get it with McCarren. At the same time he knew that all athletes were not created equal. Class would show. But the one who fell back and took their places on the bench would know they'd had their honest shot at a starting role. They would play when they could and wait until next year.

"Orientation tomorrow morning," McCarren said. "Coach Turner will see you through that."

Mitchell Winters smiled, his teeth large and square and blunt. "I wasn't thinking about taking classes this summer. I thought I'd hang around the pool all summer. That's a great pool we've got downstairs."

"Better if you do," Coach Turner said. "It'll allow you to carry a reduced load during the fall and winter, when we're playing ball."

"Coach Turner's right," McCarren said. "And besides that, how else are you going to meet some girls?"

"When you put it that way…" Mitchell Winters stretched his long legs and laughed.

Jimmy Stefano racked his pool cue. He gave Winters an exaggerated legs to head look. "I hope there are some big girls up here."

"You could fall on one and smother her."

"I've got too much grace for that," Winters said.

Theold Brown looked down at the green cloth on the pool table. He smiled but he looked embarrassed.

McCarren saw Brown's reaction. He thought. My Lord, I've got to find that boy a church to go to. I promised his mama, I would.

"Coach Turner will see that you're assigned rooms and settled in. He'll also meet with each of you in private to see if there are any problems he can help you with." In other words, he'll meet with you and see that you've got walking-around money.

"That's it," Turner said.

"We missing somebody?" Houston Tarr looked around.

"Paul Gilson's not here yet," McCarren said. "I think he's lost somewhere between the airport and here."

Theold Brown rolled the cue ball up and down the inside of his arm. "Where's the Killer?"

"He ought to be here today or tomorrow," McCarren took the folded jacket from his arm and put it on. "You looking forward to some games of Ten?"

Brown nodded. "Got to play against the best."

That was it, the word from the Mountain and the Burning Bush.

"The Coliseum will be open from four p.m. for pickup games," McCarren said. "Supper's at seven."

"This way, men." Coach Turner got to his feet.

McCarren stood in the doorway and watched them go. He patted each one on the shoulder as they passed him. Either that or a handshake.

The New Five, now that was a group. Only it was four until Paul Gilson showed up.

It was the best recruiting year he'd ever had. Better than some of the established teams, one of the sports magazines had written about it. Better than Carolina, better than State. Better than Indiana.

All of it accomplished in four years. One as a fulltime recruiter and three as a coach. His dues paid and deducted from his soul. The hard roads, the rejections, and now he had the Five he wanted.

The bus from Winston-Salem stopped at College Station, Hunt Morgan University, around five a.m. The college station didn't look like much to Paul Gilson, the young black man who'd occupied a forward seat, level with the black bus driver. In hour-or-so since leaving the the airport at Winston-Salem, the young black man and the driver had talked. It was a confusing conversation in many ways. Neither man really quite understood the other's accent and whole words and phrases seemed swallowed and lost. The bus pulled to the side of the road opposite the all-weather shelter with the roof and the glassed-in sides. The driver opened the door and got out and found the young man's suit bag and heavy new Samsonite suitcase in the luggage bay. He placed the bags next to the young man and took the baggage checks and tore them in half.

Gilson stared at the stone arch over the road that led to the campus. "Don't look like much."

"Up and coming college," the driver said. He lit a Kool and drew deeply on it. "I can't smoke in the bus. Got to catch one when I can."

"It don't look like any school I ever seen."

"Give it a chance," the driver said. "You here for an education, ain't you? If you are it don't matter."

"I'm here to play b-ball," Gilson said.

"Huh?"

Gilson lifted his hands and pantomimed a soft one-handed shot.

"Oh, that?" The driver smiled. "You see them last year?"

"The game they lost in the Mideast Regional finals."

The driver dropped the cigarette into the sand at his feet and mashed the coal with the toe of a shoe. "That wasn't the real team. The coach…"

"McCarren," Gilson said.

"I watch his Sunday night show. That coach, he took the team from nowhere to the final eight in the country last year. All in three years. And the Killer…"

"Hinson."

"It's the last year for him. He says he wants it all this year or he won't be satisfied."

"I used to watch him play schoolyard ball," Gilson said. "That's one reason I'm here. I want to play with him."

"Well…" The driver looked at the leather-cased watch on his belt. "Got to keep the schedule." He reached the steps to his before he turned back. "You going to play much this year? Ain't no use watching for you if you ain't."

"My butt wasn't made to sit on any bench," Paul Gilson said.

He found the athletic dorm and climbed the stairs to the second floor. That was the meeting place, according to the letter and the instructions that had come with the plane ticket. There was no movement on the hall. The doors were closed and it was dark except for nightlights in the hall and the lighted bathrooms. Everyone was tucked in for the night. He found the rec room. He placed his bags against the wall and kicked off his shoes. He stretched out on the sofa. In a matter of minutes he was fast asleep.

It was a small orientation group. Only the five new players and the orientation guide, Billy Stoddard, a junior small forward on the team. For Stoddard the tour of the campus was a favor for the Coach and a way of gaining a few points for his frat house, the Sigmas.

Coach Turner had breakfast with them in the makeshift training table, a large room set apart from the noisy main cafeteria where the student ate. The food was hot and cooked to order and there was no limit on it. Later in the summer, when the basketball camps opened, the training tables in the athletic dorm would be opened for breakfast. The Hunt Morgan basketball players in town for the summer would eat with the kids. In the fall, the athletic dorm cafeteria would serve three meals a day.

A cool wind rustled through the trees as they walked across campus. Later it would be warm and sunny but the mornings were always cool. Green hills towered above them in the distance. In the winter those hills would be covered with snow.

"Undergraduate library there," Stoddard said, pointing to a marble-fronted building ahead of them. "Good place to study, fine place to meet girls. That's where you'll do research on term papers."

Jimmy Stefano squinted at the building. "What's a term paper?"

"Something a girlfriend writes for you if she really likes you," Stoddard said.

"I like that." Mitchell Winters towered above the others by inches. "I'll get me two girls. One bright and one dumb."

Paul Gilson turned and watched a flock of girls crossing in the distance. "Any black girls here on campus?"

"No worry about color here," Stoddard said. "You can date a purple girl if you want to."

"Got to find me one of those purples," Houston Tarr mumbled.

"Student Union here. Meeting rooms, a lounge, a snack bar. On the other side of it the campus bookstore. After you meet your classes, you take your book list there, get what you need and sign for them."

"Anything you need?"

"Books, paper, pens, notebooks. All of it." Stoddard checked his watch. "We got half an hour before we meet Coach Turner at the gym for registration. Anybody want a Coke?"

They sat around a table off to one side of the Student Union. A striped umbrella shaded them. Paul Gilson, still needing sleep, rubbed his eyes and yawned. Next to him, Theold Brown flexed his long, flat hands. Jimmy Stefano snapped his fingers and danced to some music only he could hear. Mitchell Winters took a sip from his drink cup and pushed his chest out as he watched the girls go by. Houston Tarr stood in the shade created by the bulk of Winters, a full foot shorter than he was.

Stoddard came from the snack bar with a tall, leggy blonde girl. The girl wore tight white shorts and a t-shirt that could hardly hold all of her. The girl leaned against Stoddard, laughing. When they reached the table, the girl lifted her head and looked at them.

"These the ones you've been telling me about, Billy?"

"The freshman five."

"Nice," the girl said. Her eyes moved over Jimmy Stefano and stopped on the lean height of Mitchell Winters. "I hope ya'll like it here."

"No doubt about it," Stefano said," if there are more like you around here."

"Only one of me," she said. The slow, lazy smile that curled and brushed against Stefano.

A wave and she walked away.

"She belong to anybody?" This from Mitchell Winters.

"The Killer does her now and then," Stoddard said, "but it's nothing steady."

"I wouldn't want to get the Killer mad at me," Paul Gilson said.

"No, indeed," Billy Stoddard said. "No, indeed."

Coach Turner met them at a side door to old Carter gym. Billy Stoddard said he'd probably see them later in the day at the Coliseum for a few games of Ten. Coach Turner led the five of them past long lines of milling students. It was warm in the old gym. Turner stopped at a table that had a large printed card on it. LINE CLOSED.

As soon as they reached the table, a tall gray-haired man in a short sleeve shirt and dark tie moved the sign and sat down on the other side of the table.

"Good morning, Coach Turner," the man said.

"Morning," Turner said.

In a line at the next table a short, chunky girl and a boy with uncombed, long hair, in a chorus, chanted, "Jocks, jocks, jocks ," and held their noses pinched between fingers.

English 1 and French 1 class cards for all of them. The same courses and the same sections. Registration was over for them in a matter of minutes.

"Jocks, jocks," the chant was louder, joined in by other students as coach Turner led them from the gym, through the side door and into the bright sun.

"They like us," Mitchell Winters said.

"Kooks', " Jimmy Stefano said. "Got a few of them everywhere."

Coach Turner drew them around him in a circle. "Classes start in the morning. No cuts without good reasons. Pickup games at the Coliseum from four on. Supper from six-thirty on. Study hall from seven-thirty to nine every night except Friday and the weekends. No excuse for missing study hall."

"Looks like we joined the army," Houston Tarr said as they headed for the dining hall and lunch.

CHAPTER NINE

By late afternoon, the new players had settled in and gathered, one by one, in the coliseum for some casual play. Mitchell was the last one to arrive. He was assigned sweats, issued new basketball shoes and a locker in the basketball team room. It was all first class, green carpeting on the floor, full-sized lockers and a players lounge off to one side.

After Mitchell changed, he entered the Coliseum by the players ramp. Paul Gilson and Houston Tarr were shooting baskets at one end of the court, Brown and Stefano at the other. Mitchell warmed up for a few minutes. He did stretching exercises that would lessen the chance of a muscle pull. When he was certain he was loose enough, Mitchell took a basketball from the cart on the side of the court and dribbled to the far end of the court where Theold Brown and Jim Stefano were.

Stefano braced a basketball on his hip. "Man, show us your best move,"

Mitchell dribbled forward a few paces. He tossed the ball against the backboard, a planned miss, and sprang forward and rammed the ball through the net with one hand. Mitchell turned and grinned. "That's also my shooting range."

"You." Stefano pointed a finger at Theold Brown.

Brown had long, thin legs and a heavy chest. Fast legs, Mitchell had heard a coach call them. Brown nodded and dribbled to a spot on the baseline to the right of the basket. Twenty feet away. He lofted a smooth jump shot that hit nothing but net. Stefano caught the ball and whipped it back to Brown. Brown took a step to his left. As soon as the ball touched his hands he shot again. Straight through, almost no arc at all. Again and again, shot after shot. Brown walked the circle around the basket. Twelve shots in all and he missed only one.

"Jesus," Jimmy Stefano said. "I got to learn to be a ball handler. I'm never going to get a shot around here."

Mitchell edged toward Brown. "That's your range?"

"Sure range," Brown said. "But I try from maybe five feet more out there, if I have to."

"Hit any?"

Brown grinned, "Now and then."

Fifteen minutes passed. Mitchell was beginning to wonder where the upperclassmen were when he heard loud talk and deafening laughter. A group of the older players stopped at the head of the ramp. Mitchell recognized Robert Hinson, the Killer, and Jorge Morgan.

"New boys in town?" Robert Hinson looked even large and heavier and broader across the chest than he'd ever looked on TV.

"Some games of Ten?" Jorge Morgan had wide, sloping shoulders and slightly bowed legs. His complexion was almost freckled from his mixed blood.

"That's why we're here," Stefano said.

Besides Hinson and Morgan, Mitchell recognized Stoddard, the big kid who'd given then the tour of the campus that morning. Also Tom Alley, a six foot – four white from upper state New York and Ames Ashley, a six-eight forward.

"Old boys against the new boys?" Hinson said.

"You sure you want to give us that advantage?" Stefano laughed.

"What advantage?"

Spare balls were fitted into the ball cart. Paul Gilson and Houston Tarr joined Brown and Mitchell Winters and Stefano.

"New boys start it," Hinson said.

Paul Gilson stood just over center court, dribbling the ball in place, waiting for the matchups to be made. "Ready?"

"When you are." Robert Hinson nodded.

Mitchell Winters moved toward the lane. Hinson played behind him. Hinson's hands tapped the small of Mitchell's back, a way of checking him and at the same time trying to "feel" any move before he could make it. Mitchell tried to roll around Hinson and break for the basket. One of Hinson's elbows whacked him hard.

"Going to eat your breakfast and supper," Hinson hissed at him.

"Make sure you chew it good." Mitchell moved, a half turn and a push at Hinson's hip to free himself. Hands up, he moved for the basket. Gilson passed to Stefano. Stefano took two dribbles to his right and saw Mitchell's move that freed him. He whipped the ball past Stoddard. Mitchell got the ball one step from the basket and started up with it. A huge black arm came out of nowhere and raked Mitchell's arm, the ball fell free. Hinson's arm continued downward. It struck Mitchell a glancing blow to the side of the head.

The ball curled toward midcourt. Theold Brown reached it in a couple of steps. Two dribbles and he was close to the basket. He was in his shooting motion before Jorge could react.

Dead center. Only met and floor.

"One to zip," Stefano crowed. Fingers snapping, he danced down the floor and took up his defensive position.

Coach Jack Turner watched the games of Ten from the press box high above the court. It was dark in the press box. Without lights there was no way anyone could tell that Turner was there. Better that way. Better if the freshmen didn't feel inhibited. And better that the N.C.A.A. didn't get the wrong idea and assume this was a supervised practice.

The first game of Ten seesawed. The freshman got the first three baskets. Then the Killer's team got the next five baskets with Hinson going in low around the basket with the big kid, Winters. No doubt about it, the Killer was giving the big kid a lot of hip and elbow. Most of it might have been called in a regulation game, in a game with officials. No officials here.

At the other end of the court, Theold Brown made a running one-handed shot off the glass. Five to four, Killer's team ahead.

The next time down it was going to be the killer against the big kid again. That was written in one yard letters and carved in stone, the way the upperclassmen set up the pattern. The ball went in to the Killer at the right baseline. Dribbling, he began to back in against Mitchell Winters. The kid bumped him, the sound of flesh against flesh could be heard all the way from the court to the press box. The kid was trying to overplay the Killer and pin him against the baseline. The Killer backed toward the basket. At the same time he edged slowly away from the baseline.

Now. Now it was time. The head and shoulder fake to the right, as if the Killer were going up for the looping half hook. Mitchell Winters took the fake and moved to block what he thought would be the Killer's path. Instead, moving around Winters in the opposite direction, the Killer dribbled around Winters, down the baseline and went up for the slam dunk.

It didn't happen. Turner was so involved in the struggle between the Killer and Mitchell Winters that he didn't see Theold Brown glide down the baseline on the other side of the lane. His head seemed above the rim when he put out a hand and slapped the ball away from the Killer's grip. The ball bounded toward midcourt where Stefano caught it in stride. With a scurry of a high dribble Stefano drove down the left side of the lane and put it up off the glass.

No slam dunk. No dunk of any kind. At center court Theold Brown cupped his hands to his mouth and hooted. "White man's disease? Can't dunk."

Stefano trotted to the other end of the court, ready to take his defensive position. As he passed Brown he said, "Who you calling white? Us Italians were the first blacks..."

The Killer and Jorge leaned together, talking, setting it up. Out of the chute straight to the Killer, as if it were a repeat of what had been going on all game. The Killer against Mitchell Winters. This time two men were on the Killer, Winters behind him and Paul Gilson in front. As soon as the Killer got the ball Winters and Gilson surrounded him. Jorge Morgan cut past him and headed for the basket. The Killer gave him the blind, over the head, pass and Jorge laid it in.

Six to five, upperclassmen leading.

The next time down Winters wanted the ball. He had his pride. Turner thought, and that was good. The Killer had been working him over good. Turner liked to see that in a young player. That he didn't get intimidated.

The bounce pass into Winters. Winters, in the next few seconds, put every move he had on the Killer. Everything he'd learned in high school ball and moves that he seemed to invent on the spot. Still, when he went up for his shot, the Killer was there. He caught Winter's shot in mid-air and, falling away, passed to Jorge Morgan breaking toward the other basket. Jorge dribbled to the foul line. He pulled up there and put up a soft jump shot.

Seven to live.

Theold Brown trotted down the court shoulder to shoulder with Winters. Winters nodded a time or two and took his position. The Killer set up behind the big kid.

Paul Gilson put the ball in play at mid court. A couple of dribbles and Gilson made a hard cross court pass to Stefano in the left corner. Stefano hardly touched it. A return pass to Theold

Brown in the right corner. Brown bounce passed it in to Winters. Winters put his back to the Killer and began dribbling, working his way toward the basket. The move got Winters within five feet of the basket. At that point the Killer must have decided that war far enough. He put his 240 pounds against Winters. That far and no more.

Dumb, Turner thought. The Killer is going to slap this shot back in his face. How dumb can …?'

The Killer's weight stopped Winters. He stopped his dribble. Winters faked with his shoulders to the left and then to the right. The Killer was ready, hands up, ready to block the shot. Winters lifted the ball. The Killer left his feet. Winters brought the ball down and performed a backhanded shovel pass that went to Paul Gilson. The ball went under the Killer's arm. Gilson turned and left his feet. The ball rolled off his fingertips and through the basket.

Seven to six. Upperclassmen leading.

Back and forth. Tied at nine each. Jorge put up a soft jump shot that rimmed and bounced away. The Killer blew past a flat footed Mitchell Winters and jammed the ball through the basket with one hand.

Ten to nine, the Killer's team ahead.

Paul Gilson walked the ball down the court and stopped. After the score, it was a half-court game again. Gilson looked at Jorge. "Ready?"

Jorge said, "Ready." As soon as the word was out of his mouth Jorge lunged for the ball. He almost made the steal. Paul Gilson pulled the ball away at the last possible moment and turned and dribbled away.

Pressure Coach Turner said. They are going to pressure the kids. Jorge chased Paul Gilson. Ames Ashley stepped out and blocked Gilson's path. Surprise made Gilson pull up. Across the court, trying to help, Theold Brown let out a piercing whistle. Gilson turned and threw a pass toward Brown.

Billy Stoddard who'd been lurking in the Killer's shadow stepped between Gilson and Brown and took the pass. As slow as he was he had too much lead on the freshmen. He dribbled to the far end of the court. He banked his shot off the backboard and turned and grinned.

"That's a white man," Stefano shouted from the other end of the court.

The Killer and Theold Brown stopped at center court and looked at each other.

"That was a good block a time ago," the Killer said.

"Just luck," Brown said.

"Yes, indeed." The Killer slapped Brown on the back. "You couldn't do that to me twice."

⚜ ⚜ ⚜

Coach Turner left the dark press box. He walked down the hallway to his office. It was large and airy and spotless. Not like The old office in Carter gym. McCarren insisted on neatness and order. It made a good impression, he said. And that went all the way down to how the players dressed on road games. Jackets and ties and haircuts and no beards.

Turner dialed McCarren's office in the Ipsom Building. He got past Ellen.

"Yes, Jack?"

"You ought to be over here," Turner said. "The new boys are playing the old ones."

"How does it look?"

"There's a lot of talent on that court. Right now, they're feeling each other out, getting to know what they can do."

"You think it's worth making a highlight film?"

"There are flashes," Turner said.

"Call me again," McCarren said, "when they're ready to win the national championship."

❧ ❧ ❧

A few days later, Houston Tarr came into the Coliseum for another game of ten. As he did, he spotted a black girl in the stands. She was beautiful, with her hair done in strings and the strands strung with bright colored beads. She was seated with another black girl at the east end of the court.

Houston got a basketball from the cart and trotted to the west end of the court, away from her. Dribbling, put up his shots, getting his legs warmed up and loose. His usual shot with the flat arc. Too flat, one of his high school coaches had said, but now and then it was on track and he was good for four or five in a row.

The Killer slouched out and stood aside and watched Houston's shot. "That shot any flatter and you could hang the wet wash on it," he said after a time.

"I like the sound of it," Houston said. "Anybody can shoot those high looping ones. I like the *thuck* when the ball hits the back of the rim."

The Killer dribbled around, circling. He had a long look at the two girls at the other end of the court. "Anything special going on here today?"

"Not that I know of." Houston shook his head. "All I know is that it's Monday."

"But we done drawn ourselves an audience for some reason."

The ball *thucked* as it hit the back of the rim and went through. "Fine looking," Houston said.

"But too pure for a man."

"How you know?"

"I gave it a try once," the Killer said.

"All that means is the lady's got good sense."

"Now you watch that kind of talk." But Hinson was smiling. "I think the girl wants somebody to take her to church for a month or two and pray with her. And that's before you get the first touch of the merchandise."

"A waste."

"Ain't it?" The Killer banked in a soft shot and retrieved the ball. As he dribbled past Houston he said, "It must be you she's interested in. I know it ain't me."

Houston shook his head. "Maybe Theold."

"You." The Killer pointed a finger at him. He swung around and put up a soft half hook. "From where I stand, it looks like she has got the big eyes for you."

"Hard for me to believe that."

"One way to know for sure," the Killer said. "I'll ask her."

The Killer dribbled down to the other end of the court. Houston looked over his shoulder and saw Hinson leaning forward, talking to the two girls. Houston thought he could hear the clack of the glass beads and her high laughter. He looked away. He continued to shoot, moving to one side and then the other. A step forward and two steps back. He heard dribbling as the Killer approached and stopped directly behind him.

"It's you," the Killer said. "Now, ain't that a shame?"

Over the next few minutes, the other players wandered in. They took their time warming up. The kidding went on for a while. How they'd spent the weekend. How many girls they'd talked nonsense to. How many girls had seemed to believe that nonsense.

When it became time to start the games of Ten, the Killer said he wanted first pick. Jorge would choose the other team members.

"I'll take Houston Tarr," the Killer said. "Houston is my new star."

"Is that right?" Theold Brown and Houston had gone to church the day before and, though Houston had seemed bored by it all, it had been good to have a friend along. Now he could write his mama and say that his roommate had gone with him and that would please her.

"I take Theold," Jorge said.

"It would serve you right if I took that big slow white there." The Killer motioned at Mitchell Winters. "Instead, I will take the little slow white, Jimmy."

"Winters," Jorge said. "Thank you, Killer, for not being greedy."

"Gilson," the Killer said.

And so it went, on down the line until each team had their five men. What was becoming more and more clear as the summer went on was that Jorge and the Killer were selecting the freshman and trying to give them all the experience they could get. Some of the upperclassmen had to wait until the later games before they got to play at all.

The Killer drew his team together at the center jump circle and huddled with them. "I suppose that you are all wondering why I have decided that Houston Tarr is my new star. Right?"

A nod or two. Smiles.

"Behind me, at the other end of the court, there is a black girl I call the snake lady. For some reason I do not understand, she has fallen for my friend, Houston. For that reason alone, because she is here watching the new Romeo, I vote that we make Houston a star. An instant star."

"Second that," Jimmy said.

"Third," Paul Gilson shouted.

"Enough," the Killer said. "The motion is carried."

The game of Ten began.

Paul Gilson passed it in to Jimmy Stefano, Jimmy looped to his right where the Killer was setting up just outside the lane, near the baseline. Houston was on that side, at small forward. Jimmy passed the ball to the Killer.

The Killer caught the ball in one huge hand and dribbled, backing up alone the baseline. The Killer lowered an eyelid and nodded at Houston. Mitchell Winter was behind Hinson, hands on his lower back, trying to control him and slow him down.

The Killer said, "Shit, man, you're fouling me," and bounce-passed the ball to Houston, who caught the pass as he moved toward the lane. He raised an eyebrow as he headed toward the Killer. The Killer shook his head. Houston dropped the ball to the Killer and moved past Mitchell as if getting into position for the rebound. The Killer wheeled as if going up for the shot. Instead, he hard-balled a pass toward the backboard glass. Houston caught it in the air and slammed the ball through the net.

"Now you see why Houston Tarr is my new star," the Killer yelled. "Our one against your nothing."

The Killer's team won the first game 12 to 10. Fed and set up by his teammates, Houston scored five of his team's twelve baskets. At the final basket, after Jimmy Stefano lofted a soft jumper from the corner, Houston mumbled to the Killer, "This being an instant star is tiring."

"Oh, yes," the Killer said. "Yes, indeed. Now you know how I feel all the time," Hinson hooked a finger at Billy Stoddard. "Come sweat and give our star a short blow or two."

Houston sat on one of the front row seats at center court. He wrapped a damp towel around his neck and mopped at the sweat on his face and chest. He heard the clack of the beads and knew she was behind him. He didn't have to turn to know the girl was there.

"Hey, there. I'm Leota," the black girl said. He could smell some kind of musk-based perfume on her. "You look cool out there."

"We take turns being the star. Today's my day."

She laughed as if she didn't believe him. "I saw you at church yesterday."

Houston blinked. He didn't remember seeing her. "Just keeping my roomie company."

"Theold Brown?"

"He's the real star," Houston said.

"Better than you?"

"I'm modest about my talent."

"You're funning me." She watched as he wiped the perspiration from his face. "You ought to come to Black Studies Wednesday night."

"When?"

"Eight o'clock."

He shook his head. "Coach has us at study hall."

"We could meet later for coffee."

"Name the time."

"Wednesday night at nine-thirty. The lounge at the Student Union."

"I'll be there." He stood and dropped the towel. The second game of Ten was over. He was ready to go back into the game. "See you." He trotted onto court. He replaced Paul Gilson. Before the game he looked over his shoulder and saw Leota and her girlfriend leaving.

The Killer met him. "You doing good, star?"

"Coffee with her Wednesday night after study hall."

"I am proud of you, my man." The Killer wrapped an arm around his shoulders.

"I did it for the team," Houston said.

The Killer turned him. "Houston Tarr is no longer a star. Who wants to be a star?"

"I do," Jimmy Stefano said,

"Not you," The Killer grinned. "I am a star. Jorge is a star. Theold will be a star in time. The rest of you are twenty cent a pound dogmeat."

On instinct, just for the pure hell of it, McCarren had let himself into the dark press box and spent more than an hour watching the games of Ten. It was close and too warm in the enclosed space and McCarren loosened his tied and rolled his shirt sleeves to the elbows.

Yes, Theold Brown could play with the big boys.

Paul Gilson had the eye and the sure touch of a fine passer. He would have to be convinced to shoot more. Jack Turner would work some extra time with him on his shooting. Jack was a fine basics instructor and that was one of the reasons that McCarren had kept him on the staff.

Jimmy Stefano was a bit and a piece of almost everything. What a heady basketball player needed to coexist with all the stars. Cool and steady. The head of a chess master. By the middle of the season, he'd split time or he'd have a winning edge on playing time. At least twenty-five minutes a game for you, boy. That's next year for you.

The big kid, Mitchell Winters, was willing to butt heads with the Killer. That was balls and guts. And as far as McCarren could tell, the Killer wasn't pulling his punches with the kid. What Mitchell got he earned with bruises and lumps.

That left Houston Tarr. He'd seen the game, the charade, the Killer had orchestrated for Houston. He didn't understand exactly what the Killer was doing but it had a good team feeling about it. Minimum talent, Houston had, but he seemed to have a good effect on the players around him. Like Joe Truex at St. Joseph's. Not a talented bone in his body. But good glue in his personality. The good glue that could hold a team together during the bad times and keep the edge to it during the good ones.

Not a bad recruiting year, he told himself. Even the throw-in, the afterthought, Houston Tarr, had his real value.

Still, he saw problems. More basketball talent with some of the freshmen than the upperclassmen. But lacking the game experience. How to get the new men that experience, that game time without getting the older players, ones like Ashley and Stoddard and Regis, and their noses out of joint. Especially when it became obvious what McCarren was doing.

He'd have to plan. Perhaps he'd have a team of the older regulars. Hinson and Jorge and Stoddard and Regis and Ashley and Alley. Then a Go For It all team. The Go team. The new five players on the court for two or three minutes at a time. Going as hard as they could, A blitz of defense and a rack of points at the offensive end of the court. The steady "kick your butt" of Hinson and Jorge. Then the helter-skelter of Theold Brown, Gilson and Winters and Stefano. Two rhythms that the other team would have to adjust to and compensate for.

Might work. He'd talk to Turner. Consider some ways of making the contrast work.

Yes, it had been a very good year. He had done a good job of shaking the tree.

PART TWO

THE 1982-83 SEASON

HUNT MORGAN U. "MOUNTAINEERS"
1982-83 Basketball
Schedule

November:
Sat. 20th	Green and White Squad Game
Sat. 27th	N.C. State AWAY
Mon. 29th	Clemson HOME

December:
Thurs. 2nd	Belmont Abbey HOME
Sat. 4th	Kentucky State GREENSBORO
Sat. 11th	St. Peters MADISON SQUARE GARDEN
Sat. 17th	E. Tenn. State HOME
Sat. 25th	Georgia State AWAY
Mon. 27th	Tire Classic AKRON
	Ohio U.
Tues. 28th	Bowline Green or Penn.

January:
Mon. 2nd	Notre Dame AWAY
Wed. 5th	Northwestern AWAY
Sat. 8th	W. Virginia St. HOME
Sat. 15th	Georgia Tech AWAY
Thurs. 20th	Richmond AWAY
Sat. 22nd	William and Mary HOME (Player Family Night)
Wed. 26th	L.S.U. AWAY
Sat. 29th	East Carolina HOME

<u>February:</u>

Wed. 2nd	Furman AWAY
Fri. 5th	: Virginia Tech HOME
Sat. 6th	Wake Forest GREEENSBORO
Thurs. 10th	U.N.C.-Charlotte AWAY
Mon. 14th	Florida Southern HOME
Thurs. 17th	South Carolina HOME
Sat. 19th	DePaul HOME
Wed. 23rd	Appalachian St. AWAY
Sat. 26th	Marquette HOME

CHAPTER TEN

Tim McCarren watched as Jack Turner read the schedule card and flipped it and stared at the photograph on the cover side. Pictured there, in all his awesome power, was the Killer. He was level with the basket, doing one of his dunks, the stiff-armed thunder slam against one of the teams the year before.

"I thought you'd want to be the first to see the printed schedule. Jack."

Turner shook his head. His eyes were hooded. "I didn't like that murderers' row when you were putting it together."

"Give me a guess how you think we'll do."

"Split."

"Have to do better than a split." McCarren said.

"Sixteen and ten or seventeen and nine."

McCarren retreated to the turret window that overlooked Biddle Coliseum. He leaned on the window sill for a long time with his eyes closed. "You'll think I'm crazy." He opened his eyes. Below him, on the Biddle steps, there was constant activity. Students were returning to school this day or they arrived for their first years. Parents snapped away at them with all kinds of cameras. The Biddle had become a popular background for photo sessions.

"I know you're crazy. The University of North Carolina could handle this schedule. We can't."

McCarren looked over his shoulder. "I say twenty and six or twenty-one and five."

"What'll that buy us?"

"We win against the right teams there'll be a bid to the N.C.A.As."

"Which teams?"

"The ones in February," McCarren said. "You think I planned that part of the schedule with an empty head? Huh? We win eight of those nine that month and the selection committee can't ignore us. The bids will come wrapped in gold foil."

"And if we lose eight of those nine?"

"We stay home," McCarren said. "The weather will be fine that time of year."

"I'd rather be somewhere."

"The National Invitation Tournament?"

Turner shook his head. "Now that the N.C.A.A. has increased the field to forty-eight, that's a losers' tournament."

"A bit of cash there. Maybe a bit of prestige if you win it all." McCarren left the turret window and circled his desk. He opened the refrigerator door and bent down. When he straightened his back, he held two frosted bottles of Harp. He pried the caps away with an opener he kept on top of the refrigerator.

"The money's all right." Turner nodded his thanks as he received the bottle of Harp. "When a team reaches the quarter finals, it helps recruiting to play in Madison Square Garden. What hurts is that the tournament is for third and fourth place conference teams and independents with bad records and no real credibility."

"I don't want the N.I.T. either." McCarren tipped back his head and let a long swallow of beer roll down his throat. "But we've got to keep President Edwards happy. He wants to see us bringing in money and making the University famous."

"We play in the N.I.T. and win it he'd noticed the difference in the size of the check from the one we brought in last year, from the N.C.A.A."

"True." McCarren adjusted the cuff of his dark blue blazer with silver buttons. His pearly gray slacks had a crease like a razor edge. Since he'd been going with Ellen Fletcher, he paid more attention to the quality of his clothing and he knew he was dressing younger. Jack had mentioned the change in him once and then had backed away when he saw how sensitive McCarren was to his comment. "But, when it comes to money, we'll take the heel of the loaf rather than no crust at all."

"Whatever you say, chief."

The door opened and Ellen entered. Since she and McCarren had been going together, their relationship in the office was entirely businesslike. But there was a real warmth in the A.D.'s office. Turner had noticed it right away and that had been his first hint that their relationship had changed. Turner had never talked to McCarren about it in a man's locker room way. He was sensitive enough to know what was happening between Ellen and McCarren was not a fuck-and-run relationship.

"Coach McCarren, there's a Mr. James Vickers here from *Sport* magazine," she said. "His appointment is for three. He's ten minutes early."

"Better early than late. Tell him I'll be with him as soon as I finish discussing a matter with Coach Turner."

Smiling, nodding, Ellen closed the door behind her.

"You think you can put together a pickup game for four this afternoon?"

"No sweat."

McCarren finished his Harp and tossed the bottle in the waste can. He covered it over with a newspaper. He got a roll of mints from his desk drawer. Turner gulped back the last of his beer and shoved the empty under the same newspaper. McCarren sucked on a mint and passed the roll to Turner.

They walked to the door. Turner opened it and they passed through into the outer office. The writer from *Sport* was a tall slat of a man with a flushed face and a graying thick red mustache. McCarren shook Vickers' hand and led him toward Jack Turner.

"You'll remember my co-coach from his years at Duke?"

They shoot hands and then McCarren took Vickers to the Faculty club, getting a seat in the second floor alcove.

The Faculty Club was a recent addition to the University. For years, the campus had been dry because of its original connection with the church. There was to be no possession or consumption of beer on the campus. Two years before, the citizens voted in the ABC system and the sale of liquor by the drink. It was a minor step to the realization that the rules against alcohol on campus applied to beer only, that it did not cover hard liquor. A Faculty Club was chartered, coffee and tea was served in the morning, a good lunch at noon and cocktails after flour in the afternoon.

Vickers sipped a double martini. "Better than I expected in this part of the country."

McCarren leaned back in his chair and hooded his eyes against the slant of the sun through the window directly in front of him. "I heard someone say the other day that all journalists live under the false assumption that they really know and understand America. That they talk about the South being like this and the Southwest being this way … when, in fact, they fly over the real America on the way to New York, Chicago, Los Angeles, Dallas and Miami."

"You mind if I quote you on that?"

"Not if you can find a way to tie it in some way to college basketball." McCarren sipped a large stem glass of dry white wine.

Vickers scribbled a few words on the top sheet of his steno pad. "You've just said that most of the big time journalists fly over so much of the real America that they don't really know the quality of the basketball that's being played down here."

"Brilliant-of me," McCarren said.

Vickers smiled. "You were the surprise team in the N.C.A.A.'s last year. You didn't lose anybody important from the team. You think you're going to be better this year?"

"At least as good, I hope."

"Your freshmen. The word is that it's your best class yet."

"I wish I could be as sure as everyone else is about my freshmen class. Look, it's a big leap from high school ball to college. A coach never knows how a kid will handle the transition or if he'll handle it at all."

Vickers' pen rippled across the pad. "Theold Brown?"

"He's sky walker himself. He's the best pure shooter I've ever seen and that covers more than twenty years of really paying attention."

"A starter this year?"

"Practice hasn't started. One rule I learned as a young man just starting out in coaching. You don't usually win with more than one freshman in the lineup."

"Even great freshmen?"

McCarren shrugged. "Basketball is a game that's usually won by the team that makes the fewest mistakes. Freshmen make mistakes."

"Paul Gilson? I saw him play in the City."

"He's a whippet. In a year, after he's adjusted, he'll be eating defenses alive. It might take this year to polish him."

"The others?"

"Jimmy Stefano from Philly. He does it all. He's a hardworking Italian kid who'll do everything for a team except cook the pasta."

"But a year away?" Vickers was learning.

"At least that." McCarren waved at the student waiter and nodded toward Vickers' glass, "And there's Mitchell Winters. Big, strong, tough. He's not the Killer yet but he's a quick learner. He can be as good as he wants to be."

The pen flowed. Vickers looked up as the second double martini was delivered and placed in front of him. "That's only four. You recruited five."

"Houston Tarr. A kid from Charlotte. I'm not sure what Houston's real strength is. He's got a shot that nobody wants him to take. It's got the arc, the curve of a round of pita bread. He can't play defense. He can't dribble."

Vickers grinned. "What can he do?"

"Find a way to beat you. That's all."

Vickers finished his martini. McCarren signed the tab and left a cash tip for the student waiter. They left the Faculty Club and walked slowly across campus to the Coliseum. McCarren remained with Vickers until they reached the third tier of seats. Below them, the games of Ten had started.

"Got to leave you here," McCarren said.

"Why can't…?"

"I don't want this to be thought of as a supervised practice. That wouldn't do. You go down and introduce yourself to the Killer. Talk to Jorge. Talk to anybody you want to."

McCarren stood on the third tier of seating until he saw Vickers reach the court level. He recognized the man who stood and shook hands with Vickers. That was Jock Trimble, the new Sports Information Director. At least Jack Turner had looked ahead and prepared the for the arrival of Vickers. That was good.

McCarren walked down the long hall and entered the dark broadcasting booth. Turner was already there, seated at the counter that usually held the electronic equipment. He was leaning forward, his nose almost pressed against the glass.

"Good thinking. Jack." McCarren indicated courtside where Vickers and Trimble were talking.

"It's the proper drill." Turner motioned to a chair on his right. McCarren sat down.

On court, Regis and Mitchell Winters squared off at center. Walter Turk was playing Jorge's guard position. The Killer and Jorge were being interviewed by Vickers. Vickers had told Jock

Trimble that he didn't like flacks prompting players while he did his interviews. Trimble looked crestfallen and disturbed by his ouster.

"What kind of coach is McCarren?"

"The best," the Killer said.

"The greatest." Jorge nodded.

"Would you say the same thing if it wasn't true?"

"If it wasn't true," Jorge said, "I would not be here to say anything at all to you. I'd be playing ball at some other school."

"Listen to the man." The Killer wiped his chest and back with a towel.

"You know what this team was like three years ago?"

Jorge looked at the Killer. Jorge didn't want to do all the talking.

"It was the dirty pits," Robert Hinson said.

"Coach Turner...?"

"Hey," Jorge said," it wasn't all his fault. Coach Turner is great. His mistake was thinking you could recruit rednecks and teach them to play street ball. The real man, McCarren, knew you had to reach out and find the right players."

"You and Hinson?"

"I'm too modest to admit that," Jorge said.

"I ain't." The Killer looked past Vickers at the game of Ten in progress. "He got us and he got the greyhounds."

"Greyhounds...?"

"There." Vickers turned when the Killer pointed.

Theold Brown was driving the baseline. Gilson, guarding him, did the best he could to deny Brown the shot. Brown was almost level with the basket when he was nudged to the back side of the backboard. As he moved behind the backboard he reached back and laid the basketball on the front side of the board and rolled it in.

"That's one of the greyhounds," Jorge said. "Theold Brown."

"That shot," Vickers said. "What do you call that shot?

"It ain't got no name," Hinson said. "Theold's got so many shots he ain't had time to name them yet."

On court, Theold and Paul were matched against each other. Paul said, "Ready?" and when he got Theold's nod he started his dribble. He used a slow tap-tap dribble and moved to the head of the foul circle. Walter Turk faked away and broke down the baseline. Paul Gilson saw him and whipped the ball to him. Turk got two steps and then Bo Regis moved out to block his path. Bo played good defense. He seemed to have contained Walter Turk. That was when Turk went up for the shot. Bo made the mistake of leaving his feet. From the high point of the shot, with Regis off his feet and out of position, Turk dropped the ball in to Mitchell Winters who was behind Regis. Mitchell did a half turn and slammed the ball through the net.

"That Mitchell is trying to take my job," the Killer said. "I got to go back in there and teach that crackers some manners." The Killer trotted on court He lifted one huge arm. "Bo, you take a rest."

The reporter glanced aft Jorge. "Did he mean that about Mitchell Winters being a cracker?"

Jorge shook his head. "Mr. Vickers, those boys been banging each other like they got a hate going. Off the court they're like brothers. Take my word."

Vickers scribbled on his pad. "A good feeling to this team?"

"The best," Jorge said.

"The Killer's awesome."

"He might be the best center in the country," Jorge said.

"You believe that?"

"He proved it last year. Nobody eats his cheese crackers."

"Who else should I talk to?" Vickers smiled as he wrote "nobody eats his cheese crackers" In his steno pad.

"Theold Brown and Paul Gilson. They need the ink. The Killer and me, we're already media stars."

Jorge trotted away. After the next score, he sent Theold and Paul to talk to Vickers.

Theold Brown knew all the right buzzwords. He'd learned them from his high school coach at Society Hill. "Be modest," the coach had said, "and always talk about the team, always the team."

Vickers would have liked a good quote from the cocky new kid, the freshman who knew he was going to start and said, "To hell with the guy who started last year because I'm here and he's got to move over and make room."

Instead, Theold said, "I respect Coach McCarren or I wouldn't be here. My mama respects Coach McCarren and she wanted me to come here. I'll do anything I can to help this team and all Coach McCarren has got to do is tell me what he wants done. If that means I don't play as much as I want to this year, then that's the way it is."

Paul Gilson stood to one side. His mouth almost dropped open when he heard what Theold said. But he had an angle on Vickers and he saw the approval on the journalist's face. He heard the click-click-click in his own mind, the gearing it up, and he was ready when Vickers put the same question to him.

"I came here to play with Robert and Jorge. I'm here to learn from them and from Coach McCarren and Coach Turner. If I don't play much this year, next year's my time."

Vickers stared at both of them with amazement. The PR man Trimble had crept up the sideline toward center court. Vickers looked at him. "You can listen. But I don't want a peep out of you."

Jack Trimble nodded.

"How far can this team go, Theold?"

"As far as the Killer and Jorge take it. They're the main men."

"Paul?"

"If it was up to the Coach, we'd go all the way. But there's only so much he can do. Coach McCarren won't make any mistakes or miss any free throws or dribble any balls off his sneakers. If we lose a game, we did it. He didn't."

"You talk like Carolina players," Vickers said.

"That ain't bad," Paul said.

A game of Ten ended. The Killer took the basketball and held it on his hip. "That's enough of you two being famous," he shouted. "You will never be as famous as Jorge and me."

Theold laughed. "The Killer is right."

"Spell my name right," Paul said as he passed Vickers.

In early part October, *Sport* magazine arrived at the newsstands with their pre-season basketball rankings. The Hunt Morgan Mountaineers were ranked 14th behind the usual cream of the crop teams that were always there.

There was article by Vickers headlined "Four to Draw To." The piece was mainly about Robert Hinson and Jorge and the better known of the new freshmen, Theold and Paul. There was background on each of them, the development of Hinson and Jorge over the past three years and now the coming of the speed and the new scoring thrust. The question is, Vickers wanted to know, who is the fifth man? Who will fill in this royal flush and take the team to the championship bracket?

There were pictures that the Trimble, the team PR man, had furnished *Sport*. In a box at the bottom of the page, Vickers had put a series of quotes. At the end there was even a quote from a late-arriving Houston Tarr. He was asked "How good is this team?" Houston, waiting for his chance to get into the game of Ten, answered, "So good I don't know what I'm doing here."

CHAPTER ELEVEN

It was the final Saturday before the regular scheduled basketball practice started.

The team set out on the three mile run. It was cold. The wind raged down the streets and the walks. A few more degrees, a drop, and it would freeze, Jimmy thought. And he believed it might snow before the night was over.

On the run, the Killer moved up and down the line of joggers, urging them on. "Don't tell me you're tired. Just because I look like Superman, you think I don't get tired?"

He stopped them outside the Biddle stared down at his watch when they completed the route and. "Practice starts Monday. You know what that means?"

"The upchuck mile?" asked Billy Stoddard.

The Killer shook his head. "Not this year. We got better matters to spend our time with. I done give my assurance that my boys are in top shape. No eight minute mile run this year. Be on the court at four."

There was yelling, handclapping. Hugging. The players split and jogged toward the Coliseum entrance.

Later, the Killer, Jorge, Theold and Houston got together for dinner at one of the student hangouts. All of them except Theold had more beer than food. Theold was drinking 7-up. The Killer and Jorge and Houston were enjoying the buzz.

The Killer burped and told his three teammates: "Got to blow out the nines tonight. Tomorrow's the rest day before we start the real push on Monday."

Over their protests, Theold Brown had left them and returned to the dorm. The others cruised around aimlessly in the Killer's old battered Fairlane.

"Need to find us some sweetmeat trim," Jorge said.

"Trim" was a word that Jorge had adopted since he'd come south. That was what some of the country blacks called pussy. The term came from the fact that, in the backwoods, they called a pencil sharpener a "pencil trimmer".

Houston uncapped the bottle of wine. It was oversweet. It had the artificial flavor of some fruit, strawberries or cherries. But it was 14 percent alcohol.

"Last night to howl," the Killer said. He held his cupped hand toward Houston, who placed the bottle into his hand with the slap of a nurse handing an instrument to a surgeon. The Killer, eyes still on the road and the wipers brushing the snow away, tipped his head back slightly and let a long swallow of the wine course down his throat. "Got to howl tonight. Lord knows when we get the next chance. Not the way the Coach works us."

"That hard?" Houston took the bottle and had a sip.

"McCarren runs you until you knee-walk."

"That's right, man," Jorge said.

The Killer lifted a hand from the steering wheel and snapped his fingers. "Those nurses. We ain't blessed them for a long time."

"Not since April," Jorge said.

"And we'll take Houston along. Now that ugly girl, Ann, won't have to be alone. We make some points by bringing her a stud of her own."

"Many points," Jorge said.

The Killer laughed and looked at Houston. "We done worried our star. We tell him the truth?"

"The truth is better," Jorge said.

"She ain't exactly ugly," the Killer said. "She is more like plain."

"Exactly." Jorge nodded.

Ann wasn't plain at all. She was brown as a pecan shell and cute, as cute a girl as Houston had ever been with, and she acted a little shy, as if she didn't have that much experience with men. Maybe, he thought, maybe.

It was obvious that Jorge and Argenta had experienced each other before. Argenta had almost blue-black skin and meaty hips and buttocks that stuck out like a shelf. A little talking and hugging and fondling and Jorge and Argenta drifted away into one of the bedrooms.

The Killer and Velda didn't remain in the living room long either. Houston saw the Killer asking her the question and he wasn't close enough to hear what Robert said. He did, however, see Velda's nod. Velda was tall and slim and she had what was called high yellow skin.

Two down, Houston thought as he watched the Killer and Velda prance to the other bedroom. What Houston saw last, before the door closed behind them, was the huge hand of Robert Hinson cupping Velda's behind.

Locks snicked on both bedroom doors.

"You want coffee, Houston?" Ann asked.

"I ain't much for coffee this time of night," he said.

"A beer?"

"If you got one."

Ann laughed. "We always got one. Even if we don't have grits and eggs we got a beer."

She brought him a Strohs from the kitchen and stood in front of him. That was, he thought, so he could see that she was a fine, slim woman. Her jeans were so tight that, when he looked at the crotch, he could tell right away that she wasn't a boy. He could see the shape of the mound and the cleft there. Added to that she didn't appear to be wearing a bra and didn't need one.

He popped the tab on the beer. "Where do you sleep?"

"But I'm not sleepy." A sly smile.

"If you were sleepy."

"Two bedrooms here. Tonight it looks like I'll sleep here." She stepped around him and sat on the sofa.

"It comfortable?"

"No. It sags."

He tipped back his head and had a swallow. "You got any bad habits, Ann?"

"One or two."

"Which ones are those?"

Before she could answer, there was a burst of uncontrolled giggling from the room where Jorge and Argenta were. That was followed by Argenta's muffled, "Oh, shit, shit, shit….shit."

"You got a radio, Ann?"

"Better than that." Ann crossed the room and stuck a tape in a player. It was a Stevie Wonder. She adjusted the level to cover the sound from the bedroom. "Better?"

"Jungle noises scare me," Houston said.

"Me too." Ann crossed in front of him on the way to the kitchen. When she returned, she carried a spice jar with OREGANO on the label. In her other hand, she held a pack of double wide rolling papers. She flopped on the sofa next to him and drew a glass-topped coffee table toward her. She opened a magazine to catch the spill and rolled a thick joint. "This is one of my bad habits."

"That ain't no bad habit," Houston said.

He touched the match to the joint for her. Deep breath. Holding it and not wasting any of it. She turned and her knees brushed against him as she passed him the smoke. He tried it in small puffs. He wanted to see how good it was. Had to know that from the start unless you wanted to end up feeling like a vegetable.

Good but not great, he decided.

Ann took his beer and had a swallow. "Jungle noises bother me too." Her eyes were hooded but alert.

He watched her. It didn't matter, for her, what the real strength of the grass was. With the daily users, they could be handed rabbit tobacco and told it was grass and they'd get high. The passed the joint back and forth until it was a finger-burner. Ann let the coal die, stripped the paper away, and swallowed the remaining grass and washed it down with a swallow of his beer.

Houston stood and stretched. "What are your other bad habits?"

"Sometimes I give the best blowjobs in town."

"Now you got my attention." He leaned forward and peeled her t-shirt over her head. Her breasts were small, shaped like pears and the nipples were hard and black. He pulled her to her feet and unzipped her jeans and got them down around her ankles. She stopped him when his fingers touched her underpants.

"It's my monthly," she said.

That barrier in the way, he decided to settle for the best head in town.

It was six o'clock when Houston awoke and found the Killer and Jorge dressed and ready to go. It was hardly first light. Still stoned, Houston staggered around and got dressed. Ann wrapped a sheet around her and disappeared into the bathroom. He said his goodbye through the door and she said, "You come back sometime, you hear?"

The snow was still swirling about on the streets. Houston used a gloved hand to clear the snow from the windshield and the rear window of the old Fairlane. Robert pushed the car at a slow crawl across town to the campus.

Hardly two hours later, Coach McCarren was on the second floor of McCoy dorm. He was white-hot angry and he entered the room the Killer and Jorge shared.

Houston awoke with Jorge leaning over him, shaking his shoulder. "You got to tell him."

"What? What?"

Houston sat up and swung his legs over the side of the bed. The other bed in the room, Theold's, was empty and the covers straightened and in place.

"Coach McCarren."

"Tell him what?"

"That pig Velda's took a warrant saying that the Killer raped her last night."

Houston got into a pair of jeans and found his shower shoes. He followed Jorge down the hall to Jorge's room. Jorge opened the door without knocking. McCarren, looking tired and unshaven, sat on the edge of one of the beds while Robert Hinson dressed.

"You tell him," Jorge said. He gave Houston a push toward the center of the room.

"I was there," Houston said. He swayed. He felt dizzy but he continued. "The Killer didn't rape that girl. They went in that bedroom like they knew what they were going there for."

"And what were you doing?" McCarren asked.

"I was with Ann."

"Ann's the other roommate," Jorge said.

"And you?" McCarren turned his hard eyes toward Jorge.

"I was with Argenta."

"Jesus," McCarren exploded, "was the whole basketball team there?"

"Just the three of us," The Killer said.

Jorge watched as Robert zipped his heavy coat and pulled on a knit cap. "Hey, we told you the truth, Coach."

"I believe you," McCarren said. "The problem is that I've got to take Robert to the police station. I told Chief Baker I would. It was that or the police would have come here to arrest him." McCarren stood and shook his hat. A scattered of drops from melted snow sprinkled across the floor.

"It ain't fair," Jorge said.

"Trust me," McCarren said. "You two get dressed, have yourselves some breakfast and come back here and wait for Coach Turner. You do that?"

"Sure, Coach."

McCarren waved the Killer to the door and followed him.

Jack Turner was waiting on a bench in the hallway of the Sandersville Police Station when McCarren and The Killer arrived. Turner looked ragged and sleepy but he'd found time to remove the top layer of his whiskers with an electric razor.

McCarren motioned him to wait and walked to Chief Baker's office with Robert Hinson. He was inside the office, the door closed behind him for a couple of minutes. He returned and slumped onto the bench next to Turner.

"I'm going to put up bail for him."

"You can't do that," Turner said. "It's a violation of N.C.A.A. rules. As a coach, you can't do anything for one of your players that you wouldn't do for the rest of the student body. Are you going to come here and bail out every student gets himself arrested?"

"That's the way it is?"

Turner nodded. "Who do you know owns property who's not connected to the University?"

McCarren considered it for a moment. "Billy Markham." He owned Billy's Newsstand. He was a friend and he was a rabid fan. "He'd do it."

McCarren made his call. Billy said it was a damned shame and he'd be at the station as soon as his wife could drive from home and take over the newsstand. Sunday was a big day with the *New York Times* and the *Washington Post* for sale and the faculty almost fighting to get their copies.

McCarren returned to the bench and found Jack Turner buttoning his topcoat and adjusting his scarf. "Where you going?"

"To McCoy. I'm going to babysit Jorge and Houston. I have a feeling this is big enough for somebody to leak it. If that happens, I don't want those kids saying anything."

"Do it." McCarren patted him on the shoulder.

Turner was right. It had leaked. Newspapermen were pulling into the parking lot outside McCoy dorm as Turner climbed the front steps. A television van skidded around a corner and barely missed two parked cars before the driver got it under control.

One of the newspaper writers, a staff man from the *Winston-Salem Journal* sprinted up the steps, taking them two at the time and blocked the doorway. "What can you tell me about this, Coach Turner? Is the Killer being held?"

"You know as much as I do," Turner said. He looked over his shoulder and blinked. It looked like a cavalry charge. The news people running toward him and the television cameramen and the on-camera reporters one or two steps behind them. "Soon as I know something I'll see that a statement is issued." Firmly, using both hands. Turner eased the Journal reporter aside and hurried in.

The campus night security man hadn't left for the day yet. He was having breakfast in the training table cafeteria. Jack Turner posted him at the front door and called University security and asked for another six men to seal off the dorm. He knew reporters and he knew that some of them had trouble taking no for an answer.

President Edwards heard the news bulletin on the radio when he was about to leave the Mansion for morning church services.

There was no answer at McCarren's house. He called the police station. McCarren was still there with Billy Markham, the proprietor of the newsstand. They were waiting for the amount of the bail to be set so that Billy could use his downtown property to cover it.

"What the hell is going on?" President Edwards demanded.

"It's a frameup."

"There wasn't any rape?"

"Robert Hinson doesn't have to rape any girl. They almost rape him."

"I have your word on this, Tim? I don't want a scandal." Edwards said.

McCarren was impatient. "I think we need a lawyer."

"Reg Knowles, the University lawyer, is a top man."

"I think we ought to go outside the university system." McCarren wasn't sure that using the university lawyer was the same as putting up bail for one of his athletes. He didn't have time to check. Under that circumstances, it would be better to be careful. "You know an outside lawyer? Someone without a school connection?"

"I know one. Bob Jay Caldwell." Edwards gave him the name and address, which was address on the narrow offshoot of Ridge Road that they called Law Court. "Call me, Tim."

"I will," McCarren said.

He remained at the station with Billy Markham until bail was set at fifty thousand dollars. Billy and a bail bondsman, a man with a gun strapped to his hip and a huge wallet chained to his belt, arranged the matter.

Robert was freed.

McCarren drove the Killer to his house and told him the guest room was his. While Robert showered, McCarren tried the office number for the lawyer, Bob Jay Caldwell. He got an answering service. On Sunday, what else? He found Caldwell's home number listed in the book. An older woman said that

Mr. Caldwell was at church but she would be sure that his call was returned, probably by one p.m.

The Killer finished his shower and came down to the kitchen and raided the refrigerator. "Crime makes a man hungry," he said, waving a turkey leg at McCarren.

McCarren gave him a beer and mixed himself his first Irish and ice for the day. It was early but what the hell? It was a long way from being the start of an ordinary day.

By two in the afternoon Jack Trimble, with Turner leaning over his shoulder, had completed a statement that the PR department would read to the gathering of newspapermen and television reporters and cameras.

"And after I read this?" Trimble finished the final typed draft of the statement, rolled it from the portable typewriter and closed the case.

"Mumble a lot," Turner said. "Keep mumbling."

"Where'll you be?"

"Gone."

It was not a long statement. Too short, in fact, Jack Turner believed. But he knew that the reporters would badger Trimble for a few minutes before they realized he didn't really know anything about the situation.

Jorge and Houston waited in the Rec room for Turner. He waved and the two players followed him down the second floor hallway and down the fire escape. There was a back parking lot there, the less desirable spaces. A car from University security was waiting for them there, engine running, the exhaust billowing and scattering in the icy wind. They piled in.

The driver dropped them at the entrance to Law Court.

Bob Jay Caldwell was dark and intense. An energetic man, some part of him always seemed on the move. He was dressed in jeans, a heavy fisherman's knit sweater and half boots. A tan cowboy hat dripped water on a coatrack hook on one side of his office.

His secretary, Alice Watkins, an angular woman with a body that seemed to have the weight of green lumber, had driven in from her home deep in one of the mountain passes. What she heard, the two depositions she took down, shocked her. But, then, she had always hated and feared blacks and this was only one more reinforcement to what she felt.

McCarren and Jack Turner sat in the outer office-and waited. Caldwell took Jorge's statement first and, during that time, Houston Tarr sat with the coaches. Jack Turner had talked out most of the evening with Houston. He had the sequence sorted out. Now he pulled a chair closer to the one in which Houston sat. "Two things."

"Yes, sir."

"I don't think you ought to mention what you and the girl were smoking. I've got a feeling, if they talk to ..."

"Ann," Houston said.

"... if they talk to Ann she'll leave that out too. It's self-incriminating. It could get her in trouble."

Houston dipped his head. He understood. "The second matter's the kind of sex."

"Yes?"

"I'm not sure what the laws are. In some states, oral sex is against the law. I didn't have a chance to check." Jack Turner looked toward the closed office door where Caldwell, his secretary and Jorge were. "If I'd had a chance ..."

"I get you, Coach Turner. I just don't say exactly what kind of sex me and Ann had."

"That's it."

"But the rest of it, I tell it the way it was?"

Turner nodded.

A wall clock ticked the seconds away. A strong wind rattled the office windows in their casements.

Caldwell's secretary, Alice Watkins, kept her head bent over her pad. The wiggle-wiggle of shorthand, the many years of it, didn't distract her. She savored every nasty moment of Jorge's deposition.

"The thing between Robert Hinson and Velda Johnson had been going on for more than a year," Jorge said. "Fun and games, that's what it was."

A couple of times, when Jorge and Robert stayed the night with Velda and Argenta, they'd switched partners about halfway through the night and nobody had been upset or insulted.

"What about the night in question?" Caldwell asked.

"Well, on this night Velda seemed to be sitting on ready but she seemed a little angry." Jorge had heard her say something to Robert about how he hadn't called her all summer.

"Velda felt neglected?"

"That might be true. But during the night in question, she wasn't neglected. No way." The walls between the two bedrooms were eggshell thin and he'd heard a lot of what went on.

"Pleasuring, that's what went on?"

Damn right, he knew the difference between pleasuring and anything that sounded like it had force involved in it. Jorge, passing him, had given Houston a lazy wink and a thumb up signal.

"How did Velda Johnson receive Robert Hinson?"

"Well, she seemed to be happy to see him. At least, she jumped up on him and hugged him."

"Happy?"

"Yes, very happy," Jorge said.

Houston got his turn with Caldwell, who asked about the sounds that came from the two bedrooms. "How long did you listen?"

"Not any longer than I had to," Houston said. "It made me nervous."

Caldwell had him describe the yells, the words that were said and how they were said, and the moaning.

"And then I had Ann put on some music so we wouldn't have to listen to it," Houston said.

"And then?"

"Me and Ann got close," Houston said.

Alice Watkins coughed and looked away. Houston looked at her. He could see that she was blushing.

"The next I knew Robert and Jorge woke me up and I got dressed and we went back to the dorm."

"Did you see Argenta or Velda?"

"Not that morning," Houston said.

"Did you hear any screaming or yelling during the night?"

"Only the pleasure ones," Houston said.

"Velda didn't try to break the door down or leave the bedroom?"

"Not that I know of."

"Where were the girls when you left the apartment?"

"Ann was in the bathroom."

"Where were Velda and Argenta?"

"I guess they were still sleeping," Houston said.

Bob Jay Caldwell was done. He turned to his secretary. "Tomorrow will be soon enough on the typed transcript. Miss Watkins." Alice Watkins placed her pads in her desk and locked the desk drawer.

Bob Jay Caldwell stood in the office doorway and looked at McCarren and Turner.

"I need a few words with you, Coach McCarren. You also, Coach Turner."

Turner stopped in the office doorway. "We'll be back soon, guys."

Caldwell took a seat behind his desk. He waited until McCarren and Turner settled, McCarren seated and Jack Turner standing with a hand on the back of a chair.

"I don't have a doubt in the world. We can fight and win this one in court."

"That's good news," Jack Turner said. He turned slightly and looked at McCarren, who was staring intently at the manicured nails on his right hand. "Tim?"

McCarren shook his head.

"It's cut and dried," Caldwell said.

"Tim?" Jack Turner waited.

McCarren lifted his head. "I won't have it."

"Huh?"

"This scandal. A long and drawn out trial."

"He says we can win, Tim,"

"Win the battle," McCarren said, "but lose the war." He stood and slicked his gray hair with a hand. "You know the damage a long trial could do to this team? You think I spent four years building this team so that it could go down the toilet?"

"I don't see that you've got any choice," Bob Jay Caldwell said.

"There's always a choice."

"What choice, Tim?"

McCarren gave Jack Turner a hard stare. A tilt of his head. He motioned toward the lawyer, Caldwell.

"What choice, Tim?" Jack Turner insisted.

"I can talk to this Velda Johnson and see if she'll drop the charges against the Killer."

"Why would she drop them?"

"For the same reason that she brought the charges in the first place. She saw Robert as the money pot. Maybe she believed Robert was going to take her away with him when he goes off to play pro ball. That's big money."

"I'm not sure I want to hear this," Caldwell said.

"You're going to try to make a deal with her?"

McCarren nodded at Turner. "That's right."

"I didn't hear that," Caldwell said. "You didn't even say it in front of me."

McCarren turned slowly on his toes. There was a thinly concealed contempt on his face. "Send the bill for your work to me

personally. To my home address. You can mark it as estate planning, if you like."

"The depositions …?"

"Have them typed. I'll want them for my records."

McCarren and Jorge drove to The Snow Lodge Motel, which was
on the highway between Sandersville and Winston-Salem. Many
times, on the way to the airport or driving to Winston-Salem
with Ellen for dinner, McCarren had passed the motel and wondered about it. Whether it was legitimate or whether each room
got the sheets changed three or four times a night.

The main highways had been scraped as soon as the snow
all ended. One double track had been cleared in the snow
around the motel. McCarren followed the track and passed the
motel office. The room he was looking for, number 24, was in
the back. A green Mustang, one front wheel high on a ridge
of ice where the scraping stopped, was parked in front of the
room.

"That's Velda's car," Jorge said.

McCarren pulled in beside the Mustang but braked short of
stopping on the ice ridge. "See that the girls are alone."

A curtain moved in the window of room 24. Then it settled
back into place.

Jorge skipped across the ice and knocked at the door. He went
inside and the door closed behind him. McCarren wore a tweed
jacket under his lined raincoat. In the side pockets of the jacket,
in each pocket, there were two banded packets. Each packet,
made up from money in the war chest he kept at his office, held
a thousand dollars. In tens, twenties, fifties and hundreds. Two
packets in each pocket. Two thousand in each pocket. He would
bring out the packets one at a time, if needed. He didn't want to
encourage greed if he could help it.

The door to the motel room opened. Jorge waved McCarren in.

A color TV with a grainy picture droned away in one corner of the room. McCarren looked in the closet and then he opened the door and checked the bathroom. "You're alone?"

"Alone," Velda said.

McCarren dropped his raincoat over the back of a chair. He adjusted his tie.

"This is Argenta," Jorge said.

The heavy woman Jorge had been with that night. McCarren nodded. He looked past Argenta and saw the twelve pack of Bud with the end torn away.

Argenta offered Jorge a beer. Jorge raised his eyebrow in a question to the Coach. McCarren nodded. "Go ahead. Miss Johnson and I will have our conversation." He dipped his head toward the bathroom. "In there."

Velda walked into the bathroom with McCarren, who closed the door behind them. Velda sat on the toilet cover. McCarren leaned his back against the door. "Why did you do it, Miss Johnson?"

"I wanted him to love me."

"You thought making a charge …?"

She shook her head. "That was because I was pure mad."

"You know this isn't going to work? Maybe if you'd been at the apartment alone with Robert. This way there's a flaw. Jorge was there, Houston Tarr was there. You're going to end up looking pretty silly."

"I know." Velda lowered her head into her hands and began to cry. "I know."

Velda sobbed and lifted her head. They were real tears, McCarren saw, but he wanted to test it.

"After Robert's lawyer gets done with you on the stand, you won't have a shred of dignity left. Your reputation will be destroyed forever."

"I shouldn't have done it. All I wanted to do was hurt Robert."

"You've done that."

"I'm sorry I did it," Velda said.

"How sorry are you?"

Their eyes locked. "I want to do the right thing."

"And after you've done that, what are your plans?"

"I've been offered a job at Grady Hospital in Atlanta."

"I hear it's a good hospital." McCarren had never heard of Grady Hospital in his life. Velda nodded. "I'll tell you what. Let me help you with finances, what you'll need to get settled there," He reached into his pocket and kicked himself for having estimated too high. He separated one of the packets and drew it from his pocket. "Call this a loan. Our little secret. You get settled and ahead you can send it back to me."

Velda took the packet. She didn't count it in front of him. She did, however, flip through one end and take a rapid glimpse at the denominations of the bills.

"In the morning, you drop the charges. You say you've thought it over and you know what you've done is wrong."

Velda nodded.

"And then you're either going to have to give some interviews or stay out of sight."

"I couldn't give interviews. I wouldn't know what to say."

"If they corner you, and these news people are good at that, you tell the truth. What you told me. That you love Robert and he doesn't love you and you wanted to hurt him and that's why you brought the charges against him."

"I guess I could do that."

"If I were you, I'd be vague about the circumstances. In fact, I'd leave Jorge and Houston out of the story altogether. There's no reason to involve them, is there?"

She shook her head.

"Then it's settled?"

Velda nodded, unrolled toilet paper and used a wad of it to blot her eyes.

While McCarren and Jorge were leaving the motel room McCarren noticed that Velda held the packet behind her back. Argenta stood shoulder-to-shoulder to her and sipped a beer and winked at Jorge.

The next morning, Chief Claude Baker of the Sandersville police called McCarren at the office at the Ipsom Building.

"I thought you'd want to know, Tim. That black girl dropped the charges against the Killer."

"That's good news. Chief."

"It had a bad smell to it, Tim."

McCarren's heart lurched. Did the Chief know something? "What?"

"From the get-go this looked like a bad rap. I'm glad we're done with it."

"And now I can get back to coaching," McCarren said.

"Good luck." There was a hesitation. "You tell that Robert to keep it in his pants for a month or two, until this dies down."

"I'll quote you."

CHAPTER TWELVE

The scandal died away in time. One day it was all that they talked about across campus. The next day there was nothing new to add. Within a week, Robert Hinson decided that he didn't have to remain a hermit any longer. Until that point, he'd attended classes and he'd practiced with the team. The rest of the day had been spent behind the locked door of his room in McCoy.

McCarren opened two Harps and pushed one across the desk toward Jorge. It was dark beyond the open window of the turret office. "One won't hurt you, will it?"

"Not the way you run us," Jorge said.

Practice had gone well that day. They'd just finished half an hour before. After a shower, because he had instructions from McCarren, Jorge told the Killer he had a couple of errands to run and he'd see him at the McCoy cafeteria.

Jorge had a sip of the Harp. "I felt funny lying to the Killer."

McCarren nodded. "I understand that. The problem is that I'm not sure the Killer is leading the team anymore."

"If he's not …?"

"Then you are," McCarren said.

"Why not Robert?"

"You think this rape business is over?"

"That's my guess. Coach."

"That's here at Hunt Morgan. How's it going to be on the road?"

"I don't know."

"What's Robert going to do the first time a crowd starts yelling that he's a rapist? Not because they believe that he is but because they're trying to rattle him and take him out of his game?"

"He might go crazy."

"That's why you've got to take part of the weight." McCarren sipped his beer, swallowed and let out a long, weary breath. "You two are going to be co-captains. You're the only seniors on the team. That makes sense."

"All right, Coach."

"If the road crowds get on Robert you're going to have to keep him from blowing and you've got to keep the team from blowing as well."

"That's a big order."

"Yes, it is." The phone on the desk rang. McCarren scooped it up. "Yes, I'm having a talk with Jorge. I'll be there in half an hour. See you then, Ellen." McCarren replaced the receiver on the base. "Nothing worthwhile is easy."

"After last March I thought …"

"That was last March. This is a whole new year." McCarren tipped back his head and poured the Harp down his throat. "What are you planning after this year?"

"I'd like to get drafted by the pros."

"It'll happen. In the third or fourth round, if you have a good season and you show well in the N. C. Two A's."

"You know that much, what are my chances?"

McCarren finished his beer and dropped the bottle in the trashcan. "I wish I could lie. The truth is that you're a step and a half slow. With luck, maybe you stay on a team."

"What does that leave me?"

"The Continental League here in the States. Money's not that great. Or Italy. I've got contacts there. The money's good, you get an apartment rent-free and all the pasta you can eat."

"I'd rather the Knicks."

"Plan on Brindisi or Rome."

Jorge finished his beer. He tossed the bottle in the trashcan and stood. It was straight talk, honest talk and he could find no fault with that. "It would be better than bagging groceries at a supermarket."

"A few years of playing and I'll see about getting you an assistant's job somewhere."

"Better and better," Jorge said.

The Green and White inter-squad game was played on Saturday, November 22nd. It was one week before the opener for the season, the <u>away</u> game against N.C. State.

The Biddle was crowded with 12,000-plus fans who'd paid two dollars each to see the game.

McCarren and Turner decided to show the audience two different halves of basketball. The first half, they played the freshmen, with the three sophs as reserves, as the White team. The two seniors and the three juniors constituted the Green team.

Before the game began, McCarren introduced Jorge and Robert as the two senior co-captains. For the first half of the game, from the freshmen, Jimmy Stefano was appointed captain.

The game was rough and bruising. Theold Brown sky walked around the edges of the basket and kept the freshmen in the game. Paul Gilson, at point guard, was a dealer, with the proper pass here and there and Jimmy Stefano, not usually expected to be a scorer, dropped in four straight during one run.

On the Green team, the Killer was on his game. Nothing Mitchell Winters tried could stop him or slow him-By the half the Killer had fourteen points and he hadn't taken all the open shots he had.

In the dressing room, at the half, the student manager passed around white split tie-on vests according to a list that Coach

Turner had given him. The vests could be worn over green tops, thereby making the player a member of the white team.

McCarren mixed the team. He placed the Killer, Jorge, Theold, Stefano and Gilson on the Green team. The student manager tossed green vests to Theold, Stefano and Gilson.

The White team was Mitchell Winters, Stoddard and Ashley, Walter Turk and Tom Alley.

The Green team was the team that McCarren dreamed about late at night. Strong at four of the positions. Maybe he was giving up some size and weight with Stefano at big forward. Still, there were pluses. Stefano would bite off a hand to keep the other player, the one he was defending, from scoring.

When it was time to return to the court, McCarren stood and clapped his hands. "Good first half. Let's give them another one." He stationed himself at the door and patted backs as the players trotted down the hallway toward the ramp.

Something was off in that moment. McCarren didn't know, at first, what was wrong.

It was the silence. The players had stopped at the mouth of the ramp. McCarren pushed his way past them and reached the edge of the court. Two cheerleaders moved aside. He could see center court.

A demonstration was in progress. About a dozen older women and young girls about student age marched up and down the basketball court. They waved placards on sticks high above their heads.

THE WOMEN CAMPUS ORGANIZATION
SAYS NO TO RAPE
SICK MINDS RAPE WOMEN
THE KILLER REALLY KILLS
RAPE IS KILLING

There were other signs McCarren didn't bother to read. He looked around and spotted one of the Coliseum security guards. He gave the guard a "come here" gesture. While the guard crossed to him, McCarren yelled to Jorge, "Take them back in the dressing room."

The security guard stopped in front of McCarren, who took him by the arm and turned him around so that they stood shoulder-to-shoulder.

"One thing you can say for them," the guard said. "They're peaceful."

"I want them off the court."

"I can't do that."

"They're wearing the wrong kind of shoes. The soles are marking up my court floor. If they want to remove their shoes, I think they can protest another five minutes."

"Right, Coach." The guard moved away and gathered three or four guards and a couple – of ushers. He stepped on court and approached one of the older women, the one at the head of the line of demonstrators. He said a few words and then pointed at the woman's shoes. She laughed. He laughed with her. Then she leaned over and took off one shoe. It was then that she seemed to get angry. She threw the shoe at the guard as hard as she could. He turned and it hit him on the shoulder.

A woman next to her screamed and hit the guard with a placard stick. An usher grabbed her and pulled her from the court. A young girl fell on the floor and had to be dragged away. Another woman, this one in her forties, saw McCarren and made a run for him. Her hands became claws. She tried to rake McCarron's face with her nails. But before she could, one of the security guards grabbed her around the waist from behind and carried her away.

The student manager stood a step behind McCarren.

"Tell them the court's clear," McCarren said.

After the protest, the Killer was shaky. He missed his first three shots, one of them a slam dunk that hit the back rim and bounced to the roof of the Coliseum.

For all that, the Green team was a good blend.

McCarren thought the Killer worked well with Theold. Jorge was at shooting guard, not his real position, but he was adequate at it. Paul Gilson was the difference. He was the speed, the quickness, the team needed, he could penetrate. One step and he was past the defender and into the area of the foul circle. There were a lot of things a quick guard could do in the lane and most of them were good. And there was Stefano. The puzzle. The quiet one. An invisible man. So much in the flow of the game, doing all the right things, the unspectacular defense, the rebounding, that almost nobody realized he was in the game.

By the final buzzer, McCarren thought he knew pretty well what his mid-season starting team would be. The Green team, the team that started the second half with the Killer and Jorge. But he knew he'd have to work them in slowly. He had to season the freshmen. The Go team idea, that was a good one. Start the upper-class men. Spot substitute the freshmen. About twice a half, at unexpected times, put in the freshmen as a unit. Two minutes at the most at a stretch. The Go team all out, blitzing, playing helter-skelter, trapping, double-teaming, gambling on defense. Trying to score off the other team's mistakes and the Go team gambles. And in time, slowly and surely, Theold and Paul and Jimmy would find themselves with more and more game time.

The players left the court to shower. McCarren put a hip on the scorer's table where the reporters were and said he'd answer a few questions, if they were nice questions.

"The Green team you started and stayed with most of the second half, that your starting team?"

McCarren shook his head. "Call it an experiment, trying to blend experience with inexperience to see how that looked."

"You sure it's not your starting unit?" The sports writer from the *Charlotte News* didn't seem convinced.

"My starting unit, unless there's an injury between now and next Saturday, will be Robert Hinson at center, Ames Ashley at power forward, Billy Stoddard at small forward and Jorge Morgan and Walter Turk at guards."

A pudgy man with a wet slouch hat grinned at McCarren. "You remember me?"

"Sure, Frank. I remember King Kong too."

"Then you know I'm with the *Raleigh Times*. You wouldn't be trying to send some false messages to the State coach through me?"

"You a betting man?"

Frank hesitated.

"A friendly wager. A dinner?"

"Done."

The questions were a scattering. The *Charlotte Observer*, because Houston Tarr was from there, wanted to know what his chances were for much playing time. Another reporter wanted him to assess the progress of Theold Brown. Was Paul Gilson as quick as he seemed to be? Mitchell Winters came with good press from high school. After all that, why was he having trouble playing against the Killer?

McCarren answered each question calmly, fairly.

He was ready to end the makeshift press conference when the young woman stepped forward. McCarren had noticed her earlier but he thought she was with one of the male sports writers, a wife or a girlfriend.

"I have a question."

"I don't know you," McCarren said to her. "Which paper are you with?"

"*The Appeal*."

A couple of the sports writer groaned and backed away.

McCarren looked around. "I don't know the paper. I don't think…"

"It's a pinko paper," one of the writers said.

The girl gave the writer a hard look. Her lips started to move but she checked herself in time. Her eyes whipped back toward

McCarren. "What did you think of the demonstration here tonight?"

"I said I'd answer the nice questions, the friendly questions."

"You act like you don't believe women have the right to protest against Robert Hinson."

"I thought it was unfair. If you read the papers, you know it was all a mistake and the charges were dropped. Robert Hinson is no longer on bail. He is not charged with any criminal act. He has not been tried or found guilty of any crime. At this moment, unless you have some information I don't have, Mr. Hinson is just another American citizen with all his rights intact."

"The woman wasn't pressured to drop the charges?"

"Oh, come off it," the columnist from the *News and Observer* hissed at her.

"She wasn't pressured by me or anyone on my staff."

"But you orchestrated the brutal way in which the demonstrators were removed from this court?"

"We have rules about what kinds of footwear can be worn on our court. Black rubber soles is a no-no. The demonstrators were told if they'd removed their shoes, they could stay for a few more minutes."

"Is your floor more important than the American right to demonstrate peacefully?"

"It's according to where a person stands. I'm sure, the way you see it, the right to demonstrate is more important. From where I stand, the condition of the playing floor is more important."

The sports writer from the *Charlotte News* had heard enough "Robert Hinson has his rights, too. One of those rights is that he is to be presumed innocent …"

"And he has a right to rape any woman he wants to because he is a basketball star?"

"… until he has been tried and found guilty."

It was getting out of hand. "That's it," McCarren said. "See you after the N.C. State game Saturday."

"I didn't get to make my protest," the girl from *The Appeal* said.

"What?"

"My protest." The girl lowered her shoe and turned it on the side so the edge of the sole touched the highly polished floor. She drew the shoe toward her. A wide black mark streaked the floor.

Starting Monday the Go team worked as a unit.

Jack Turner designed traps and gambles that sent the forwards into the passing lanes. An intercepted pass and they went for the fast break. On offense they looked for the quick scores, the high, lobs to Theold breaking for the basket, and the variation from that: Gilson faking the pass to Theold and keeping the ball. The drive down the lane.

The feeling on the team was good. The upperclassmen had read McCarran's starting lineup in the Sunday papers after the Green and White game. They knew they weren't being pushed aside by the freshmen. The freshmen, because they saw the weaknesses of the upperclassmen, knew and told themselves that it was only a matter of time before McCarren had to make the changes.

Thursday afternoon, after practice, McCarren stopped by his office and picked up a few things and jammed them in a briefcase. He was headed down the front steps of Ipsom when he saw Robert Hinson waiting there for him.

"I forgot to tell you," McCarren said. "You're on the pro coaches pre-season All-America team in this week's Basketball Weekly "

Robert brushed that aside. "I need to ask you something."

"Walk to the car with me."

"It's this. I thought I was captain. Now, last Saturday night, you announced Jorge was co-captain with me."

"That's right." McCarren nodded.

"What's it mean?"

"Both of you are seniors. One or the other is going to be in a game at any given time."

"Be level with me, Coach."

"All right. It's the rape charge."

"I didn't rape anybody."

"You know that and I know that and half the country, the part that gives a damn either way, knows you didn't rape anybody. Think a minute. You saw those women Saturday night. And that was here on our campus. You want to make any educated guess about how some students at the other schools are going to get on your case?"

"Hard, I guess."

"Nasty is the word. They're going to try to rattle you. They want you off your game so they've got a chance to beat us. And they will get to you. It'll happen. And when it happens, I want Jorge in there to take up the slack, to have the authority to handle it."

"It won't bother me."

"Easy to say. It won't be just the fans. The players'll get their words in."

"I'll take that as long as you tell me when I can get even, when I can get mine back."

"Agreed."

They reached McCarran's car. He unlocked the door and placed the briefcase on the seat.

"Basketball Weekly, you say?"

"Got you a copy." McCarren opened the case and dug out a folded copy of the new Weekly. He handed it to Robert.

"It's going to be a long year."

"Tough it out," McCarren said. "Next year this time you'll be playing power forward on a pro team and nobody will give a crap about this year."

✤ ✤ ✤

They left Sandersville early the next afternoon after loosening up drills in the Coliseum. The team bus, with the players dozing, carried them to the Triangle area. That was Raleigh-Durham-Chapel Hill. State-Duke-Carolina.

McCarren had decided not to stay in Raleigh. He had Ellen make reservations at a motel on the outskirts of Chapel Hill. For no special reason, he told himself. Except for the fact that he wanted the players away from all the people who'd tell them how great they were and away from all the pretty girls who'd want to meet them. A pretty girl, the thought of one, could get a player away from the concentration he needed.

So, off to Siberia this time. An early dinner at a steak house that wasn't more than half-a-mile from the Carolina Motel. Back to the motel and a slow walk around the area to stretch the kinked legs and settle dinner. Television and card games until ten. Then lights out.

The opening game, the next day was an afternoon game.

The Mountaineers left their dressing room at noon and trotted, single file onto court for the first part of their warmup drills.

McCarren stood near mid-court. It seemed a well-behaved crowd. A team never knew what to expect when it came into Reynolds Coliseum. Rowdy and obscene or polite and pleasant.

After the running drills ended, the ball cart rolled on court and the players began to take shots from different angles, different spots on the floor. Each player had his time on the free throw line. Twenty shots, trying to get a touch a sense of the basket rims.

At 12:30, McCarren waved at Robert and the Killer took the team into the dressing room for the short break that came before the introduction of players and the tipoff. Fifteen minutes to rest, to have a Gatorade or to relieve a nervous bladder in the bathroom and they trotted on court again.

Final sharpening up on the shooting. McCarren saw that only Theold Brown seemed to have his eye. The rest of them seemed to have what could be first game jitters. It would end with the first contact and with the elbow a player caught when he went strong for a rebound.

McCarren sat the players down with three minutes to go. At one exactly, the introductions began. Introductions were handled, as they usually were in the A.C.C, in the international way. One of their players and one of others'. The third player from the Mountaineers introduced was Robert Hinson.

As the Killer trotted toward center court it happened, almost as if by signal. The women's underpants and bras appeared in the hands of students. The students stood and waved the underwear wildly.

And the chant began:
"Rape 'em once,
Rape 'em twice.
The Killer don't know
Rape ain't nice."

The chant was repeated a second time, louder, and then the underpants were balled up and thrown from the stands onto the Coliseum floor. They landed in colorful splotches, whites and reds and blues and greens.

The crowd counted, "One...two..." The bras drifted down from the stands. "Three," the crowd yelled as the bras hit the court.

The Killer, standing there at center court, thought an hour passed before the announcer introduced the State center, Billy Byrd.

The Killer slapped hands with Byrd and joined Stoddard and Ashley near the Mountaineer bench. He looked down at his hands while the guards, names called, trotted to mid court and slapped hands.

Ushers moved the length of the court and collected the underwear and stuffed it in a laundry bag.

The Killer was flat-footed on the jump ball.

He rebounded a missed State shot and was called for walking. He'd taken an extra step before he passed to Jorge. The first time down the court on offense the Killer took a high pass from Walter Turk and slammed the ball through the net so hard, with so much anger, that two State men covered their heads and backed away from the ball.

Both teams showed nerves. It was the opening game for each team. After five minutes, the score was even, 12 to 12.

McCarren tapped Turner's shoulder. "Try the Go team."

The five freshmen were in a line to Turner's right. He used his finger as a pointer. "One-two-three-four – five … report."

The freshmen checked in with the scorer and crouched, one knee on the floor so they would not block the view of the fans or the officials.

State scored. Foster banked in a long shot from the corner. Foster was the big scorer that the Killer had guarded in the surprise matchup the year before. This year, McCarren had decided to let Ashley try to guard Foster head-to-head.

Jorge brought the ball up the court without looking at the bench or noticing that the Go team was ready to enter the game. He crossed mid court. He dribbled toward the foul circle. One fake to his right and he spotted Walter Turk in the free slot on the left side of State's zone. Turk took the pass and shot in the same motion.

The ball went through without stirring the net.

The Go team only put token pressure on State as they brought the ball over center court. The State point guard headed directly for the foul circle. A fake to Foster. Jimmy Stefano jumped in front of Foster. The point guard smiled and turned and passed to the small forward on the right. The ball never reached him. Theold had cheated a step. He cut across the passing lane and took the ball in the air, on the run. No State player was within ten feet of Brown when he coasted, slowed and rolled it off his fingertips rather than dunking it.

This time the Go team put on full court pressure. Five men playing four men because they didn't guard the State player who was out of bounds, trying to find a man to pass the ball to. The five second call, which would have given the ball to the Mountaineers, was about to be made by the ref. The State guard panicked and tried to lob the ball over Houston Tarr's head. Tarr deflected the ball enough to direct it toward Theold. Theold tap-passed it to Paul Gllson. The speed man circled. A slow State forward and dropped the ball through untouched.

Paul waved the pressure off. The Go team dropped down court and took defensive positions. The State point guard looked shaken, wary.

McCarren let Robert get his breath evened. "Keeping your cool, Robert?"

"Doing my best."

The student manager passed and dropped a fresh towel in the Killer's hands.

A groan from the State crowd. McCarren saw enough to realize that Mitchell Winters had blocked Byrd's short jump shot and the Go team was running once more. State got back this time. Two men. Paul Gilson pulled up and slicked a pass to Jimmy Stefano. Jimmy took a dribble. A blink of his eyes while Jimmy made certain Mitchell was in rebounding position. He put up a flat shot and it rattled through.

The Go team blitz lasted three minutes. State never seemed to know how to handle it. The starters replaced the Go team with an eight point lead. The Killer steeled himself for new abuse. He wasn't disappointed. Bright colors of underwear fluttered in the crowd.

McCarren waited and watched for his moment to insert the Go team once more before the half. The State and Mountaineer starters matched baskets. Hunt Morgan was still ahead by eight points when the State coach, with less than five minutes to go, sent in three subs to give his front line starters a breather. McCarren waved the freshmen team to the scorer's table. In the first minute, they were in the game the Go team scored two unanswered goals. The State coach wavered. He wasn't sure he wanted to panic and return the starters. He gave his starters another minute. Theold Brown missed a sure shot from twelve feet that should have run the lead to fourteen.

The State starters returned. McCarren left his freshmen team on the floor another minute. He rested his starters and used his Go team to wear the State players down.

At halftime, the Mountaineer lead was twelve points.

McCarren took his slow rounds of the dressing room. He saved Robert Hinson for last. He put a foot on the bench where the Killer was seated and leaned forward.

"Looking good," he said.

"Byrd's got a rotten mouth. Coach."

"Tell me about it."

"He tells me he hears I'm going to make the All-Rape team even before the season's over."

"That bother you, Robert?"

"Some."

"Stay cool," McCarren said. "I'll tell you when you can have him."

The Killer sucked on an orange half and looked at the dressing room floor.

N.C. State burned to the touch at the beginning of the second half. Before the Mountaineers could settle into the pattern of their game, State had scored six straight points and they'd cut the lead to six points.

McCarren went to the Go team early. He hoped that new personnel and the helter skelter style of play might spoil State's concentration. It didn't work. State handled the Go team much better this time and McCarran had to attribute this improvement to a couple of adjustments the State coach had made at halftime, more movement and "help" on the inbounding plays and patience and care in the passing game after the State guards crossed center court.

The Go team played for three minutes and then McCarren ran the starters back in the game. During the central ten minutes of the game, McCarren sent in the freshmen one by one, mixing and blending the seniors, the juniors and the freshmen to see how they fitted together in a real game situation. Like a new jigsaw puzzle, McCarren thought. Like it is the first few times until the machine-cut edges on the pieces smooth and wear down and the fit is assured.

Planning ahead, with four minutes to go, the freshmen were on the bench and had been for two or three minutes. Jack Turner studied the five of them. He looked for signs of fatigue. He didn't see any. Like the Killer said, these guys could run all day and all night.

"Report." McCarren sent the Go team in for the final time this game with three and a half minutes to go. The Killer stalked stiff-legged from the court and sat in the empty seat on McCarran's right.

"Byrd's still bothering you?" McCarren felt very, very tired.

"It goes against me. I owe that sucker."

"Him or the whole crowd here?"

"Both," the Killer said.

"How about letting it go and pointing at the score when the final buzzer sounds?"

"No."

"Try it," McCarren said.

"I got your promise. You said you'd tell me when."

Boxed. He was boxed. "If you've got to, you've got to. But make it look good. This is enemy country."

A groan from the crowd. Houston Tarr batted a State pass away and Jimmy Stefano scooped it with one hand and tossed it to Paul Gilson. Gilson and Theold Brown broke away against a single defender. Gilson and Brown against the one State forward, the ball whipping back and forth over the defender's head. Gilson in the right lane and Brown in the left. Gilson had the shot. He was almost against the backboard when he tapped the ball to Theold who slam-dunked the ball and had to duck and twist to miss the backboard.

McCarren sent in the starters. The Killer waited his time. He wanted the right situation. When he realized that Byrd wasn't playing his usual game, that he wasn't pressing for the ball, the Killer sucked him in. He let Byrd, the next time the State center touched the ball, dribble around him. Byrd almost stumbled. He must have been thinking, hey, what is this free lane to the basket doing here? At that moment, two steps from the basket, he went up for the shot. He was like that, arms extended, ball over his head, when the Killer, stumbling as if trying to recover from a bad defensive mistake, hammered him. He hit Byrd in the back of the head, the arms and the shoulders. Byrd hit the floor face first.

"Jesus," the Killer said, "I'm sorry." He leaned over the State center and held out his hand when the big man turned over and blinked at the Coliseum ceiling. "Let me help you,"

"Get the fuck away from me." Byrd slapped Robert's hand aside.

Foster, the State forward Robert had guarded the year before, had received a smashed cheek in the same kind of get-even move by the Killer the first time they played. The Killer's roughing of Byrd shattered Foster's resolve to leave his past anger in the dressing room. He let out a yell and ran up Robert's back. He took a wild swing that hit the Killer on the ear and stunned him.

"You bastard. You did that on purpose."

Robert whirled and swung his right hand. He hit Foster across the mouth with the back of his hand. That alone was enough to knock Foster to the floor.

"Out of the game, you two." The official pointed at Foster and the Killer. "Walk 'em off," he said to the other two refs. Each ref took a player by the arm and led that player toward the bench.

Robert reached the Mountaineer bench and shook the refs hand from his arm. McCarren met him there and put an arm around him and patted his shoulder. "Take it easy. That's all for tonight." He motioned the Killer to a seat and sat beside him. "You see what I mean?"

Robert nodded.

"Mitchell, you in for Robert."

Winters stripped his warmup pants and jacket.

"Brown in for Stoddard."

They reported. McCarren stood in front of the bench with them, one on each side, huddling. He still had a few seconds left on the time given him to select a replacement for the Killer. "Now they think they've got an edge on us with the Killer out of the game. They'll want to work in close to Byrd. Don't let them. Foster's gone so we don't have to worry about his replacement. Let's do it this way. Mitchell, you back Byrd. Theold, you cheat and front him the best you can. Watch for them to try the lob over you. We got to hold on and ..."

McCarren looked up. The ref was motioning. Time to resume the game.

Mitchell checked the score as he entered the game. The Mountaineers were up by six. That score was deceptive. When the ball was ready for play the State center, Byrd, was at the foul line shooting two. That was from the in-the-act-of-shooting hammering the Killer had put on Byrd before he and Foster got into it.

Mitchell took position in the front slot on the right. Theold, after a word with Ashley, took the rebounding slot directly across from Mitchell. Byrd made the first foul shot. He put the second one up long. Mitchell was out of the slot and into the lane in a split second. He backed away, keeping Byrd from charging down the lane and trying to play tip ball with the rebound. Theold soared high in the open space created by Mitchell's bulk and strength. He took the rebound as soon as the ball dropped below the edge of the basket rim. He came down with the ball and faked the outlet pass to Jorge. The move froze two State defenders and Theold dribbled out of traffic and down the baseline. He had every intention to pass. But he sensed it. The State players expected him to pass to the ballhandling guard. They expected the Mountaineers to set up, to run the clock with a five point lead.

Theold broke and turned up court. He reached mid court before the State players realized that he wasn't going to stop. One State man was back, a guard, and he tried to move in front of Brown and draw the charging call. Theold went up, he seemed to hang there, and when the State guard planted himself in what he thought was the path, Theold rolled around him, twisting in the air. He changed hands and dropped the ball through the net. The State guard swore at him in amazement.

The Mountaineer lead was seven.

The sandwich defense, with Byrd the meat between Mitchell Winters and Theold Brown, worked so well that the State coach was on his feet before State got off a shot. He made the "T" sign and called his team to the bench.

The Mountaineers huddled around McCarren. "State's losing patience. Might make a mistake soon. If they continue to try to force the ball to Byrd we'll steal it. My guess is State has a wrinkle on this stored away. Maybe a guard drives the lane and drops to Byrd in low." He tapped Brown on the arm. "Watch for it. Jorge, you see that play developing you cheat a step or two toward mid court and get ready to break. One more basket and this game is wrapped in gold foil."

Play resumed. State tossed in the ball just inside center court. Time was running out. A bit over two minutes remained in the game. Once, twice, a third time, the State guard tried to work the ball to Byrd. Each time the pass wasn't there.

Here comes the wrinkle, Theold thought. The way the Coach called it.

The State guard passed to the other guard, stepped past Jorge and was in the foul circle. The return pass came and he started a drive toward the basket. Theold cheated a step toward him. He was patient, waiting for the proper moment. At the last moment, as he left his feet, the State guard saw that he'd drawn Mitchell Winters to him. He dropped the pass toward a waiting Billy Byrd.

Theold Brown stepped behind Mitchell Winters and took the ball on the run. He turned up court and saw Jorge over the center line, breaking for the basket. He one-handed it The pass hit Jorge's hands while he was at a full run. He controlled the ball, slowed the dribble to let the clock run, and cakewalked to the basket. No slam, no gaudy dunk. He went up, almost as if doing a slow motion demonstration and laid the ball in.

Up by nine.

State got a basket on a fifteen foot shot from the big guard. Theold matched it from seventeen.

The clock ran out with Jorge and Paul Gilson playing keep away and the State players chasing them and trying to commit a foul and stop the clock.

Right at the buzzer, the State guard caught Jorge and gave him a hard push that sent him sprawling. Jorge leapt to his feet, his fists at the ready. Mitchell caught him around the shoulders and dragged him toward the Mountaineer bench.

"Easy, man," Mitchell said. "We just ate the red off their candy and they're hot about it."

"One and zip," Jorge said.

The State coach muffled his disappointment and met McCarren at center court. A handshake. "That Theold is a player. I'll trade you six horses and my wife for him."

McCarren smiled. "No deal."

McCarren turned away.

The State coach followed him. "Sorry about that underwear crap. I didn't know anything about it."

"Thanks." McCarren stopped. He said then what he'd say later at the press conference. "As far as I'm concerned, they can do that at every road game. It gets Robert mad. Any team that wants to play Robert while he's mad knows how now."

CHAPTER THIRTEEN

The team bus arrived at Sandersville early in the evening. The student manager ran ahead to open the dressing room and make the call to the cooks at McCoy cafeteria. The after game meal would be on the grills in five minutes.

McCarren put his topcoat over his arm and stood in the aisle at the front of the bus. "That was a good effort today, men," he said. "Especially in the surroundings where it was played. One down and twenty-six to go. See you Monday."

Some waves, some goodbyes and the players filed from the bus after McCarren. The players carried their travelling bags to the dressing room and stored their personal gear in their lockers.

The excitement of the afternoon hadn't passed yet. Turner followed the players from the Biddle and the cook was nice enough to put another steak on the grill and cook it to order, medium rare.

He ate at the table with the upperclassmen. The Killer and Jorge and Stoddard and Ashley and Alley.

Something is wrong. Turner could sense it.

The sophs were at a table together. Regis and Case and Walter Turk.

Like they're in no man's land. That's how the sophs carried themselves. Neither fish nor fowl, heroes or goats.

There wasn't much talk at the upperclassman table. Jorge proudly displayed a pair of red panties that he'd scooped up from the floor and kicked under the bench. Hidden there until halftime when he'd taken the underwear into the dressing room and tucked it in his travel bag.

The Killer examined the underpants with an expert's eye. "Last worn by a woman with an ass like an elephant."

"No matter," Jorge said. "It is a different kind of trophy. Of the win rather than a fuck."

"How'd you think the freshmen did?" Turner asked.

"Great," Jorge said.

"Number one." The Killer dipped a huge spoon of ice cream in his mouth and sucked the spoon clean.

Turner sat back and waited. The upper-classmen left together. The freshmen, the last to be served their steaks, sat over their ice cream. Jack Turner got himself a refill of hot tea and carried it to the table where the five freshmen were.

"Join you?"

"Sit, Coach," Jorge said.

Turner squeezed in lemon and added a dash of sugar. While he stirred the tea he looked around the table, from face to face. "I'm getting bad vibes tonight. After a big win, that's an odd time for the feeling to be bad."

Paul Gilson lifted his head and stared at Turner. "What's bothering you, Coach?"

"Let me turn that question around, Paul. What's bothering you?"

"I didn't like today."

"Playing time? If t's playing time don't worry. You'll be leg weary before the season's over."

"It's not playing time."

"If it's not playing time, then what is it?"

"Today … is that what the rest of the season's going to be like?"

"In one respect. We'll win."

"No, that goddam underwear waving. It made me want to puke."

"When we continue to win, when the other schools see that it's not working, it'll die out."

"I didn't come here to join the circus," Gilson said. "I came here to play some good basketball."

Stefano stacked his dirty plates on a tray. "It bothers me a lot too. I don't feel as strong about it as Paul here does."

"Mitchell?" Coach Turner nodded at the big center.

"I like the Killer. This isn't his fault. He's getting a raw deal."

Houston shook his head slowly. "He ain't guilty of any rape. I was there and I know. It comes down to it, I got to back Robert."

Turner looked at Theold.

Theold spread his huge hands on the table top. "I wish you'd forgot about me. I came here to play. That's all. Nothing else. Houston says he's innocent. I take his word for that. If he was guilty ,I'd try to forgive him. Since he ain't guilty, I don't see what this is all about. I guess it's just those crazy people in the stands."

"You're splitting the team, Paul." He nodded at the freshmen. "You splitting this team. It's a rank business."

"That's the way I feel today. I don't play basketball wearing clown white for anybody."

"One game and you'd flush this team down the tubes?"

"I didn't say that." Paul stacked his dishes on a tray and stood. "Anybody for a cold one?"

He got no answer.

"You see?" Turner said.

"Suit yourself." Paul carried the tray to the washer room window and shoved it in the chute. So hard there was a crash of broken dishes.

Turner finished his tea with the four remaining freshmen. Turner took the game apart for them, and put it back together: what they did right and the mistakes. After a few minutes, with Gilson gone, he could feel the others relaxing.

Maybe it wasn't too late.

The call from Turner disturbed McCarren. He made an appointment to meet Jack for breakfast at the Rebel Cafe at nine-thirty or ten, or whenever the Highlights Taping, scheduled for that morning, was over.

McCarren was on the bed, on top of the covers, dressed in a robe. Ellen sat in a chair beside the bed. He turned to her. "Gilson? Do I know which one he is?"

"He's the speed. He's quick as a cat. Quicker than that. "What's his problem?"

"He's the purity and the corruption," McCarren said.

"That's a deep answer."

"For this boy, basketball is all he wants and all he will ever want. It's music and literature and dance and art all rolled into one. It's emotional, it's played with blood and guts, but to him it has the purity of a perfect chess match."

"And the corruption?"

"I can't talk about that yet." He couldn't tell her about the lawyer uncle in New York, the money that was channeled through him. He couldn't explain the blind spot Paul Gilson had, where he insisted on the purity of the game and at the same time saw nothing wrong about being paid to play the game at the amateur level. Nothing wrong in demanding to be paid for his skill.

"Tomorrow," he added. "If I can't work it out tomorrow, I'll explain it to you. If I work it out, I'm going to forget I ever said a word about it."

"You're an odd man, Tim."

"As long as I'm odd enough for you, lady."

The Rebel Cafe was empty except for the help, two farmers and two long haul truck drivers when Jack Turner arrived there the next morning. He had breakfast, even the ever-present bowl of grits with the pat of butter, and he sat over his second cup of coffee. He'd bought a *News and Observer* at Billy's and tossed everything but the sports page in a sidewalk trashcan.

What the two Raleigh sports writers saw in the N.C. State and Hunt Morgan game the day before was essentially two different games. "On the one hand," one of the writers noted, "an exciting contest between two talented and explosive basketball teams. But, on the other hand, the specter of all that is sick and rotten about the game, the brutality, the violence and the win-at-all-costs philosophy."

Turner lowered the paper and watched McCarren rush in and hang his topcoat on the rack near the front door.

"What the world needs is a good one-armed sports writer," Jack Turner said.

McCarren blinked. "Say again?"

Turner folded the paper to isolate that part of the game write-up and tossed it to McCarren. Seated, McCarren passed the *Washington Post* to Jack. "See if we made the northern papers."

"It's here." Jack Turner ran his finger down one section of an inside page in a roundup of games. The Mountaineer win over State got about four paragraphs. There was no mention of the fight or the ejection of the Killer and Foster. There was, however, a couple of sentences about the play of Theold Brown, Paul Gilson and the other freshmen , who were described as "the Kamikaze Kids at War on the Court."

"Good quote," McCarren said. "You like Kamikaze Kids better than Go team?"

"More colorful."

"I guess that's what they pay the writer for."

Turner passed him follow-up article in the *News and Observer*. In an interview after the game, the State coach said that he thought Theold Brown was already a "franchise" and that he could go pro hardship anytime he wanted to. "Think of the worries and gray hairs it would save a lot of coaches over the next four years."

"Nice of him to plant the idea in Theold's head." Jack Turner's tone was dry as dust.

"Don't let it worry you." McCarren knew that Theold Brown wasn't going to turn pro before his time was up, before he graduated. His mother there in Society Hill wouldn't allow it.

McCarren finished his breakfast and pushed the plate away. "What are our options with Paul Gilson?"

"Apart from suspension from the team?"

"I won't consider that as an option."

"You talk to him and turn him around," Turner said.

"You think I can?"

"He respects you. That's more than I can say for anybody else in the world."

"Give me another option. Jack."

"You can reward him for being a rotten kid. You move him to the starting unit and play him more. Maybe his attitude will improve."

"That goes against the grain."

"It's your ball and your ballgame, Tim."

"Think of a good reason why I ought to stop by McCoy dorm this afternoon."

"I'm winging it. After yesterday's big game, the Sports Information office wants to do a press release on the new freshman. Nobody questions that. Everybody likes a little ink."

"Set it up."

"A writer?"

"A writer and a photographer," McCarren said.

"They're going to be screaming."

"Let them." McCarren held out his coffee cup as the waitress passed in the aisle.

Jack Turner used the phone at the cash register. He returned after five minutes. "They're screaming."

"When?"

"They'll be there at two. Trimble and his boys don't like it."

"They'd like being unemployed even less," McCarren said.

The Sports Information director's office, on Turner's instructions, telephoned the McCoy and arranged for the five freshmen to assemble in the game room at two. Casual but neat dress, the caller said. Joe College. What the well-dressed jock wears around campus.

The photographer took one look at the pool table and devised his first shot: Houston Tarr shooting while the other players stood around with cue sticks in their hands.

Under ordinary circumstances, McCarren thought, it might have been a good photo. From his vantage point against the wall, he saw how uncomfortable Theold Brown was. It took him a few seconds to realize why that was. His mother, that was it. Theold didn't want his mother to see him playing what his mother considered a gambler's game.

McCarren drew the photographer aside. After a few words with him, the shot was rearranged. Four of the players, Gilson, Winters, Stefano and Tarr, were depicted in a friendly game of 8 Ball while Theold Brown, seemingly unaware of the game behind him, twirled a basketball on one finger in the left foreground of the shot.

Three variations on this and the photographer split the team and took individual shots.

Ben Wiggins, the writer Jock had assigned, was a young man two years out of the U.N.C. Journalism School. He'd worked most of that two years with the Durham Morning Herald on the sports beat. He'd covered the Bulls games, college baseball, black college basketball and women's A.C.C basketball. In another ten years, he'd figured, he might get his shot at what he really wanted to write about. That was men's ACC basketball. The job offer from the sports publicity office at Hunt Morgan came about the time he'd decided that ten years was too long to wait.

Ben Wiggins thought he had the angle for the press release. "This early in the season," he told McCarren, "the big question is how the new five feel after their baptism under fire against N.C State."

"Run with it," McCarren said. The truth was that McCarren didn't care how the story came out. That wasn't why he'd arranged this.

Wiggins used a small tape recorder. He hadn't been in the business long enough to rely on his memory or his ability to reconstruct quotations.

While Wiggins moved around the Rec room and asked his questions, McCarren stood back and watched Paul Gilson. Paul was sullen, withdrawn and downright unfriendly. When Wiggins asked his first question of Gilson, the answer should have been predictable. Paul said he thought the team had played well considering the circumstances.

Wiggins looked past Gilson and caught McCarren's slight shake of his head. That wasn't an acceptable quote. It opened a can of rotten worms about the way the Killer had been treated at Reynolds that McCarren didn't want touched. Wiggins was quick enough to understand. He worried at Gilson, using this question and that one until he solicited a response he could use in the release.

Yes, the team had played well and Paul thought the team would improve as the freshman gained experience. As it was, the overall team speed with Theold Brown in the game, created problems for defenses.

A nod to Ben Wiggins. That was what McCarren wanted.

Wiggins switched off his tape recorder. "Thanks Gentlemen and I'll see you at the game tomorrow. Good luck."

McCarren followed the players into the hallway. "Paul. A word with you."

Gilson stopped and waited until McCarren was abreast of him. McCarren led him down the hall to the fire exit and the escape landing outside. McCarren stopped there and leaned on the railing and looked across campus. Biddle Coliseum was a glistening, snow covered dome in the near distance.

"You pleased with your play yesterday, Paul?"

"What playing time I got, Coach."

"You don't like your minutes?"

A hesitation and then a shake of his head. "The Go team idea works. At least, it works now. It might not when the other clubs expect it."

"If it's not playing time, it's something else. What's in your craw, Paul?"

"Come on, Coach." Gilson was impatient. "You don't have to pretend with me. Coach Turner talked to you, didn't he?"

"All right. No pretense."

"I didn't like that circus yesterday. I've been thinking about transferring."

"Just like that? You're kidding."

"I made a call or two last night," Gilson said.

"How many calls?"

"Two."

"Which coaches?"

"I don't know if I ought to say. Coach."

"You can say. No harm done."

"Lemonella and Carteret."

"And ...?"

The fire exit door opened behind them. Stoddard and Ashley passed by, headed for the Coliseum. "Going to work out the kinks," Stoddard said.

"Good idea," McCarren said.

Paul Gilson waited until the two players reached the bottom of the fire escape. "Lemonella said if I didn't like it here, with you, that I would hate it there with him."

George Lemonella was the new head coach at St. Vincent's in Boston. He and McCarren went back together for a number of years. What Gilson couldn't know was that McCarren had been instrumental in Lemonella getting the head coaching job. "What George means is that he doesn't want a ballplayer who's unwilling to unpack his suitcase."

"I guessed as much." A shrug. "Carteret said he wanted to be sure I was sure. If I was, he'd see I got a plane ticket. However it was handled, I'd have to sit out a year."

Carteret was a new man. He'd been an assistant coach for a long time. Templeton University was his first head coaching job. He'd been there two years and he was thin on talent. He could use the speed and know-how of a Paul Gilson. McCarren doubted that the offer had been restricted to a plane ticket and nothing else.

"It's what I'd say if a player called me," McCarren said evenly. The only sign of the frustration in him was the grip he put on the fire escape railing and the shake he gave it. "Tell me one thing, Paul. You think the Killer raped that girl?"

"No. I believe Houston. He ain't bright enough yet to lie and get away with it."

"Robert's your teammate. You feel right backing away from him when he's under pressure?"

"You know I don't like that," Gilson said.

"That's the difference between you and the Killer. Even if Robert thought you were, he'd back you all the way to hell."

"Damn it, I don't like playing ball the way it was yesterday. It made me sick."

McCarren took a deep breath. He let it out in a slow hiss. "I was talking to someone who is close to me about you last night."

Gilson nodded. Waiting.

"I tried to explain to her that you were both the purity and the corruption of the game."

"That's past me."

"It was past her, too. I didn't explain it all. Only the purity part."

"You brought it up. I guess that means you're going to explain all of it to me."

"The purity part. You've got basketball somewhere up there in your head so that it's like going to church. The holy of holies. The ultimate good. Grace and skill and brains and talent all wrapped up in one perfect ball of wax. Not just a way out of the ghetto. Maybe that was part of it in the beginning. No more. You probably don't even remember when it stopped being a sport and became a way of life, the only life."

Paul didn't answer. He was staring across the campus toward the snow on the mountains that formed a cup edge around the University.

"But you're also the corruption. The brown spot on the apple that hides the rot inside. Or points to it."

"Run that by me again."

"Five of you came in as a class this year. You're the only one in this group who's paid to play ball. Your uncle, George Marks, saw to that."

"Theold Brown ...?"

"What the N.C.I.P allows and some under-the-table."

"Theold could have got what he wanted. All he had to do was ask for it."

"You're not as pure as he is."

"And more corrupt?"

"You said that."

Below them, the Killer and Mitchell Winters emerged from the shadow of the corner of the dram. They walked together slowly toward Biddle. They appeared unaware that McCarren and Paul Gilson stood on the fire escape landing behind them. The Killer wrapped a long arm around Mitchell's shoulder, leaned toward him and said something. The Killer reared back, laughing, his face pointed toward the sky. Mitchell faked a punch at him and they went into an elaborate routine of punch and counterpunch.

"A good feeling there, Paul." A nod toward the two centers as they moved away.

"You should have been a priest, Coach."

"It was that or black eyes and skinned elbows and knees. I suppose I decided I liked the black eyes and the skinned places better than the Church."

"Maybe we're a lot alike. Coach. The corruption too."

"A white cracker like me?" McCarren snorted.

"Let me use your idea. In the purity part of it, skin color don't matter."

McCarren gave the iron rail a shake and backed away. "I'll tell you what. Take a day or two. Handle the Clemson game. There's no hurry. If you transfer you've got to sit down for a year. One more game won't matter. If your decision is that you want to leave, if that's what you want, I'll buy you the ticket from my own pocket. I'll drive you to the Winston-Salem airport and carry your bag. And when you fly away, I'll think good riddance."

"You'd do that?"

"A happy ballplayer is a good ballplayer. I don't want you here fucking up my team. That's right, my team."

"No bluff?"

"Let me tell you a story. There's a coach I know. I won't name him. You know who he is. Now he's won everything there is to win. A clutch full of conference championships, the N.I.T. when it meant something, coached his team to the N.C.A.A. championship, and coached the U.S. team in the Olympics and won that, too."

Paul thought he knew which coach McCarren was talking about. If McCarren wanted to leave his name out of it, then it would be that way.

"Along comes this kid. Maybe the player of the decade. All the schools want him. He's eighteen, he's got all the tools in the world. All he needs is polish, taking the rough edges away. The recruiting is so hot and heavy the kid's high school coach steps in the middle of it. He establishes rules about the way the kid is going to be recruited. This includes an interview with the coaches at the schools that the kid is interested in. Each college coach is required to appear before a board composed of the high school coach, the high school principal, the kid's preacher and the kid himself. The board will ask the college coach about academics at his school, how many of his players graduate and other matters like that."

Gilson nodded. Besides his guess about the coach, McCarren had mentioned he had an idea which highly-recruited player the story concerned. In fact, he'd played against that player in an all-star game and the kid was all that his press clippings claimed he was.

"So here we've got this great coach and he's got to go before a board. He's got to go there like an unemployed office clerk, his hat in his hand. It's like he's begging for a job. It's degrading and it's humiliating. Shit, you know that much. Anyway, this great coach goes before the high school coach, the high school principal, the preacher and the kid. He's got the figures on how many of his players graduated, how many didn't but are still working on their degrees during the summer, and how many of his players are in the pros, how many are doctors and lawyers and dentists. As far as academics go, he points to the fine ranking his school has, how certain departments are ranked."

"Boring," Paul said.

McCarren nodded. "After he's answered all their questions, the board gives him a couple of minutes to say anything he wants to say. You want to make a guess what the coach said?"

"Please, please, please come play for me?"

"Not exactly. He starts out by saying that he'd like the kid to come to his school and play for him. He thinks he could help the boy reach his full potential as a basketball player and a person. It's a tradeoff. The kid can help him win games. Then came the ass-kicker. He says that his school won games even before the kid was born and it will continue to win without him if the boy decides to play somewhere else. End of it."

"You're confusing me."

"No, I'm not. The story's got a message in there."

"I'll bet you twenty bucks the kid didn't pick that coach's college."

"You'd win the twenty," McCarren said. "But the coach was right. He's still winning and he's still winning big."

"You're talking to me?"

"The indirect method." McCarren opened the fire escape door. "I've got some work to do."

"Your offer of the ticket still good?"

McCarren's stomach almost dropped to his shoelaces. "You say the word."

"I won't say it this year. I'll stick the year."

They entered the hallway. Paul stopped at the doorway of his room.

"You're sure, Paul?"

"Ninety-three percent count?" Paul unlocked the door. "I think I'll shoot some baskets."

"See you." McCarren was in the lobby on the main floor of McCoy when he began to shiver. It had been close. Could have gone either way. Eighty years ago, he told himself, I would have been selling patent medicine.

CHAPTER FOURTEEN

From the opening tip of the Clemson game, it was obvious that there was some problem with Jorge. He threw one pass away, toward the corner when Stoddard broke, instead, down the baseline toward the basket. Another time he let the Clems on guard steal the ball from him near the foul circle and had to hammer the man to keep him from going in uncontested for a layup.

Jack Turner eased around in his seat and stared at McCarren. McCarren looked down at the floor. He wasn't about to embarrass Jorge by substituting for him early. He'd wait and see if Jorge settled into a rhythm.

Another turnover. Jorge lofted a pass toward the Killer and the Clemson big forward batted it away.

Clemson was up by 6.6 to 0.

McCarren said, "The Go team."

As the team passed McCarren, he caught Gilson by the arm. "Get those points back."

"No sweat."

The teams switched. McCarren patted Turner on the shoulder and moved him down a seat. Jorge jogged toward the bench and stopped when he saw the Coach nod toward the space to his right.

The crowd roared. Gilson stepped into a passing lane and bumped the ball downcourt to Theold Brown. Sprinting, bobbing, Theold drove the length of the court and slammed the ball through the net.

6 to 2.

"Tell me about it." McCarren studied Jorge's face. There was a cold, slick sweat on his face.

"Something I ate. Coach."

"At the training table?"

"Chili at the Student Union snack bar."

McCarren waved a hand at the trainer. "Take him to the dressing room and get a doctor."

The trainer and the student manager walked Jorge up the ramp and out of sight.

The Go team blitzed. On defense, Stefano rebounded a miss by the Clemson big forward. On offense, at the other end of the court, Mitchell put a hip on the Clemson center and bumped him away. The push wasn't called. Mitchell took the high pass and stuffed it.

McCarren moved down the bench. He asked the same question. "Anybody eat at the Student Union? Anybody eat the chili?"

All head shakes. No yeses.

"Robert."

The Killer eased into the seat on McCarren's right side.

"You four back in. Gilson stays in at point."

The starters trotted on court. Gilson saw them coming and headed for the bench. The Killer stopped him. Gilson looked at McCarren.

McCarren stood in front of the bench and patted each of the four members of the Go team leaving the game. "Good work. You got us moving."

Theold stopped. "Where's Jorge?"

"Upset stomach."

McCarren returned Paul Gilson's stare. You want playing time. Here it is. Get a bellyful.

Gilson played well. His one shortcoming was that he was not accustomed to playing long stretches. No amount of practice and conditioning could prepare a player for actual game time. The chemistry was different. At the five minute mark, five minutes before the end of the half, playing on the starting team and the Go team, he was sucking air into hurting lungs. He swayed slightly while he stood on the foul line and prepared himself to shoot – a one and one.

"Stefano."

Jimmy's head jerked up. He ran to McCarren.

"Theold."

Theold Brown joined them.

"Jimmy, you give Gilson blow."

"At point?"

"You can do it." He tapped Stefano on the shoulder with a fist. "Theold, you're in for Stoddard."

Gilson slumped into the seat next to McCarren. He took a deep breath and shuddered. "I've got … to get … in shape."

"You're in shape. Take slow, even breaths."

The student manager returned and leaned over the Coach. "They took Jorge to the infirmary. I'm thinking they're going to pump his stomach."

Gilson chewed on an orange wedge.

"You got fifteen more minutes in those legs?"

"At least that."

Stefano was a step and a half slower than Gilson or Jorge. He made up for it in effort. Heady too, McCarren thought. He drove the lane twice and passed back to Theold who made both shots. He bumped bodies and rebounded like a big forward.

Another time, Stefano drove the lane and faked to Theold and passed under the basket to Ames Ashley. Ashley went up for the layin free and untouched. In front of him the Killer cleared the Clemson center away.

Stefano played well enough so that McCarren didn't have to play Gilson the rest of the half. Paul rested and felt the strength flowing into his legs.

At the buzzer, the Mountaineers were up over Clemson by five points.

McCarren placed a folding chair near the bench where the Killer, Theold, Paul and Jimmy Stefano were seated. The student manager passed by and handed around orange halves or Gatorade. "We've got to take them out of the zone. If Theold hits three or so more, and we play good defense..."

Orange juice ran down Paul's chin. "Give me Walter Turk instead of Ashley and we'll have Clemson man to man in three or four minutes."

"What?"

"We give up some height. But say we put Walter in the other crease in the zone, the one opposite Theold. Theold and Walter give an exhibition."

McCarren smiled. "A promise?"

"Count on it."

"Get Turk."

They found Walter in the bathroom. He came in rubbing wet hands on his uniform top.

"How're you shooting, Walter?"

"Don't know. But I got an eye like a hawk."

McCarren grinned. He pushed the blackboard flat against the wall. "We'll call this one the Zone Buster." The chalk stick squeaked as he drew the half court set.

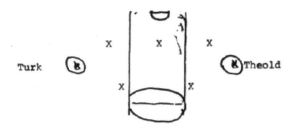

The Clemson zone shift, cheating toward Theold in the crease on the right. Gilson faked a pass toward Theold and saw the Clemson adjustment. He passed to Alley and got the ball back. He took the dribble to the left, toward Walter Turk. He was three paces from Turk when he faked the pass to Theold on his right, saw the zone shift in that direction, and dropped the ball to Turk. Turk's shot was a "rimmer". It bounced from rim to rim before the momentum died and it dropped through.

The next time the zone floated with the ball. No cheating toward Theold. It was honest now.

A duck shoot, McCarren thought. Theold got his open shot. He faked taking it, brought the ball down, and dribbled three steps before he took it.

In. Clemson scored. The Mountaineers led by seven.

Theold took a pass from Paul a few feet over mid court. Instead of returning the ball to him, Theold whirled and drove for the basket. Clemson wasn't prepared. Theold brushed past the guard on his side of the court. The Clemson center moved away from the basket and challenged him. In stride, Theold bounced the ball past the Clemson center. The Killer took the pass knee high and extended his arms. He dropped the ball through without leaving his fleet.

The Clemson coach called a time out. After the time out Clemson was in a man to man.

Stefano and Gilson split time at point guard. At the buzzer the Mountaineers had won 74 to 70.

Paul Gilson sat in the folding metal chair in the shower long after everybody else had finished and left to dress. The water pounded him. There was a roaring in his ears like the sound of the ocean.

"There you are." The Killer leaned into the shower and turned the knobs and cut the water flow "You so skinny, I thought you washed down the drain and nobody noticed."

"God, I thought…"

The Killer leaned over him. "You stand 7"

"I don't think so."

"Don't go anywhere." The Killer left. When he returned he carried three large towels. He wrapped Paul in the towels and lifted him as easily as if he were a baby. The student manager jerked his head around. He'd been pushing the laundry cart down the aisles between the lockers in the dressing room.

"You want the doctor?" he asked the Killer.

"No. What you can do for me is put some towels on the training table. Spread them out."

"Sure." The manager ran ahead of Robert.

When the training table was covered with towels, Robert lowered Gilson to the table and stripped the damp towels away. He covered him, head-to-foot, with dry towels.

"You rest, my man, while I get dressed."

Paul closed his eyes. He seemed to drop into the darkness as if he'd rolled over the edge of a table.

Over an hour had passed when Paul awoke. The Killer sat in a chair that was titled back against the wall. He sucked on a bottle of beer. He raised the bottle and nodded at it. "Sent that manager boy out for provisions in case we had to stay the night."

"I feel better." Paul pushed away at what he thought were towels covering him. The towels were gone. Robert had covered him with a blanket. He heard the dry croak, a voice he didn't recognize as his own, "I could use a brew myself."

Robert tipped the chair forward. He got to his feet and reached in the small refrigerator that held medicine. "The shape you're in, it can't hurt you."

Paul pushed the blanket aside. He sat forward and swung his lees over the side of the table. He was stiff but he thought he was stronger.

The Killer twisted the cap from a throw-away Bud. Paul poured down about a third of the beer. It hit his stomach like a rock. Paul wobbled his way into the dressing room and stopped at his locker. He started dressing. A sip of beer, a piece of clothing went on. The Killer put a foot on the floor and watched him. He'd put the remaining bottles of Bud in a bag.

"Thanks, man."

"For nothing," the Killer said. "You wasn't so tired I might even get you laid tonight"

"I ain't <u>that</u> tired."

Robert took him to a black tavern in the northeast part of town, near the city limits. There weren't that many blacks in the mountains. In the beginning, from slavery times, blacks worked the lowlands, the sandhills and the coastal jobs. Only with the expansion of Hunt Morgan University, the admission of black students and the required recruitment of black faculty, had the obvious influx started. Still, in terms of the whole state, the percentage of blacks to whites was about half what it was elsewhere.

A neon sign blinked outside. EVE'S PLACE.

The inside was knotty pine walled, early 1950's juke joint design. The tables and bar tops with scarred and knife-carved names and initials. A long beer box extended the length of the bar counter. At the rear of the bar an old iron grill smoked. Fatty hamburgers hissed on the grill. A huge stainless steel pot bubbled with plump, watery hot dogs.

The Killer swaggered to the middle of the bar and planted his elbows there. "Eve, I'm hungry. I done worked up a good hungry.

I'll have three of those burgers with everything and four of them dogs. That'll start me."

"Beer," Paul said. The croak was gone from his voice. His thirst, even with the second bottle he'd drunk on the ride, hadn't eased.

"Beer for me and my man here," the Killer shouted.

Everyone knew the Killer. A tall, elderly black man in a sweat-stained felt hat said, "Those beers are on me. Eve. I can't afford to feed him but ..."

"Tall ones," Robert said. He wagged a hand at the black man. "Thanks, Bob."

"Heard you win on the radio tonight," Bob said.

"You heard the game you heard about this man. He's my speed man, Paul Gilson. Paul played extra time tonight because Jorge ate himself some bad food."

"I got my wish I'd see you play one night."

"You want your Christmas present early?" The Killer laughed. "How about the game Thursday night?"

"Huh?"

"We're playing this little Catholic school Thursday. You come by the ticket office at the Biddle. I'll leave you two tickets there. The name's Bob ...?"

"Turley. But I don't need more than one ticket."

"Take a sweet woman with you. Take Eve,"

"I don't know." Bob rubbed his face.

"One ticket or two?"

"Two," Turley said.

The Killer popped the tabs on two tall Buds. Behind the bar, at the grill. Eve turned the burgers and pressed the fat from the patties with a spatula. The grease spattered. The door opened and a cold wind blew in from the outside. Robert looked over his shoulder, The Killer pushed one tall Bud toward Paul.

"Eve, you hold them onions. I decided I want to taste good tonight. Here come the Honey sisters."

Paul eased around and braced an elbow on the bar. Two young black girls, in their late teens, entered and stood in the doorway looking around. As his eyes adjusted, Paul saw that both girls were attractive. Foxy girls.

The Killer leaned toward Paul until his shoulder touched Paul's. "You tired?"

"Not anymore."

"Honey girls," the Killer yelled, "here I am." Both girls squealed and ran against him. The Killer wrapped a huge arm around each of them.

Jorge was back for the Belmont Abbey game five days later. The Go team was used as a unit for three minutes stretches five times during the game. Turner charted the effectiveness of the maneuver. Each time the Go squad held their own or bettered the opposing team in scoring margin. Four and six-tenths points each entry into a game. That was amazing. Turner thought.

Gilson, besides his stint with the special squad, split time with Jorge who was not back at full strength yet. Theold Brown logged his minutes as well. About equal time with Billy Stoddard.

It was no contest. The Killer dominated both ends of the court. Late in the second half McCarren cleared the bench and the final margin was eighteen points.

At the postgame press conference, Bo Willis, the Belmont coach, said that McCarran was a true gentleman and a kind-hearted man. Shaking his head sadly, he said, "He could have won by a hundred if he wanted to."

The Kentucky State game was played on a neutral court at the Greensboro Coliseum. The Mountaineers seemed flat after the win over Belmont Abbey. What resulted was a close game. Headed into the last two minutes of the game, Kentucky State was in front by four. Gilson fed Stefano on a baseline drive. Jimmy took an off balance shot that slid across the rim and was rebounded and tapped in by the Killer. Down by two. Mitchell Winters, in at big forward, blocked a shot attempt. On a Fastbreak, Robert filled the center lane and dunked the pass from Theold over the Kentucky State small forward who took one look at the Killer and rolled out of his path rather than taking his position to draw the charge.

Even. 71 to 71.

The Kentucky State called time with fifty-three seconds left. On the Mountaineer bench, everyone knew that State would run the clock until it ticked under the ten second mark. Perhaps as low as five seconds before they tried the shot. That way, if the shot missed, the Mountaineers wouldn't have time for a winning basket and the game would go into overtime.

McCarren looked at Jack Turner. "What do you think?"

"We trap."

"Listen up," McCarren said.

"We don't play the man bringing in the ball from out of bounds. Robert, you start at center court. If they inbound the ball, you drop back and play goalie. Jorge and Gilson, you play the other guard. Mitchell and Jimmy, be here, there and everywhere. I want a steal. If not a steal, I want them to waste a lot of time getting the ball across mid court. I don't want them to have enough time to set up a good shot. A bad shot won't beat us."

The buzzer sounded. The ref moved down the court and motioned at the Mountaineer bench.

"But no foul," McCarren said. "Foul shots can beat us, too."

The hustling defense the Mountaineers showed Kentucky State forced the inbounding guard to bounce the ball off Mitchell Winters and out of bounds again. It was that or have the five seconds call that would have turned the ball over to Hunt Morgan.

"Catch it this time," Jorge shouted at Mitchell.

Still the postage stamp defense. The Kentucky State guard didn't have a certain and clear pass in and called time with four seconds gone on the ref's five second arm count swing.

"Good defense," McCarren said, leaning over the players.

"That was their last time out," Turner said.

"Same tight defense. If they call a time out now, it's a technical and we shoot it."

"No passing lane for them," Turner said.

McCarren ran his tongue across dry lips. "Can't get it in, not in two tries. They might have a number hidden away somewhere."

Turner closed his eyes. When he opened them he said, "I can't see them changing the inbounding man. He is cool, got the experience. They might try to free the small forward on a sprint over the middle toward center court."

"Theold," McCarren said, "you stay with him."

"Mitchell, that leaves you watching the center and the big forward."

Mitchell laughed. "All by myself?"

"What's wrong, white man? You got slow feet?" The Killer cracked up and almost fell out of his seat.

The whole team whooped and yelled. On the other side of the scorer's table, the Kentucky State coach, about to send his team on the floor, looked at the Mountaineer players like he thought they'd cracked under the strain.

The buzzer sounded. Turner caught the Killer by the arm. "Watch their center. Could be he'll break with the small forward. If he does, you…"

Robert nodded. "Got you."

It was almost the way Jack Turner predicted it. With Jorge and Paul clamped on the other guard like a vise, the in-bounding guard knew he didn't have a good pass there. The small forward slid along the baseline, as if positioning himself for the pass. Then he whirled and broke diagonally downcourt. Without

Turner's warning, Theold might have been fooled. With it, he was one step ahead of the small forward. He slowed, seemed to break stride. That was what the inbounding guard was looking for. He threw the pass toward the small forward. As soon as the ball left the Kentucky State guard's fingers, Theold sprinted. He timed it to the second. All the small forward saw was a dark blur as Theold stepped in front of him and jerked the ball out of the air.

McCarren jumped to his feet. He was about to call time. He wanted to set up the shot. Turner edged to his side. "Let them do it."

Theold dribbled down the side of the court. Jorge moved to meet him and receive the ball. Jorge whipped the ball to Paul Gilson.

The clock was down to forty-one seconds.

Jorge backed toward the Mountaineer bench. "One shot," McCarren shouted.

A nod and Jorge moved forward again.

Paul passed the ball to Jorge. Jorge held it, a standup, waiting dribble. Paul checked the clock above the floor. Twenty-three seconds.

A Kentucky State guard jumped out and made a cut at the ball. Jorge backed away and flipped the ball to Gilson. He moved to get an angle on the clock. Sixteen seconds.

"Fifteen," he shouted at Paul.

Paul moved to the right, flipped the ball to Mitchell and got it back. He reversed his dribble and moved toward the full circle. Jorge brushed past him. "Ten seconds."

Paul looked at Theold.

Theold was on the left, guarded by the small forward. Theold tapped his chest with a finger twice. Paul nodded. That meant, in the signals between them, the second move.

"Six," Jorge said.

Theold jumped out as if headed for the corner. The small forward charged after him. Three steps and Theold planted a foot and spun around. He passed the small forward and broke across the middle of the lane. The pass from Paul reached him when he was high in the air. He hung there, turning and banked the shot through.

No time left. The game was over.

CHAPTER FIFTEEN

The scheduling took over, the way McCarren liked to pace his games during the early part of the season. The team flew into New York a week after the Kentucky State game and played St. Peter's in the Garden as a part of a doubleheader. The *Times* called the game the homecoming of Timothy McCarren, the scrappy little guard from the early fifties at St. Peter's who now brought his southern powerhouse to the big city to play the college he still loved and donated money to.

A few hundred to Annual Giving got a man good press, McCarren decided.

It was a blowout. The Killer decided he wanted to look good and he scored forty-one points while playing less than twenty minutes. Theold was nervous and missed his first three shots before he made eight of his next nine.

During the game, the Mountaineers used the Go team only once. McCarren thought of it as a demonstration, showtime, and he smiled to himself when he saw how much it rattled the other team.

He pulled them after two minutes. He wanted to win. He didn't want to humiliate.

In the last seven minutes, he played the low end or the bench. But he watched the score. He knew, from the paper, that the Mountaineers were favored by eighteen points. He maintained the margin at twenty-two most of the game and won by twenty.

There. Nobody could get mad at him for not covering the points.

When the polls came out the following Tuesday the Mountaineers were ranked 12th in both the AP and the UPI.

The team was 5 and 0 and one of the *Charlotte News* said he thought the Mountaineers looked unbeatable.

The East Tennessee State game was, for all intents and purposes, really two games. In the first half the Mountaineers couldn't do anything right and the East Tennessee team did everything right. It was a measure of the half to come that, as poorly as they'd played. Hunt Morgan was only down seven points.

In the dressing room, McCarren raged and stormed all over the players. "All you thought you had to do was throw your press clipping on the court and that team would roll over and play dead dog, right? Well, you thought wrong. You're stinking up the Biddle. Another half like the last one, and I'm going to make you buy tickets. Yes, tickets. You're not playing, so you must be watching. We charge people to watch a game, don't we?" With that, McCarren stormed out of the dressing room and slammed the door behind him.

To further humiliate the starters, McCarren started the Go team at the beginning of the second half. The Go squad blew past East Tennessee and, in two minutes, made up six of the seven points.

As if reluctant, unwilling, McCarren allowed Jack Turner to insert the starters. Motivated, Jack Turner thought. He made a mental note of McCarren's dressing room blast.

The starters pulled past East Tennessee and roared to a big lead. By the ten minute mark, the game was out of reach. McCarren did some spot substituting and let the margin fall. The Mountaineers won by a respectable twelve points.

The East Tennessee coach said afterwards, "We won the first half and then they won the second. They won the second half by more points, so that means we lost."

McCarren walked around the dressing room after the game and chatted with the starters. He wanted to see if there was any resentment toward his tirade. He didn't notice any. Winning healed every scar. A loss and even the minor sores began to fester.

The team broke for Christmas that night after the East Tennessee game. The next game scheduled was for December 27th and the players were to gather in Atlanta on the afternoon of the 26th for a short workout. The opponent was Georgia State, an inner city school in Atlanta. McCarren had chosen the team with care. He didn't feel Georgia State was in his class as far as talent went. With his players coming back after a six day layoff, he wanted a tune-up, not a testing of his team.

It was an indication, McCarren thought, of the new respect the Mountaineers had achieved that Georgia State asked if the game in Atlanta could be shifted from their small gym to the Omni. The original suggestion had been made by Omni management. McCarren agreed to the new location with the proviso that a new contract be drawn up that would assure Hunt Morgan a reasonable split on the increased gate.

Georgia State stayed with the Mountaineers during the first half. The 12,000-plus fans had to settle for "close." The Mountaineers were ragged during that twenty minutes, the result of the holiday, the overeating and the poor training habits of some of the players.

The second half all the kinks were gone. The team flexed and cowed. The Killer went at the smaller Georgia State center and muscled him on both ends of the court. At one stretch Robert scored five straight baskets. Close in dunks, turn arounds from in the lane and even one jump shot from the free throw line.

McCarren used the Go team three times in the second and each two minute episode was a blitz and a point spurt for the Mountaineers.

Even with the poor first half start, the Mountaineers won by twenty-one points.

In the morning paper, the Constitution, the Atlanta Hawks scout and coaches were interviewed. The scout said that he thought he could start a new franchise in the N.B.A. with the Killer, Jorge, Paul Gilson and Theold Brown. And maybe he'd take Jimmy Stefano as well, for plain hustle and savvy.

The Hawks coach said that he projected Robert Hinson as one of the dominating power forwards in the future of the N.B.A.

"Too bad," he said," that we'll be drafting so late that it would a miracle if Hinson were still available."

The assistant coach, tongue-in-cheek, said that he was angry with the old Gray Fox, McCarren. "All he had to do was keep the Killer under a basket another year and we might have got ourselves a ballplayer. As it is, Robert ain't no secret anymore. Or he's the best known secret around."

The team flew from Atlanta Hartsfield International the following morning. Their destination was Akron, Ohio. On the 29th, one day later, they were to play in the Tire Classic there. Their opening round competition was the host team, Ohio University. The other game would match Bowling Green and Penn.

A sudden blizzard struck Akron while the plane was still an hour away. Due to the heavy snow and the deteriorating visibility, the pilot considered a landing at an alternative field three hundred miles south of Akron. When McCarren received that word, he ranted and raved. He stomped up and down the aisle. He insisted, if it was possible to make a landing within the safety limits/ he wanted to continue to the original destination. The pilots conferred. Weather control at Akron decided that visibility was satisfactory. The landing was a slipping, sliding and skidding affair and the players and the press entourage were shaken and relieved when they stepped from the plane.

There was some grumbling about the risk, the gamble that McCarren had taken with their lives.

The bitching and the grumbling ended after they spent nearly three hours on a bus in a massive traffic snarl, just getting from the airport to the hotel downtown.

Jack Turner explained to the Killer and Jorge, as captains, why McCarren had made the decision he did. "If you liked almost three hours on a bus getting to a hotel, how would you like to spend the whole night getting here from East Jesus Airport?"

Snow swirled and billowed and piled all down the street. The wind gusted at more than twenty-five miles an hour. McCarren stood at a lobby window and decided that he would not try to reach the Coliseum for the planned evening workout. The next morning, if the streets were clear, if the weather was better, he'd try to fit in some loosening up and some shooting c drills. It would still leave them the afternoon for rest before the seven o'clock game against Ohio University.

While the team ate in a private dining room at the hotel, McCarren and Jack Turner had supper with a couple of sports writers from the area papers. The Tire Classic was fairly new as a Christmas season tournament and it needed all the press and publicity it could receive.

Frank Watley was with the Cleveland Plain Dealer. Over drinks, the menus spread before them, he asked, "Tell me about this team, Tim. Is it as good as the out of town papers say it is?"

"What you'll see is what we've got."

"I covered you in the Mideasts last year … well, last march. You had all the making then."

"Picked up some speed," McCarren said, "but it's young, a year away from taking control."

Watley drank his dark rum straight. He finished his drink and handed the glass to the passing waiter. "I saw some clips of the North Carolina State game. I haven't seen so much women's underwear since laundry day in the slums of Chicago in the 1930's."

"I thought Robert Hinson handled that as well as anyone could under the circumstances. I felt for him. It's a blessing he's matured as much as he has. Two years ago … well, I'd hate to think what might have happened with the same provocation."

The blinds were open on their side of the restaurant. Snow continued to fill. Jack Turner stared at the snow for a time. "I wonder how it is in California today."

"Better," Frank Watley said. The waiter brought Frank's dark rum refill and took McCarren's glass away for another Irish.

"You think anybody will dog sled over to the Coliseum to see my country boys play Ohio University?"

"Country boys?" Watley smiled at McCarren. "It's the only game in town. It's that or stay home and shovel snow."

"That's reassuring."

"Ain't it?" Watley said.

McCarren was restless. He'd tried to sleep and couldn't.

The wind whistled around the hotel, a howling, wheezing wind that sounded like it belonged on the soundtrack of The Call of the Wild. He stuffed his feet in the fur-lined slippers Ellen had insisted on packing for him and belted his robe and went prowling.

Normally, on the night before a game on the road, there would have been a bed check. Not tonight. It was like the Russian steppes inches outside the hotel entrance. McCarren was fairly certain that he hadn't recruited any retardates for his basketball program.

He saw lights above the transom in one of the rooms down the hall. He knocked and the door was opened to him. The Killer and Jorge and Houston Tarr and Paul Gilson sat around a bed playing poker for matches.

"Care to sit in, Coach?" The Killer asked.

"I got all the matches I need," McCarren said.. He pulled a chair to the end of the bed and looked at Gilson. "How are the legs?"

"Hanging on the bones." Paul smiled.

After the hassle of almost a month ago, Gilson was fitting in. It pleased McCarren to notice that he and the Killer were tight now, hanging around together.

The Killer called. Gilson showed two pairs, aces and kings. The Killer had three deuces. He raked the small pile of paper matches toward him.

Gilson shuffled the cards and placed them for Tarr to cut. "Next year. Coach, can we go to California? Please."

"Could be. We're working on the Rainbow in Hawaii."

"Better and better."

"I think I'll redshirt the rest of the year. I want my chance to see Hawaii."

McCarren shook his head. "Too late. You remember we're seven and zip? You've played too many games. You can't redshirt."

"Don't worry, man," Gilson said. "If that Hawks coach is right, you're going to be so heavy in the pocket you can pay your own way there next summer."

"True, speed man."

"You get back, maybe you need a driver." Houston stretched and rubbed his neck. He yawned.

"You too bored to be my driver." the Killer said.

For a nightmarish moment, McCarren thought it was a rerun of the Western Arkansas game in the Mideast final back in March. Ohio University had speed. Good team speed. He blinked and yes, it was Ohio University instead of Western Arkansas. Another day, another chance to deal with that bad dream.

Ohio U. was ahead by four and the game had hardly started. He motioned toward the bench. "Theold, Paul."

Gilson in for Alley and Theold in for Stoddard. The game changed. His team didn't appear to be moving in slow motion. "Show me something else," McCarren mumbled as he stared past the scorer's table toward the Ohio U. bench.

It was a good crowd for the weather. Almost ten thousand people had courted fever, chills and frostbite to reach the Coliseum. The Tire Classic director had walked by prior to the game and said, "Thanks for coming. I think your team drew the crowd."

Speed countered speed and then talent became the only real factor. Theold Brown took it to the small forward at both ends of the court. He blocked shots and had a steal on defense. On offense, he split the lane wide open and put up a running shovel shot that rolled in. When the small forward bumped him and denied him the drive, Theold reversed his dribble, backed away to fifteen feet, and put in the soft jumper. Ohio U. tried to adjust their defense to control Theold. Paul Gilson, managing the point, fed the Killer in low until Ohio U. double-teamed him and used the big forward to front him. The small forward cheated a step toward the basket so he could help out. Gilson saw this the second time it happened. The next time down Gilson faked to the Killer and, when the small forward took a step away from Theold, he dropped the ball in the open slot on the left. Theold took it in stride, went up and put in the thirteen foot shot.

The second half, up by twelve and the score mounting, McCarren decided to try a big front line. It was a concept he'd considered late one sleepless night. Sooner or later, down the road, he thought he might encounter a team that had recruited for size rather than pure quickness.

The Killer at six-ten at center. Bo Regis at six-nine at one forward and Mitchell Winters at six-ten at the other. In the backcourt, to add speed, he tried Theold and Paul. It was awkward at the beginning. It took getting used to. Five minutes passed and the flow was there. The big men crashed the boards. The Killer scored. Mitchell scored. The Ohio U. team, bumped and hipped and elbowed aside, didn't collect a rebound at either end of the court.

Jack Turner had his doubts about the experiment. He'd wanted to argue but hadn't. When the flow was there, he turned in his seat and looked at McCarren. His mouth moved without sound. Awesome.

McCarren changed the lineup. He substituted his usual starting team. No reason to show a wrinkle that he might want to save for a special day, a special time.

With the clock at ten seconds and winding down, Theold stole a pass and broke the length of the court. He brought the crowd to their feet with a twisting, behind his head two-handed slam dunk.

The Ohio U. coach met McCarren at the scorer's table. "Like the man in Atlanta said, get yourself an N.B.A. franchise." There was no sting to what he said. He was nice about the way the game had gone, only disappointed.

On his way from the court, McCarren looked at the score on the clock. Won by eighteen. He'd wanted to hold the margin down. He'd played the whole bench.

Some days all the peaches fell from the tree. Even when you'd rather save a few of those peaches for a day when you were really hungry.

❧ ❧ ❧

The nightcap between Bowling Green and Penn was a deliberate, control game. Bowling Green had racehorses and Penn decided that was a kind of game they couldn't win. Penn wanted the good shot and didn't, as far as McCarren remembered later, take a single bad one. Bowling Green, frustrated all evening, wanted to racehorse back and forth, end to end, but nothing they could do forced Penn into their tempo.

The game ended, Penn over Bowling Green 56-52, and McCarren stayed on court for the press conference.

McCarren furnished the sports writers some good quotes for the morning and afternoon papers. About the snow: "If I'd wanted to ski, I'd have stayed home and saved the plane fare."

About his fine showing against Ohio University: "We were playing over our heads. My boys are all from the country. They were looking forward to seeing a big city for the first time. They got mad when they got snowed in last night and they didn't get to see Akron. I guess they took it out on these nice people from Ohio U."

About the Killer: "He's such a friendly guy that I have to threaten to keep his meal money if he doesn't throw his weight around three or four times a half."

McCarren remained after the Ohio University coach left. He wanted a look at the new Penn coach, Kelly. New to the East but not new to coaching. A good record in the W.A.C. A fine Christian gentleman. Very big in the Christian Athletes Association, what some coaches and players called "Jocks for Jesus." Kelly was young, tanned. He wore his hair short, almost in a crew cut. His face, when he responded to questions, was open and revealing.

Later, riding the team bus to the hotel, McCarren rubbed his eyes and yawned and said it had been a long, long day.

"But you're still thinking?"

"On one cylinder."

The bus ground and crunched its way across the icy streets. Snow banks, like small mountains, glistened where the snow plows had created them along the gutters.

"What will Kelly do?"

"He'll sit on it," McCarren said.

"Like tonight?"

"Tonight will look like run-and-gun compared to what he'll probably do tomorrow night."

Jack Turner sneezed and blocked the spray with a hand. "He had a rep for using a modified four corners the last place he coached." The four corners was a slowdown game where the team that wanted the slowdown jumped into a lead and then pulled the ball out and ran the clock, protecting the lead and looking for only the perfect shot, the high percentage shot. The other team, because it was behind in the score, had to chase the ball. It was the chase, the man to man that was forced on the trailing team, often led to the open layup, the clean drive to the basket. "How do we play them. Jack?"

"We use the speed early and we don't let them get the lead. We insist on the tempo we want."

It was after eleven when they arrived at the hotel. The manager wanted to do his best for the Tire Classic and the teams but he hadn't wanted to keep the kitchen open until midnight. McCarren settled for a late supper of soup and a buffet of cold meats and salads.

The waiters cleared the tables. McCarren ordered an Irish over ice for himself, a scotch and ice for Jack Turner and one bottle of beer for any player who wanted it.

The student manager closed the double dining room doors and stood with his back to them.

McCarren sipped his Irish and frowned. "Eight wins without a loss ain't cabbage soup."

"It's damned near perfect," the Killer said.

Some of the players clinked beer bottles in a toast and laughed.

"You're talkative for this time of night, Robert. You give us a scouting report on Penn."

"They can't match us on the front line."

"Go on."

"The small forward has a good shot, some quickness."

"The guards?"

"The point's quick, protects the ball well, doesn't make many mistakes."

"The big guard?"

"He's the danger," the Killer said. "I figure he hit ten of twelve."

"Eight of twelve," Turner said. He tapped the stat sheet he kept of the game.

"You know I can't count."

McCarren rattled the ice cubes in his glass. "What do you think Penn will do against us tomorrow night?"

"Your guess is as good as mine, Coach."

McCarren stared at him for a long moment. "Penn came close to matching up with Bowling Green. Even then, they wanted a control game. If they can't match up with us, what do you think?"

"I think you're saying they'll let the air out of the ball."

"Talk about guessing. That's my guess."

CHAPTER SIXTEEN

The consolation match between Bowling Green and Ohio U. was run and gun basketball at its best. Both teams had been hurt by the game a night earlier. They took it out on each other and the scores were in the middle nineties. Bowling Green won by three points.

In the dressing room before the game with Penn, Jack Turner said that he sure would like to know how the Penn coach, Kelly, was going to play them.

"I'll ask him."

"The hell you will."

"The hell I won't," McCarren smiled.

When the players returned from their initial warmups, McCarren had the backboard positioned. He'd set up a team one and a team two.

team one	team two
Hinson	Hinson
Stoddard	Regis
Ashley	Brown
Morgan	Morgan
Alley	Gilson

"You'll notice," McCarren said smiling, "I made it easy for Jorge and the Killer to remember which team they're on by putting them on both." He looked at his watch. "It's time."

McCarren picked his moment. He wandered along the front of the Mountaineer bench. On the court, the players from both schools took their last shots. On the other side of the scorer's table, Coach Kelly happened to face McCarren. That set McCarren in motion. He drifted along the sideline and stopped at the scorer's table. He leaned forward and asked how long before tipoff. The Penn coach, Kelly, wasn't certain what McCarren wanted at the scorer's table. He knew, however, that no coach ever let the opposing coach work the scorer or the timekeeper without being there to protect his own interests. He rushed to the table and stood shoulder-to-shoulder with McCarren.

"One minute to tipoff," the timekeeper explained and touched the buzzer button. Satisfied that McCarren wasn't trying to steal an edge away from him, Kelly backed away. McCarren followed him and offered his hand.

"Good luck," McCarren said,

Kelly stopped. He stepped forward and extended his hand. He was pleased. "Thanks, Mr. McCarren."

McCarren turned him, still holding his hand, and put an arm around Kelly's shoulders. He leaned close. "You going to hold the ball on me?"

"What?" Kelly was shocked. He pulled away from McCarren's arm and jerked his hand free. He stormed down the sideline.

Enough. McCarren joined Jack Turner and said, "Team two."

"You did it?"

"Another guess."

Turner carried the new lineup to the public address announcer.

On the opening tip, assuming that the Killer would control the ball, McCarren called one of the set, special situation plays that he sometimes worked on during practice. The moment the official stepped forward and tossed the ball between the two centers, even as the centers jumped and extended themselves, Theold Brown broke for the basket.

The Penn small forward who'd been jockeying for position with Theold a moment before was caught flat footed. The Killer won the tip and batted the ball downcourt. Theold had only to adjust one step to his right to take the ball. Three dribbles and he scooped the ball, one-handed, and soared. He slammed the ball through the rim. The Penn small forward was four or five strides behind him.

Up by two. Not decisive yet. Too much time.

"Let's see if you can shift rears," McCarren mumbled to himself as the Penn team brought the ball past his bench. Penn was cool, the players were confident. It showed in the way Penn took their time looking for the good shot. McCarren's game was to make certain they didn't find the shot they wanted and had to settle for one they didn't want.

Paul Gilson dogged the Penn point guard. He worked him into a hot sweat and lather. As it should be. But the point guard retained his mental coolness. He didn't make a mistake. But, from where he sat, McCarren thought he could see the tension building in the Penn player. Take two aspirins and a neck rub, McCarren thought.

Three minutes passed before Penn small forward freed himself for a shot he wanted. It was good shot selection, a good shot. The ball dipped into the net and popped out. The Killer rebounded.

McCarren stood and shouted at Jorge as he passed the bench. "Four I."

Jorge nodded.

Paul Gilson curled back to take the ball from Jorge. Jorge moved his lips, repeating the instructions, and Gilson smiled. Paul dribbled across the centerline. He looked toward Theold.

"Four eyes," he said. Paul started his dribble to the right and turned and moved left. About the time he reached the back of the left side of the circle Theold broke toward him. He had a step and a half on the Penn small forward. Paul stopped his dribble and tossed the ball, belly high, to Theold. Paul planted his feet. Theold took the ball and dribbled around Paul. The Penn small forward, sprinting after Theold, didn't see Paul until the last second. The Penn forward broke stride and swerved aside to avoid charging into Paul. Freed, far ahead of his roan, Theold performed a ninety degree turn and drove the lane, the "I" designated in the call, and laid the ball in off the backboards.

4 to 0.

Penn didn't rattle. They were patient. The small forward used a pick on Theold to shake him. The shot, from twelve feet, on the baseline, dropped through.

4 to 2.

"Stefano." Jimmy jumped from the bench and positioned himself on one knee in front of McCarren. "In for Jorge. You're at small forward. Play Dilmore tight. Don't let him get a run going. Theold moves back to guard and chases their point guard."

The whole first half McCarren kept fresh men on the Penn point guard. Gilson, Jorge, Theold and even Houston Tarr for a short period of time.

The scoring was low by most standards. 20 to 15 at the half, the Mountaineers ahead.

Leaving the court, McCarren stopped in the ramp and watched the Penn point guard pass him. The kid was almost exhausted, sucking air and trying to hide it.

"Got 'em," McCarren said.

In the second half, Coach Kelly had to go to his bench and relieve his point guard. Gilson rattled the replacement, caused a walking call and stole the ball from him.

Butcher ball, McCarren told himself. It ain't pretty but it works.

The Mountaineers won by six, 51-45.

The Most Valuable Player voting took place with minutes to play in the game. Robert Hinson and Theold Brown shared the honor.

While the teams waited at courtside for the presentation of the championship and 2nd place trophies, McCarren strolled along the sideline and found Coach Kelly.

"Forgiven?"

"Cheap trick," Kelly said.

"It was only worth two points." McCarren smiled. "You've got to play more poker."

McCarren gave the team New Year's Eve off.

New Year's Day, with its day and evening of football bowl games, was to be recovery day, January 2nd there was a full scale practice and "devil take the man" who wasn't in shape for conditioning wind sprints.

The team practiced on January 2nd and 3rd and flew into South Bend on the afternoon of Sunday the 4th. Check-in completed at the hotel, they unlimbered at the Student Convocation Center. The game did not go well from the get-go.

It was what they called "home cooking" in most parts of the country. The home team got all the calls from the officiating crew. Both the calls that could have gone either way or even outrageous ones. Most of the time, the home coaches had nothing to do with "homer" games, at least in no direct way. To some degree, a rabid crowd could influence the officials more than anything else. Even a ref wanted to be loved.

In the first two minutes of play, the Killer had two fouls called on him. Touch fouls. No harm done fouls that wouldn't be called anywhere else.

On the second call against the Killer, McCarren drew his first technical. He knew he had to do something to make his point, to show that he knew what was happening. After the call, he stood in front of his bench and waited until one of the refs fogged by in hearing range.

"Hey, I'm Catholic too." He raised his hands toward the ceiling. "Give me a call too."

"You've got it," the ref shouted. He blew his whistle and stopped the game. He made the "T" sign with his hands toward the scorer's table.

Notre Dame had been leading by six. After they shot the two technical, and made both, they were ahead by eight points.

McCarren pulled the Killer and substituted Bo Regis for him. He saw that Robert was getting angry and frustrated and he didn't want to risk another foul. The Killer slumped into the seat on McCarren's right. "They're screwing us," he mumbled.

McCarren agreed. "We'll try to hold you out the rest of the half. Regis and Mitchell can split time."

"Holding me out won't make any difference. I'd need ten more fouls to last this game."

Regis played the big Notre Dame center well for a couple of minutes.

Sending Mitchell in, McCarren said, "Bang on the kid some. I don't want him to think he can rest while he's out there."

"The elbow trick I showed you," the Killer said.

Mitchell lowered an eyelid in a wink.

The elbow trick worked off a set play. Theold, on a drive down the baseline, tried to get in as close as he could for the jump shot. Or, if the crack was there, he made his flash move toward the basket. Mitchell's job was to clear the opposing center from his path. At the end of the play, as if he didn't know exactly where the center was, Mitchell would turn, his elbow slicing, and head for the basket as if getting position for the rebound.

The elbow was called. Theold's shot was put up about the same instant the elbow was thrown. It went it clean. The two points weren't allowed.

McCarren had the satisfaction of seeing the Notre Dame center rubbing his ribs.

The game tilted back and forth. Notre Dame kept a lead that moved between four and seven points.

At the half, when the teams left for the dressing rooms, Notre Dame was ahead by seven.

It didn't get any better.

Killer picked up his third foul before he broke a sweat the. It was a cheap trick. The Killer was backing up, setting up on defense. He was near the foul circle, blind to what was behind him. The Notre Dame big forward slipped into the lane and took his position. The Killer backed into him and knocked him off his feet. The whistle blew. Charging was called.

McCarren was on his feet, screaming. "We've being jobbed."

Jack Turner kept him from charging onto the court. "One more technical and you're gone and I'm coaching the team the rest of the night."

"Maybe that's what I want."

Turner shook his head slowly. "You're the miracle man. We need you here."

McCarren signaled that he wanted a timeout to the Killer. The Killer, calmer than McCarren thought he'd be under the circumstances, motioned to the nearest official. The whistle blew. McCarren watched the listless trot of his team toward him. With Robert in foul trouble the team was sleep-walking through the minutes.

Mitchell substituted for the Killer. He stayed with the rest of the upperclassmen starters. Another five minutes of play, and McCarren knew that they weren't gaining ground on Notre Dame. By then, Regis was in at center and Mitchell had taken a breather. McCarren sent in the freshman five.

Over the next two and a half minutes, Paul and Theold chipped away at the Notre Dame lead Down to five and back to seven Down to four with a shot by Gilson and the foul shot that went with it.

McCarren huddled with the Killer. "How you feeling?"

"Rested," Robert said.

"I think we've got to take a chance. Sometimes these homers get the guilties and start trying to even up the calls after the game's out of reach. You willing to take the chance?"

"I ain't worth squat on the bench. I might as well spend my fouls."

"All right then." McCarren lowered his voice. "But if you have to give a foul, make sure it's a real foul. You hear me?"

"Loud," the Killer said.

There was a roar from the crowd. Theold put a move on the small forward that turned him completely around. Even before Theold put up the shot, the whistle blew. The ref called him for walking. It wasn't walking. It was a fast half-step takeoff. The ref hadn't seen a step that fast and didn't believe the blur.

Theold followed through, completed the shot, and it dropped through.

The ref waved the score away. Notre Dame got the ball out of bounds.

"Go." McCarren sent the Killer in before Notre Dame could inbound the ball.

As the game moved up and down the court, McCarren decided that he'd been right about the officiating crew. They felt the guilty over the bad calls that got the Mountaineers away from their game in the first half and most of this one. Now they were doing a make-up. The Killer turned the animal loose. He powered over the kid center twice. Notre Dame answered once, a pull up bank shot from the side by the big forward.

Down to five.

Theold Brown's touch had deserted him. It happened when he was called again for the half-step movement. He lost his shooting rhythm. The next shot he took was off by three or four inches. He'd lost his concentration. He was waiting to hear the whistle. Or, McCarren thought, he was thinking too much. Or he was telling himself, my feet are doing this and now I bring up my hands …

It didn't work that way. The shot had to be a flow, an unconscious movement. The great shooters learned the techniques and then forgot them. When a shooter started taking his shot and his stroke apart, it led to failure.

McCarren replaced Theold.

Theold sat next to his coach and his head was down. "My fault. Coach, my …"

"The hell it is." McCarren patted Theold on the back. "The calls against you are wrong. You relax for a minute. When I put you back in, you blank your head. You take your shot. Let them blow their fucking whistles if they want to."

"You. You. You." The crowd chant drew McCarren's attention to the court again. The Killer" had drawn his fourth foul. The Notre center was sprawled on the floor, feeling his mouth.

Winters went in for the Killer. Theold moved over one seat to make room for Robert next to the Coach. Robert sat down and looked at his elbow. There were teeth marks on it. "I think I need a rabies shot."

"One more and you're gone. You want to give it now, sit down and wait for a shower? Or you want to hold it in case we cut it to two?"

"What chance we got of doing that?"

"None or slim," McCarren admitted.

With the Killer out, Notre Dame ran a string of six points and led by ten. With two minutes to go, Theold entered the game again. Theold hit two straight. He made the shots while he stood flat footed, not moving. Another shot, missed by Stefano on a break after a steal, was tapped in by Mitchell. The Notre Dame lead was four.

"Time for it," McCarren said. He sent in the Killer. A chorus of boos greeted him when he reached center court. Robert paused long enough to pat Mitchell Winters on the back. Then he turned and blew the crowd a double handful of kisses and bowed.

Notre Dame wanted the Killer out of the game for good. They wanted the fifth and last foul. The big forward took it straight at Robert and he had to back away. The big forward grinned at the Killer as the ball dropped through the net.

Out of Sense, the Killer hooked from eight feet. Down to four points once more.

The Notre Dame plan was the same as before. Take it to the Killer. The power forward again. The Killer didn't want to allow the easy shot this time. He stepped to the side and tried to block the shot from that angle. The whistle blew. It was the fifth foul. The Killer was disqualified.

The Killer took a couple of steps toward the Mountaineer bench. He turned and went back to the ref who'd made the call. His lips moved. He snarled. Nodding, he backed away and trotted to the bench.

McCarren met him and put an arm around his shoulders. "What'd you say to him?"

Robert smiled. "I told him he called a great game." McCarren laughed. It was his first laugh since the game started.

The teams traded baskets. Notre Dame won by a margin of four.

The team spent a sullen, angry night in South Bend. After they showered and dressed, McCarren sent the players to the hotel with Turner for a late meal. He remained at the Convocation Center for the press conference.

He couldn't say anything about the officiating. That would sound like sour grapes. He batted those questions aside from the local reporters. "The refs in our area allow a little more contact," was all he'd say.

The *Sports Illustrated* writer tried to bait him into saying that the officiating was one-sided.

"Let's just say my boys were tight playing up here for the first time. They never did get untracked. We didn't play our game and we got beat by a very, very good Notre Dame team."

Two nights later, at Evanston, the team regrouped and blew Northwestern out of their socks by thirty-seven points while the Killer had twenty-eight of those and fourteen rebounds. "No mercy, no mercy," the players whispered among themselves. "No fucking mercy from anybody from now on."

McCarren could have halted the slaughter if he'd want to. He didn't. He let it happen. To him, it was a way the team vented their anger and frustration over the loss to Notre Dame. The rule was that a team won, even with the homer refs, IF that team played well and if it was a great team.

A hostile Chicago-area press gave him the stone looks and the hard question about why he'd run the score that high. Oh, sure he was ahead the whole time and the game was never in doubt, but...

"I didn't score a single goal or grab a rebound all night." McCarren said.

"Come on, McCarren. We know you. We know your reputation. You don't rub anyone's face in ..." The Tribune sports writer was impatient with McCarren's answer.

"All right." McCarren nodded. He paced away from the mike and returned. "You guys ever take off the record answers? Call it background for your story."

He saw a head nod or two. He waited. There was another nod and a few yeses.

He directed his answer toward the Tribune writer. "You know that much about me, you also know I accept getting beat. I try not to alibi. I try not to blame it on the officiating."

"Now we're getting to it," someone said.

"What you're getting to is the off the record part."

He paused and looked around, seeing the dozen or so faces. "Agreed?" No answer. "Who doesn't agree?" No answer. "I'll assume we're in agreement." A pause while he rubbed his eyes. "Two nights ago my team got jobbed. Not by Digger, not by Notre Dame, but by an officiating crew that had nothing to win or lose by the outcome of the game. Maybe they wanted the fans to love them. I never saw kids, my kids, try so hard against such odds."

"Tonight....?"

"Tonight my players were mad. If I'd tried to hold them back, they'd have stoned me."

"You're saying you don't have control of your team?"

"Maybe I was angry too."

"I noticed the officiating too," the Tribune writer said.

"Write about it," McCarren said. "But don't quote me." Early the next morning, they flew to North Carolina.

The record was ten wins and one loss. They were headed toward the midway point of the season.

West Virginia State came to town the following Saturday for a home game at Biddle Coliseum. A vestige of the Notre Dame anger remained. The Killer raged up and down the court. He scored forty-three points and still didn't seem satisfied when he was substituted for with six minutes left in the game.

"Let the kids play some," McCarren said. "Mitchell needs the experience unless you're planning to stay around another year."

He led the Killer to a seat and leaned over him, soothing words and touches pouring over him like warm oil.

Mitchell and Bo Regis finished the game. The Killer grumbled as he watched the time tick off the scoreboard clock. "I could have scored a hundred tonight."

The Mountaineers won by twenty-eight.

The team had a rest break, a week, before the next came on the schedule. That would be in Atlanta at Alexander Coliseum against Georgia Tech. McCarren relaxed the practice routine. Twelve of the twenty-six regular season games had been played. Now, with the rest of the stretch ahead of them, he worried about their legs. He didn't want the players losing leg spring and endurance.

The latest issue of *Sports Illustrated* arrived on the stands the Monday after the West Virginia State game. There was a three page spread on the Mountaineer-Notre Dame matchup a week earlier. It was headlined: "Ambush at the (South) Bend."

> Something not so funny happened to the Hunt Morgan "Mountaineers" on their drive for a national championship, some national respect and a better place in the polls. They ran into an eight man team at South Bend. 'Five Irish players and a three man officiating crew were just too much for the tall and talented team that the Gray Fox, Tim McCarren brought to town with high hopes.

And later in the article:

> Each time Robert (the Killer) Hinson looked toward the basket or moved into a defensive

position, a whistle seemed to blow by magic. All the important calls went against the "Mountaineers" And, if picking on Hinson wasn't enough, the officials broadened their scope by calling walking on young Theold Brown until his touch and his confidence deserted him during one sustained run at the Irish. The essential damage of the night was done to Robert Hinson. Harried on all sides by the Furies of officials ,he played roughly one-fifth of the game. For all but eight minutes of the contest he hatched splinters on the "Mountaineer" bench.

McCarren noticed that the photo of the Killer with the Golden Dome over his head like a halo wasn't used. That was the selection, he decided, if we'd won. What they used was a picture of Hinson that had been snapped near the end of the game. He was on the bench, hunched over like a beaten fiend, and his head was lifted. The fierce, destructive look on his face would have cleared a room in any city in the world.

The caption: "Restrained by fouls. The Killer surveyed the bleak past."

CHAPTER SEVENTEEN

What worried McCarren as he approached the halfway mark of the season wasn't the one loss at South Bend. In some odd sense that loss toughened the team. The media reaction was mostly sympathetic. The Tribune writer mailed him a column dated on the 9th of January. It was his regular feature, Talking Sports , and this particular column was headed: Home is Where the Homers Are.

He had respected McCarren's off the record status and he offered a relationship between the "stolen" game at South Bend and the pitiless blowout of Northwestern as an insight.

The column ended with a warning. "If I were Digger and the Irish I'd think twice about playing a return came in North Carolina. They've got refs of their own down there in the sticks. Even the most impartial and respected basketball officials in the area might decide that turnabout is fair play or is that foul play?"

What really worried McCarren was the stamina of his young players. He didn't want to risk burning them out or wasting their legs. With that caution in mind he gave the team Sunday and Monday after the game with West Virginia State as a break. He told them he didn't even want to find them playing pickup games. The court was off-limits to them.

It wasn't sudden. Jorge knew.

The game wasn't sweet one day and sour the next. Not that way at all. All that trust he'd put in Coach McCarren, all the faith that he'd given no man except for his father. His father, the round-faced Irishman, who was the Rock, who sang him to sleep as a boy and awoke him with "The Wild Colonial Boy." Who put a basketball in his hands when he was five and said, "Yes, this is your sport," that judgment delivered on the basis of four awkward dribbles before the ball rolled under the dining room table.

The game was sour now. The trust and faith in McCarren was spoiled.

And the reason he felt betrayed?

The coach was using him, a senior, as if he were a freshmen and he was using the freshmen as if they were seniors. It was all there, in black and white. The game by game notation of his playing time, how many minutes he played. Not as exact as the logs Coach Turner kept. But he thought he was within five percent either way. Marking the time he went in and marking it when he came out. That was two minutes and twenty-eight seconds. He compared that to the running total that he wrote down each night in his room saw a pattern in his declining time. More playing time for the kid, Paul Gilson, and less for him. It wouldn't be long, the way he saw it, before McCarren replaced the starting backcourt. That smartass kid, Gilson, for him and Theold Brown for Tom Alley.

No good would come of talking to McCarren or Turner. He knew the answers he'd receive. That McCarren was experimenting with new combinations, that he was seasoning the freshmen for the stretch run toward the N.C.A.A.'s.

Sheeeeeeet, if that Gilson got any more experience, Jorge thought, he'd have more than I have.

And there was the Killer. The last three years, it had been him and the Killer against the whole fucking world. The old men, the seniors, the leaders. Now the Killer preferred the company of

Gilson and that no-talent, Houston Tarr over his. No time for the half-Spic. Only all the time he had for the new niggers.

Fuck it. That was the way felt about it now. He'd show them what they could do with their basketball. The first time he got a chance …

The chance came in Atlanta. They flew into Atlanta Hartsfield International on Friday, 16th and checked into the Italian Villa Motel on Peachtree Road. It was almost dark by the time they were assigned rooms. After a wash, the team bus took them to the Coach and Six, a restaurant famous for the roast beef. The team didn't skimp, that was for sure. There were double cuts of the beef all around and the Coach had arranged for seconds for anyone still hungry .

The bus returned them to the motel. Coach Turner drew the players around him in the lobby. "Any of you want to see Atlanta, you've got until eleven. I'd rather you didn't have anything to drink. But if you get thirsty, one beer. No more than two. Check-in at eleven. And that means eleven on the nose."

The game against Georgia Tech the next day was an afternoon match, set for two p.m. Coach Turner didn't want them to leave their legs on the concrete streets of Atlanta.

Room assignment placed Jorge with the Killer. The Killer said, when Jorge asked him, that he didn't feel like any short tour of the town. In a year or two, when he was pro, he'd probably do the town with real time and real money to spend. Tonight, he was going to watch some TV and play cards with the guys.

A cab Jorge flagged on Peachtree Road carried him north, away from the center of town. Twenty blocks or more clicked away on the meter. The cab turned into a driveway on the left of the Road and braked in front of a low flat structure. Blocky neon letters flashed in the front window. BAD NEWS.

"You sure this is the place?" Jorge read the meter and added a fifty cent tip.

"This is where the office girls go for fun on Friday night. It's Friday night, ain't it?"

It was.

Jorge stepped out and looked around. Cars of every make and model clogged the parking lots on the street. The bar itself looked like a converted greenhouse. Black trim work held together panes and panes and sheets and sheet of glass. Inside ceramic pots held plants of all kinds Real plants, Jorge decided after he reached up and punched a fingernail into a leaf.

Loud music. A dance floor near the back of the bar. Couples showing it like they thought they were on Broadway. Oh, yes, this was the place.

Jorge bought a beer and stood at a narrow space at the bar wedged for himself with a shoulder. He was wearing his green Hunt Morgan travel blazer. The University crest with Hunt Morgan under it on the breast pocket of the jacket. Only a matter of time now ....

Sucking slowly on the beer and waiting for somebody to notice. When it happened it wasn't a girl who recognized the crest. Two slicks stopped next to the bar. One looked at Jorge and then the jacket pocket.

"Hunt Morgan? Hey, you're down for the game tomorrow?"

"Yeah."

"Big fan, huh?"

Jorge shook his head. "Not a fan. A player."

"That right?" The slick peeled back a cuff and looked at his watch. He had trouble reading the time in the dim light. "I thought you guys had ..."

"Thought I'd break training." Jorge introduced himself.

"Hey, yeah. You and the Killer, you're the seniors."

"Right."

"Where's the Killer?" The slick looked around.

"Back with the team, resting for the both of us."

The two slicks, Bobby and Tub, invited Jorge to join them at their table, where two girls waited. Bob and Tub introduced him and he danced with both girls. Other girls passed and stopped and remained a time and flitted away.

The evening blurred. It seemed every time he turned around there was another bottle of Bud at his elbow.

Somewhere around midnight, he and Bob and Tub and two girls who weren't the same girls the two slicks had started the evening with, left Bad News and drove to an apartment about a mile away. They blew some weed and drank some more beer and there was nose candy, cocaine, to snort. One of the girls remained in the bedroom for a long time and then appeared, stark naked in the doorway, and wobbled and said, "Who wants it first?"

Bobby and Tub and Jorge took turns with her. The other girl, a strange one, didn't join in. She kept her clothes on, but now and then she walked in and stood by the bed and watched and giggled.

The girl in the bed was young and had a chunky body and real blonde pubic hair. She had a pussy like a rubber glove and Jorge fucked her twice. He might have gone the third time. What stopped him was that he had a look at her from the side of the bed and her eyes were rolled all the way back in her head. Jorge guessed she was on drugs and he liked his lovers conscious.

He dressed. When he entered the living room, the strange girl, still fully dressed, was giving head to Tub.

"Got to play tomorrow," Jorge said to Bob.

Bob drove him to the Italian Villa Motel. Jorge had Bob drop him half a block from the Motel. "Great night," he said.

"Ain't over yet for me," Bob said.

Jorge thought he might be able to slip in. He didn't make it. Coach Turner, bleary-eyed grumpy, sat in the hallway next to the room Jorge shared with the Killer. Turner tipped the chair forward when he stood. He glared at Jorge eye-to-eye.

"You want to explain this?"

'Lost track of the time, Coach."

Turner grabbed the chair back and headed down the hall. He waved Jorge along with him. He motioned Jorge into his room and closed the door behind him. He sat on the side of one of the twin beds. A turn of the travel alarm clock on the night table and Turner said, "Maybe you can find it now."

It was twenty past two.

"That late?" Jorge smiled.

"No use talking to you now." Turner nodded at the other bed. "You sack out there. No reason to wake the Killer. I'll have to see what Coach wants to do with you in the morning."

Jorge sat on the edge of the bed and kicked off his shoes. "The Killer told you I wasn't back?"

"You kidding? He was trying to make excuses for you for an hour." Turner draped his robe over the foot of his bed. He was wearing green and white striped pajamas. "We had a bed check, remember?"

Jorge showered. He wanted the smell of the pig woman off his body. When he returned to the bedroom, Coach Turner was in bed, curled away from the light of the table lamp.

Jorge felt a thick darkness around him. He fell asleep the instant his head hit the pillow.

Wakeup was at eight. Breakfast at eight-thirty.

Jorge was groggy, hungover and he had the smell of weed trapped in his nose. He wobbled when he walked. His hands shook. All that and he was still certain that he couldn't notice the players acting any differently toward him. The word on his late hours hadn't leaked. He could say that much for the coaches. No snap judgments with them. No useless badmouthing. They'd take their time and decide. The decision would then be carved in stone and placed on the mountain.

After breakfast Coach Turner pushed back his chair and said, "Let's take a walk to shake this meal down." He led the team through the lobby. Heads turned and there were blinks at the tall group of young men. They reached Peachtree Road. Coach Turner set a fast pace. Jorge lagged behind. He felt sick to the stomach, like he was going to vomit.

"Let's walk in that direction." McCarren said, startling Jorge.

McCarren stood on the sidewalk behind him. It was the first Jorge had seen of him since the day before. He hadn't been at breakfast.

"Whatever you say, Coach."

They matched strides. "You like going off in opposite directions anyway, don't you?"

"You're talking about last night?"

"Unless you want to confess some other nights you broke training." It was a cold, sunny day. McCarren pulled his hat low over his eyes to shade them. "What am I going to do with you, Jorge?"

"You can bench me," Jorge said.

McCarren stared straight ahead. "Or I could ship you home this morning on the first available plane."

"Home?"

"To Hunt Morgan."

They stopped on the street for a red light. Brookwood Station, the old Atlanta train depot, was in front of them. "What the hell is wrong, Jorge? You're a co-captain. I could expect this crap from anybody but you and the Killer. You're supposed to lead by example. You're supposed to show these kids what's expected of them."

"Nobody knows but you and Coach Turner?"

"And the Killer. "McCarren nodded. "He was worried sick about you."

The light changed. They stepped from the curb. "Bench me today."

"That doesn't answer my question. What's wrong?"

"It's those goddam freshmen. You're turning your back on the guys who've been here two and three years."

"You believe that?" McCarren sounded stunned.

"Yes."

"What makes you think that?" McCarren stopped and turned.

They'd walked five or six blocks from the Motel.

"Playing time. I think you've decided to hedge your bet, Coach. Maybe you think this isn't your year. Maybe you think next year is."

"And you really believe that?"

"I don't want to," Jorge said.

"Let me tell you this. You're one thousand percent wrong. Without you and the Killer we don't stand a chance."

"You've got the big white kid."

McCarren shook his head. "You and the Killer. You're the core to the team. "

"You're got Gilson and Theold."

"Gilson's the one sticks in your craw, right?"

"Maybe."

"Next year they start. They've got the rest of this season and the summer to mature. This year they start in certain situations and they fill holes."

"I knew you'd say that."

"You wonder why I said that." McCarren waited.

"Huh?"

McCarren took Jorge's arm and turned him and they walked back toward the Motel. "You've got a good basketball mind. Right now you're letting what you feel warp what you know. Think about it. You're saying I'm playing the first year guys because I think they've got more talent, right?"

Jorge nodded. "That's what I think."

"We've lost one game. Got it stolen. I think we can afford to lose one or two more. Three losses and the right wins from our schedule and we're a shoo-in for the N.C.A.As. And I'll gladly lose those other two games if it means we go to the playoffs with an experienced team. Say we get to the playoffs, how many games to win a national championship?"

"Without a bye in the first round we'd have to win six."

"That's right. And we've been getting good press. We might hustle a bye this year."

"Five game then," Jorge said.

"Say you pull a muscle. Say we've got to play without you two games. How many games did you say to win a national championship?"

"I won't pull no muscle. You got my promise on that."

"Early foul trouble then. Three fouls in the first ten minutes. Say we get a ref who calls every finger touch a foul."

"It could happen."

"The bench is the key. Damn few teams can win a championship with five starters and a one man bench. A team's got to have more experienced depth than that. Pat Ewing against Sam Ferkins in the Georgetown and North Carolina finals last year."

"I remember it."

"What happened?"

"Ewing ate him alive."

McCarren shook his head. "Nibbled at him. Maybe that. Carolina had the starters but a thin bench. Nobody who could really replace Perkins if he got in foul trouble. I think I'd make a bet on what Coach Smith told Perkins. He told Sam to take his open shot when they were there, to get his rebounds, to block out, to try to deny the ball to Ewing. But, under no circumstances, to get in a muscle contest with Ewing. Two things could happen there and only one of them is good. Ewing might foul out. He's had a tendency for that anyway. And that would be good. Perkins might foul out and that would be bad. Especially bad because Carolina didn't have an experienced backup center."

"It could have been that way."

"Our bench. Gilson, before he leaves here is going to be a hell of a player. Better than you are at the same point. Part of that is speed and quickness. Theold is already in a class by himself. Unlimited talent. The problem is that they're just making the leap to college ball. No real way of knowing when they're going to blow apart on us. The big kid, Mitchell, he'll be a player in a year or two. The Killer's getting him ready. If I've had one disappointment this year it's that you're not doing the same with Gilson. You're not teaching him what you know and making him the player he ought to be by next year."

"I guess I screwed up, Coach. With Gilson and last night."

"As long as you realize that."

"I do. I swear it."

"You don't play tonight. You don't even dress. You don't even sit on the bench. And you're suspended for one more game, the Thursday game at Richmond. You don't make the trip, either. You stay on campus and study. Understood? Accepted?"

"Right, Coach."

They reached the motel lobby before the rest of the players returned with Jack Turner. They'd hardly settled into chairs when the team filed in, laughing and talking, and milled around the magazine and notions stand. There was a run on *Atlanta Constitution*s.

McCarren put a hand on Jorge's arm. He stood. "Now's the hard part. You've got to explain the suspension." He dipped his head at Jack Turner, who gathered the players and led them across the lobby.

"I've got something to say," Jorge said.

McCarren took Turner by the elbow. "A few last minute notes about today's game."

They reached the elevator. Behind them they heard Jorge say, "I broke training last night. I got caught."

The elevator arrived. McCarren and Turner got in and punched the button for their floor. The doors closed.

It was a better team that Tech put on the floor that afternoon than the one from a year before. It should have been a closer game than it was. The Mountaineers ware in a kind of rage, an angry high, on this day. Perhaps it was anger at Jorge. McCarren didn't think that was it. No, McCarren thought, it was probably that the players wanted to cover for the missing Jorge. They didn't want Jorge to feel that he was responsible for a loss. Paul Gilson filled in and started at point guard. He ran the offense like a surgeon.

At the half, the Mountaineers were ahead by fifteen. They won by twenty-eight.

Jorge sat in the stands, three rows up and directly behind the Mountaineers bench. He suffered through the game, the good and the bad plays, the incredible passes and the impossible ones that didn't work.

At the end of the game, he walked outside and stood by the side of the team bus. He waited for the team to shower and dress. The wind that blew across the parking lot was cold and ice-edged. He hardly felt it. He'd never been so alone in his life.

⚜ ⚜ ⚜

Jorge listened to the Richmond game on a radio in his room. During the broadcast Hub Wilson, the Mountaineer radio network play-by-play announcer, mentioned his name several times. Wilson said there were two stories that explained why Jorge had not made the trip. One was that the senior guard was sick with a virus. The other rumor was that Jorge had broken training rules and he was being disciplined by the coaching staff. Coach McCarren would say only that Jorge was not ill but he would not comment, because it was a principle with him, on any possible rule infraction. "That is between the young man and the staff," he said.

That was more than fair of the Coach, Jorge thought. He wouldn't lie about it but he wasn't out to embarrass anybody either.

Richmond usually liked to run. It was their game. With a week between their last game and the one against the Mountaineers, they decided to put in a surprise for McCarren. The control tempo they used kept the contest close most of the way. That was the idea, keep it close and pray for a good break or two at the final buzzer.

At the half, the Mountaineers were ahead by four, 32-28, and the Spiders strategy was working. The control game put a special pressure on McCarren's guards. Gilson had to chase the ball and disrupt the careful flow of the Richmond game. At the halftime buzzer Paul had three fouls on him. Early in the second half Gilson drew his fourth foul and McCarren had to bench him and play Theold Brown in the backcourt with Tom Alley.

Without being there, Jorge knew what McCarren was thinking. You see, see what you've done to the team? When we need you...

Not that McCarren would say that. Not aloud. Perhaps by a look. McCarren knew that Jorge realized how much the team missed him and that was enough. No words were necessary.

At the two minute mark, the Mountaineers led 51-49 and the game almost turned in the wrong direction. The Spiders took their time. They set up for the shot they wanted. The shot that would have tied the game and placed Richmond in the position where they could head into overtime if the Mountaineers didn't score the next time down the court. Or, if time remained on the clock, the Spiders might get downcourt and try for the winning basket. One of the Spider guards got around Tom Alley. He was clean and untouched and headed down the lane when Theold

Brown left his man and sky walked the baseline. He blocked the ball out of bounds. Less than half a minute remained when Richmond inbounded the ball. The shot was rushed. The Killer cradled the rebound until he was fouled. An intentional foul, the refs decided. Robert made the first of the two shots and the Mountaineers were up by three.

The Killer missed the second free throw. The Mountaineers fell back on defense. McCarren was on his feet yelling. "No foul, no foul."

Jack Turner was next to him. "Let them have the shot. No foul. No three point plays. "

Richmond got off a shot with five seconds left that went in. The Mountaineers were ahead by one. The Killer inbounded to Theold Brown who dribbled the clock away.

The Mountaineers were 13 and 1 and over the halfway point of the season.

CHAPTER EIGHTEEN

The team returned to Hunt Morgan that same night. Coach McCarren scheduled a short workout the next day, Friday, and released them to meet family members who were coming in for the Family Day game against William and Mary on Saturday.

Paul Gilson reserved rooms at the College Inn for his mother and his uncle, George Marks. They flew into the Winston-Salem airport early in the evening and George Marks rented a car and drove to Sandersville. After dinner in the hotel dining room, Paul's mother said she was tired. Paul and his uncle left her to rest. After a walk around campus, Paul took his uncle to McCoy dorm and introduced him to the other players. It was obvious, after his early doubts about Hunt Morgan, George Marks was pleased with his nephew's play and happy with the facilities and the way Paul lived.

"Top drawer," George Marks said about the dorm and Biddle Coliseum. Paul wondered where his uncle had learned the phrase.

Mrs. Brown arrived by bus from Society Hill. On the way from the bus station to the College Inn, she admitted to Theold that this was the first time in almost five years that she had been out of her hometown.

McCarren called in an I.O.U. from Theold's pastor and Mr. Boswell visited Mrs. Brown in her room at the College Inn for almost an hour. There was talk about the love and respect the other church members had for Theold and, at the end, Pastor Boswell and Mrs. Brown prayed together because he thought that was what she wanted.

Starting time for the game was two in the afternoon. The Biddle was packed to the rafters. The pep band blared, the cheerleaders and the pom pom girls danced along the sidelines.

William and Mary kept the game close for the first ten minutes. The depth and the talent of the Mountaineers blew the game wide open in the last ten minutes of the half. It was no longer a contest. It was, as planned, a celebration. Every member of the squad had played. McCarren and Turner had tried their best to make certain that every player scored at least one goal.

Now the team was 14 and 1.

Afterwards, there was a buffet luncheon at the faculty club for the players and their families, hosted by the Educational Foundation.

McCarren got to his feet. He adjusted his tie. He smiled. "I only have about fifty badly chosen words to say. I know you, the players and you, the families, want to spend time together." He smiled. "And I think I've already used twenty of my words."

He waited for the laugh.

"All of us know that this team wants to go all the way this year. We were close last year. This year we want the watches and the rings that go with being national champions. That's the reason for having this season. That's the reason for all the long hours and the hard work these young men have put in on the courts. But if we don't go all the way, if we stumble, it won't change one basic fact. The young men are already true champions."

He grinned. He waved as the applause began. "Anyone count my words?"

He left the head table and walked around the banquet room. He had handshakes for the men, kind words for each of his players and a courtly kiss on the cheek for each of the women.

McCarren's final stop was at the table where the important members of the Educational Foundation were seated. He knew all of them by name and he respected most of them as men and as successful businessmen. There was one exception. There, big as life an red-faced, sat Frank Sellers, the man he'd had all the trouble with at the Mideast Regionals back in March. Since their encounter, President Edwards had acted as a buffer between them.

When McCarren left the table Frank Sellers followed him and held out his hand. "Bygones are bygones, Coach?" Sellers swayed slightly. There was an oily line of sweat on his brow and his upper lip.

"You know they are," McCarren said. He gave Sellers hand a brief squeeze and dropped it.

"That Queen boy in Sumter ..."

"What about him?" Joe Queen was one of the top power forwards in the south and McCarren had hopes he could talk Queen into signing a letter of intent when the time came.

"Well," Sellers said," you could say I'm talking to him."

"I'd rather you didn't, Frank."

"I don't see why not. I'm in Sumter about once a month on business and his coach is an old buddy of mine."

"Then be cool, "McCarren said.

"What does that mean?"

McCarren stepped close to Sellers and lowered his voice. "It means don't make him any promises, It means that I don't want you to give him any money."

"You must think I'm stupid."

It wouldn't do to say what he really thought. "It's got to be handled right or we'll lose him."

"You do think I'm stupid." Sellers whirled and stomped his way to his table. He stood there, eyes on McCarren, and threw back a drink in one gulp.

McCarren sat at his desk in the Ipsom Building. He hadn't had a drink all day. That was because, while he didn't mind the players seeing him have one or two while he was on the road, he knew that some of the parents expected him to be a holy man, to teach their sons by example.

After the encounter with Frank Sellers an hour ago, he wasn't sure he could handle just one drink. Later, when he was with Ellen. That was the right and proper time.

He opened the refrigerator and found a Harp beer. A couple of sips and he dialed Coach Vincent's home number in Sumter, South Carolina.

"How'd it go?" Vincent wanted to know.

"A piece of cake." That was what the Family Day game was supposed to be. Picked and scheduled that way. A loss on Family day was a disaster.

"You are calling for any special reason, Coach?"

"It's touchy," McCarren said.

"Between us? Go ahead."

"Has Frank Sellers been hanging around there?"

"Was he supposed to be?" Vincent sounded cautious.

"No."

"I didn't think that was your style. Yeah, he's been around the gym some."

"No matter what he tells you, he's not talking for me or the program here."

"I guessed as much."

"Discourage him, if you can."

"I wanted to be sure," Vincent said. "Now I'll feel free to use a tire iron if I have to."

"Do that and I'll owe you one. How's Joe Queen?"

"Thought that was why you called. He's fine. In fact, he's too much man to play in this league much longer. They'd outlaw him."

"You can mention I've got a spot for him here," McCarren said.

"He knows that, Coach."

"You and the kid pick a time for a visit?"

"February," Vincent said. "You pick a weekend."

"Will do."

After he ended the call, McCarren made a note to decide on which games he'd offer Coach Vincent and the Queen kid for their allowed campus visit.

He sipped the last of the Harp. The call had reassured him. It was comforting to know that assholes didn't always spoil everything. Damn Sellers anyway.

Injuries are part of the game, McCarren told himself on the trip back from Baton Rouge. A good team with the right kind of coaching could fill the gap and continue to win. He told himself, he told Jack Turner. The problem was that he wasn't certain that he believed it.

Not when that injured man was the Killer.

Hardly five minutes passed before it happened. The Mountaineers had the ball. A pass from Jorge, intended for the Killer, was deflected by the L.S.U. center who was playing behind Hinson. He reached a long arm over Robert's shoulder and batted the basketball. That touch changed the path of the ball. Robert lowered his hands at the last moment. The basketball struck the end of Robert's little finger on his right hand. There was little pain at first. Only numbness. The Killer looked down at his hand. The little finger was bent to the side, like the angle on a child's jigsaw puzzle.

The team doctor thought it was dislocated. He seated Robert on the bench and leaned over him. He grasped the finger and pulled at it. When he released the hand the finger was straight. "Move the joint," he told Robert.

Robert held out the hand and moved the joints of the little finger. It jumped out again. The same twisted, bent angle. Three times the doctor pulled the finger into place and each time the finger returned to its grotesque shape when Robert worked the joints. Heavy perspiration flooded the Killer's face. He bit into his lower lip so hard tiny drops of blood stained his teeth.

The doctor backed away. McCarren leaned in.

"It could be broken," the doctor said. "I'll need an x-ray."

The second half was underway when the doctor and the Killer returned from the hospital. The Mountaineers were still in the game but losing and losing ground. McCarren had hoped the Killer could return to the game. When he saw that Robert was in street clothes he knew that the game was over. Maybe even the season was over.

But no McCarren-coached team ever gave up. He wouldn't let them. One more ploy, he thought, and he gave the timeout signal to Jorge. The players sprinted to the bench'. McCarren sat Robert in the middle of the huddle. Jorge looked down at the metal splint under the Killer's little finger.

"Sheeeet, Killer," Jorge said, "you human after all."

"Be the first one-armed center," Gilson said.

Laughing, loose and down by eight points.

McCarren gave them that much time to get it out of their systems. "As you can see the Killer here wants his night off. Jorge's had his three nights off and that adds in the one with food poisoning. Guess we got to play without Robert. Anyone believes we can't win without him, I want out of the game. I don't want that man on the floor."

Shouts. "We can win. We can win."

"Show me," McCarren said. "Make me believe it."

The team almost made a believer of him.

Theold Brown was hot. He went on a shooting spree. Whirling, diving, flying across the lane. One shot, an under-handed scoop, went in and no one, even after they saw the film later, ever thought such a move was possible. Not the move and certainly that such a shot wouldn't drop in. It did.

Jimmy Stefano banged the L.S.U. small forward so hard and so often that the small forward dropped out of the game and didn't even look for any of his usual shots. With the small forward backing away, Jimmy added a driving layup and a short jumper on a pullup.

Almost wasn't enough. The L.S.U. center was experienced and he was the true difference. No matter how Mitchell Winters or Bo Regis played him, he always had another kind of move they couldn't handle.

At the final buzzer, the Mountaineers were down by four.

14 and 2, that was the season so far.

The next game was three days away. That didn't leave time, he and Turner agreed, to retool completely.

"What do we do?" Turner asked.

"A big front line?" McCarren yawned. He hadn't slept much on the plane or after they arrived back in Sandersville. Turner didn't hesitate. "Why not?"

They had a short practice on Thursday, the day after the loss to L.S.U. Then a longer one on Friday. They drilled with Mitchell Winters at center, Bo Regis and Jimmy Stefano at forwards and Jorge and Gilson at guards. Theold Brown was to be the swing man. He'd spell Jorge and Gilson from time to time at guard and alternate at small forward with Jimmy Stefano. Ames Ashley and Billy Stoddard would enter the game for brief periods and give Regis and Winters a breather.

"Boards. Boards. Boards." McCarren paced the edge of the practice court and yelled himself hoarse.

On Thursday, when he was satisfied the flow was developing, he turned practice over to Jack Turner and kept his appointment in the sports medicine room upstairs in the Biddle.

The team doctor, Claude Western, and the trainer, Sarg Williams, waited there for him. Robert Hinson sat across the room on the training table. The splint was in place, the finger swollen and discolored.

"Give me a guess," McCarren said.

"We'll know better in a week or so."

McCarren turned away from Dr. Western. He looked at Sarg.

Sarg nodded. "The doc and I agree on this. We need at least a week to let the bone start knitting. Less than that and we run the risk permanent damage."

"All right." McCarren thought ahead a week. Furman at Furman, Virginia Tech at the Biddle, and Wake Forest at the Greensboro Coliseum. "You know me well enough to know I won't risk a player."

"One thing we can try, "Sarg said. "After the swellings reduced, we can experiment with a plastic sheath."

"I want to play," the Killer said.

The three men ignored him. Sarg held out his right hand. "We try it one way or the other. The broken finger taped against the finger next to it or two fingers. We cover the fingers with a foam pad. Then we see which method absorbs most of the bumps and hits."

McCarren looked at the Killer.

"I want to play. I want to play Saturday." Hinson was almost pleading. "Give me a painkiller or numbing shot and I'll—"

"No shots," Dr. Western interrupted. "I can't go along with painkiller shots."

Sarg agreed. "The big job is to get Robert back to one hundred percent. With a painkiller, he might further injure the hand and not know it. That might put off full recovery for another two weeks or more."

"No shots," McCarren said. "Killer, if you can play with discomfort or some minor pain, that's fine with me. Otherwise, it's a no go. And if he plays, I want one of you to check the finger at intervals."

Dr. Western nodded. "That's the only way I'd have it."

"One of us will be on the bench," Sarg said.

"Both of us." Western nodded at them.

McCarren walked together with the killer to the dressing room. He left him at the doorway. "I want you running."

"Today?"

"Unless the finger bothers you."

"I'll try it."

McCarren left him to change to workout clothing and returned to practice.

The big lineup the Mountaineers put on the court surprised East Carolina. They'd come to the game expecting only that there would be a replacement for the Killer. And they came breathing fire. With the Killer on the bench this was a good chance to pull off an upset that would make all the Sunday papers across America.

What East Carolina found was a trio of Mitchell Winters, Bo Regis and Jimmy Stefano banging them and the boards. And just when they thought they'd adjusted to the muscle, in came Theold Brown. With Brown at small forward, it was all speed and quickness and daring.

The spirit dwindled in East Carolina by the middle of the first half. Midway through the second half, the game was out of reach. Theold left the game with twenty-six points and was replaced by Houston Tarr. Coach Turner told Houston to take the open shots and he did. The flat arc shot was on and he scored six goals, five of them in a row at one stretch. It was his high point total.

When Houston left the game, he was hugged by the Killer. The Killer didn't seem to mind that Houston was perspiring all over his best blazer. "Kid, you remember I told you to stay with that shot, don't you?"

"I owe it all to you. Killer," Houston said.

CHAPTER NINETEEN

About the same time that Coach Turner was putting the Mountaineer players through their practice drills at the Biddle, Tim McCarren landed at the airport in Columbia, South Carolina on a private jet that had been made available to him by a retired banker who was a close friend of President Edwards. He gave himself a bit of lag time and still set a return flight time for the pilot.

Less than an hour later, he parked the rental car on the street outside the Edmunds High School gym and entered through the front door. A wave at Coach Vincent and he sat in the stands and watched the practice. One thing you could say for Vincent, he would sacrifice something for the sake of his players. He refused to play a kid out of position. With a kid as big as Joe Queen, there was a temptation to play him at center. Instead of that, Coach Vincent used a man two or three inches shorter at the post and played Joe Queen at his natural position, the position he'd play at the college level. That way, Queen wouldn't have to make a difficult transition. He wouldn't have to go from playing with his back to the basket to playing facing it.

Until this day, all McCarren had seen of Joe Queen was the usual game footage and the scouting reports. Yes, he told himself as he watched the skins and shirts scrimmage, this kid was a player. He reminded McCarren some of James Worthy, the power forward at U.N.C. Queen was almost six-eight and might grow another inch. About two hundred and twenty pounds and he had the same two and three step quickness that Worthy had.

He needed polish, some refinement. Some work on his shot selection. But the rest of it was already there.

At the end of practice, McCarren joined Coach Vincent and Joe Queen on the court. He gave the kid his best handshake and his best Irish smile. Some general talk about basketball, a few words about Hunt Morgan and McCarren shook Queen's hand and let him head for the showers.

"Dinner, Coach?" McCarren said. "My treat."

"Let me call my wife."

"Bring her along."

Vincent laughed. "Not enough warning. She'd need half a day at the beauty parlor."

They had their dinner at a barbecue place on the edge of town. It was famous for its ribs and the sliced pork and the coarsely chopped salad. It was the real article and McCarren, though he'd never really got used to southern barbecue, had a heaping plate and about a dozen of the hush puppies.

They sat a time over their coffees. Coach Vincent had brought along a copy of Joe Queen's grades. They looked good. Some A's, mostly B's and a few C's. McCarren said he was impressed. The truth was that grades on the high school level didn't mean much. Good athletes usual got favorable nudges from the teachers, perhaps as much as a letter grade upward when it became clear that the kid had a chance of going away to college on an athletic scholarship.

At eight, Coach Vincent drove McCarren to the Queen home. Without totally ignoring Joe Queen, McCarren spent most of his attention on the family. He was warm, down to earth and completely charming.

Around the room, as if placed there carefully, he noticed books and magazines. For my benefit, he thought. Neither Joe's mother or father seemed highly educated. Joe's father worked for the highway department and his mother was an L.P.N, at the hospital. Neither, he thought, had probably finished high school.

Still it was hopeful. That the parents were concerned enough about his visit to stage the charade for him.

Half an hour after McCarren arrived, the Queens left McCarren and Coach Vincent with their son and closed the kitchen door behind them.

For a time, there was gentle sparring with Joe. Joe knew that McCarren had an opening at big forward the next year, didn't he?

"Yes." Joe said that Hunt Morgan was high on his list of schools.

"At the top?"

"Near," Joe said.

"That's good to know." McCarren grinned.

There was a pause. Joe Queen opened his mouth a couple of times and closed it, as if he wanted to say something and didn't have the nerve to do it. Money, McCarren thought. Now we tap dance around the money.

"I got to ask you something, Coach McCarren. That man comes by the gym. His name is Sellers…"

"He doesn't represent me or the school."

"He took me for a ride in his Coupe de Ville."

"Did he now?"

"He said if I came to your school I could have that Couple de Ville or one just like it."

"What did you think?"

Joe cut his eyes toward Coach Vincent. "I'd like to have one of those."

Coach Vincent got to his feet. "Maybe I ought to visit some more with the Queens."

"No." McCarren stopped him. When Vincent was seated once more McCarren said, "I can't make you that kind of promise. In fact, if you arrived at my school driving a 1983 Coupe de Ville, I'd probably tell you to turn it around and drive back here."

"That's not what Mr. Sellers …"

"He doesn't speak for me or the school. Look at it this way. You come and play for me and you'll have everything you need. All expenses. And I mean all expenses. In four years, after you're a number one draft in the N. B. A., you can buy any car you want, just on the basis of the expected contract. I'll arrange it for you as soon as the draft's held that June."

"I wanted that car."

"A lot of coaches want you at their schools. They might offer you this or that under the table. That goes on. But I don't think any of them are crazy enough to buy you a new car. The first time you drive that car on campus, the investigators from the N.C. A.A. will be half a block behind you."

Coach Vincent leaned in. "The school will be put on probation. That means no chance to play in the post-season tournaments or to be seen on national TV."

"That right?" Joe looked at McCarren.

"And it's an even money bet that I would be fired by the school. A more than even money bet."

"But you say this Mr. Sellers ain't connected with the school. How could …?"

"The school is responsible for any illegal activity of a booster. You understand that?"

"Yes, sir."

"In one year, we can arrange some kind of wheels for you that are tuned like a stock car."

The conversation changed directions. McCarren could see that the car was still on Joe's mind. McCarren pretended not to notice. He talked about the social life at the school. How much fun his young men were having. The travel. "We might go to Hawaii next Christmas. How'd you like that?"

Joe brightened some at that prospect.

It was time to leave. McCarren gave Joe a packet of information about the school and the athletic program. There was a brochure with color photographs of McCoy dorm and the living spaces and the dining room.

The Queens came from the kitchen. There were goodbyes. While McCarren spoke to the mother and father, Coach Vincent was at the doorway with Joe. McCarren came back in time to hear the last of what Vincent said.

"...ought to think about making a verbal commitment to Hunt Morgan. The sooner the better. It will take the pressure off you. And, let's face it, you want to play pro ball. McCarren is the man to get your ready for that. Look what's been done with the Killer in three and a half years."

McCarren saved his best shot for last. Before he left, he told Joe that Theold Brown said to say hello. Theold and Joe had played against each other and they'd spent some summers on the courts. They were, from all accounts, fast friends.

"How's he doing?" Joe grinned.

"Great and he loves it there. I'll have him give you a call. What he says he wants now is for you to play the big forward on the other side of the front line. He says, that way. he wouldn't mind playing the Lakers."

A final handshake and McCarren and Coach Vincent went into the icy cold night. On the drive back to the gym where McCarren had left the rental car, McCarren told Vincent that he appreciated the good words that he'd put in with Joe Queen. He thought it had been helpful.

"I'll call the I.O.U. in a week or two," Vincent said.

McCarren pulled up behind Vincent's car and kept the engine running. "Tell me about it."

"There's an opening for an assistant coach at U.N.C.-Charlotte."

"Odd how the timing works out. We play U .N.C.-Charlotte on February 12th."

"I know that."

"I'll make you smell like a rose. Put me down as a reference. And I'll make a call as soon as I get back to Sandersville.

"I've applied. But I didn't put you down as a reference, not until I talked to you."

"Do it." McCarren smiled. "you'd have better bargaining power if you could deliver Joe Queen with you."

"That's true. But Joe's already made up his mind, whether he knows it or not. He wants to play up with Theold and those four studs."

"That's good news."

McCarren waited until Coach Vincent drove away. Then he started the drive for Columbia.

On the return flight, he thought about Joe Queen. He wasn't sure he'd succeeded in recruiting him. There was still a chance somebody would get to Joe Queen and offer him a Coupe de Ville.

The Killer didn't make the trip to Greenville for the game against Furman. He remained behind and had the finger fitted with the plastic sheath designed by Sarg. The finger was then covered with a foam pad and taped to the adjoining finger. Robert met a graduate assistant on the court. For most of an hour, he and the graduate assistant passed the basketball back and forth and engaged in a session of one-on-one that gave the Killer a chance to try his shots and his rebounding.

The hour's workout left the graduate assistant exhausted and complaining of sore ribs. A dull ache extended from the finger to the elbow of the Killer's right arm. In the sports medicine room, the pad and the sheath were removed. There was only a minimum of new swelling. Sarg seemed pleased.

That night, the Mountaineers had trouble with the Paladins. They played over its head and they played like they wanted the game more than the Hunt Morgan players did.

The game was decided in the last two minutes on a quick step drive by Theold Brown and a blocking call against the Furman small forward who was guarding him. The shot went in and Theold made the free throw as well. Those three points pushed the Mountaineer lead to five points . The Paladins never got close again.

On the return bus trip from Greenville, Jack Turner leaned over McCarren. "We've got to get the Killer back soon. These teams are beginning to think they can beat us."

McCarren agreed. "The one thing you can't let another team have is hope."

McCarren met the Killer on the court an hour before the Thursday afternoon practice at the Biddle. He examined the sheath and the padding. Satisfied, he stood six feet from Robert and tossed and caught the basketball with him. He progressed from soft and easy to a quicker pace and a chest pass that put more and more strength behind the toss.

He stopped when he saw that the Killer was trying to catch the pass with his left hand and the palm of his right. The Killer was perspiring and there was a thin pain line around his mouth.

"Hurts some, huh?"

"A little," the Killer admitted.

"How's your left-handed hook shot?"

"It ain't the shot that bothers me. Left-handed dribbling makes me move like a sick turkey."

"Wind sprints." McCarren nodded at the near baseline. "Fifty each way. You'll dress tomorrow but I don't know that you'll play. I'd like to hold you out until Saturday."

"I'd play even if I knew the finger would fall off."

"It just might." McCarren dropped the basketball in the ball cart and stayed long enough to see Robert begin the wind sprints.

Upstairs, at the office level of the Coliseum, he stopped in Turner's outer room and told the receptionist: "Honey, if Jack's not on the phone, get me Coach Barstow at the University of North Carolina at Charlotte."

The receptionist nodded and buzzed him a moment later.

McCarren grabbed the phone receiver before Turner could. "Have to pay back on the Joe Queen deal." He put the phone to his mouth. "Hello, Joel. McCarren here. I guess you've heard the good news that the Killer's got a broken finger? That ought to save your coaching career for you, a win over a ranked team."

He laughed and grinned at Turner.

"You want his leg broken too? You know there's no honor in whipping up on cripples." He paused, listening, nodding to himself. "Yeah, there's one other matter. I've been talking to Coach Vincent at Sumter. He mentioned that he's being considered for a position with you. Is that right? You couldn't do any better. If the people here would let me add to my staff I'd hire him in a flash." He listened. He smiled. "You know better than that, Joel. Hell, I'm not even sure that Joe Queen's coming here. I'd like to have him. I've got a letter of intent dusted off and gold plated for him." He lifted his coffee cup and took a small sip. "Sure. Let me write you a letter if that's the way you want to handle it. And, when I'm in Charlotte, maybe we could have a minute or two to talk." He put his cup aside. "Say hello to Mary and the boys."

He said goodbye and placed the receiver on the base.

"That's a reference?"

"That's a reference," McCarren said.

❧ ❧ ❧

16 and 2.

That was the team record before the game against Virginia Tech the next night.

The Killer dressed for the game and warmed up with the squad. Seated on the bench, McCarren saw the huddle of the Tech coaches when they recognized Hinson. Burn, baby, burn.

The Mountaineers started their big lineup. He felt the Tech staff relax when the Killer wasn't in the starting five. Without Robert it was a neck and neck contest. Close and even, the score never more than two points in difference for the first half. At the halftime buzzer the Tech shooting guard put up a shot that scraped around the rim and fell through. The gobblers led by two at the break.

While Turner huddled with the starters in one corner of the dressing room, McCarren searched for the Killer and found him at one of the urinals.

"We got to stop meeting like this," Hinson said. "You gonna ruin my reputation."

"How's the finger?"

"Let's try it."

McCarren nodded. "We need some kind of edge. It's getting so nobody's afraid of us anymore." He followed the Killer into the dressing room. "Maybe we ought to set up something for you. What do you feel comfortable with?"

"How about some taps off the glass?"

"That might be it." McCarren pushed his way into the huddle next to Jack Turner. "Listen up. About three minutes into the period I'm going to put the Killer in."

"About time he earned his supper," Jorge said.

"The tap drills. We set up those for the Killer. Right?"

Jorge nodded. Gilson asked, "Which hand?"

"Either," the Killer said.

The home crowd stood and screamed and stomped when the Killer entered the game. "Kill, Robert, kill," was the chant.

Sixteen minutes remained in the final period.

On the defensive end of the court Regis positioned himself for the rebound while the Killer used his size and bulk to box the opposing center. On offense, the first time down, Theold took a pass from Jorge and moved along the baseline. The Gobbler small forward stepped out to challenge him. Theold went into his shooting motion. It was a fake. At the high point of his leap, he dropped a pass toward the far side of the backboard. The Killer lifted his left hand. He nudged the ball once, a second time. It went through with a soft roll. Two for the Killer.

"Kill, Robert, kill."

The Tech center, backing away, heading up court, swings a hand at Robert. The Killer blocked the hand with an elbow. The Tech center's swing had been aimed at Robert's right hand. "Watch that, sucker," Robert yelled at him.

It was going to be like that. He knew what to expect. He'd have to protect himself. No quarter on the floor. No easing up on an injury. The Tech center was telling him, if you're not healthy, stay off my court.

At the defensive end, the Killer chased down a missed shot and grabbed the ball with his left hand. He bounced it to Jorge and sprinted down court. On the way he passed Theold. "Blow by me. I'll sweep the lane for you."

Theold nodded. There was a question on his face. That wasn't what the Coach had called for.

The Killer prowled the lane, in and out of it because of the three second zone. He had the Tech center, big and white and with the chest of a weightlifter, on his back. All the time the Tech center was banging him, slapping at the bandaged right hand. The Killer kept the hand cradled against his chest, shielded from the blows.

Theold took a pass from Gilson on the run and started in. The Gobbler small forward thought he was going immediately for the shot. Theold flashed by him and left him gawking. Theold went toward Robert. The Killer turned and rammed into the Tech center. He saw the surprised and frightened look the center gave him. The center backed away a step. That step was all that Theold needed. He dribbled past the Killer and rammed the ball down through the rim.

When the Killer left the game a minute later, the Mountaineers led by six.

McCarren patted the empty seat on his right. The Killer slumped into it and looked at his bandaged hand. "A risky move there. That one you put on the center."

"Had to get his attention," Robert said.

"Rest. We might let you have another chunk of him in the last two or three minutes, if we need you."

The way the game went from that point on, McCarren didn't have to insert Robert again. The damage was done. The Mountaineer margin remained at six or seven the rest of the contest.

The Virginia Tech coach was quoted in the next morning paper. "You see that out there? The ghost of Robert Kinson freaks out a team even when he's not in the game."

CHAPTER TWENTY

It was early bed check that night for the team. The bus would leave the Biddle for Greensboro at nine the next morning. The game against Wake Forest was scheduled for one that afternoon and would be carried on a regional basis on the east coast by CBS.

Jimmy Stefano got a call from his mother as soon as he walked into the room he shared with Mitchell Winters. .

"It's your grandfather, Jimmy." She said. "He's had a stroke."

"I'll be there as soon as I can get a flight," he said.

Still half an hour before bed check. Jimmy tried Coach Turner's apartment. There was no answer. It meant he was probably on the way or he'd stopped off for a drink somewhere. He placed the next call to Coach McCarren. From the way Coach McCarren sounded, he knew he'd awakened him. But as soon as the Coach heard the reason for the call he was alert and brisk.

"Pack a bag. I'll call the airport and see when the night flight's available."

Twenty minutes later, McCarren trotted down the hallway and stopped in the room doorway. "If we hurry we can make the last flight tonight."

McCarren. had already stopped by Ipsom and raided the "war chest." They made the drive to the Winston-Salem airport in record time. On the way, they were stopped by a North Carolina Highway Patrol car. When the two patrolmen understood the situation and recognized McCarren, they radioed in and received permission to escort McCarren to the airport.

McCarren paid for the ticket from his own pocket. He hurried to the gate with Jimmy. At the barrier he reached into his topcoat pocket and brought out a fold of money. He stuffed the cash in Jimmy's pocket. "Call me as soon as you know something."

"First thing in the morning. Coach."

"Tonight. Or early in the morning."

Jimmy nodded. The flight attendant waited for him.

"And don't worry about the Wake game. We'll win it for you."

Jimmy followed the flight attendant across the tarmac. The plane was being held for him.

He landed in Philadelphia a little over an hour later.

He took a cab directly from the airport to Philadelphia General. After a hurried meeting with his father and mother, he rushed to his grandfather's hospital room. He sat in a chair beside the bed. He listened to the shallow breathing. It hurt him. All his life, especially his childhood, his grandfather had been his hero, his light, his image of what a dignified man ought to be. He'd never seen his grandfather without a coat and tie, except at bedtime. He wore a hat when everyone else didn't.

His mother begged Jimmy to wait at home for news. Jimmy refused. He watched the time while he waited in the room or in the lounge. At eight o'clock, he placed a collect call to Coach McCarren. He'd just completed the call when his mother found him.

"He's awake. He's been asking for you."

Jimmy leaned over his grandfather. "Granddiddy, Granddiddy, I was never ashamed of you."

The old man blinked as if he were trying to focus his eyes. He whispered. "Jimmy, look under the Christmas tree. See what Santa left you."

"Granddiddy, I was always proud of you."

"I will...bet you...it is a...bicycle...if you...have been...good boy..."

The doctor forced Jimmy to leave the room. He leaned against the corridor wall and cried. Around nine that morning, while he was eating a doughnut and drinking coffee in the hospital cafeteria, he was told that his grandfather was dead. The priest was with him, giving him the final rites, when it happened.

While his father made the funeral arrangements, Jimmy's mother fixed him pasta and red clam sauce. He tried to eat to please his mother. He'd only taken a few bites when his mother wheeled the television set into the dining room and plugged it in.

"I don't want to watch it," Jimmy said.

"Your grandfather was planning to watch you today. He was so proud of you. He bragged to everyone."

"He did?"

"All week. He loved you so much. He was waiting to see you."

Sobs clawed at Jimmy's chest for release. He wouldn't let them out. He left the table and hurried to the bathroom. He washed his face and held a cold cloth to his face for a time. When he thought he had himself under control, he returned to the dining room. His mother had taken the pasta away and replaced it with a scoop of ice cream.

His mother switched on the TV set.

The question Jimmy had was answered during a brief interview before the game with Coach McCarren. "You may have heard," McCarren said, "that Jimmy Stefano's grandfather is ill and he's not with the squad today. It's even sadder than that. I've called the hospital and they tell me Mr. Stefano passed away after we left Sandersville. It goes without saying that our team is in mourning with Jimmy. "

"Could you tell us the status of Robert Hinson, your All-American center?"

"I'd rather not play him," McCarren said. "I want him to heal for the stretch run."

"Of course, this game against a strong ACC team is important to your showing to the N.C.A.A. selection …"

McCarren shook his head. "No more important than the health of a fine your ballplayer."

"Still, with two losses already and your season ..."

McCarren looked past him toward the camera. "Jimmy, the team's with you. And I'll call as soon as I can get to a phone after the game."

The color man sputtered. He was speechless.

The Mountaineers started the game with the Killer on the bench. The team seemed shaky without either Hinson or Stefano. Wake Forest had a point run early and led by eight points, 8 to 0, before Theold Brown took a tipped pass from Jorge and charged the length of the court and jammed it.

Wake Forest changed up their defenses sometimes two and three times while the Mountaineers looked for a shot. The change ups bothered Paul Gilson more than they bothered Jorge. That was the inexperience. In another year, McCarren was certain, he'd read the defenses in a split second and react. Faced with the complex shifts Gilson threw the ball away several times.

The Wake center was six-nine or listed at that. He was probably six-ten. With his long arms he seemed about seven feet tall when he moved around the basket.

"Got to have you in there," McCarren said. He tapped the Killer on the knee. "Without you, their center is playing the court like a soccer goalie."

Regis came out. The Killer moved to big forward and Mitchell remained at center. Now the Wake center, Bickman, had to play both Mitchell and Hinson. After a few minutes, the Wake center began to lose his leg strength. He was tiring. On the defensive end of the court, Mitchell and Hinson banged him every chance they got.

The Wake center needed relief. He was replaced by a freshman who hadn't played that much during the year. Mitchell and the Killer played tip ball over the new center and scored four baskets. Two by each. They closed the gap. At the buzzer Wake forest was up by two, 43-41.

They were on the ramp that led to the dressing room when Coach Turner noticed that Walter Turk was limping. He was trying to hide it. Turner caught him by the arm. "What is it?"

"I've hurt the knee again."

With Stefano gone, McCarren was using Walter Turk to spell Theold Brown and the two guards. Gilson and Jorge. Another injury? They were snake bit. Turner thought.

Sarg checked the knee in the examining room. He came out shaking his head. "It's not bad. But I wouldn't play him anymore. I've wrapped the knee."

"Houston." Turner shouted across the dressing room.

Houston Tarr jumped to his feet.

"How's your shot today?"

"I haven't tried it yet." That answer was getting to be a joke around the team. How's your cock today? How's the chow tonight? How's the beer? Does Emmalou give good head? All these and a hundred more to be answered with Houston's response.

"We need your shot," Turner said.

McCarren returned from the examination room where he'd spoken to Walter Turk. He stopped in front of Coach Turner.

"Houston's going to demonstrate his clothesline jump shot."

"Hit eighty percent," McCarren said.

McCarren began the game with Regis, Winters and Brown across the front line. The Killer had a seat on McCarren's right. Houston was next to the Killer.

The Killer learned toward. "They put you in; we get to see if you really want to be a star."

The game remained close. Up two points, even, then down two points. Mitchell and Bo Regis couldn't handle the Wake center now that he'd had a rest in the dressing room.

McCarren nodded at Hinson. "Need you in there. Report."

The Killer examined the tape and the pad over the broken finger.

He checked in with the scorer. He waited on one knee in front of the table.

"You too, Tarr. In for Theold."

When Houston squatted next to the Killer the big center grinned at him. "Let's see you make that shot, boy."

"Yes, sir."

The Killer laughed. "And keep calling me sir."

On court, Theold tried for a steal and saw that he couldn't keep the ball in bounds. He turned in the air and bounced the basketball off the leg of the Wake center. The clock stopped. The Killer and Houston entered the game, replacing Bo Regis and Theold Brown. The Killer loped toward the offensive end of the court. Houston followed and set his position on the left side. Joe dribbled left, toward Houston, and then looked right. Mitchell Winters broke for the basket. At that same moment, Houston slipped in two steps. The pass from Jorge, after the fake to winters, was crisp and fingertip high. The Wake small forward whirled and adjusted. Houston put up the low, flat shot. It hit the far side of the rim with a _thuck_ and fell through.

The Killer passed Houston on the trot down court to set up on defense. "My man, my man," he murmured," your star is looking brighter every moment."

Houston lifted his head and read the overhead clock. Even. 56-56. He set himself to play defense. He hand checked the small forward. Bumped him. Banged him with a thigh. The Wake point guard looked in the direction of his small forward and backed away. The high pass went to the big forward who made the catch and tried to turn on Robert Hinson. The Killer hit the power forward with a shoulder and bumped him off stride. The near official called the Wake big forward for walking.

The Wake Forest bench was on their feet, screaming about the call.

"You got one more?" The Killer passed Houston at mid court. Houston nodded. "Good man."

Houston blanked his mind. He waited while the ball moved, rotated. Gilson to winters to Jorge and then to him. He was seventeen feet away when he went up with the good stroke, the easy. This time the Wake small forward was closer and Houston had to lean slightly to his right to avoid an outstretched hand. The shot looked short. It didn't appear that it would reach the basket. It barely did. It hit the backboard on the short side of the basket and banked in. No *thuck* this time. A net whisper.

In a five minute stretch, Houston sank four of his six shots and he had one assist. When he left the game, Theold, entering, took a wide turn and patted his back. Bo Regis replaced Mitchell Winters. The Killer remained in the game.

McCarren patted the seat on his right. "Deep breaths, Houston. I want you in for Jorge in a couple of minutes."

By the time clock, two and a half minutes later, Houston went in for Jorge. His man, on defense, was the Wake big guard. Paul Gilson was needed against the quick Wake point man. That created a problem for Houston. The Wake big guard was three or four inches taller than Houston. Wake saw the mismatch, the advantage, and went to the big guard. They cleared a side for the Wake guard to go one on one against Houston. The larger man used his size to work for an easy shot.

Houston looked toward the Mountaineer bench. McCarren was facing away, talking to Jorge. He looked unconcerned. The Mountaineer lead was two points.

On offense, Gilson did most of the ballhandling. He worked the ball to the Killer. The Killer turned and made his move toward the basket. The Wake center threw a block at the legs of Hinson and knocked him down. The Killer twisted, trying to land on his left hand. He didn't turn far enough. He hit the floor on his right side and his right hand. He kicked out his legs and grunted. He rolled to his back and pressed the hurt hand under his armpit.

McCarren and Sarg, the trainer, were on the court at a run. Sarg put a knee on the floor beside the Killer and learned over him. McCarren stood there for a few seconds and then went chest to chest with the closest official.

"You let this crap go on?"

"Intentional foul," the official said and walked away. He held up two fingers toward the scorer's table.

McCarren stared at the ref's back for a long time. He did his slow burn. Then he walked over and stood next to Sarg. "Can you shoot, Robert?"

Sarg looked over his shoulder at McCarren and shook his head. "Got to check his hand. Coach."

The rule was, if the man who was fouled couldn't shoot the shots, and then McCarren had to pick a man from his bench, a man not in the game at the time. McCarren walked to the bench. He stopped beside Walter Turk. "Can you make two foul shots and then come out?"

Turk limped to the line. He made both foul shots. He hobbled from the court. Jorge entered the game, along with Bo Regis. Gilson left for a rest.

The Killer watched the free throws at the mouth of the ramp. He waved at Houston and backed away.

Jorge tapped himself on the chest and pointed at the Wake small, quick guard. That meant Houston was still on the big shooting guard. When that was obvious to the Wake team, it was a replay of the last time down the court. Wake cleared a side for the big guard and he went one on one against Houston. He muscled his way past Houston for a short jump shot in the lane.

Wake had cut the lead to two points.

Jorge got a jump on the Wake point guard and made his drive for the basket. At the last moment he decided to drop the basketball to Mitchell. Mitchell wasn't expecting it. He juggled it and, by the time he had control and attempted to put up the shot, the Wake center recovered and batted the ball away. The Wake big forward took the rebound and slowed the tempo.

Jorge passed Houston at center court. "Foul the bastard," he hissed. "Make him get the points at the line."

Back to what worked. The Wake big guard took the pass and started his move against Houston. Dribbling, backing in. Houston banged him from behind and stuck a hand in his kidney. The whistle blew. The foul was called on Houston. Wake was given the ball out of bounds. They weren't into shooting the one and one yet.

Again. Wake isolated the big guard on Houston. Houston fought him for each inch. Jorge moved over and tried to help out. The big guard found Jorge's man, the point guard, alone and flipped the ball to him. The Wake guard banked the ball off the backboard.

The game was tied.

McCarren substituted. The starting lineup was on the floor. Regis Winters and Brown on the front line. Gilson and Jorge at guards.

Houston slumped into the seat next to Coach McCarren. "My fault, Coach."

"How's that?" McCarren patted him on the back. "Because you didn't grow five inches overnight?" McCarren dropped a fresh towel in Houston's hands.

Back and forth. Even. Wake up by two. Even. The Mountaineers up by two. Even.

Five minutes remained when Sarg leaned over McCarren and shook his head. "No new damage. But I don't think we ought to risk it. I've told him to shower and dress."

"That's for the best," McCarren said.

Sarg returned to the dressing room. McCarren rubbed his eyes and put his attention on the game. It was shifting. It was changing. Without the Killer, without that threat inside. Wake clogged the middle. Their center and big forward formed a wall across the lane. Neither Winters nor Regis could get inside. What was left of the Mountaineers was the fifteen foot and anything beyond that.

Theold hit one from seventeen and missed another.

Wake was up by one point when the clock touched the two minute mark. Mountaineers ball. McCarren stood and gave the signal for the timeout. Jorge turned to the official and asked for it.

McCarren didn't want to use the timeout. He had to. Bo Regis and Mitchell Winters were almost staggering with fatigue. As the players jogged toward the bench, McCarren made another decision. He sent Stoddard and Ashley to the scorer's table to report.

McCarren stood over his players. "Regis and Winters, you relax. You've got the timeout and maybe another thirty seconds of rest." He turned to Stoddard and Ashley. "Give me all you've got for thirty seconds."

Winters squirted water on his face and let it run down his uniform front.

McCarren looked at Theold. "You got a shot you haven't shown us yet?"

Theold sucked in air. "I'll think of one."

"Our ball. We need this basket. Stoddard and Ashley, I want you after the rebound if the shot doesn't fall.

Stoddard and Ashley nodded.

"All out?"

"Yes, sir," they said.

Jorge brought the ball straight down the middle of the court. He pulled up near the free throw circle. The Wake small forward positioned himself to deny Theold the baseline. Theold faked a run at the baseline and whirled and moved back toward Jorge. Jorge saw the cut and fed him the pass. Theold moved toward the lane. The Wake big guard slid over and tried to block his path. Theold stopped his dribble and went up high for the shot. The Wake small forward recovered enough to move behind Theold. He took a giant leap and slapped the ball away. There was the sound of flesh on flesh. The Wake big guard put out a hand and grabbed the ball.

Theold looked over his shoulder at the nearest official. He made no call. The official shook his head and started toward the other end of the court. No reason to stay and bitch. Theold sprinted down court to play defense.

Wake was still ahead by one point. 74-73.

The Wake coach moved along the side of the court. He held up one finger.

The number of a play? Or, McCarren thought, the Wake team will hold for one shot.

One minute and twenty seconds showed on the clock.

McCarren turned to Jack Turner. "How are we on fouls?"

"Over the limit."

They were trapped. If Wake decided to hold for the one shot, the Mountaineers were caught with the smaller lineup on the court. Stoddard and Ashley instead of Regis and winters. While Wake had the ball, while the clock was moving, there was no way that McCarren could call a timeout.

The clock reached the one minute mark and ticked passes it.

Turner leaned toward him. "Foul them."

McCarren jumped to his feet. He yelled at Jorge. "Give the foul."

Jorge lunged toward the point guard. He took a swipe at the ball. He caught arm and hand and ball. The whistle blew. The official held up a finger on each hand. That meant it was one and one. They hadn't called the intentional two shot foul.

Winters and Regis sprinted to the scorer's table, reported and went in for Stoddard and Ashley.

The Wake point guard made the first free throw. He got the chance to try the second and made that one as well. Wake was ahead by three with forty-seven seconds to go. 76-73.

Gilson rushed the ball down the court. He tossed it to Jorge. On the left side Theold faked the move toward Jorge and sliced down the baseline. He got the pass on the run and went up over the Wake center for the shot. He had to adjust to get it over the long arms. The ball hit the rim and rattled around. Mitchell Winters, overeager, moved behind the Wake center and tapped the ball in. The whistle blew even as the ball fell through the net. The official ruled that Mitchell had touched the ball while it was still in the cone over the basket. It was called basket interference and the goal wasn't allowed. It was Wake's ball with twenty-eight seconds to go.

"Foul," McCarren shouted to Gilson.

Paul heard him and ran the Wake point guard down. This time the official ruled that it was intentional and held up two fingers on one hand. Two shots.

The Wake point man made the first shot and missed the second. Winters boxed out the Wake center and Bo Regis grabbed the rebound.

Wake led by four points, 77-73.

Twenty seconds on the clock.

No time to work for the shot. Theold took the shot from twenty feet and it went in. Wake led by two. "Foul."

Jorge grabbed the Wake big guard as soon as the ball was passed over the end line to him. The foul was called intentional again. Two shots.

The pressure affected the Wake big guard. He missed the first shot and made the second. Wake was up by three points.

Gilson made one long pass from the baseline to Jorge at center court. He turned and tossed the ball to Theold. Theold drove straight for the basket. The small forward gave ground, backing away. The Wake center curled away too. The shout from the Wake bench was to let Theold have the shot. "Don't foul him and give him a chance at the basket and a free throw."

Theold stepped around the small forward and slammed the basketball through.

Wake led by one.

The final seconds Wake played cat and mouse with the ball Passing it from player to player. No player held it long enough for a Mountaineer to run him down and foul him. The final buzzer sounded as Paul caught the big guard and fouled him. No call was made. The game was over.

The Wake fans celebrated in the stands.

The Killer was dressed in his street clothes. His travel bag was at his fleet. His left hand crossed his chest and pressed a plastic bag of ice against the point of his right shoulder. He lifted his chin from the elbow of the arm that held the ice bag and looked at Jorge when he entered the dressing room. The answer to his question was in the way Jorge moved.

"One lousy point," Jorge said. "One fucking point."

Paul Gilson stopped beside Hinson and nodded at him. "You all right, man?"

"I was," the Killer said.

"One lousy point." Jorge removed his basketball shoes and threw them against a locker.

Mitchell Winters staggered into the dressing room. He was totally exhausted. As soon as the door closed behind him, he leaned his back against the wall and stood these, eyes closed and his mind a dark tunnel.

"You." A hand rammed Mitchell in the chest. He blinked and opened his eyes. Jorge rammed the hand against him again. "That shot by Theold was going in. Damn you, we needed that two points. It made all the difference in the fucking world."

Theold got to his feet and ran toward Jorge. "It wasn't going. I tell you it wasn't …"

Jorge turned on him. "You fucking hotshots. All you know is how to lose. The Killer man and me, we don't like it. We say fuck losing. The Killer man and me, we …"

Mitchell stepped forward and put his arms around Jorge, pinning his arms to his sides. "We don't like it either."

Theold stepped in and wrapped his arms around Winters and Jorge. "Listen to this man. Captain."

The Killer dropped the plastic sack of ice on the floor and crossed to them. He approached from the other side, facing Theold, and swept the three of the others into his huge arms. His voice was almost a whisper, so that only the four of them could hear him. "We're forgetting two things. I ain't playing worth shit hurt. It ain't my fault and it ain't yours. And that Jimmy-boy ain't with us today. We're forgetting him."

"Jesus." Jorge blinked and closed his eyes. His head dropped on his chest. "We forgot Jimmy."

They were standing like that, in a human knot, when McCarren entered and stopped. He stared at them. "Bus leaves in twenty minutes," he said.

The Killer lifted his head and looked at McCarren. The look was calm and distant.

The funeral for Jimmy's grandfather was held the following Monday. Coach McCarren and Jack Turner, with Jorge representing the team as Captain, attended the services.

There was a wreath from President Edwards of the University and one from the players.

That night, after dinner with the Stefanos, the two coaches and the two players flew to North Carolina. McCarren asked Jimmy if he wanted to stay a few more days. Jimmy said he thought he'd better return with them. There was school work, he said. Unstated but there, almost in the open: and games to play and try to win. Six games remained to play in the regular season. Three of those games were the hard part of the season.

The drive from McCoy dorm, where McCarren had dropped Jimmy and Jorge, was quiet. Jack Turner seemed withdrawn. Or he'd noticed the mood McCarren carried with him like a shroud.

McCarren braked in the parking lot outside Turner's apartment. It was after midnight. A light icy rain fell. The windshield wipers clattered and skipped.

Turner opened the car door on the passenger side. "I'll see you in the morning."

"I think I need to talk, Jack."

"Come on in then."

"You got any Irish?"

"I might have a dram or two." Since working for McCarren, Jack Turner had added Irish to his bar shelf.

They sat at the kitchen table. Turner passed McCarren a strong Irish over the rocks and poured himself a short scotch over ice.

"What is it, Tim?"

"You see those kids in the dressing room Saturday after the game?"

Turner had missed the early part of it. He'd arrived in time to hear McCarren announce the bus would be leaving soon and he'd seen the body knot beside the entrance to the dressing room. "They were comforting each other?"

McCarren shook his head. "They were almost fighting each other. Until cooler heads changed it."

"Jesus."

"A hard thing for me to admit. Jack. Bitter as gall. I got outcoached the last two minutes of the game."

Jack Turner hesitated. He worked for this man and he learned from him and he even loved him. As much as he wanted to he couldn't lie to him. He nodded. "Yes, Tim."

"Why? How?"

"I think that's Atlantic Coast Conference ball. Situation basketball. A coach who plays an independent schedule usually meets a wide range of kinds of coaches. And he plays the other team once a year. A coach like the Wake one plays the seven other schools twice a year, home and home. Used to play them in the Big Four tournament before Christmas too. And then there's a big chance they meet again in the A.C.C. tournament at the end of the regular season. That's a lot of head to head."

"Situation basketball?" McCarren sipped his Irish.

"Like Saturday. In a certain situation, say two years ago. Dean Smith catches the Maryland coach with his big horse on the bench getting a breather. He's up one point and he plays four corners against Maryland and won't let Maryland get their big center in the game. It becomes a foul earner as it did with us Saturday. The next year perhaps Maryland does the same thing against Wake. Wake turns right around, this year, and finds the same situation and puts that script into the works against us."

"You knew this was possible?"

Turner shook his head. "No reason to think Wake wouldn't play with us."

"No reason?"

Turner gulped his scotch. "No tendency toward the slow-down game this season from all the scouting reports. What happened was that we got into a certain situation and the Wake coach said, hey, let's do what Maryland did to us last year."

"I guess that means we file this away and wait until next year and we get to use it on somebody."

Turner smiled. "It might be more than a year. It was an odd combination of factors. The Killer hurt, Stefano not playing. The inexperience of Winters."

"Those kids ..."

"Yes." Turner brought the Irish bottle to the table and poured a trickle into McCarren's glass.

"They were about to fight each other over whose fault it was they lost the game. I almost stepped into it and told them it was my fault."

"No, Tim. Not now. At the end of the season, if you still have it bothering you. But not now. Those kids have got to believe in you. They've got to know you made the right move, that you played the percentages."

McCarren laughed. "I could blame it on you."

"I'd rather you didn't. With you around, I've got enough trouble getting any respect."

"They're good kids."

"The best," Turner said. "If they hold together."

"They will." McCarren started to toss back the drink. He thought better of it and had a long swallow. He pushed the half-filled glass toward Turner. "Sorry to waste good Irish. It just doesn't help tonight."

He stood and walked into the living room. He put on his scarf and hat while Turner got his topcoat from the closet. Jack held the coat for him while he worked his arms into it.

"We need to win at least twenty."

"At least four of the last six would be better." Turner stepped away.

"The right four of them."

"We win twenty and they owe us a return," Turner said. "We were there last year."

"It doesn't work that way."

"The U.N.C. at Charlotte game…?"

"Mastermind the game for me," McCarren said.

"One. We keep the Killer out for the next two games. No more risks. We don't use him at U.N.C at Charlotte or against Florida Southern. We hold him for South Carolina. That meet with your approval?"

"What else?"

"Without the Killer inside, they're eating us alive in there. We've got to change that."

"How?"

"We put in a control game."

"Why?"

"This must be the Socratic method." Turner smiled. "One thing, we might conserve some energy. No racehorse ball that drains the players. Two. We take only the perfect shot, the high percentage shot. We work for it for five minutes if we have to. We take less shots and we make more of them and they can't score on us while we're working for that perfect shot."

"I don't like the control game." McCarren took a deep breath. "Oh, shit."

He stripped off his topcoat and dropped it over the back of a chair. He returned to the kitchen and got his unfinished drink from the table. He walked back into the living room.

"What else we do is start screwing around with the heads of the other coaches. The ones we play down the line, the rest of the season and in the tournament."

"How?"

McCarren already knew the answers. Turner thought. He wanted Turner to defend his concept. "We put in the control game. They won't know how to prepare for us. They won't know what to expect. Right now everyone knows we run and gun. We racehorse. What happens if, for two games, we don't run and gun?"

"It's not our game," McCarren said.

"No. It's not the game we've played. That's a different matter."

"They'll say we're going to it because we don't have the Killer."

"The Killer comes back and we still do it. What happens to the thinking then?"

"Two days to put it in. Tomorrow and Wednesday. That enough time?"

"Maybe. I'll dream some patterns tonight. Jorge and Gilson handle the ball well. So does Theold. Tom Alley's questionable. So we try Houston Tarr. Walter Turk, if his leg is better."

"Two games? Against U.N.C. at Charlotte and Florida Southern."

"For starters. Maybe one more later if we get the chance. That's to show that it wasn't to cover the Killer being out."

"Map it out," McCarren said.

CHAPTER TWENTY ONE

Two days of practice and they took the team bus to Charlotte. While the team walked around the campus and stretched their legs after the long bus ride, McCarren visited Coach Joel Barlow to complete the rest of his promised push for hiring Coach Vincent as an assistant.

"All I can tell you is that he's one of the final two," Barlow said.

"He brings Joe Queen with him?"

"I wish." Barlow shook his head. "But there's a guard at Camden and a small forward from Bennettsville …"

"Sounds good," McCarren said.

"You go after either of them?

"No. A token gesture or two."

"Recruiting five great ballplayers in one year can be a liability." Barlow said.

"So I hear." McCarren hesitated. "Who was the fifth one?

"Houston Tarr."

McCarren shook his head. "He was the throw-in."

"If you don't want him you can throw him to me."

"Finders keepers," McCarren said.

"The problem with some coaches," Joel Barlow said, "is that they've got a warped yardstick. Your warped yardstick is Theold Brown. A Theold Brown is a once in a lifetime. Gilson you might recruit twice in a lifetime. Maybe three times. The same with winters and Stefano. The Houston Tarrs you recruit all the time but they're the ones you win with year in and year out."

McCarren smiled. "I feel like I got here in time for the sermon "

"I watched the Tarr boy for three years. I wanted him. I still do."

"Why?"

"One reason. When everybody else gives up, when they've all mentally packed their bags and gone home, he'll still bust his ass for you."

McCarren put on his coat and found his hat. "Thanks for reminding me."

"My pleasure."

"What should I tell Vincent down in Sumter?"

"That you made your best pitch."

"He's a good recruiter. Or will be."

"A designated recruiter?"

"It might be a good idea."

"Amen. Tim," Barlow said.

At the final buzzer that night, Joel Barlow met McCarren at the edge of the court, near the scorer's table. He was shaking his head. He appeared puzzled.

"What's going on, Tim?"

"What do you mean?" McCarren took Joel's hand and clasped it.

"You beat us 55 to 50 and you ask what I mean?"

"Blame that on Jack Turner. He decided that we ought to install a delay game and see how it works."

"It looked good to me," Barlow said.

McCarren shrugged. Might as well seem modest. The truth was that the control game had worked very well indeed. At the beginning of the game, the Mountaineers got a couple of quick baskets. They retained that margin through the first half and into the middle of the second half. With ten minutes to go, Jack Turner nodded to McCarren and got to his feet. He got the attention of Paul Gilson. He held out the crooked thumb and finger that formed the "C" and set the team into the control game. Only the open shot, only the high percentage shot. Nothing else.

The Killer sat at the end of the bench in his street clothes. He scowled. He didn't like the control game and he didn't like not playing.

At the Friday afternoon practice, Turner continued to work with the control game. Only now, with one ten minute stretch under game conditions behind them, he enlarged the concept. Not just control now, but an out and out stall. "Nothing but a layup," he shouted.

McCarren scowled. "Pull Winters to midcourt," he said.

"He's not a good enough ballhandler ..."

"Try it anyway. Let's see what happens if the other center comes out and tries to guard him."

"Got you, Tim."

Turner huddled with his starting five. Winters, Regis and Brown across the front line and Jorge and Gilson at the guards. "No dribbling about," he instructed Mitchell Winters. "Paul, Jorge, you two make sure he doesn't get trapped into a jump ball. Always have a passing lane for him."

He sent them back to the floor.

Perimeter passing at first. Careful to pass or move the ball over the time line when the ballhandler was being guarded.

"Now, Mitchell."

Mitchell trotted to midcourt and took the pass from Jorge. He was unguarded. He put the ball on his hip and looked around. Ames Ashley, the opposing center in the workout, was still under the basket.

"Ashley, come out and guard your man."

When Ashley was a step away from winters, Mitchell flipped the ball to Jorge. Jorge turned and spotted Theold flashing across the open lane. He threw the high lob pass to Theold who caught it in the air. Completed a half turn and slammed the ball through the basket.

"All right," McCarren said. "That's one way. But it might be one pass too many."

Turner understood. He stepped close to winters and said a few words. "Same as before."

This time, when Mitchell took the pass from Jorge at mid-court he didn't look for the return pass to one of the guards. He waited for Ashley to move away from the basket to confront him. As soon as Ashley broke past the free throw line Mitchell saw Theold flashing across the lane. He passed to Theold. The lob was high but Theold adjusted for it and guided it into the basket.

"That's it," Turner said.

"One more," McCarren said. "They see Theold do that once or twice, they'll try to close it off." He designed two more patterns off the flash across the middle of the zone. On one. Regis broke down the opposite baseline and took a dish off pass to Theold. On the other Jorge trailed Theold, a couple of steps behind him, and took Theold's behind the back pass as Theold drew the defenders toward him.

McCarren still scowled.

The next night against Florida Southern, the opposing coach and players probably expected the Mountaineers to play control ball. Instead, McCarren and Turner turned the team loose to play run and gun, racehorse, basketball. The Mountaineers blew the game wide open near the end of the first half. There was a run of six straight baskets, four by Theold and two by Jimmy Stefano, and the game was beyond any comeback attempt Florida Southern tried. The score mounted in the second half. In the final ten minutes, McCarren emptied the bench and played the second line team members. Florida Southern, against these players, cut the score and made the final seem almost respectable. At the final buzzer, the Mountaineers had won by sixteen.

19 wins and 3 losses, that was the record so far.

The polls came out that night and were published in the morning papers. Hunt Morgan was 19th in both the AP and the DPI. "Just as long as we stay in the top twenty," Jack Turner said.

Four games remained on the regular season schedule.

"Suicidal," the sports writer from the *Winston-Salem Journal* wrote about the final four games on the Mountaineer schedule.

"A mistake?" the columnist from the *Charlotte Observer* questioned.

"A horrible blunder," a staff writer from the *Raleigh Times* called it.

"I planned it this way," McCarren insisted. "I wouldn't change it if I could."

What McCarren wouldn't say was that he'd planned to have the twenty wins under his belt before he started the final run of four games. At the least he expected to be 20 and 2. The difficult schedule was intended to impress the selection committee of the N.C.A.A. Other independent teams might soften their stretch run schedule; he seemed to be saying, so they could make a strong final showing. Not Tim McCarren. This was the way McCarren did it.

Too much pride. He'd outsmarted himself, he knew.

Four games to go and he had to win at the least two of those to have any chance at all to go the N. C. A. A's. That was his private estimate. In public, he said that he had to win all four. And that was what he told his team.

He sat the Mountaineers down before the Tuesday practice.

"The Killer and Jorge and I made a promise to ourselves that we'd go back to the Big Dance this year. Right, Killer? Right, Jorge?"

"If you ain't been to the Big Dance, you ain't been anywhere," Robert Hinson said.

"Nineteen and three. Will that get us invited to the ball?"

"No," the Killer said.

"Nineteen and seven?"

"No way," the Killer shouted.

"Twenty-three and three?"

"That's the magic numbers, Coach."

McCarren nodded at Jorge. "Tell them about the Big Dance, co-captain."

"The food is great."

"The best hotels," the Killer said.

"All the press and the attention," Jorge said.

"The beautiful girls."

Jorge stared at the Killer. "What girls were those?"

"The ones they furnish the players."

"I didn't get no girl," Jorge said.

"And here I've been wondering all year why I got two girls."

Jorge threw a basketball at the Killer. The Killer, without thinking, caught it with his right hand. He didn't flinch. If there was pain he didn't show it. He stood and dribbled the ball, using his right hand, toward the nearest basket. "Twenty-three and three. That's the ticket to the Big Dance."

He slammed the ball through the net.

On Tuesday and Wednesday, before the Thursday game against South Carolina, they worked on the control game and the stall game.

All through the drills the shouts cascaded. "Twenty-three and three."

McCarren smiled.

"That's the ticket," the answering yell was.

The Killer started the game. The roar from the crowd shook the Coliseum walls. The Killer was ready to play.

"He's kicking ass and letting Mitchell take the game," Billy Stoddard whispered to Jimmy in an awed voice.

The Killer's touch was off the first two or three times he put up shots. But Mitchell was there, playing the big forward, and he rebounded and fed Hinson for second shots, for close in slam shots that the Killer never missed.

Added to that, Theold was hot. His shot had never been so pure, so easy. No rim, no backboard, only net.

The Gamecock small forward started a shooting tear. After he hit three shots in a row, McCarren reached down the bench and called for Jimmy Stefano. "Cool off number twenty-two," McCarren said. "Do it quick."

Stefano moved to small forward, replacing Theold who dropped to the backcourt. Paul Gilson left the game for a breather. Jimmy played the Gamecock small. Forward chest to chest. He denied him the ball most of the time. Using his hands, hips and body he jogged the small forward until, when he did touch the ball, he was beyond his effective shooting range.

The South Carolina coach left the court shaking his head. Twenty minutes of play behind them and the damage had already been done. The small forward had missed his last three shots and the guards weren't even looking for him anymore. The Killer was regaining his touch. Theold Brown wanted the ball every time down court on offense because the blessing was on him tonight and he couldn't miss.

After the first half, the Mountaineers led by twelve points.

In the first minute of the second half, the Killer broke the back of the Gamecock team. On an inbounds play, he lost the South Carolina center in a crowd and broke for the basket and slammed the ball through with both hands. The next play, he blocked the power forward's shot, recovered the ball and tossed it on the fast break to Jorge. He trailed the play and filled the center lane. Jorge's shot, taken from four or five feet when the small forward challenged him, rimmed and fell away. The Killer soared over the small forward and around him and rolled the ball up the side of the backboard and down through the net.

The margin was sixteen points and the Gamecock spirit faded.

At the post-game interview, the South Carolina coach, Timmons, said that all he could do now was head for home and plan an ambush for next year when the Mountaineers arrived in Columbia without Hinson or Jorge.

"But let me tell you this. This Mountaineer team is playing better ball than they were at the beginning of the season. And that's scary for the rest of the teams in the country."

"It's a good quote," McCarren said when it was his turn. "I'm not sure it's true, but it's good of Jim Timmons to say nice things about our little team."

"You're twenty and three now," the writer from the *News and Observer* said. "Do you think this assures you a spot in the big show?"

"Twenty?" McCarren smiled. "Did we reach the magic twenty tonight? I must be short one finger or toe."

The press group laughed. The *News and Observer* writer repeated his question. "Do you think this win assures you and the team a berth in the N.C.A.A.'s?"

"I can't speculate on that," McCarren said. "But I'll say this. If this is the way Robert Hinson plays after he breaks a little finger and takes a few games off, then I'm going to break one of his thumbs."

DePaul was riding a wave, a winning crest, when they arrived at Sandersville to play the Mountaineers. They'd won their last six games and there was talk, no matter what the rest of their season was, that they were sure to be invited to the N.C.A.A.'s again this year.

It wasn't a friendly game at all. It resembled a grudge match.

The Killer and the DePaul center, Fred Carson, had played pickup games on the playgrounds in New York and hadn't liked each other much then. Now, this year, the Killer was getting all the good press and the mentions for All-America teams. Carson thought he was being slighted and he wanted this game to be for the bragging rights.

It almost started with a fight in the hallway outside the dressing rooms at the Biddle Coliseum. As they usually were, the Mountaineers were in their locker room, ankles taped and getting into their uniforms, when the Blue Demons arrived by bus from their motel. The exception was Robert Hinson, who'd been upstairs in the sports medicine office. He'd had the finger checked. The break was healing well. And he'd been fitted with a new plastic sheath that replaced the old one which was too large now that the swelling had gone down. As it happened, he was at the Mountaineer dressing room door when the DePaul team came down the hallway in a file. Fred Carson stepped from the line of players and looked at Robert. "Hello, Killer." He didn't offer to shake hands.

"Good to see you," Hinson said.

"You say that now," Carson said. "Let's see what you say when the game's over."

"Put your mouth on the court," the Killer said. "Let's see how well it plays basketball,"

"My mouth ain't what it's about," Carson said. Carson wore his hair in a stiff afro that made him seem about two inches taller than Hinson. They were, in fact, about the same height. There was a horseshoe mark burned in the dark flesh of Carson's right arm, a gang symbol.

"All I hear is mouth now."

"You want more than mouth?" Carson took a couple of steps toward Hinson.

A DePaul assistant coach stepped between them and gave Carson a push. "Save it for the game."

❧ ❧ ❧

The Killer dressed in his uniform and his warmups. He found McCarren in the training room. "This time it's my question. You want to take a piss with me?"

Sarg, who was working on Walter Turk's knee, gave them a strange look and turned away.

"Sure," McCarren said.

Billy Stoddard was in one of the stalls taking his pregame, nervous piss. McCarren and the Killer waited until he left the bathroom. McCarren leaned against one of the urinals and waited.

"That Carson…"

McCarren nodded.

"We've got an old dislike working. It almost got spread around the hallway a few minutes ago."

"What you want me to do about it?"

"I want his ass stuffed in a garbage can," the Killer said.

"You want my permission to do that?"

The Killer shook his head. "We got to win this game. If we don't win, nothing else matters."

"What do you want?"

"I want Mitchell banging him with me. At least for the first half. He'll blow up. He's got a short fuse."

"Spell it out for me, Robert."

"I plan to play this straight. No fouls. I want Mitchell to clobber him every chance he gets."

"That puts Mitchell on the spot."

"You mean foul trouble? Well, we spell Mitchell with Regis. Maybe even throw in Stefano a time or two for his licks."

McCarren closed his eyes and considered it. "But we win?

"We win."

"Set up your deal with the guys.

The Killer grinned.

Each time the DePaul center, Carson, touched the ball he thought two or three cinderblock walls fell on him. He attracted elbows, fists, shoulders and hips.

Ten minutes into the game, it appeared that the two centers, Hinson and Carson, were holding their own against each other. Each had four baskets, eight points. Robert had two blocked shots to Carson's one. Each had five rebounds.

The difference was that the Killer was smiling and relaxed. Carson was puffy-faced, had sore ribs and a split lip. The sore ribs came from a collision when Jimmy Stefano rammed into him while trying to fight through a pick Carson set.

DePaul was up by three points but no one seemed to care about the score this early in the game. What was really happening on the court was the dismantling of the DePaul center. The Mountaineer front line concentrated on that.

Heading into the final five minutes of the first half, the Killer heard Carson complaining to one of the officials that he was getting fouled two and three times each time he touched the ball.

Only one foul was being called. He was, he said, "being killed by four players."

Theold Brown wasn't part of the hatchet job on the DePaul center. He prowled the perimeters and took his shots when he had them and he kept the Mountaineers in the game.

At the half, Fred Carson staggered from the court and wobbled up the ramp to the dressing room. The Killer stood at center court and watched him.

In the dressing room, McCarren leaned over the Killer. "We're down by two. When do we start winning the game?"

"Soon. You wait and see."

Jimmy walked by. The killer slapped him on the rump. "Good work in there, young man."

"We owe you. Killer."

According to the statistics Jack Turner kept, there were two fouls on Hinson, three on Regis and three on Mitchell Winters. Stefano had two. No trouble yet with fouls. If it didn't get out of hand. McCarren was worried.

"How soon do we start winning?"

"Soon as Freddy-boy loses his cool."

Carson came out of the dressing room fresh after the half-time rest. A couple of stitches had been taken in his lip. From the opening tip of the second half, he used his elbows. One elbow struck Bo Regis in the mouth and knocked out a tooth. Regis hit the floor and rolled over. He spat the tooth on the floor.

The official blew his whistle and pointed at Carson. It was Carson's third foul.

"He was on me," Carson yelled. "He was on my back the whole time."

The official didn't back away from him. "Watch those elbows. That's a warning."

"You tell that to …"

The official walked away.

The next time down the court on offense, Robert Hinson took the ball directly at Carson. One dribble, two, a third while Robert swept across the lane. He went up for the soft finger roll shot. Carson had it timed perfectly. He went straight up. He would have blocked the shot and never touched Robert. At the last moment, with the official screened, Mitchell Winters brushed against Carson and threw him off balance. Carson fell into the Killer. The official who'd been screened blew his whistle and called the fourth foul on Carson.

"With the body," the official said.

Carson whirled on Mitchell and threw a fist at him. Mitchell expected it and slapped the hand away. The official stepped between them and tooted his whistle again. "You calm down, thirty-four. You hear me?"

The Killer circled the official and stopped beside Mitchell. "You okay, white hope?"

The official was still warning Carson. He didn't see Hinson and Carson lock eyes. He didn't see the sneaky grin the Killer gave Carson. That grin was the final straw. Carson let out a bellow and pushed the official aside. He charged the Killer. The Killer dodged him.

"That's it, thirty-four," the official said. "You're out of the game."

With Carson on the bench, and the substitute center in for DePaul, the Mountaineers made up the margin of points. It remained fairly even until Theold hit three straight jump shots and the Killer sucked it in and powered his game against the new center.

At the final buzzer, the Mountaineers had won by eight. They were twenty-one and three.

Appalachian State ran scared against the Killer and the Mountaineers. That was all the edge that McCarren needed.

Varsity Gym was packed to the rafters, all 8,000 or so seats taken. The Killer, now that the hand was better, went on a scoring rampage. He had twenty-eight points by halftime and he added another twelve in the early part of the second half before McCarren decided the score was too lopsided and benched the starting unit.

It was still a rout. The Mountaineers, even with the reserves in the game, scored their highest point total of the year. The final was 123 to 83.

"Would you say you're peaking at the right time of the year?" the sports writer from the *Winston-Salem Journal* asked McCarren afterwards.

"You're judging on the basis of tonight's game?" McCarren shook his head. "This was a fluke, one of those crazy games that take place every two or three years. Appalachian is a better team than they showed tonight and we're just not this good, though we'd like to be. Some nights one team can't do anything wrong and the other one can't do anything right. It worked out we held the dry end of the stick and they had the wet end."

"Would you say you're expecting a bid?"

"Right now, all I'm really expecting is for Marquette to show up in Sandersville on Friday. And I'm expecting them on the court on Saturday."

"The Killer …" the *News and Observer* columnist began.

"Ain't Robert something else?"

"He was awesome."

"See?" McCarren said. "You can answer your own questions."

"Tonight he scored forty points."

"Most of you have watched the Killer for almost four years. By now, you ought to know that Robert could score thirty point a game if he wanted to or if we asked him to. On another team, where we didn't have balanced scoring, we might need those thirty points a game from him. Robert is an unselfish player, a complete player. And he runs that team out there on the court.

He takes his shots when he's open and he makes sure the other players get the ball when they're open."

At breakfast the next morning, Robert read the quote in the *Winston-Salem Journal*. He drew himself to his fall height and puffed out his chest. "Don't call me Killer anymore. Call me Unselfish Killer."

Jorge laughed and tossed a toasted English muffin at him. Robert caught it, inspected it closely and took a huge bite from it. "And call Jorge unselfish too."

CHAPTER TWENTY TWO

The Marquette team arrived Friday afternoon and worked out on the court within an hour of checking into their motel rooms.

While Marquette was in the Coliseum, McCarren sat in his office and ran the Marquette highlights film that Turner had put together for him.

Player by player, strength to strength, weakness to weakness.

The centers. Bozeman, the Marquette center matched up pretty well with the Killer in size and talent. The main difference was that Robert had two years of experience on him. In a couple of years, with the tough schedule Marquette played, Bozeman would be a terror at both ends of the court. Not this year. McCarren decided he'd try to work against Bozeman with both the Killer and Mitchell Winters, alternating them. Mitchell had surprised McCarren with his progress as a player. He'd developed faster than he or Turner expected him to. He could credit that to the Killer and the one on one work the Killer had put in with Winters.

The guards. Marquette, as it usually did, had quick guards. The point man was, perhaps, a step and a half quicker than Jorge. The shooting guard was about as quick as Paul Gilson. But he had better range as a shooter than Gilson. That was because Paul was playing out of position. He wasn't a big guard, a shooting guard. Next year, he'd be the point man and Theold would move back from small forward and fill the role of shooting guard. So McCarren knew he lost a little something with Jorge on the point. But, during the game, he could move Paul to point and drop Theold back to shooting guard. That would even it out to some degree.

Power forward. Ben Pickett, the Marquette power forward was going to be the real problem. Big at six-eight and two-fifteen or twenty. Probably too big and quick for Bo Regis to contain him. Might have to play Mitchell Winters on him part of the time. The risk was that Mitchell might get in foul trouble and be unavailable for backup duty with the Killer. Perhaps the best hope was to start Jimmy Stefano on him. Jimmy gave up a couple of inches to Pickett but he would make up for it with aggressive defense and hustle, with toughness.

The idea was to start Jimmy on him, spell him with Mitchell and Regis. Keep showing Pickett new bodies every minute or two. Try to keep him off balance, off stride. Make him start thinking.

Small forward. When Theold was there, it was no contest. Their small forward couldn't stay with Theold. The truth was that almost no small forward in the country could match him step for step. Maybe Mike Jordan over at Carolina. No, not just maybe. He could. Jordan and Theold were two of a kind, from the same mold. And then they broke the mold or hid it away for another ten years.

McCarren stopped the tape and switched off the Betamax. He opened a Harp and leaned back in his chair. He turned and watched the twilight settled across the slopes. It was a beautiful sunset.

Play it as it comes, he told himself.

A coach, like a player, could think too much.

It was the final home game of the season and, therefore, Senior Night. There were only two seniors on the team, the Killer and Jorge Morgan. They were the fruits of the first recruiting trip north.

Robert was introduced first. Hands high, he trotted onto court. While the ovation continued, a little girl dressed in a lone white gown ran onto the floor and handed Robert a large bouquet of long-stemmed red roses. Robert leaned down and took the bouquet and kissed her on the forehead. The little girl scampered from the court, all blushes and happiness.

Jorge was next. The ovation seemed, if anything, to increase. A second little girl, also in a white gown, ran to Jorge and gave him the roses and took his kiss proudly.

Jorge and the Killer stood shoulder to shoulder at center court and waved and waved. Jorge turned toward Robert and said something. Robert grinned and nodded. Then both of them unwrapped the bouquets of roses and walked around the edges of the court, tossing single roses into the stands.

The game began. Watching the Killer, at first McCarren thought the excitement and exhilaration of Senior Might had got to him. That he was so high on that and it had made his game flat. His game was off. He didn't have his usual intensity. That happened now and then to a player, McCarren knew.

Robert wasn't dominating the kid, Bozeman, the way the game plan had established it. Boseman matched the Killer basket for basket and rebound for rebound. Some games a coach accepted the draw, when the players were of equal ability and experience. That wasn't supposed to happen tonight. No way was that kid supposed to stay with the Killer.

To compound the problem with the Killer, Theold Brown was having his worst shooting night of the year. The magic touch had disappeared. At the half, Theold was three for nine, not the equal fifty or sixty percent he shot.

McCarren had a look at the scoreboard over the court before he headed for the dressing room. Marquette led by five. That indicated that the other players on the Mountaineer team were trying to take up the slack. Stefano and winters and Gilson had been scoring well, rebounding fiercely.

The Killer, at the Gatorade cooler, saw McCarren heading for him and shook his head. "I don't need to."

McCarren pointed in the direction of the bathroom. "Then you just come alone and whistle the school fight song," He led the way and stood in the center of the bathroom, head down until he heard the *squeek-squeek* of Robert's basketball shoes.

"Coach, that Boseman kid is a player."

"You've been standing around watching him long enough to see that."

"In a year or two ..."

"This is <u>this</u> year. You remember the first time we made the trip in here?"

"The Citadel game, my first game here."

"And you haven't learned a thing since then? Is that what you're telling me?

The Killer didn't answer. He looked at the tile floor.

"Well, let me tell you something. If you've learned anything, it was the wrong thing. Bozeman looks like the senior and you look like the rookie."

"There's room for both of us on the court."

"There's only one top dog," McCarren said.

"Then I'm the top dog."

"Not tonight. Tonight that kid is eating your headlines and your supper."

"That's not true," Robert said angrily.

"Ask Jorge. Ask winters. Ask Gilson."

McCarren turned and walked into the locker room. He stood back a time and watched Jack Turner at the blackboard. Turner was drawing a couple of zone traps. McCarren walked through the players and took the eraser from Turner and wiped the blackboard clean.

"There's nothing wrong with our approach to the game. What's wrong is that this team doesn't want to win tonight. They're tired of winning. They want to roll over and show they can lose and be good sports about it." He threw the eraser against one of the lockers. A huge cloud of chalk dust settled to the floor. McCarren turned to the student manager. "On the court in five minutes."

He and Turner left the dressing room and he reached back to slam the door.

"What's going on, Tim?"

"Let's see. Let's wait and see."

Five minutes later, by the clock, they stood at the bench and waited. It was then he heard the first low rumble of it. The shouting and yelling and screaming. The team was coming out. The crowd heard it also and they were on their feet when the first of the players reached the end of the ramp and headed for the court. Robert and Jorge led the team.

McCarren felt an icy chill down his back.

He'd done it. Now he'd have to wait and see what he'd really done.

After the warmups, the shooting at the far basket, the players to the bench. Robert sat down without looking at McCarren. Jorge was sullen. His mouth was a hard line that could have been drawn with a ruler.

The first ten minutes of the second half was a bloody butcher shop job. The Killer was back to his peak, going up and over and around Bozeman. His slams and his rebounding were so fierce, so intense; that Bozeman seemed to back away and let him have what he wanted.

Theold still didn't have his touch. An off night, McCarren decided. Theold did his other kind of game. He drove the baseline. He got his points on layups and rebounds of missed shots.

The Marquette coach used all his timeouts trying to blunt the charge. The Mountaineers wouldn't let down. The last five minutes, with the score mounting, McCarren sent in Houston Tarr for Jorge so he'd get his final home court ovation. McCarren met Jorge at the edge of the court and hugged him while the crowd stood and cheered.

The next time the clock stopped, McCarren sent in Bo Regis for the Killer. The crowd reaction to the Killer's exit from the game was even wilder. He trotted from the court with forty-two points and fifteen rebounds. At the edge of the court, still a few feet from McCarren, he slowed and almost stopped. When McCarren stepped forward, as if to hug him, the Killer put out his hand and shook McCarren's. Robert backed away from McCarren and, after a final wave to the crowd, sat on the bench and covered his head with a wet towel.

The Mountaineers won by eighteen.

The team left the court. The crowd was filing out. McCarren remained at the bench and waited for the postgame interview. Usually he liked to go with the team to the dressing room. This night he hadn't. The way Robert acted after the game had troubled him. Hell, all the players knew that a coach jumped on them now and then. Most of the time the resentment didn't last past a win.

The Marquette coach had the floor first. He said he'd never seen a performance like the one Robert Hinson had put on against his team. "I'm almost tempted to ask for a saliva test." He laughed. "No, that's not serious. We all know how good Hinson is. We just happened to catch him on Senior Night, on his last home game." He smiled. "Wasn't that something with the roses? I think I'll do the same with our Senior Home Game Night next year."

When it was McCarren's turn, he had the obligatory kind words for Bozeman. "For one half, he played Robert as tight as any center in the country has. Why, Robert told me himself at the half this kid was great."

"What happened in the second half?" This from the *Raleigh Times* sports writer.

"You've been dodging this question for a month." The *News and Observer* columnist was the last questioner. There was an early deadline for the morning paper.

McCarren smiled. "Can I answer it without having to hear it again?" Yes, he did expect to be invited back to the N.C.A.A.'s. The Mountaineers had been ranked all year. They'd played a fairly representative schedule and they were 23 and 3 at the end of regular season. In fact, 23 and 3 ought to be good enough to rate a chance at a first round bye.

The interview ended. With a wave McCarren left by the side entrance and headed for Ipsom. A brief stop there and he was expected at Ellen's for a late supper. He was half way to Ipson when he heard the footsteps behind him. He turned and stopped. The Killer was there.

"You got another one of those beers in your office, Coach?"

"One or two."

When they reached his office, McCarren switched on a lamp and motioned Robert to a seat across the desk from him. He opened two bottles of Harp and passed one to Robert.

The Killer drank most of the first bottle in one swallow. "Thirsty," he said.

McCarren laughed and got another Harp and placed it on the blotter in front of Robert. "That was a second half you had yourself tonight."

Robert picked at the label on the bottle. "Some ways I'm glad this is my last year. I could get to dislike you in another year."

"That right?"

Robert nodded.

"That's what college is about. Growing up. I think that's what happened to you."

"I'd rather think it was that I don't want any more piss room talks with you."

"There's still the tournament," McCarren said.

"I won't need talks tor that."

"After you leave here, there won't be any piss room talks at all. Place a bet on that. Nobody is going to give a crap about you. You won't matter to them one way or the other."

"Say that again."

"You'll be a pro. You won't get the piss room pep talks. Either you put out for the team or you won't last. You get dropped or you get traded down. Traded to another team." McCarren sipped his Harp beer. "Let me paint you a picture. Life in the pros. You've just played a game in the Meadowlands in Jersey and the next night in Madison Square Garden. You leave that game and hurry to catch a flight to Chicago. Say that game in New York was an afternoon. You get supper on the plane. You're tired but there's no way to get some sleep. You reach Chicago and check into a hotel. You're too tired, too restless to sleep. You do a bit of the town. Have some drinks and maybe bed down a girl. Then back to the hotel for some sleep. But your head's back in New York. You're on New York time. You roll around more than you sleep. Up at one in the afternoon and have breakfast. You loaf around the hotel. You're trying to save your legs. The season's getting old. It's harder and harder to get any spring in your legs. A light pre-game meal at six. To the Coliseum by seven. You dress and wait. You're bored. You've heard all the stories your teammates have to tell, you've heard all their bitches and moans. One or two of them have a cocaine problem or some other drug trouble. Maybe pills. And those guys are trying to figure some way so they can be sick and not have to play. A bad cold or flu or a virus. Something like that. Maybe you're shaky too. Jet lag or those drinks last night and not enough sleep. You get the picture so far, Robert?"

"Yeah." Robert nodded.

"The Coach has his own problems. If the team's winning, he's worried that it'll take a tailspin. If he's losing, he knows his head's on the block. He hasn't got time for your problems. He's got a wife and kids and a mortgage and he's making half the money you are. He knows what every player on the team did right or wrong in the case against the Knicks. He knows who fucked up. He knows which one of you shot beyond your range. He knows which one didn't hustle. Does he say anything about it? Not very likely. He knows you're a pro and you know exactly what he knows. He's not going to take you into the piss room and talk to you. What you do this game, this night, is up to you."

Robert opened the second Harp. He was listening.

"And there's the pro sports fan. The home team fan is supposed to love you, right? And the fans of the opposing teams admire you, right? Don't count on it. He's sitting in an overpriced seat. He's paying an outrageous price for a cold hotdog and half a cup of foam on his beer. He's parked in a lot down the street and he's not sure the car will be there when he leaves the game. Or if he'll get mugged on the way to the parking lot. You think he cares that you're tired? You think he cares that you're far from home? Check the no on your questionnaire. What he wants to see you do are all those beautiful, graceful moves you used to have in college when you were playing twenty-five or thirty games a year. Now you're playing close to ninety. You do anything less than what he expects and he'll spit beer in your ear." McCarren took a deep breath, followed by a swallow of Harp. "So you're in the dressing room and it's almost time to head for the court. What do you do?"

Robert grinned. "I ask if I can be the one with the flu tonight and sit out the game."

McCarren gave him a steady, serious look. He shook his head.

"I look around the dressing room. I look at those other dudes and I say to myself, fuck you, I came here to play."

"That's it."

"I think there's a meaning in there somewhere, Coach."

McCarren nodded.

"I guess I'm not too old to learn. I'll take that back what I said about if I stayed here another year I'd dislike you."

"Don't mellow too much," McCarren said. "I want you mean on the court."

"I owe you, Coach.

"Let's say we owe each other."

The Killer stood. He drained his bottle of Harp. He dropped the bottle in the trash can. "Where'll I go in the draft?"

"Right now, in the middle of the first round. You played at a small school. You didn't play in one of the big conferences. But you played for me. That means I put pro standards on you. That'll keep you in the first round."

"That high?"

"Maybe higher. Say we win a regional. Say we get to the final four or the championship game. You play five or six great games and you'll leap frog some of the better-known players who didn't have good tournaments or whose teams didn't make the big dance. You might move to where you're the fifth or sixth, man picked in the whole draft."

"That's what I want."

"It's up to you," McCarren said.

"No more talks in the piss room?"

"Never again," McCarren said.

They shook hands on it.

The following Tuesday morning, the final polls before the N.C.A.A. tournament were in the papers. The Mountaineers were 14th in the AP and 15th in the UPI.

The office picnic on Selection Day was on the way toward becoming a tradition. This year, Ellen planned the menu and prepared the food. There was sliced cold roast pork, two kinds of chutney, a potato salad made with sour cream and green pepper corns and a bowl of artichoke hearts tossed with romaine lettuce.

Jack brought three bottles of white wine. McCarren made sure the refrigerator was stocked with beer. Harp and Guinness and Carlsberg.

It was Sunday, March 6th, eight days after the final regular season game against Marquette. There had been practice all week, loose, brief drills. Enough running and shooting to keep their wind and their touch but not enough to tire their legs. That was important, McCarren knew. Just enough to keep the honed edge. Nothing more.

As usual, there was a game on TV. This one was between two Big Ten teams, Michigan and Purdue. The outcome would have no effect on the N.C.A.A. selections. It might mean, however, a berth in the N.I.T. for the winner.

The real reason the television was in place was that the pairings for the N.C.A.A.'s would be announced at halftime. At least, the main bids would be given and the others, some at-large selections, would be disclosed at the game's end.

Ellen arranged two days before for two tables to be placed in McCarren's office at Ipsom. A small table held the television set that was usually out of sight in the closet. A larger table had been covered with a cloth and table settings placed on four sides.

They began the meal at two. The game was on but the sound was tuned to a whisper. Ten minutes of the game passed. McCarren was at the refrigerators uncorking a second bottle of wine when the phone rang. He waved Ellen to remain in her seat. He answered it himself.

"McCarren here."

The caller was John Pullen, athletic director with one of the Big East schools. He'd moved so often that McCarren wasn't exactly sure where he worked now.

"We're running behind with the invitations," Pullen said. "So far, in my experience, nobody had turned down a bid."

"We accept," McCarren said. "Where are we this time?"

"The Eastern Regionals."

"Who do we play?"

"That's the good news. We don't know yet. That's our way of saying you got a bye this year."

"We'll take that present, too," McCarren said.

"You watching the game?"

"Waiting for the half, John."

"You can see the brackets then," Pullen said. "I've got other calls to make."

McCarren said his goodbye. He placed the phone on the base and looked down at his desk. Then he lifted his head and smiled. "The Easterns and we got a bye."

Ellen ran to McCarren and hugged him and then hugged Jack. When the laughing and yelling and shouting was done, McCarren passed the bottle of wine to Jack. "You open this. I've got a call to make."

"Two calls," Ellen corrected him.

McCarren called President Edwards first. Edwards was proud and pleased, especially with the bye. That meant, to him, that the program had arrived on the national scene.

The second call was to the Killer at McCoy. The Killer wasn't in his room. McCarren reached him in the Rec room where the team was watching the game and waiting for the halftime announcements of the brackets. He waited while the Killer shouted for quiet and gave them the information about the bid and the bye. Robert returned when the shouting died down. "What time is practice, Coach?"

"None today. We don't know who we'll play. How about some shooting and running instead?"

"Wind sprints?"

"Fifty down and fifty back. A four mile jog."

"Fine."

"No scrimmage. I don't want any twists or sprains," McCarren said.

"You got it," the Killer said. "Everybody stays healthy."

Earlier that day, Jack Turner used a ruler to draw up the empty brackets for a single region. Now he placed the sheet of poster paper on the desk and filled in the slots when the pairings were flashed on the screen during the half.

EASTERN REGIONALS
Thurs, March 10th

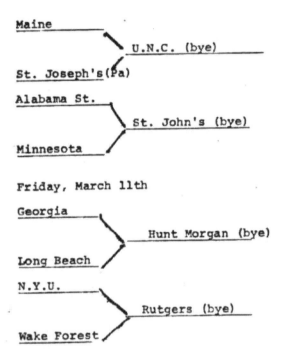

The excitement spoiled McCarren's appetite. McCarren leaned over the pairings with Jack Turner. "What do we know about these teams?" He tapped Georgia and Long Beach.

"Not as much as I want to," Turner admitted. "From what I remember, Georgia is twenty and nine. They split with Kentucky and L.S.U. in regular season play. Lost to Kentucky by less than ten in the conference tournament. I don't think they've got a center who can match up with the Killer. Haven't really replaced Wilkins who went hardship. Not a disciplined team. I think they can be taken out of what they want to do. Their tendency is to freelance. Some speed."

"Long Beach?" McCarren looked across the desk and caught Ellen's smile.

"Childers is there. Remember him?"

Childers was a big center from inner city Pittsburgh. Big and black and strong. McCarren had tried to recruit him two years before but he'd wanted warm weather and the beach and the California lifestyle.

"How's he doing?"

"Maybe fourteen points a game and ten rebounds. Blocks his share of shots."

"He the real horse for them?"

Turner shook his head. "I think they've got a junior college transfer from one of the small schools there in the state. I forget his name. I think he scores around nineteen a game. Plays small forward."

"Guards?" After the game in the Mideast finals McCarren still had nightmares about quick, speedy guards.

"I'll make a call. I know an assistant at U.S.C."

"Do it today."

Turner nodded. "I'll use the phone in my office at Biddle." Turner lifted the poster paper from the desk. "I'll have some copies made of this. And I'll call you later, Tim."

Turner walked out and the office door closed behind him

Ellen reached into a back corner of the refrigerator and bought out the champagne. It was California again. "Next year, you ask for another raise so we can drink vintage French champagne at these celebrations."

"I might have more expenses next year."

Ellen smiled. "Do you think so?" She left him to ease the cork from the champagne. She returned with two tulip glasses from her desk in the outer office. McCarren poured.

"To this year," he said.

Ellen drank. "To a better year than last year."

"Amen," McCarren said.

CHAPTER TWENTY THREE

McCarren and Turner flew into Atlanta Hartsfield International early Friday afternoon to watch the first round game between Georgia and Long Beach. They'd also decided, since they were there, they might as well scout the Wake forest and N.Y.U. game. If the Mountaineers got past the winner of the Georgia-Long Beach contest on Sunday, they'd have to face the winner in the other bracket.

A few minutes before the seven o'clock game time, McCarren presented himself to the tournament officials at the Omni and was given tags and passes. The seats were at midcourt.

There was a tide, a flow, to the game. Georgia jumped ahead early. It was run and gun and speed basketball, what Coach Hugh Durham liked. But Long Beach remained close, down by four or five, no more than that, and they were behind by four at the half time buzzer.

A writer from the Atlanta morning newspaper, the *Constitution*, recognized McCarren as he passed in the aisle. He followed McCarren and Jack Turner to the concession stand near the top of the aisle.

"What you doing here, Tim?"

McCarren took a chew from a hotdog and swallowed. "Just trying the hotdogs here. Got to do something about the ones we serve at Biddle."

"Come on, Tim. Give me something I can use."

"Call it a busman's holiday. I can't watch enough basketball. If there's nothing on the cable networks, I'll travel three or four hundred miles to watch a game."

"Let's say, instead, that you're scouting Georgia and Long Beach. How do you see the game so far?"

"What I've seen has my poor little team worried."

"You forget I've seen that poor little team of yours. Twice. Which team would you rather play, Tim?"

"You think I'd answer a question like that? And give the other team a quote they can stick on the dressing room wall? Not very likely." He nodded at Jack Turner. "And don't ask Jack. He taught me everything I know about public relations."

The sports writer turned his attention toward Turner.

"I understand. Jack, you're in the running for another head coaching job."

"It's too early to say." Jack ducked his head and wheeled and headed for the concession stand. He remained there, waiting to order a couple of Cokes.

"I'm not getting much out of either of you. How do you see the game?"

"We make a deal?"

"What kind of deal, Tim?"

"Quote me only if it turns out that I'm right. Otherwise, no quote. I like to act like I know what I'm talking about. I don't like looking foolish."

"All right. A deal." The writer pulled a pad from his coat pocket.

"I expect Tay Childers to go on a tear this half. If he does, then it's Katy-bar-the-door. I'll be playing Long Beach on Sunday."

"Thanks, Tim."

Jack returned with two Cokes. He passed one to McCarren. "It's John, isn't it?" he said to the *Constitution* writer.

The writer nodded. "John Gaithers."

"That talk about a heading coaching job, that's speculation and nothing else. I won't even make a decision about it until our season is over. As a favor, I'd rather you didn't print it. If you do write about it, I'll have to turn the job down and close that door completely."

"Why?"

"Our players, that's why. I can't have our guys thinking about anything but the next game. I can't have them worrying part of the time why I'd leave them and go somewhere else. That make sense to you. John?"

Gaithers nodded. "I'll bury it."

McCarren watched John Gaithers walk away and become swallowed up by the crowd. He sipped his Coke.

"I know the timing's bad," Jack said. "But I didn't apply. They came to me. It's not even far enough along so I'd feel the A.D. ought to talk to you, Tim."

"It's not a matter of permission and you know it."

"Maybe not. Still, I'd want your blessing."

They entered the Coliseum and walked down the steps to their seats. The teams were already on the court, warming up.

"Which school, Jack?"

"Southeast Florida. They've seen what you've done. They think I might have learned enough to build a program there the same way you did at Hunt Morgan."

"You get the itch again?"

"To head coach? I guess I did."

They found their seats. "You could do better, Jack. There are going to be some jobs available after the season. I could ask around."

"Don't laugh," Turner said. "I've got an urge to do it your way."

McCarren nodded. "We'll talk when the season's over."

"If it ever ends."

"It always ends. That's the final truth."

It was a McCarren predicted. In the second half, the Long Beach team worked the ball into the low post to Tay Childers. He scored twenty-five points in the second half alone. The Georgia center couldn't handle him. Long Beach won by seven. During the break between games, John Gaithers passed them in the aisle. He waved to get McCarren's attention. He made a writing motion, one hand scribbling in the palm of the other, and nodded.

McCarren waved and nodded. The quote was fine with him.

The Mountaineers had one day of practice before the game against Long Beach State.

On the morning flight to Winston-Salem, Jack Turner prepared his scouting report on the Long Beach starters while McCarren mapped their offensive sets and a breakdown on their defensive tendencies.

The practice was held early Saturday afternoon.

In his office at Ipsom, McCarren had prepared his chart. Strength against strength: that was the Killer and Tay Childers. The Killer might have a slight edge because of his experience. Two more years of the backboard wars that Childers didn't have. But Childers was playing well for a second year man. If anything, McCarren might accept a draw at the center position. The two centers could negate each other with equal scoring, rebounding and defensive play.

The Long Beach small forward, Greg Bender. He was the scorer. Twenty-three points against Georgia. Normally, Theold Brown would be matched against him. McCarren decided on a switch. He wouldn't waste Theold on defense against Bender. No, he'd place Jimmy Stefano on Bender. To bump and bruise him. And then, when Bender thought he had Stefano figured, he'd spell him with Jorge to give the small forward another look.

With luck and hard work ,Bender might be held to fifteen and that would be an edge to the Mountaineers.

Theold moved to big guard, shooting guard. An advantage there, McCarren thought, to the Mountaineers. Theold would get his shots against the Long Beach big guard.

On defense, Long Beach had a tendency to use a midcourt trap about a quarter of the time. The Long Beach guards would try to double team Paul Gilson as soon as he crossed the center line. They'd try to force him into mistakes. Gilson was quick enough to handle the pressure and cool enough to find the open man. If two Long Beach players double teamed Paul, that meant at least one Mountaineer player would be open. Paul would find that man. That first pass to the open man could create havoc and result in uncontested baskets.

Those were the keys.

Before practice, McCarren took Jorge aside and explained that Theold would have to start at big guard if the team was to have a chance to win the next day. Jorge would play some small forward and spell Gilson and Brown in the backcourt. It was a sacrifice he asked of Jorge. Jorge said, "We go to the dance I don't care who my partner is."

Most of the brief practice was spent working against the midcourt trap. When Paul Gilson was at the point, Jorge and Houston pressured him, taking the roles of the Long Beach guards. When Jorge ran the point, Gilson and Houston worked against him.

Jack Turner stood at center court and directed the pressuring double team.

McCarren took a position near the basket and developed a series of plays that followed the first pass from the point guard. In the short time, he had he established three basic movements. Each had a number of variations that depended upon how the defense played the first pass from the point guard.

The team spirit was good. McCarren was satisfied. He sent them to the showers. The team bus, already loaded with the players' belongings, waited outside Biddle.

The players dressed in their green blazers and tan trousers. After the drive to Greensboro they checked into the Ramada Inn near the Coliseum where a two-day reservation had been made for the team by the tournament committee.

As a result of the pairings St Joseph's Pennsylvania faced North Carolina that afternoon. North Carolina, starting slow, won by three. In the same bracket Minnesota, having defeated Alabama State in the qualifying round, played St. John's in the late game that afternoon. Minnesota, with superior height and rebounding, defeated the smaller and quicker team. Both games had ended by the time the Mountaineers reached Greensboro and checked into their motel.

The one o'clock game between Hunt Morgan and Long Beach State was a national game, telecast over a broad section of the country.

"Last year's miracle team," the network color man called the Mountaineers.

"And they're even better this year," the announcer who did the play-by-play added.

The game began. During a period of five minutes, all the play seemed to revolve around the two centers. The Killer and Tay Childers went at each other like heavyweight boxers. It was hips and shoulders and elbows. Neither center backed away from it, neither was intimidated.

"Hardball," Turner said, leaning toward McCarren.

"Now you see why I tried to recruit Childers."

Jack nodded.

After five minutes, McCarren sent in Bo Regis and moved Winters to center and brought the Killer from the game for a breather and a rest. The Long Beach coach saw McCarren's thinking, that he wanted to keep the Killer fresh, so he sent in his second team center and matched him against Mitchell. It wasn't a good move. Mitchell had the size and the weight on the Long Beach substitute center. On both ends of the court, Winters used his advantage to clear the other center away and leave the rebounding to Regis and Stefano and the tap-ins to Theold Brown.

Long Beach had to return Childers to the game. He and Mitchell Winters banged bodies for another minute or two before the Killer returned to the game and Winters got a rest.

During the first half, the Killer got two long breaks. Childers had to settle for the one short rest early in the half. In the second ten minutes of the half, the focus shifted. The Long Beach offense turned its attention toward the small forward, Greg Bender. Jimmy and Jorge took turns on him. It was tough, hardnosed defense. Denying him the ball where he wanted it, in close, and making sure that when he got the ball he was out of position. Bender never worked so hard for eight points, his total in the first twenty minutes, in his whole career.

Theold Brown started well. He had the twelve and fifteen foot shot. His touch was back. When the Long Beach big guard tried to play him tight Theold used his quick first step to blow past him and, once he was past the Long Beach big guard and in the lane, he could wreck a defense. He drove for the basket. If the path was open he dunked the ball. If he was blocked, if another defender tried to help out, he found the Killer or Mitchell for layups.

At the half, Theold was eight for ten and had seventeen points.

The Mountaineers left the court leading by eight. The second half was almost a replay of the first one. The point edge remained, most of the game, between eight and ten. At one point when Theold needed a rest McCarren sent in Houston Tarr. The Long Beach big guard had four inches on Tarr and it might have been a dangerous substitution for McCarren. McCarren countered by telling Houston to take his shot. In a three minute stretch Houston matched the taller guard basket for basket. His low, flat shot was on. The Mountaineers didn't lose any ground to Long Beach using Tarr.

At the middle of the final half, McCarren gave the Killer a three minute break. He re-entered the game with seven minutes to go. Childers was obviously tired. The Killer wanted the ball and Gilson and Theold got it to him. Robert took the ball straight at Childers until Childers drew his fourth foul and had to head for the bench. When Childers returned at the two minute mark the game, for all intents and purposes, was over.

"Chalk this win to the Mountaineer depth," the TV color man said. "That and some very, very good defense."

The Mountaineers won by seventeen.

The Eastern Regionals were at Raleigh, on the campus of North Carolina State. The site was Reynolds Coliseum. The Mountaineers travelled by team bus to Raleigh the morning of the game and checked into the motel around lunchtime.

Their game with Wake was the second one off the evening. It would begin twenty minutes after the final buzzer of the game between North Carolina and Minnesota. Except for short walks after lunch and the early pregame meal, the players remained in their motel rooms and rested.

The team was late arriving at Reynolds because the bus driver took the wrong route and found himself entangled in the traffic snarl near the Coliseum. The Mountaineers entered the Coliseum during halftime of the game between Carolina and Minnesota. By the scoreboard, they could see that Carolina led by six points.

Seats had been reserved for the teams. McCarren allowed his players to watch the first ten minutes of the second half. He led them from courtside to the dressing room. North Carolina led by five points at that time in the game.

The tournament official tapped on the dressing room door. "Ready for you. Coach McCarren."

"Lead them out," McCarren told Robert and Jorge.

McCarren followed the players down the chute to the court. He'd reached the edge of the playing floor before he realized something had changed in Reynolds. The crowd was stunned, silent. The tournament official pointed Robert and Jorge toward the basket at the near end, closest to the entrance. Robert clapped Jorge on the shoulder and they sprinted onto court. As soon as the players moved, McCarren saw the Minnesota players dancing and hugging each other at center court. Jumping up and down, screaming, their faces brilliant with emotion.

McCarren felt Jack Turner touch his arm. He followed Jack's pointing hand. He'd indicated the scoreboard clock.

U.N.C.	Minnesota
71	73

All week the newspapers in the area hadn't taken either the Minnesota Gophers or the Hunt Morgan Mountaineers seriously. All the kind words didn't change that. The sports writers who mainly covered the action in the Atlantic Coast Conference expected Carolina to play Wake in the Eastern Regionals finals on Sunday afternoon.

The crowd was split between Wake and Carolina supporters. Now, during the warmup drills, McCarren realized that the Carolina fans shifted their ground. With the Carolina upset, they'd pull for Wake and the honor of the ACC conference.

McCarren sat on the bench near the scorer's table. He watched the Wake team do their drills. The Wake center looked even bigger than he remembered him from the earlier game. An arm wing span like a 747. He judged the quickness of the Wake forwards. Frightening.

Have fun now, McCarren mumbled toward the Wake team. Especially you, big center. The Killer is back and healthy. Have your fun now.

The Wake small forward was showboating. He made incredible dunk shots on the lapup routine. He flew past the basket and backhanded the basketball through the net. Those don't count, McCarren whispered to himself. You'll wish they did because Jimmy Stefano is going to chew off your fingers to the elbows.

Enough. McCarren stood and walked across court. He took his team from the floor early, while Wake was still practicing their jump shots.

He stood before them in the dressing room. "By now you know Carolina lost."

Nods, a few "yeahs" from the players.

"That's a hostile crowd out there. Half of them came to root for Carolina and they'll stay to do the same for Wake,"

"Fuck 'em," the Killer said.

"My sentiments exactly," Jorge added.

"I was outcoached last time. It won't do that again. You can believe that. You take care of your business and I'll take care of mine."

McCarren pointed them to the dressing room door.

As they had planned; the Killer took the ball directly at the Wake center from the first time the Mountaineers went on offense. It was different this time. Robert had the use of both hands and the Wake center had to play him honestly. That honest defense opened other lanes to the basket. The Wake center couldn't sit back and play soccer goaltender. He had to come out and work against Robert. The creases were there at the backboard and Robert dished off to Mitchell Winters and Theold and Jimmy Stefano.

The Wake small forward must have believed he was playing not an entirely different team. The open shots were/not there now against Jimmy and every time he looked for the ball he found Stefano bumping into him. "I don't remember you, man," he mumbled at Jimmy.

Jimmy nodded. He didn't answer. He'd been in Philadelphia during his grandfather's illness the other time they'd played at Greensboro.

Theold Brown and Paul Gilson started in the backcourt. Jorge Morgan relieved one or the other from time to time. And a couple of times, after a rest break, he substituted for Stefano and Theold moved to small forward. This change gave the Wake small forward problems on defense as well as offense. Theold's quickness was more than the Wake small forward planned on. He'd geared himself, during the first few minutes for Stefano, and here he found himself faced with Theold.

At the half, the Mountaineers led by nine. The sports writers were composing their lead-ins to the opening paragraphs of their accounts of the night in Raleigh. "If you thought Black Sunday was bad, Black Sunday when both Carolina and Duke lost in Greensboro, then you hated Black Friday."

Variations on that theme.

Nobody ever said that sports writers were imaginative.

The partisan crowd began to leave Reynolds early and the Coliseum was almost empty by the time the final buzzer sounded. The Mountaineers won by twelve. Carl Tacy hadn't outcoached McCarren this time. A healthy Robert Hinson had scored twenty-seven points and grabbed twelve rebounds.

The finals of the Eastern Regionals weren't until Sunday afternoon. The day gave the players a chance to stroll around the State campus and rest their legs. McCarren gave Jack Turner the job of riding herd on the team. There was a lunch on Saturday at noon, followed by a press conference, that McCarren had to attend.

Plates holding the remainders of Maryland Chicken, green peas, buttered carrots and salad bowls were cleared away from the head table. The crowd quieted. The TV camera lights were switched on. The writers placed their pads on the tablecloths and uncapped their pens.

Tim McCarren took the podium and stood behind the row of microphones first.

"To tell the truth," he said, "I didn't see very much of the Gopher team. I missed the first half of the game because my bus driver took a wrong turn in your wonderful Raleigh traffic and almost ended up at the Coliseum without the team in the bus." He grinned. "You've got some wonderful cops directing traffic too."

The crowd laughed.

McCarren sipped his glass of water. "To compound my problem, I left with ten minutes still to go in the second half. I accompanied my team to the dressing room. I would have stayed and watched the rest of the game but all the sports writers and sports TV people had assured me that Carolina was going to win." McCarren ducked his head when some of the press writers hooted at him. "It's true. It's really true. Some of my young players read what you'd written and they weren't even sure it was worth the long trip here. Before I could leave Sandersville, I had to flush two of my players from hiding. Imagine how surprised my players were when they came out for warmups and found that Carolina had been upset. Why, that alone gave my team heart. You see, they decided if all the experts could be wrong about the outcome of the Carolina and Minnesota game, then they might also be wrong about our game as well."

The *Raleigh Times* writer got to his feet. "I think you've skinned that dead horse, Tim. Your point's taken."

"Ask your question," McCarren said.

"From what you say of the Minnesota team, what was your impression?"

"They're too big for us. I can't match up with them. No way. Stop me if I'm wrong. Their center is seven or seven-one. The power forward is six-ten or eleven. The small forward is six-nine. Against that I've got a six-nine center..."

The Minnesota coach interrupted him. "Unless he's shrunk, Hinson is six-ten or eleven."

McCarren grinned at him. "Tell fibs on your own time, Jim."

The Minnesota coach nodded and took his seat again.

"Against that front line, I've got a six-nine center, a six-nine big forward when I'm playing Winters or Regis and six – five or six-seven small forwards, according to whether I'm playing Theold Brown or Jimmy Stefano. And I've got to underline the fact that Winters and Brown and Stefano are all freshmen. It's a truth as old as the first peach basket that got nailed to the wall of the gym that you just don't win with freshmen."

"You're twenty-five and three," the *Times* writer said, "and that's using freshmen."

"Blind luck," McCarren said. "Now, when you write this story, the kids are going to find out they're not supposed to win. I shoulda kept my mouth shut."

"Tell us how you plan to play Minnesota," the *News and Observer* columnist said.

"Hold the ball," McCarren said. "If their big men don't touch the ball they can't score."

"How do you predict the score?"

"Two to nothing."

"Which team?"

"That's why we'll play the game. To see which team gets the one shot."

"You trying to drive the crowd away, Tim?"

"I don't expect anybody here at all. You remember how it was after Black Sunday?"

That bit. The area remembered how the fans had stayed away in the thousands after Duke and Carolina lost in that single afternoon.

The Minnesota coach lumbered around the table. McCarren shook his hand and backed away to find his seat. The Minnesota coach blinked into the TV camera lights.

"I never heard so much poor-mouth in my life. Tim's got one of the premier centers in the country. And those freshmen he's worried about. If the N.C.A.A. allowed it I'd swap him any three of my freshmen for any one of his. You saw what Mike Jordan did to us last night? Well, Theold Brown is a secret that's not that well-kept anymore. That point guard, Gilson, is a blur. Winters is the most improved center in the country. And Stefano might be the best defensive player I've watched."

The Durham Sun staff writer stood. "Tell us how you're going to play the Mountaineers, Coach?"

"I'm going to circle the wagons. I'm going to line my three big men up in front of the defensive basket and give them the twenty foot shot."

And that's probably the truth, McCarren thought.

"You expect a crowd, Coach?"

"A few hundred fans are flying in. Then we'll have a scavenger hunt in the parking lot for the tickets the Carolina and Wake fans threw away." The Minnesota coach spread his hands. "Look, anybody with a ticket who misses this game is going to be sorry."

Not the twenty foot shot, McCarren decided. Give me the fifteen foot one and we'll burn you.

He sipped his second cup of coffee and smiled.

CHAPTER TWENTY FOUR

It was far from an empty Coliseum. The tickets that could be had were bought up by Hunt Morgan fans and the stands and seats were a sea of the green colors, of shirts and jackets, sweaters and banners.

McCarren and Turner sat on the bench and watched the Minnesota team warm up. God, the height was awesome. It was the tallest team McCarren had ever coached against and that included the pros when he'd been with the Ironmen.

A last time in the dressing room before the tipoff. McCarren nodded at Theold Brown. "How's your fifteen foot shot today?"

"It's there, Coach."

"It's a perimeter game to start with," McCarren said to the team. "If the shot's there from fifteen or closer in, I want Theold with the ball. When they challenge you, I want the ball to the Killer and Winters and Regis. If Theold's shot is dropping, we'll warp their defense out of shape. Soon as that happens, I want the Killer with the ball."

The Killer nodded.

"Who wants a trip to Albuquerque?"

"Us.Us.Us ......"

"Show me on the court." McCarren pointed them to the door.

The Killer stole the opening tap from the seven foot center, Brassler. Minnesota fell back on defense quickly. Paul Gilson walked the ball over midcourt. He dribbled to his right and faked a pass to Mitchell Winters. Winters moved toward the lane. Paul whirled and dropped a short pass to Theold on the left side of the lane. Minnesota's big guard was out of position, moving inside, when Theold caught the pass. Theold took his one step and went up for the shot. The seven foot center, Brassier, was emotionally high. He went above the rim and batted the ball away. The whistle blew. The near official called it goaltending and awarded the two points to the Mountaineers.

At the defensive end of the court, the ball was passed to Brassier. The Killer and Mitchell Winters surged around him. In the tangle of arms Brassier took one step too many and was called for walking.

The second time down, Theold got his shot again. This time, also, Brassier batted it away while it was still in the cone. Goaltending once more.

The Mountaineers were ahead by four points.

Six minutes into the game, Hunt Morgan had outscored Minnesota sixteen points to four. Jack Turner knelt beside the court, his knee on a towel. He watched the game with a puzzled look on his face. McCarren noticed that stare.

Turner looked over his shoulder at McCarren. "Let's call a timeout, Tim."

"Huh?"

"I see something."

"Call it. Jack."

Turner stood and made the "T" sign to the Killer. The Killer flagged the trail official. The whistle blew. As soon as the starters were seated Turner and McCarren stood over them.

"They're flat, aren't they?" Turner said.

"Huh?" The Killer blinked at him.

"They're flat. They're flat-footed and they don't have energy enough to piss on themselves. Right?"

McCarren leaned in. "What are you talking about?"

"Minnesota left it on the court in their game against Carolina. They can't get it up again. They're going through the motions."

"Could be," the Killer said. "They ain't bruised me any yet."

"No more perimeter game," Turner said to McCarren. "Give it to the Killer in low. Make them prove they're not flat."

"Do it." McCarren nodded.

Theold inbounded the ball to Gilson. Gilson stood at the head of the free throw circle, waiting. The Killer moved into the lane and took the high, crisp pass from Gilson. Even as he moved, he heard the labored breathing of Brassier, the Minnesota center.

Brassier moved in close and took a position directly behind the Killer. The Killer timed it right. Before Brassier had his feet set, before his arms were fully extended, the Killer turned under him and underhanded the basketball. The ball had spin, English on it, and it skittered up the side of the backboard and rolled across the rim and fell through the net.

"How about you, kid?" Robert asked Mitchell as they trotted downcourt to take their defensive positions. "You want to be a star today?"

"My daddy is proud when I score a basket now and then."

The Killer smiled. "Let's do the tap drill on that big sucker."

The next time the Mountaineers had the ball, after the Killer caught the pass as he moved into the lane, he showed Brassier the beginnings of the same move as the shot before. The big center stepped forward, trying to get his position. At the last possible moment, Robert hesitated and then wheeled. He flipped the ball toward the rim, just below it on the other side of the backboard. Mitchell Winters knew it was coming. He stepped around the Minnesota big forward and caught the ball with both hands, went up and slammed it through.

The rout was on.

Everybody on the Mountaineer team played and everybody scored. Jack Turner orchestrated that, insisted on it. He wanted every player on the team to feel he was a part of the big win.

❧ ❧ ❧

It was early evening by the time the team bus approached the city limits of Sandersville.

The Killer was slumped to the side, asleep, with his head against the window until the bus hit a pothole and he was jarred upright. He rubbed his eyes and got to his feet. He wobbled up the aisle and leaned on the back of the seat that McCarren shared with Turner. "Coach?"

Both coaches turned to face him.

"I've been taking this course that's got a part of it about Roman history. You ever heard of a triumphant return?"

"Say whatever it is you want to say, Killer."

"I'd rather show you," Robert said to McCarren.

"It's your day," McCarren said.

The Killer laughed and stepped forward. He touched the driver on the shoulder. "Pull to the side of the road."

"Do what he says," McCarren told the driver.

"Yes, sir." The driver found a wide spot on the shoulder and pulled from the highway and parked.

The Killer trotted up and down the aisle, rousing his teammates. "On your feet, get up, got this idea."

Jorge staggered to his feet. "You gone nuts, man?"

"Not yet." The Killer ran to the back of the bus and reached above him to unlock the escape hatch on the roof. He gave the hatch cover a push. Turning to Jorge, he said, "Give me a leg up.

Jorge put his hands together. The Killer stepped into locked hands and pulled himself through the hatch to the roof of the team bus. A deep breath and he bent over the hatch opening, extended a hand to Jorge, and pulled him through. Jorge offered an arm to the next man.

In a couple of minutes, the thirteen players were seated on the bus top. Only the student manager, the driver and the coaches remained inside.

An iron railing that held luggage during long trips formed an outside border and a safety screen. The players gripped the rail and held on when Robert yelled, "Drive on, my man."

They made a slow drive down the center of town. Townspeople and students flocked from the shops and restaurants and lined both sides of the street. At first the onlookers gawked and then a cheer went up.

The players waved and bowed to the ovation.

One slow pass through the town and the bus headed for the campus entrance.

A crowd of better than five thousand students and faculty had waited in front of the Biddle for more than an hour. When the bus approached the Coliseum, an enthusiastic chorus of shouts and screams greeted the players. The Killer struggled to his fleet. Jorge grabbed one leg to steady him and Mitchell Winters grabbed the other.

"I am the general," Robert shouted. He waved and blew kisses.

"I wish I was one of them," Jack Turner said. "I'd like to be up there."

"It's their day," McCarren said.

Students surrounded the bus when it stopped in front of the Biddle. The players leaned over the side of the bus to touch hands. Robert recognized a pretty girl and caught her under the arms and yanked her from her feet. He swung her to the bus roof and kissed her and passed her back to Jorge. He took his kiss and dropped her in Mitchell Winters' lap.

"Yours," Jorge said.

The celebration lasted for almost an hour.

The final four pairings had been settled by games in the Mideast Regional and the Mideast Regional on Saturday and the East and the West Regionals on Sunday.

Hunt Morgan (East) / San Francisco St. (West)

St. Louis (Mideast) / Loyola-Detroit (Midwest)

A chartered plane left the Winston-Salem airport Thursday morning. Besides the team and coaches, space was allotted to President Edwards and his group, a number of prominent boosters, the cheerleaders and a small Mountaineer pep band. This time McCarren insisted that Ellen accompany them.

The plane landed at Albuquerque International Airport a few minutes after two in the afternoon. They left the plane and stood on the tarmac under the highest and bluest sky any of them had ever seen. It was, McCarren told Ellen, like standing under an overturned blue porcelain bowl. A brisk wind tugged at them, an ever constant wind. Sand swirled around them. The weather was like early spring in the east.

A bus furnished for them took them to the AMFAC Hotel on Yale Boulevard, not far from the University Area which had been nicknamed "The Pit" by the University of New Mexico students. Later, within an hour and a half, after they'd been assigned rooms at the AMFAC, they travelled by the same bus to "The Pit" for a scheduled workout.

"The Pit" was located in what appeared an unlikely part of the University. The Arena was in open desert and brush country. It was a low, flat adobe structure, one level above the ground. Concrete parking lots surrounded the Arena. The seating and the court itself were underground.

The city skyline stretched to the west. To the east were the Sandia Mountain ranges. The Manzanos Mountains, blue and angular, dominated the view to the south and east. From the parking lot beside "The Pit," the players felt they could look a hundred miles in all directions.

Once the players were on the court, they knew why it was called "The Pit." Jorge punched the Killer in the ribs and pointed upward. "They ought to call it the Snake Hole," he said.

McCarren sat high above the floor, in the stands, and watched the limbering up workout. The floor was trimmed and accented in red. McCarren knew the seating capacity. He'd checked. "The Pit" usually seated 17,126. For the N.C.A.A.'s the capacity would be reduced about a thousand by the demands of press and television coverage. But they were selling standing room.

McCarren had a warm feeling. Forty-eight teams had been in the field a couple of weeks before. Now only four teams remained in the running for the honors, the watches and the rings. Just to be there was almost the end of a dream. No matter what happened on Saturday or on Monday.

It was better than any dream he had ever had or might ever have again.

Below him, Jack Turner put the team through its paces while McCarren nodded and almost dozed away.

CHAPTER TWENTY FIVE

Jorge spotted it first the next morning in the gift shop in the AMFAC Hotel. It was in a huge stack next to the cash register when he stopped by after breakfast for a roll of mints.

There was the Killer on the cover of *Sports Illustrated* and he was making his power move over the big Minnesota center, Brassier. The low angle of the shot suggested that Robert Hinson was as big and twice as mean as the man he was going against.

Under the cover photograph was the caption. "New King on the Mountain?"

The Mountaineer players crowded the narrow shop within minutes and all of them bought a copy to put away in their rooms.

"It is not cool," the Killer said, " to carry a copy around in your hip pocket."

McCarren had advance notice about the cover photo and the cover story inside. He'd wanted to keep the news of it from the players and he'd even hoped that the magazine wouldn't arrive on the stands until after their game on Saturday. But that was good business, he guessed. *Sports Illustrated* wouldn't reach most outlets until the following Monday. Some bright distributor had seen to it that the magazine arrived in Albuquerque a couple of days early where there was particular interest.

It wasn't that McCarren regretted the publicity that the Killer and his team received. Not at all. He wanted it for them. The problem was that, at an event like this, there were too many distractions at a time when the players ought to be concentrating on their next game. It was bad enough for the coaches, the final four. The demands on their time were incredible. There were interviews and press conferences and requests for exclusive interviews from the big sports writers and the prominent magazines.

He'd already rejected ten requests for interviews with the Killer. "Not until after our last game," he said. "Whenever that is."

And the pro scouts were everywhere. Not that they contacted the players. That was against the rules. Still, they were around and the players knew they were there and that disturbed their concentration.

McCarren and Jack Turner tried to keep it in good balance. If he'd had his druthers, McCarren would have brought his team in town an hour before the game and played the game and left again. Only to return if they won their semi-final game. Otherwise, he'd have flown the team back to the east coast.

A part of the tournament was the annual meeting of the Coaches Association. There were panels and seminars on everything from ethics to sports medicine to recruiting. Some of the coaches did have ethics, McCarren thought, but those were usually the ones who'd paid their dues and could afford ethics now that they recruited the players they wanted without all the underhanded dealings.

There was a lot of concern about recruiting at the meeting. It was the dirty business that meant the difference between having a job and losing one.

McCarren used the upcoming game against San Francisco State and the other demands on his time as an excuse to miss most of the Association meetings.

It was mild weather. Sunny and warm during the day and cool and windy at night. It was good weather for walks around the city and strolls across the University of New Mexico. Elms and cottonwoods budded across the campus. Trash floated in an absurd duck pond.

McCarren filled the Friday after their arrival in Albuquerque as full as he could. The visit to the campus, pictures taken beside the duck pond and in the cactus garden beside the library, among the huge yucca and cholla. An afternoon tour of downtown Albuquerque and a bus ride through the surrounding country-side. Sandwiched in the middle of the tours was the real business at hand: a brisk workout at "The Pit." A practice just long enough, McCarren decreed, to get the perspiration flowing and warm the muscles but not enough to tire the players.

There was an early supper at the hotel where they were staying. McCarren and Jack Turner sat with the team and McCarren had an Irish over ice and Jack had a frosted mug of draft beer.

After the dishes were cleared from the long table, the waiter brought McCarren a second Irish. McCarren took a sip and stood, a hand on the back of his chair.

"Tomorrow's the whole ball of wax. Don't concern yourselves with what happens on Monday night. You don't win tomorrow afternoon, then you can forget about Monday until next year. That is, the ones who'll be with us next year. All of you but Robert and Jorge. This is their shot at it. No second shots." He looked at Jack Turner. "Tell them the starting lineup for tomorrow."

McCarren sat. He drew his drink toward him. He was watching Jorge's face.

"The Killer at center. Mitchell Winters at big forward and Stefano at small forward."

McCarren had a long swallow of the Irish.

"Gilson at the point and Jorge at shooting guard."

Jorge blinked. It came then, the beam of light that crossed Jorge's face and almost lit the dim dining room.

"Jorge and Robert are the co-captains."

"Bed check at eleven," McCarren said. "Jorge, Robert, you see to that."

"Done, Coach." Jorge reached across the table and slapped palms with the Killer.

"How long?" Turner asked McCarren later in the lobby of AVFAC.

"Jorge in the game after starting?" McCarren nodded at a couple of coaches who were in town for the Association meeting. One said, "Good luck tomorrow, Tim." McCarren thanked him. The smile faded when he faced Jack. "Two or three minutes. What I want to explain is that I'm not doing it this way because this is Jorge's last shot, because he's a senior or anything like that. I'm doing it for a selfish reason. I don't want Theold under the pressure early in the game. I want him coming off the bench, loose and easy, after the tempo of the game's set."

"You say." Turner shook his head. "Winters is a freshman and so's Stefano. You're not worried about them under pressure?"

"Jimmy's got ice water for blood. And Mitchell... well, he's got the Killer in there next to him and the Killer will keep him from blowing apart. Theold's the key," McCarren said. "I don't want a freshman to know he's the key. I'd rather he thought of himself as another substitute stepping into the game when I need him."

Turner tapped the side of his head. "Always thinking. That's one thing I like about you, Tim."

It was McCarren's night to do the bed check.

He got off on the floor where the team was quartered after midnight. He took his slow, listening walk down the hall. Lights burned only in the room the Killer shared with Jorge. He knocked and Jorge opened the door to him. McCarren entered and stood with his back to the closed door.

"You two having trouble sleeping?"

"Haven't tried, Coach," Jorge said.

"But you're going to try soon, huh?"

The Killer nodded. "Soon."

"How's the rest of the team?"

"Looser than I expected, but they missed their beer ration."

McCarren crossed the room and eased himself into a soft chair. "Tomorrow we'll have a few." McCarren rubbed his eyes "How do you explain them being loose, tonight of all nights?"

"They're ready. They know you've got them ready. And they trust you." The Killer peeled his t-shirt over his head and flexed his back muscles, stretching.

"You trust me?"

"Got to," the Killer said.

"You, Jorge?"

"You're aces with me, Chief."

"I thought you might have second thoughts, especially when I started Theold down the stretch."

Jorge shook his head. "I can't say it didn't hurt. Got to admit that. But I know my basketball. I understand what you were doing. You taught me my basketball, remember?"

"I've got a feeling about you, Jorge. I think you're going to make a fine coach someday."

"I'd rather play for the Knicks."

"I said some day."

"How about me, Coach?" The Killer gave McCarren his lazy grin. "I feel left out of this heartwarming conversation."

"No chance of you becoming a coach. I see you owning apartment houses and condos and a stock portfolio that won't quit. That is, if you don't throw all your money away."

The Killer laughed. "I like gypsy fortune tellers."

McCarren laughed with him. "Get some sleep."

McCarren couldn't sleep. He rolled about in his bed for more than an hour. One side and then the other and on his back staring at the dark ceiling. No help for it. He dressed and left a note for Jack. Gone to visit. You know where. He placed the note on the dresser and, a couple of minutes later, he knocked on the door to Ellen's room.

Perhaps Ellen hadn't slept well either. She answered the door on the second knock. She stood in the doorway. Her hair was mussed and her nightgown wrinkled.

"Are you the man I ordered from room service?"

She waved him into the room and locked the door behind him. He waited in the center of the room and watched her, through the open, bathroom door, comb her hair and wash her face. "I'm not the one you ordered, but will I do?"

"You'll do fine." She rinsed her mouth with Listerine. She switched off the light in the bathroom and glided across the room on bare feet. She put her arms around him. "What's your problem, big boy?"

"I can't sleep." He could feel the shape of her breasts through the sheer nightgown. Her heart beat against him with a soft touch, like a finger tapping against his chest.

"I think I expected you. Perhaps that's why I couldn't sleep myself." She placed her head on his shoulder so that he couldn't see her face. "But I thought you'd come to ravish my beautiful body."

"It is beautiful," he whispered.

"Let me give you a back rub."

He undressed. He stretched out on his stomach in bed, wearing only his boxer shorts. Ellen leaned over him. Her strong hands moved over the bunched muscles in his shoulders. "Relax, Tim. You're like a rock wall. I've never seen you so tense."

"They trust me. They believe in me."

"They're supposed to."

"But, damn it, I'm scared."

Her hands moved the length of his spine. "You should be. I'm not sure I'd want to be with a man who couldn't win a national championship. That would be degrading."

"Degrading, you say?"

He caught her by the shoulders. She was laughing, at first, when he kissed her. Then he laughed too and they were blowing their breath into each other's lungs. They made love that way, half-laughing, half-giggling all the way through it. Serious only at the end when the ecstasy clawed at them and all the silliness blew away.

CHAPTER TWENTY SIX

At eleven-thirty the next morning, the Mountaineers boarded the bus in front of the hotel and rode to "The Pit" in a tense silence.

A wide band of paper circled the dressing room. On it were the signatures of Hunt Morgan students and well-wishers. The names had been collected in two days at the Student Union, with each signer paying a dime to cover the cost of the rush shipment by Federal Express. The huge roll was delivered that morning to McCarren and he'd delegated the display problem to the student manager.

The players walked around the room, looking for names they knew. McCarren allowed them five minutes and then he said, "Get dressed and get your ankles taped."

At twelve-twenty, the team trotted on court and began the layup drills. And McCarren strategized in his mind.

In any game plan, McCarren always started with the center matchup. That was a luxury that he wouldn't have next year with the Killer in the pros.

The San Francisco State center was a junior college transfer. Six-eight or nine. He gave up an inch or two to the Killer in height. Not in size. He was as wide as a door. Almost two hundred and sixty pounds. Built more like a tackle or a tight end than a basketball player.

Biggers. They called him "Dirty" Biggers.

For a man as big and heavy as he was, Biggers was deceptively smooth. Opposing centers started out laughing at his chunky body and thick legs. The next thing they knew they were behind ten points and Biggers had six of those points. Off the court, he was a jolly black man. A guzzler of beer a prodigious eater. On court, he was all business and he didn't like anybody making him look bad. He had elbows like concrete.

Call the center position a bloodbath and a draw.

Mitchell Winters and Bo Regis, when he was in there, had an edge at big forward. Size and quickness as well.

With Theold Brown at small forward, it was a draw in quickness. Would start Jimmy Stefano there. Couldn't let the State small forward, Cater, jump off to a good start. Gave up some quickness with Jimmy there but compensated with his defensive quickness. Give with one hand and take away with the other.

Gilson and Jorge at guards. Jorge a step slower than the State big guard. Would see how it worked. Might switch Gilson on the big guard and let Jorge bump the point guard.

Theold the first man off the bench. Relief for Jorge at first. Could spell Stefano if necessary. Next Regis, if Mitchell needed a rest. Or in for the Killer, with Mitchell moving into the center slot. Houston Tarr, if needed, at the proper time, the proper situation.

Eight men deep. Deep enough.

The first time down the court on offense, McCarren saw what San Francisco State wanted to do all afternoon. "Dirty" Biggers popped into the lane, down low, and took a pass from the point guard. When he made his move toward the basket, the Killer stepped out to challenge him. At the last moment, Biggers dropped the pass to his small forward and used his weight and size to clear the Killer from Cater's path. The sheer size of Biggers body created a problem for Jimmy Stefano as well. He lost the small forward in the same moving pick that swept the Killer aside.

Cater slammed the ball through the basket.

No call. McCarren was on his feet. He shouted at the trailing official. "Get number 20's tag numbers. He's running over my center." The referee hesitated, looked at McCarren. For a moment, he probably considered calling a technical. He didn't. He smiled and shook his head.

"Calling it loose." Turner took McCarren by the arm and eased him back into his seat. No time for a technical.

"Go at him," McCarren yelled at the Killer as he came by the bench.

The Killer nodded. The ball came into him. "Dirty" Biggers put his bulk against Robert and stopped him in his tracks. The Killer saw Stefano open, heading toward the basket. The pass was high, juggled slight, but Jimmy tapped the ball toward the rim and it fell through.

At the other end, the State big guard got a step on Jorge and blew past him. Jorge recovered enough to force the man to slide in a circle, away from the basket. The State guard put up a running shot, falling away, and it settled on the rim. It remained on the lip. Mitchell stepped around his man and slapped the ball away. The whistle blew. Goaltending was called against winters.

4 to 2, State leading.

On offense, the Killer cut across the lane and took the pass from Gilson. Two dribbles and he turned against Biggers and the basket. The Killer had more spring in his legs. He soared above Biggers and rolled the ball off his fingertips. The ball went in. The Killer came down close to Biggers. He staggered away and rubbed his mouth. He'd taken an elbow from Biggers and his lips felt crushed and numb.

No call this time either.

Well, McCarren thought, at least the officials are calling it in a consistent way. McCarren stepped away from the bench and squatted at courtside. The Killer saw him and made a loop that took him past McCarren.

"Make it rough," McCarren said.

The Killer lowered his hand and showed the smear of blood from his mouth. "It already is." But he nodded.

With five minutes gone on the clock, McCarren called his first timeout. He sent Theold Brown to the scorer's table to report. He replaced Jorge at big guard. During the timeout, McCarren leaned over his seated players. "I want Theold to try a couple and see how his eye is. Fifteen feet and in. That might unclog the middle." He touched Jimmy Stefano on the shoulder. "With that monster pick there you've got to try to keep Cater from touching the ball. He makes that move toward the basket without the ball, bump him, knock him down if you have to."

Jimmy nodded. "Right, Coach."

"Besides that, you've got to help out with Biggers. You too, Mitchell. When Biggers gets the ball, I want all three of you on him like a brick wall. A falling brick wall. I want Biggers hurting by half time."

What McCarren wanted he got. Each time Biggers reached for the ball, he was hit from three sides. Hands and elbows and hips and knees. The Killer rammed him from behind. Mitchell from one side and Stefano from the other. It was a bloody war, with no quarter given. While that struggle continued, Theold Brown, cool and easy, put up his short jumper.

At the half the score was tied 46 to 46 and more lumps and bruises had been recorded than assists.

In the dressing room, the Killer rubbed his body with a cold wet towel. "That is one tough sucker," he said around the remains of an orange slice.

"Not tougher than you," Jorge said.

"Almost. Almost."

"Listen up." Turner had the stat sheet. "Killer, you've got two fouls. Got to hold back a bit or be sneaky. Can't afford that third one yet." He looked around. "Ames."

Ames nodded.

"I want you in the game to start the second half. At big forward. Mitchell, you move over and play the center spot. We hold Killer out for four or five minutes or as long as we stay close. That'll keep the Killer fresh and we make Biggers work hard. I want it rough out there. Ames, I want you all over Biggers. You hear me?"

"Yeah, Coach."

"Stefano, you've got three fouls. I can't risk you. I'll hold you out with the Killer. You step in at small forward, Theold. But watch yourself. I don't want you running into any Biggers elbows. You hear me?"

Theold said he did.

"Gilson and Jorge at guards. Houston, you take a chair by me. Might need you to give one of them a blow." He looked at McCarren.

McCarren came forward and stood with his back to the blackboard "This twenty minutes tells it. We either go to the dance Monday night or we sit down. You got to prove to me what you want to do. You're playing good ball. Now you gut it up, you play another good half and I'll find a way for us to win." McCarren looked around. "Anything else?"

The Killer threw the wet towel against the wall. "Ames, you kick that sucker's ass or I'll kick yours."

Ames Ashley nodded and swallowed hard. He wasn't too fond of contact. Now the Killer said he was going to be watching him. He'd have to work hard.

"You too, Mitchell," the Killer said.

"I'm doing it," Mitchell said. "I got teeth marks and bruises you won't see until tomorrow. But if you want to kick my ass, you come over here and try and do it."

"Hey, hey." The Killer stood. He wobbled across the room and grabbed Mitchell and hugged him. "I know it, my man. I know it. Just keep your mean going until I get in there. Right? Right?"

Mitchell nodded.

"Enough," McCarren said. "When we put Robert in, if we' been roughing Biggers and he doesn't get a blow, he ought to be tired. Robert goes in and we make a hard run at them. We take it right at him, Killer."

"Fucking, yes," the Killer said. He backed away and patted Mitchell on the shoulder. "Mean, mean," he hissed.

"Mean as you," Mitchell said.

"Rest," Jack Turner said. "Five minutes."

Two minutes into the second half, Mitchell Winters picked up his third foul crashing the boards against Biggers. He bounced off Biggers and staggered and hit the floor. Too much pride to stay down. He jumped to his feet and shook his head as clearing it. Blood began to drip from both nostrils. It splattered the floor at his shoes. He reached up and wiped the blood, smearing it across his cheeks and his chin. Bigger gave him a hard stare before he walked to the free throw line. Two shots, in the act of shooting. When Mitchell wobbled past him on his way to take his rebounding position, Biggers said, "More where that came from."

Mitchell stopped and pulled out his uniform shirttail. He pawed at the blood. "Enjoy it now. The Killer's coming."

"Brine that asshole on," Biggers said.

"Any minute."

The official with the ball stepped between them. "Let's play ball. Cut the chatter, huh?" He looked at the blood on Mitchell's face. "You want a timeout?"

"Naw," Mitchell said.

Biggers made both free throws. State led by one.

Another minute passed. Mitchell couldn't breathe through his nose. His throat was dry and raw. He knew his nose was broken. He wanted to protect himself. He couldn't take another blow on his nose. But he had to keep the pressure on. He went up and over Biggers and slammed the ball through. Arms up, chest unprotected, he knew Biggers would pay him for the move. He caught an elbow in the ribs .Nothing broken but he lost what little breath he had in him.

When he turned downcourt, he saw the Killer at the scorer's table. Before State could inbound the ball, the Killer trotted in and took his place. As they passed, the Killer hesitated just long enough to stare at the blood on Mitchell's face.

"Jesus," he said.

Mitchell took a seat. The student manger passed him a cold, damp towel. Mitchell cleaned his face. Then he bent his head over the towel and blew his nose. He almost passed out from the pain. When he lowered the towel and looked inside, it was filled with clotted blood.

"How you feeling?" Turner stood over him.

Mitchell tried to wad the towel. Turner stopped him. A look and he said, "My God, boy."

"You asked how I feel. I feel mean as a snake."

"You're not going back in," Turner said.

"I got to." Had to lie. "Sure, Coach."

"Take your blow. We'll see." Turner moved away.

The score flipped one way and then the other. Each team led by a point or two or trailed by a point or two. With just over three minutes to go the score was tied 78 to 78.

Bo Regis and Ames Ashley had spelled each other at the big forward slot. Mitchell hadn't played at all since the early minutes of the half. Mitchell could see that both of them were tiring. They weren't effective.

Turner made another trip down the bench. "Might have to use you after all."

"Fine with me."

"When I say," Turner said.

With forty seconds to go, the score was tied again. 83 to 83. The Mountaineers had the ball. As they moved toward midcourt, McCarren stood and gave Jorge the timeout signal, the "T" of crossed fingers.

They'd crossed center court when Jorge got the official's eye. Thirty-three seconds remained on the clock when it stopped. Turner patted Mitchell on the shoulder. "Report"

Mitchell returned and sat next to the Killer. McCarren stood over them. "Who's got the hot hand?"

"I have," Theold said.

The Killer nodded. "Him or me, that's your choice."

"All right. Theold passes in and cuts behind and goes left. I want the shot at five seconds. No earlier. Can't give State a chance at a shot. No later because I want the Killer on the boards in case Theold misses. I want a tap-in." He dipped his head at Mitchell. "That's where you come in. You've got to box out Biggers, keep him away from that rebound. But it's got to be clean. No foul. No holding. If they beat us, it's somewhere else but the free throw line."

Mitchell nodded.

"Good position. Body only." McCarren leaned close. "In feet, draw a foul if you can."

Back on the court. Mitchell's legs were strong. He felt steady. But he couldn't draw a full breath. His lungs burned. His mouth tasted of blood and ashes.

It began the McCarren outlined it. Pass from Theold to Gilson. Theold cut in front of Gilson and headed toward the left side of the court. Gilson hesitated and allowed Theold to pass. The court was in his head.

Twenty-six sounds.

"Dirty" Biggers rambled at Mitchell, "Whiteass, don't you get in my way."

Twenty seconds.

Paul Gilson walked the ball toward the free throw circle and drifted left. A look toward the Killer.

Eighteen seconds.

Biggers didn't react when Paul nodded his head at the Killer. In fact, Mitchell realized, Biggers took a step toward the left side of the court, placing himself between Theold Brown and the basket. That move allowed Mitchell to step behind Biggers and plant his feet. Now.

Fifteen seconds.

The moment Theold reached the slot fifteen feet from the basket, the small forward streaked from the corner and placed himself directly behind Brown. The big guard backed up and fronted Theold. He was sandwiched.

Twelve seconds.

Theold glanced to his left, toward the lane. Biggers was there, huge as a house. The flash across the lane wasn't there.

Ten seconds.

Paul dribbled slowly. A look toward the Killer. The State big forward was behind the Killer. The glance from Gilson set the big forward in motion. He bumped the Killer and his arms reached across Hinson, there to deflect any pass.

Eight seconds.

"Dirty" Bigger swung: an arm. A way of finding where Mitchell was. The hand caught Mitchell in the groin and doubled him over.

Six seconds.

Gilson saw that Theold couldn't free himself. At the same moment, he realized that Jimmy Stefano was open. The man supposed to guard him was planted behind Theold.

Paul yelled, "Jimmy," and whipped the pass to Stefano on the baseline twelve fleet from the basket. Jimmy caught the pass set, in the proper shooting position. He hardly kept the basketball an instant before he shot.

Four seconds.

Mitchell ignored the pain and straightened himself. He prepared himself as Biggers whirled toward the basket. The ball hit the near side of the rim and teetered there.

One second, two seconds.

Biggers stopped and his arms fell to his sides.

Mitchell turned and watched the ball.

The seam on the ball turned. A slow turn. The ball dropped through the net as time ran out on the clock.

85-83. The Mountaineers had won.

Now there were three teams in the hunt for the national championships. After the St. Louis and Loyola-Detroit game there would only be two teams left. One of those was Hunt Morgan.

"It's broken," Sarg said. "I might be able to fix you some kind of protector."

"I used one once," Mitchell said. "It limits my vision."

Sarg shook his head. "If you want to play, you need one."

"Let me go without it," Mitchell said. "I'd play that game with a broken arm and a broken leg."

McCarren stood in the training room doorway. He smiled. That was toughness. That was the stuff of champions. To hell with what they said about Wheaties.

CHAPTER TWENTY SEVEN

A couple of minutes before the first half of the game between St. Louis and Loyola-Detroit ended, McCarren left his seat beside Ellen and walked through the press section to the side of the court. He was fitted with a lapel mike. He watched the final seconds of the half from the floor level. At the buzzer, Loyola-Detroit led by five points.

The color man joined him. He was a former college coach who'd decided he'd rather talk about basketball than coach it. His name was Tony Wilhelm.

The floor manager cued Wilhelm. "I guess you're happy now, Tim."

"I feel like it's Christmas Eve," McCarren said.

"What?"

"I know there's going to be something under the tree Christmas Day. What's killing me is that I don't know if it's a championship or a second place."

McCarren went on to compliment the State team. "This was such a great game I'm willing to pay for a ticket," he said. And later: "Biggers is probably a first round pro draft pick. He's a one man wrecking crew on the floor."

Wilhelm smiled. "In the N.B.A.?"

"Or the National Football League," McCarren said.

Loyola-Detroit spurted in the last five minutes of the game and won by twelve points.

That was the matchup for the national championship. One of the writers from a midwest paper called it the battle between "the city slickers and the rednecks" in the Sunday edition that covered the semi-finals. The *Detroit Free Press* wrote that "it's the old boys against the new kid on the block."

Sunday was a rest day for the teams.

The N.C.A.A., never against money, allowed the networks to assist in the scheduling. The game would be played Monday night and would be televised during prime time.

Sunday was the Coaches Association day. As a part of it, there was an all-star game. The players were all seniors on teams that hadn't made the final four in the tournament.

McCarren, telling himself that he was basking reluctantly in the spotlight and the attention that went with making the finals, went to the game with Ellen. He was glad-handed all around. All the well-wishers swarmed over him. He was even approached, obliquely, by a number of Athletic Directors at schools that had fired their head coaches. They were feeling McCarren out, to see if he might be interested in a move "upward."

Jack Turner's business meeting was with Seth Alcott, the A.D. at Southeast Florida College. Alcott had seemed willing enough to wait for Turner's answer a couple of weeks before. Now, at the championships, he was impatient. He was afraid that Turner might reject his offer and he wouldn't have time to use his position at the convention to hire a coach for next year.

Alcott took him to lunch at the AMFAC Hotel dining room. Seth was a huge, florid man who'd been All-SEC back in the 1950's as a tackle and he'd played five years in Canada before a shoulder injury had forced him out of football. After that, there had been a series of assistant coaching jobs and, in time, that had led to him being hired as A.D. at Southeast Florida three years ago.

Over a crabmeat cocktail, Alcott asked his first question. "Could you build a winning basketball program at my school?"

"If I had all I needed to get the job done."

"You didn't win at Hunt Morgan as the head coach," Alcott said.

"I didn't stay with McCarren for the money. The money wasn't good. I stayed on to learn from Tim McCarren."

Alcott chewed a wedge of lettuce. Flakes of crab meat and sauce spotted his tie. "McCarren that good?"

"Better," Turner said.

"What would you need?"

Turner told him. Seth shook his head, ending the conversation while he inspected the bottle of wine the waiter brought. The bottle was opened. Alcott tasted it and said, "Fine."

Turner watched the waiter move away. "You've got a new coliseum?"

Alcott nodded.

"Specials dorms for the athletes?"

"Basketball has a floor at the new John D. Towers high rise."

The waiter brought their steaks. The meat sizzled on the metal platters. Alcott cut a wedge from one side and lifted the bleeding slab toward his mouth.

"I'm waiting."

"I'd need a private war chest." Turner lowered his voice. "The first two or three players we go after we might need to encourage. After we start winning, we can recruit on our own, without the inducements."

"How much?" Alcott looked around and over his shoulder.

"Twenty-five thousand to start. And a budget on a month-to-month basis that furnishes walking-around money for the players. Pocket money. "

"Where'll you recruit?"

"New York and Washington in the beginning. I'll need, from what you've told me, a center and some speed at guard."

"You have the contacts? Can you deliver?"

"I've met the body brokers," Jack Turner said.

"Will McCarren think you're poaching?

"No. In fact, he'd help. He doesn't have to deal with the brokers anymore. After a year like this one, he can recruit any player he wants."

"What else?"

"At least forty-five thousand a year. A house. A new car."

"The house and the car. That's easy. Forty-five thousand. That's as much as the football coach makes. I don't know I could go past thirty-five."

Jack Turner cut his steak. It was pink at the center, the way he wanted it. He chewed on a slice and waited.

Alcott said, "I might be able to go as high as forty."

"Split the difference?"

"Forty-two-five?" Alcott nodded.

"And I'd expect special perks if I start a basketball camp. Use of the coliseum free. Low rent and use of the dining facilities for the kids who'd attend the camp.

"Possible." A nod.

"A four-year contract. It'd take at least that to get the team winning."

"I would have gone for five years," Alcott said.

"If you're not happy with me after four years there would be no reason to stay the fifth year."

The waiter leaned in and refilled their glass with the Bordeaux.

"You'll come then, Jack?"

"I'd like to see the facilities."

"Take my word. But, in case you're not completely satisfied, we have some money from the building budget. You can make changes that are within reason."

A moment. Turner let him wait that moment. "I'll come." He put out his hand and Alcott grabbed it eagerly.

"When can I make the announcement?"

"After tomorrow night's game. Not a minute before. If the story leaks before then, I'll deny that I've taken the job and I won't take the job at all."

"It won't leak. What's so important about withholding the story?"

"The players. I owe them. I don't want them confused. I don't want to hurt their concentration. They've got to believe that McCarren and I are a team, the way they're a team."

Alcott nodded.

"Muddy the waters some," Turner said. "Spend the rest of the day and all day tomorrow asking around for a coach. Even do some interviews if you like."

Seth Alcott smiled. "You're not afraid I might find a better coach?"

"If you can, I'll release you from our agreement."

"Cocky?"

"That's from being around Tim."

Alcott laughed. "Does McCarren walk on water?"

"A few steps."

McCarren left the all-star game at halftime. Like most of those games, it was every man for himself. The players wanted to impress the pro scouts, especially the ones who hadn't been impressive over their four year college careers. It was run and gun of the worst sort.

"Enough of this," McCarren said. He took Ellen's arm and they returned to the hotel. What McCarren wouldn't admit was that he wanted to know what the outcome of the meeting with Alcott had been.

He had mixed feelings. He wanted the best for Jack. At the same time, he hated to lose him. Still, a coach was known by the success or failure of the men who'd worked under him and had gone on to head coaching jobs. Look at Bobby Knight.

McCarren met Turner for drinks in the lounge.

"Did you get what you asked for?"

"Down the line," Jack said. Once he and McCarren, during an early recruiting trip, had discussed his talk with President Edwards and how McCarren had handled it. Turner had used that account and followed it to structure his interview with Alcott. "I got everything I wanted but the A.D.'s job. Seth Alcott's not about to give it up to me."

McCarren laughed. "The rumors are already around town. I got approached in two ways today. There were those who wanted to hire me away and the unemployed who want to make application for your job."

"Shit." Turner looked down at his scotch. "Well, I was afraid of that. I told Alcott not to leak it and to pretend to still interview for the position."

"You're learning," McCarren said.

"You going to schedule me, Tim?"

"You think I'm crazy?" McCarren smiled. "In four years, we can set up a series of games. But not until this freshman class leaves. I don't believe in sending players against a coach who recruited them and helped coach them."

"That's fair." Turner gulped his scotch. "I'm going to need a big man."

"You've got the phone numbers in New York."

Turner nodded. As soon as he signed the contact with Seth Alcott, he'd make that trip to New York and perhaps to Washington. "I'll give your best to Abe Stein."

"Watch out for cripples."

Yes. That was true. The first time on his owns, without McCarren, he'd have to be certain he got his money's worth. The program would depend on that.

Loyola-Detroit was a throwback, a team that reminded McCarren of the past, the 1940's and 1950's, before basketball was a bigtime sport. A miracle team. Loyola-Detroit didn't have all the talent in the world and it had no depth at all. Perhaps it had less talent than any team that had reached the final four in the last fifteen years. When Loyola-Detroit received a bid to the tournament, one national writer said the team had a snowflake's chance in Death Valley. Since that time, the Friars had pulled two major upsets.

Loyola-Detroit liked to set a slow tempo, a pace that allowed them to conserve their players. And they played mainly zones on defense so they could cut down the chances that their starting five would get into foul trouble.

Have to set a quicker tempo, McCarren thought. Have to get them to running with us. Have to sucker them into that in some way.

McCarren and Turner returned to the hotel after dinner and locked themselves in the room with a couple of six packs of beer and discussed the starters for Loyola-Detroit.

Bill Tufts, the center. He had none of the ability the Killer had. But he was a determined player. And he was on a roll. Luck seemed to be with him. Could expect to do a bit better than a draw at the center spot. Depth might be a factor. Could bring in Mitchell and spell the Killer. Could even use Regis at center if necessary. However, if the Friars controlled the tempo, the pace of the game, numbers might not matter.

The power forward, Jesse Jeters. Too strong and experienced for Mitchell or Bo Regis to handle. The best bet might be to put the Killer on him from time to time and see if Robert could shut him down. But they had to be careful that the move didn't backfire, that the Killer didn't get into early foul trouble guarding Jeters. Unless Jeters was off his game, unless he could be controlled, the edge went to Loyola-Detroit at big forward. Five or six points.

The small forward, Jimmy Touchette. The same size at Theold. Not quite as quick. Could play Theold against him most of the time. Could put Stefano on him if he got hot. Jimmy might cool his game for him. A point edge to the Mountaineers. Might balance the point edge the Friars had at big forward.

The big guard, George Tuttle. A decent shot. Fair speed. Could try Jorge on him. If that worked, could keep Theold at small forward. Could spell Jorge from time to time with Stefano and let Jimmy bang him some. Might disrupt Tuttle's concentration that way.

The point guard, Tim Carpenter. The real worry that McCarren had. Speed to stay step for step with Paul Gilson. Had to have a good night from Gilson. Had to make sure that Carpenter didn't drive the lane on them.

The sixth man. A thug, a bruiser. Chan Lane. Should be playing football rather than basketball. Six-eight and around two hundred and forty pounds. No talent except for a high threshold of pain and a willingness to mix it with anybody.

That was the team. The rest of the bench didn't matter. That was all the Mountaineers had to worry about.

Enough to worry about, McCarren said. That and their damned luck.

For all McCarren knew, this Loyola-Detroit was a team of destiny. The kind that emerged every twenty years or so, won a national championship and then disappeared for another twenty years.

⚜   ⚜   ⚜

Sarg called Mitchell Winters into the training room and tried to fit him with a nose and face guard he'd prepared. It was awkward, it was painful and Mitchell knew that it limited his vision. Jack Turner came and had a look at it and asked if Mitchell thought he could play with the nose and face guard.

"I'll play without it," Mitchell said.

"That's risky." Turner looked at Sarg, who shrugged his shoulders.

"Let me try," Mitchell said.

"It's up to Coach McCarren. We'll see."

CHAPTER TWENTY EIGHT

McCarren sent the team on the court at six-fifteen, led by Jorge and the Killer. McCarren followed and stood beside the bench assigned to the Mountaineers and watched. He appeared to have his eyes on the whole team. The one he really watched was Mitchell Winters. He seemed to breathe well. But that swollen nose was an inviting target. The Pit was filling fast. Game time was seven. Nine on the east coast. Damn the networks for jerking the N.C.A.A. around. Bad enough to try to get accustomed to the time zones. Sometimes had to play an early round game at eleven in the morning to fit into a television schedule.

No problem, this time. Likely that Loyola-Detroit was bothered more than Hunt Morgan.

The final warmups. No pep talk in the dressing room. Lineups only. Time for the players to concentrate. Prepare themselves.

Time to reach inside themselves and tear out everything that wasn't connected to the game.

At nine o'clock, McCarren looked down the bench and saw the two broadcasters and their crew. Cued by the floor manager, the announcer began his intro. McCarren didn't have to hear him to know what he was saying. That it was an unlikely matchup for the national championships. Last year's almost-miracle team against this year's miracle tear.

"Has true parity really come to basketball this year?"

Not bloody likely, McCarren thought.

During the player introductions, McCarren stood by the bench and sent each of them on the court as their names were announced. A pat on the back, a good word.

Across the front line, Stefano and the Killer and Mitchell Winters. Backcourt, Jorge and Gilson.

Theold Brown and Bo Regis waiting to enter the game when they were needed.

McCarren saved his last words until the tear, trotted back to the bench. The network gave him that moment while they crammed two more commercials into the time slot.

McCarren leaned over his starters and Theold Brown and Bo Regis. "This is what the Killer calls the Big Dance. Most teams never get here. We're the lucky ones. And since you're here, you might as well win it all. I want everything you've got tonight. No reason to hold it for tomorrow. You won't need it then. If you leave it all on the floor and can't walk away I'll personally carry you into the dressing room. That's my promise."

The head official walked toward the bench. He bounced the ball a time or two and waited. "Ready?"

McCarren nodded. He sent the starters onto the court.

The opening tip was controlled by Loyola-Detroit. From their first offensive sequence, McCarren knew what the Briars wanted to do. Either they'd had the same thoughts and the same nightmares or that coach had been reading McCarren's mail.

Call the center spot a draw. Place the emphasis on the big power forward, Jeters. Let him get the points while the Killer and Bill Tufts fought under the basket.

Touchette, the small forward, and Jimmy Stefano were banging from the tipoff. Bruises all around and blood might flow before the game ended.

At the big guard, Tuttle and Jorge step for step. Tuttle had an inch or two on Jorge.

The point guard position was a war. Paul Gilson against Carpenter. So evenly matched that it was hard to say where the edge was.

The edge is the bench, McCarren thought.

The early jitters passed. Each team turned the ball over a time or two.

The Killer went over Tufts and slammed the ball through the net with a shot that rattled the backboard. At the other end, Tufts moved outside and put up a soft jump shot that hit the back rim, the front rim and dropped through the net.

Respect for the Killer. Tufts didn't want to challenge Kinson early.

The Killer moved across the lane and put up a slow half hook that went in.

Enough misdirection, the Loyola-Detroit coach must have said at that point. Show them what we're going to do to them.

Jeters against Mitchell Winters. Jeters had such a quick first step that Mitchell Winters couldn't stay with him. He was late getting to Jeters and was called for blocking. The inbounds pass went to Jeters. Jeters started his drive, pulled up and dropped in a short jump shot from six feet.

Four minutes gone. Jimmy Stefano, using his size, bulled past Touchette and laid the ball in while the Killer screened Tufts.

McCarren watched the clock. The network would call a timeout soon if neither team did. It was an "extra" that all the coaches liked to wait for, while they saved their allotment for crucial moments in the game.

"Time." The official called it and indicated that it was charged to the network.

McCarren nodded at Theold Brown and Bo Regis, "Report."

When they returned from the scorer's table, he motioned them to seats. "Theold, you're in at small forward. Jimmy you move to backcourt and work on Tuttle a bit. Winters, you take a blow. Regis in at center." He turned to the Killer. "Robert, you've got to clamp yourself on Jeters. Can't let him do a run on us."

Back on the court, the Killer made Jeters work both ends of the floor. He had to work for his shots and he had to struggle against the offensive pressure the Killer exerted on him.

The Loyola-Detroit coach saw the new alignment and reached down his bench for his sixth man. Chan Lane. Lane was the bruiser, the thug. Six-eight and two-forty or so.

Lane replaced Tufts at center. The next offensive series, Lane set a pick on Bo Regis that knocked him to the floor. Regis got to his feet and shook his head. He looked stunned.

McCarren tapped Mitchell on the shoulder. "How's your breathing?"

"I'll breathe tomorrow."

"In for Regis. Watch yourself. You can bet that Lane knows your nose is broken."

Loyola-Detroit had scored on the pick Lane set on Bo Regis. The score was 18 to 14, Loyola-Detroit leading.

Mitchell reported and sat on the floor in front of the table and waited for the next time the ball was out of play. He watched Theold Brown drive the baseline. A fake got him around Touchette. Chan Lane stepped to the line to block Theold's path. Brown left his feet two steps away from Lane and curled around him in the air. He turned almost a hundred and eighty degree and pushed the ball toward the basket. It dropped through without touching the rim.

Mitchell Winters replaced Bo Regis. He moved to the defensive end of the court and set up. Chan Lane jogged toward him. Lane's eyes were on Mitchell's nose. He smiled.

Now he wants the ball, Mitchell thought. Wants to take it right at me.

Mitchell played behind Lane. At the last possible moment, when he saw the pass headed for Lane, Mitchell reached across Lane and batted the ball away. It bounced toward center court. Mitchell saw Paul Gilson lunge for it. He saw Theold Brown streak for the basket. The pass led Theold by a step. That was the last thing Mitchell saw for about a minute. Chan Lane, as soon as the ball crossed midcourt grunted and turned and threw an elbow at Mitchell. The officials were gone, headed to the other end of the floor to cover the fastbreak. They didn't see the elbow. It struck Mitchell across the bridge of his nose and floored him. He blacked out even before he felt himself touch the court.

When he opened his eyes, McCarren and Sarg squatted over him. Past them he could see the scoreboard. 18 to 18, the score was tied. Mitchell gagged. He could feel blood running down his face and he could taste blood in his mouth. He turned to the side and spat blood into a towel that Sarg held toward him.

"Help him." McCarren motioned Ames Ashley and Billy Stoddard from the bench.

Mitchell covered his face with the towel while Ashley and Stoddard guided him toward the dressing room.

The Killer circled them and put a hand on Mitchell's shoulder "I'll get that cocksucker," the Killer said.

McCarren stepped forward. "Easy."

The Killer stared at winters. "You all right?"

"Listen to the Coach," Mitchell said.

Jack Turner and Sarg leaned over Mitchell. Winters' legs dangled over the side of the training table. Through the bowels of the arena, Mitchell could hear shouting and yelling. There was no way of knowing which team was doing what.

"I don't think he ought to play anymore," Sarg said. "This nose is a disaster area."

Turner nodded.

Mitchell pushed Sarg's hands away and sat up straight. "Where's the face guard mask?"

Sarg shook his head. "It won't fit anymore. There's more swelling."

"Then another mask."

"I'll see." Sarg moved away.

Jack Turner put a hand on Mitchell's shoulder. "Let it go. You've got your whole life to play basketball."

"And I've got eight or nine months for this to heal. I'll play."

Sarg returned with a heavy plastic face mask. "You said you couldn't see. Exactly where...?"

"Can't see down." Mitchell looked at the mask. "Can you enlarge the eye holes?"

Sarg reached for his pocket knife. He began to cut larger openings for the eyes. Jack Turner watched. Half a minute's work and Sarg passed the mask to Mitchell Winters. "What do you think, Coach?"

Jack Turner shook his head. "It's up to McCarren."

There was a loud shouting, the stamping of feet. "I wish I knew what the hell was going on," Mitchell said. He held the mask over his face. Sarg tied it in place.

The Killer had watched Mitchell half-dragged, half-led from the court. He watched while blood was scrubbed from the floor. It was then he turned and looked for Chan Lane. The Loyola-Detroit coach was one step ahead of him. During the injury timeout, he'd sent in Bill Tufts and put Lane on the bench.

Lane sat there, grinning at the Killer.

It took Bo Regis, Jimmy Stefano and Jorge Morgan to keep the Killer from charging the bench and taking on Lane.

"Easy," Jorge said. "That's what they want."

"What we did to those other centers," Jimmy said, "that's what they want to do to you."

McCarren passed by on his way to the bench. "Wait your time," he said. "It's coming."

"Wait, shit."

From that moment on, the Killer opened the bottle and let the demon out. He played in a frenzy, in a controlled anger. He took the basketball directly at Tufts. He banged him with a shoulder and elbows, he walked on his feet, and on offense he scored over him.

Near the five minute mark, Sarg and Jack Turner returned to the bench. Mitchell wasn't with them. McCarren leaned toward Turner.

"He's all right. He says he wants to try to play the second half." Turner stared at the scoreboard. The Mountaineers led 38 to 31.

With four minutes left in the half, the Loyola-Detroit sent Chan Lane into the game to replace Tufts. His plan was to Jive his center the four minute breather and the whole halftime to recover his strength and prepare for the second half.

Lane took his position at the Friar offensive end of the court and waited for the Loyola-Detroit guards to bring the ball across the center line. The Killer was behind him with his hands high. Lane looked over his shoulder at Robert.

"How's your buddy with the funny nose?"

"Watch your mouth, dogsucker. You don't know what rough is yet."

"You want to show me nigger?"

"Not yet," the Killer said. "Right now, I'm just happy they didn't hide you away the rest of the game."

"Hide? Why, you black son…" Lane whirled and took a swing at Robert.

The lead official who'd taken a location under the basket blew his whistle. The call was against Lane. The Killer, walking away, heard the referee say,"....again and you're out of the game for good."

The Killer waited until Jorge crossed center court. Then he popped out of the pack. Jorge passed to Paul Gilson. Gilson whipped the ball to the Killer. Lane was a step behind him. Robert dribbled across the lane. As he went, he nodded at Gilson. Lane trailed him by two steps when the Killer stopped. Paul streaked around the other side of the Killer. The Killer dropped the pass to him and stood his ground to screen Lane. Chan Lane slammed into his back. A hand struck Robert in the kidney. Gilson had an open path to the basket. He laid the ball in the basket with the ease of a layup drill.

Lane wanted the ball. That was obvious from the way he took his set in front of the Killer and waved his arms at the guards bring the ball down court. The Killer yelled, "Dealing the cards, Jimmy."

Jimmy Stefano understood. He cheated a step toward Lane. "Card dealing" meant that, because Lane wasn't a threat as a shooter, he'd take the pass and try to occupy Robert while he looked for one of his teammates breaking for the basket. Then he'd deal the ball off and box Robert.

The pass didn't reach Lane. Jimmy, at the last possible moment, stepped in front of him and stole the basketball. Surprise gave him several steps on the Loyola-Detroit players. He was across midcourt, dribbling, with Theold Brown on his right, filling that lane, before the pursuit began. Robert charged after them and filled the lane on the left.

"Coming up," the Killer yelled.

Jimmy dropped the ball to his left and curled away. The Killer took the pass in full stride. One step and he took the ball in both hands and slammed it through the rim.

The Loyola-Detroit coach had seen enough. He returned Tufts to the game. For the remainder of the half, Tufts played smart ball. He didn't get rattled. He matched the Killer basket for basket.

When the teams jogged from the court for the half time break, the Mountaineers led by nine points.

Mitchell Winters stood in the examination room. The mask was strapped in place. He moved from side to side, trying to see the tile floor. The enlarged eye holes helped some but he had blind spots, areas, close to him where he would not be able to watch an opposing player's footwork. He'd have to attempt to keep his distance. He'd have to guess part of the time and hope that he guessed right.

The Killer watched him from the doorway. "I didn't know you could dance, my man. How you feeling?"

"Rocky," Mitchell said. He leaned against the training table. "It hurts but I can stand it."

"I've called the hospital." Sarg stood next to the Killer. "After the game, or the next time that nose gets hurt, you're headed straight for the Emergency Room."

"You'd better zig and zag," the Killer said. "Rest some now, Mitch."

It was the first time anybody had ever called him Mitch. Not even his father called him that. He decided he liked the sound of it.

"I think I've got enough left to give you a couple of breathers this half."

"Good man."

The other players filed by the door. Good words, kind words. All asking how he was. He rested on the table and felt his strength returning.

His eyes were closed when McCarren looked in and shook his head. Sarg nodded and followed him from the room and closed the door behind them.

McCarren checked his watch. "Five minutes," he said to the team. He nodded at the student manager who moved around the locker room and picked up the Gatorade cups and the orange peels. "So far, so good."

"We're kicking their butts," the Killer said.

"Put that thought out of your head," Jack Turner said.

"Coach Turner's right." McCarren nervously smoothed his hair. "They're going to make three or four runs at you in this half. Nine points aren't enough. We've got to fight back each run at us. We've got to keep a working margin of five points at least. More if we can. Otherwise, you can kiss this championship goodbye and prepare yourselves to stand around and look silly when they award the second place trophy."

"No...no....NO....No.... no second place," the players shouted at McCarren.

McCarren smiled. "Warm up." He pointed the team toward the dressing room door.

It was a badly pinched nerve in Theold's back. It happened to him in the last minute of the first half. He'd hoped it would pass or he'd be able to play with it and bear the pain. Now the nerve throbbed. It was like a hot needle jab. The pain pulsed so regularly he could have set a watch by it. Every thirty seconds or so. A jab and a burn that last for a couple of seconds and then was gone. Then another thirty seconds and it returned.

He had hurt it on a rebound. High around the rim, off his feet, his right hand on one side of the ball and the power of the big forward, Jeters, on the other side. He felt the sting at that moment and he thought he heard a tearing sound.

He tried his shots during the warm up period. Lifting his hands in the shooting motion aggravated the injury. The nerve seemed on fire. His shot was off. He could hardly reach the back-board.

McCarren met him as he walked from the court. "Tell me about it, Theold."

"What?"

McCarren put an arm around him and led him toward the bench. "Tell me, boy."

"Nothing's wrong, Coach. I swear it."

McCarren led him toward Sarg. "Where does it hurt?"

Theold told them finally. How he'd hurt his back and where the pain was and what it felt like.

"You play?"

"I want to try, Coach."

"I'll give you a minute. Two minutes. If you can't hack it, you'll have to come out."

"Sure, Coach."

McCarren started the Killer at center, Regis at big forward and Theold at small forward. He paired Jorge in the backcourt with Gilson.

As the team headed for the floor to begin the second half, McCarren motioned Stefeno, Houston Tarr and Mitchell Winters to seats on his right.

The Killer controlled the tap. He batted it toward Theold. Theold was on a breakaway, alone, headed for the basket and the layin, when the pain almost doubled him over. The ball slipped from his numbed hand and rolled out of bounds. Theold turned and looked toward the bench. He shook his head at McCarren. One hand dug into the pain in his back,

McCarren tapped Jimmy. "In for Theold."

"What?"

"Report," McCarren said. He called down the bench. "Sarg. Over here."

Loyola-Detroit knew something was wrong with Theold.

Touchette asked for the ball and received it along the baseline. He went around Theold and banked the shot off the backboard from five feet. The Mountaineer lead was cut to seven points.

Stefano replaced Theold.

Sarg squatted beside McCarren. "I can give him a shot for the pain. See what that does. Even if he can't play, at least we need to deaden the nerve."

"Try it," McCarren said.

Sarg took Theold by the arm and headed for the dressing room.

At the other end of the court, the Killer slid into the lane and took a pass high on his fingertips. He turned on Tufts and underhanded the ball toward the rim. The ball bounced on the rim and wobbled there. Tufts was impatient and reached across the Killer and knocked the ball away. The official blew his whistle and ruled it defensive goaltending. Tufts didn't argue. He trotted downcourt. The Loyola-Detroit coach raged along the side of the court. He stamped his foot and yelled. The trailing official pointed at him. A warning. No technical this time. "No more," the official said.

The Friar assistant coach tugged the Loyola head coach toward the bench, whispering to him the whole way.

The Friars, well-schooled, went back to their strength. The power forward, Jeters, whirled across the lane and took the ball and completed a half hook that dropped through. Regis was a step behind him, out of position.

"Mitchell," McCarren said. "Report. You're in for Regis. The Killer moves over and takes the big forward."

"Yes, sir."

"And watch yourself."

Mitchell said he would. He reported and waited for the dead ball time. By the clock, the Mountaineers still led by seven. Stefano put up a shot that missed. The Killer touched it last before it went out of bounds. The ball belonged to the Friars. Mitchell entered the game. As they took their defensive positions Mitchell passed the changed assignment on to the Killer.

Loyola-Detroit went back to Jeters. This time Jeters tried a soft jump shot from twelve feet. The Killer batted it away. Carpenter recovered the ball and dribbled to the right.

"Won't try that shot again," McCarren said to Houston Tarr.

Tufts, now guarded by Mitchell Winters, moved in and out of the lane. Carpenter faked a pass to Jeters and dropped the ball into the lane to Tufts. Mitchell moved in close to play Tufts. As he'd feared, the mask obscured his lower vision. He couldn't watch Tufts' feet. Tufts gave him a good head fake to his right and, when Mitchell reacted in that direction, he turned to his left and put up the shot. It dropped through without touching the rim.

The Mountaineer lead was now five points.

The teams traded baskets for the next two minutes. Tuttle, the big guard, took Jorge one on one and used his extra height to muscle a shot against him. Stefano rebounded a missed shot by Gilson and slammed it through against Touchette.

Jeters used an elbow to free himself from the Killer and claim the baseline. Mitchell tried to challenge him but Tufts boxed him but Tufts boxed him away from Jeters. Two dribbles and Jeters rolled the ball over the rim and through.

The Killer, at the other end, used a pick from Jimmy Stefano that delayed Jeters. He went up and over Tufts and slammed in the basketball in with a force that shook the backboard.

The margin was still five points, the Mountaineers ahead.

There was movement on the Loyola-Detroit bench. The Killer stood with his hands on his hips and watched the big man, Chan Lane, report at the scorer's table.

He slouched onto the court, rolling his shoulders, swinging his arms across his chest, as if warming up. He passed Mitchell Winters and said, "Hi-yo, Silver."

At the far end of the court, as Lane set up on offense, he looked over his shoulder at Mitchell. "'Who is that masked man?"

Lane was the card dealer a gain. The ball came into him and he dealt it away to the shooting guard, Tuttle. Jimmy Stefano had cheated toward Lane and made a swipe at the pass. Now, as Tuttle drove around Lane and headed for the basket, Stefano planted his feet solidly and took the charge. The whistle blew. The call was made against Tuttle. The ball went over to the Mountaineers.

During that collision, unseen by the officials, Lane whirled around and swung a high elbow at Mitchell's face. The elbow missed Mitchell's nose and landed across his mouth. Mitchell felt his lower teeth shift slightly. He pushed past Lane and headed for the other end of the court. On the way he could feel his lips begin to puffs and swell.

McCarren stood in front of the bench. "Three," he shouted. "Three."

It was the Killer's play, designed for him. It had the look of the play where the Killer flashed across the lane, took the pass and turned and put up the shot. This time, the Killer would put the ball on the floor, dribble in past Mitchell and lay the ball in.

That's the good news, Mitchell thought. The bad news is that Mitchell was supposed to screen the center, this time Lane, away from the Killer. He knew he was going to get hit this time and it would be a good lick, the best Lane had in him. He braced himself for it. The pass went to Robert. Jeters anticipated the shot and moved into rebounding position. As the Killer dribbled past him, Mitchell turned and put his back to Lane. He pushed Lane away, struggling for rebounding space. Jeters saw the Killer's move too late and made a move to block the shot. Chan Lane rammed into Mitchell's back. An open hand swung over Mitchell's shoulder, as if by accident, and banged him hard across the nose and face mask.

The mask absorbed part of the impact. Still, the blow jarred Winters and he heard the nose bones grind together. His knees buckled and caught. He pushed away from Lane and ran for the defensive end of the court. He could taste blood in his mouth. He didn't know if it was from his mouth or his nose.

"Hang in there," Jack Turner encouraged him from the bench as he passed.

Easy for him to say. Mitchell lifted his hand and waved that he understood.

Jeters this time down. Lane set a solid pick on the Killer and that left Mitchell to switch and play Jeters. Jeters rolled around winters and banked the shot in.

Back down to five points.

McCarren waited for the TV timeout and got it.

Jorge slumped into his seat. "Need a blow bad."

McCarren tapped Houston on the shoulder. "Report." McCarren nodded toward Paul Gilson. "How about you?"

"I can go another minute. Until Jorge comes back in."

"Good man."

Sarg and Theold walked past the scorer's table and stopped beside the team huddle. McCarren turned the team over to Jack Turner and went to Sarg. "How is it?"

"Ask him," Sarg said.

"I want to try it again," Theold said.

"Better to know now than later." He nodded. "Report."
McCarren returned to the huddle. "Jimmy, you take a rest. Sit by me."

Stefano nodded. He gulped air. His body shook with fatigue.

Mitchell leaned forward and spat blood into a towel.

McCarren looked at the clock. 14 : 55 to go in the game.

The near official waved the Mountaineers onto the court.

It was a set play. The pass in to the Killer. He backed in and drew the defense in around him. Then, when Theold stepped toward him, the Killer fed the ball to him high and soft so that Theold took it in the shooting motion.

Coach Turner had warned them the shot might be off. He urged strong rebounding. By now, all the players knew about the pinched nerve. The Killer held his position as long as he could. He released the moment the ball left Theold Brown's hands. He whirled around Jeters and went for the basket.

Theold's shot was short and didn't hit the front edge of the rim. The Killer, in the middle of his leap, cupped the ball in his hand and pushed it up and over and through the basket.

"Good pass," he shouted at Theold.

Theold smiled. He knew better. As he ran past the Mountaineer bench, he caught McCarren's look and shook his head. McCarren took a quick look at Jorge and Jimmy. "Another minute," he shouted. "Hang tight."

Touchette, the small forward, took it straight at Theold. Theold got his body between Touchette and the basket and stopped his drive. His right arm was late getting raised and the shot was clean, through the net with a hiss.

The Mountaineer lead was five points once more.

The Killer and Houston Tarr played catch. To the Killer and back to Houston. To the Killer. "Do one," the Killer said when he returned the ball to Houston.

Houston shot without thinking. The low flat arc of the shot barely cleared Jeters's raised hand. There was the satisfying <u>thuck</u> as the basketball hit the back rim and ricocheted through.

McCarren stared at the clock. Touchette received the ball near the left corner and tested Theold again. Robert left Jeters and stepped in that direction to help out. Touchette dragged a foot and put up the short jump shot. With the Killer out of position Jeters grabbed the rebound. He pumped once and slammed the ball in.

"Report," McCarren said to Jorge and Stefano.

This time down on offense Houston was thinking. The motion wasn't correct. The arc was low. The ball hit the front rim and bounced directly into Lane's hands. He held the ball and slowed the tempo.

With the substitution of Jorge and Stefano, Houston had moved to small forward. The Killer patted Tarr on the back and pushed him toward Touchette. "Play the sucker tight. You've got some fouls to waste."

Touchette flashed across the lane. Houston rammed into him hard as he put up a soft jumper. Touchette went down hard and got up slowly. He looked like he thought he'd been mugged.

He stood at the free throw line and made both foul shots. The Mountaineer lead had been cut to three points.

There was a trough in the action. For a matter of two or three minutes neither team seemed able to score. The Killer missed a short hook. Jeters, tiring, jerked a jump shot to the right and hit the side of the backboard. Jorge dribbled the ball off his foot and out of bounds. Stefano, helping out Houston, stole the ball from Touchette as he drove for the basket.

"I'll take this," McCarren told Jack Turner. But both of them knew that it wasn't really being offered. Both teams were too good to remain scoreless the rest of the game.

Three points. That was the margin.

The Loyola-Detroit coach weakened first and called the timeout.

CHAPTER TWENTY NINE

Mitchell Winters thought he was choking. Blood was draining into his mouth. He spat into a towel. To one side, Jack Turner watched him and moved away. He returned with Sarg, the trainer.

"Take Mitchell into the dressing room and check the nose."

"Aw, Coach, I can..."

"Do it," Turner said. He turned his back to them and pointed a hand at Regis. "In for winters, Bo."

Jorge and Gilson at guards, Stefano at small forward to help with the rebounding, Regis at big forward and the Killer at center.

The Loyola-Detroit saw the new alignment and grabbed Chan Lane and pushed him toward the scorer's table. He replaced the power forward, Jeters. McCarren watched and understood the move. Regis wasn't a scoring threat. Lane could match against him well. Jeters could find a two minute breather before the final run.

The clock showed 9: 58 remaining in the game.

Regis braced himself to take the punishment. He held his ground and drew a charge on Lane. Another time he was called for a block, though the second decision could have been a charge as well.

It was brutal. As if neither team seemed concerned about scoring. Elbows and hips and hands flying. Lumps and bruises and no points.

"Take it, Bo," the Killer said. "Stand in and I'll treat you to an iced cold one after we win."

Regis nodded. His breath was ragged. His ribs ached.

Lane pounded Regis. The Killer banged at Tufts. Tufts backed off half a step. The Killer took a pass from Jorge and slammed it over Tufts.

The Mountaineers led by five points again.

Mitchell sat on the table and waited for Sarg to unstrap the nose and face mask. The inside of the mask was coated with blood.

"It's a mess," Sarg said. "It's spread across your face. I've got to get you to the hospital."

Mitchell shook his head. Blood dripped on the tile floor. "Shoot it with something and clean it so I can breathe."

"That's not the way I do sports medicine." Sarg shook his head. He dropped the mask on the table behind Mitchell.

"Some kind of local shot. What they'd give me if I went to the hospital."

"The Coach and the doc will have my hide if they knew I did that."

"Between us," Mitchell said. He was pleading.

"They can win without you."

"They don't need me and I won't play. But I got to be ready if the Killer needs a two minute blow."

Sarg hesitated. Finally he lifted the medical case and placed it on the table. He took a small bottle from it and a sterile, wrapped needle.

"Marcaine," he said. "Ought to be good for four hours." He tore the wrapping from the needle and filled it through the top of the bottle. "This could mean my job." He leaned over Mitchell. He clamped Mitchell's upper lip between his fingers and pulled it upward. He inserted the needle under the lip, toward the nose. There was a jab, a pain, and the numbness began. Sarg stepped back. He waited. Seconds passed. He leaned over Mitchell once more and used the needle to inject Marcaine inside the nostrils.

"I'll clean out the blood." Sarg reached for a bundle of cotton-tipped swabs. "You kids are crazy."

The teams matched baskets. With 7:22 remaining the score was 75-70, the Mountaineers ahead. The beating had sapped Regis' strength. He wobbled up and down the court.

Turner touched McCarren's arm. "Got to go to Ashley?"

"Might have to."

McCarren looked toward the entranceway that led to the dressing rooms. He saw Sarg and Winters. No mask. Tape and a bandage Out of the game? Damn. Returned only to watch the game? What caught his attention next was that Winters was trying to smile. The smile was crooked. The shot to deaden his nose had numbed some of his facial muscles.

Mitchell sat next to McCarren. "When you need me, I can go until I take another lick."

"We'll see."

There was a groan on the court. Regis had held his ground and another charge was called on Lane.

"How many on Lane?"

"That's four," Turner said.

Regis rubbed his ribs.

"Lane'll come out now. You and Ashley report. You in for the Killer. Ashley in for Regis." McCarren motioned them toward the scorer's table.

Chan Lane argued the call. He stopped just short of a technical. He swaggered from the court. Mitchell reported and was followed by Ames Ashley. The Loyola-Detroit coach witnessed the substitutions and sent his power forward, Jeters, in to replace Chan Lane. Then he hesitated. Tufts was tiring. With the Killer on the bench, this was the best time to give Tufts a rest. The Friars bench was thin. He didn't want to use Lane yet and risk the fifth foul. He went to the end of the bench and selected Fitzgerald, a thin white freshman he'd used very little during the season.

McCarren watched Fitzgerald report and Tufts leave the game. It wasn't the perfect matchup, McCarren knew. Even hurt, Mitchell should be able to dominate the thin kid. But that left Ashley against Jeters. Jeters would eat Ashley alive.

McCarren patted the seat next to him and waited until Robert was seated. "You've got a minute."

The student manager dropped a damp towel in Robert's hands. The Killer wiped his face and nodded. His breath came in gagging sucks.

"That foul on Lane," Turner said. "That's the big one. Next foul we're in the one and one."

Gilson brought the ball across center court. He curled to the left and they set up the triangle. Gilson outside and Stefano near the baseline and Mitchell moving in and out of the lane. From Gilson to Stefano and then in to Mitchell. Back out to Gilson. Waiting for the open shot, the mistake. When it came, the freshman center, Fitzgerald, was out of position. He'd tried to step in front of Mitchell and intercept the pass. He was too slow and awkward. Gilson bounced the pass past him. Mitchell took it, dribbled twice and, using the rim to block Jeters, jammed the ball in.

Seven points. A good cushion, McCarren thought.

Jeters stepped around a slow Ames Ashley and took a pass near the rim and guided it in. Back down to five points. Ashley shook his head at Mitchell. He was saying there was nothing he could do.

At four minutes, that would be when McCarren inserted the Killer again. Had to keep the working margin until then. Next to him, even with the crowd noise, McCarren could hear Robert's breathing steady and slow. Almost there. Then, with the Killer in the game, the Mountaineers would make their final charge at the Friars and try to pull away from them for good.

The triangle again. Gilson to Jimmy Stefano and back. Gilson passed in to Mitchell. All the time watching, working. Out from Mitchell to Stefano. Gilson saw Jeters move over a step, ready to help out with Mitchell if he turned toward the basket. Touchette gave ground, moving back a step so that he could form the front half of a sandwich on Mitchell.

From Stefano to Gilson. Gilson in to Mitchell. Touchette backed away another step. Gilson nodded at Jimmy. Mitchell dropped the ball to Stefano. Jimmy was free and open. He took the pass ten feet from the basket and went up. He released the ball when he was at the level of the rim.

In. Back to seven points.

The Loyola-Detroit coach had seen enough. He jumped to his feet and signaled for a timeout. Tufts went to report. He'd replace the big kid, Fitzgerald.

McCarren nodded at the Killer. The Killer stood and grinned. "That was almost a full night's sleep," Robert said.

Another minute passed. The lead was cut to five points on a long half court pass from Tufts to Jeters who'd lost Mitchell when he stumbled and dropped two paces behind him.

McCarren sent Houston in to spell Gilson. "One minute," he told Paul. "We might do the delay game to them."

"I'd hate to," Gilson said. "This has been an ass-kicker of a game so far."

"We'll see. Rest."

Jorge brought the ball up court. He swung toward the bench. He looked at McCarren for instructions.

"Slow it down. No hurry."

Jorge nodded. He looked at the clock. Up by five. He dribbled across center court and tossed the ball to Houston and got it back. He circled to his left and they set up a triangle with the Killer at one corner of it. In to the Killer, back to Jorge.

Touchette, who'd been fooled by Stefano before, moved as if he were dropping back to "front" Robert Hinson. Just before Jorge released the ball toward Jimmy, Touchette stepped out and stole the pass.

"Plenty of time," the Loyola-Detroit coach yelled.

Mitchell and Jeters pushed and shoved for position. Nothing was called. Jeters received the pass. Mitchell played him tight, the best defense he could. Jeters had to pull up eight feet from the basket. He turned, off balance, and put up an awkward one-handed shot as he fell away. It was an impossible shot. It banked in off the backboard.

"In now," McCarren said to Paul Gilson. "And watch for the fist." The clenched fist was the signal to start the stall game.

Up by three. 2 : 57 remaining on the clock.

Gilson waited for the dead ball so he could enter the game. On offense, the Killer called for a clear out on the right side of the court and went one on one against Tufts. He took his time. He backed in, dribbling. When he was close enough he turned and tried his hook shot. The ball hit the rim and bounced away. On the other side of the court Mitchell boxed out Jeters. Houston Tarr saw the clear lane and went up for the rebound. He slapped the ball once, twice, a third time before it dropped through.

Gilson started on the court. At that moment another television timeout was called. The official gave the signal.

McCarren leaned over his players. "Up by five. Winters, you all right?"

"I've got another minute or two left," Mitchell said.

McCarren nodded. "That's all it takes."

Jack Turner thrust his clipboard forward. He flipped until he reached a clean page. He sketched in half a court. "If we're ahead three with one minute we go to the delay, the stall."

Nods. A couple of groans. It wasn't going to be popular with the capacity crowd.

"Killer, you move out here." Turner drew an "x" just inside the center court line. "Either Tufts has to leave the basket and guard you and you stand there and dribble the minute away. If you're guarded, remember the five second rule and cross that marker line. "He turned to Jorge. "You're on the right baseline. Don't get trapped there. No five second counts and jump balls."

Jorge nodded.

"Stefano, you're on the left baseline. Meet the ball if they try to trap Gilson or double team the Killer."

"Right."

"That leaves you, Mitchell. You're running the baseline, looking for the opening."

Mitchell dipped his head. He couldn't breathe well enough to speak and waste air.

"What we want is the perfect shot," Turner said, "The hundred percent sure shot."

The buzzer sounded, calling the teams to the court for the final two minutes and twenty-one seconds.

The Friars had the ball. The last instructions to Jorge and Gilson as they left the bench were from McCarren. "Press them. Make them work to get the ball across mid court." The idea was to make Loyola-Detroit use as much time as they could. The more the Friars used during this attempt, the less they'd have the next time they got the ball. If they got the ball at all.

The tactic worked to a degree, Gilson and Jorge played the guard without the ball and forced the small forward to remain and handle the inbounds, rather than sprinting to the offensive end of the court. Touchette dribbled across the center line, clawed at by Jimmy Stefano who tried to scrape the ball away from him.

Tufts took a pass near the free throw circle and drove for the basket. The Killer got there in position and set himself to take the charge. Tufts pulled up. It was one and one time and Tufts didn't want to give the Killer a chance to make any free throws. Tufts turned and pass the ball to Carpenter who dribbled to his right and looked for Jeters. Mitchell played him close and Carpenter looked across court for Touchette.

McCarren looked at the scoreboard clock. It ticked to two minutes. And then to 1 : 59.

Jeters banged against Mitchell and freed himself. That quick first step separated them and he whirled toward the basket. The pass from Carpenter was on target and Jeters soared toward the basket. The Killer fell away from Tufts and stepped toward Jeters. At the last moment, he decided that it was better to let Jeters have the basket. The risk was that the Killer might be called for the foul. That way, Jeter might make the basket and have a chance for a free throw.

Jeters laid the ball in.

Down to a three point lead.

McCarren felt Turner tapping him on the shoulder. He turned to face him.

"Now," Turner said, "no matter how much time is left."

McCarren hesitated.

"Now," Jack Turner insisted.

McCarren stood and showed Jorge the clenched fist. Jorge saw the gesture and tossed the ball inbounds to Gilson and showed the clenched fist to him. As Gilson dribbled down the court, Jorge moved in front of him, making sure that Mitchell and the Killer and Stefano knew the delay game had started early. He got an indication from each of them.

McCarren checked the clock. 1: 48 remained in the game when Paul crossed the mid court line and stopped. The Killer saw Jorge's nod and jumped out and moved to just inside the center court line. He took the pass from Gilson and stood there with the ball on his hip. A loud booing began from the fans who knew the delay game was on.

Screw you, the Killer thought. And your mama too.

The Loyola-Detroit coach was on his feet. He waved at his center. Tufts, motioning that he was to leave the basket and guard the Killer.

When Tufts was two paces away from Robert, the Killer turned and tossed the ball to Gilson. Gilson dribbled past the five second mark and turned back toward mid court. Jorge stepped toward Paul and took the pass from him. After a look at Tufts, how close he was playing the Killer, Jorge whirled and faked a move toward the basket. Tufts sprinted toward the basket. That left the Killer unguarded again. Jorge passed the ball to the Killer and smiled.

Jorge looked at the clock. 1: 28 remained in the game.

The Killer stood with the ball on his hip and waited until Tufts ran toward him once more. Then he took two dribbles to his left and handed the ball to Paul Gilson. Gilson dribbled across the time line and, when Jimmy Stefano pushed away from Touchette, he passed the ball to him. Jimmy turned as if he intended to drive toward the basket. Then he bounced the ball to Gilson. Gilson moved back toward the center court line. As he circled the free throw line he took a look toward Mitchell Winters. Jeters was playing him close and tight. No opening there. He passed the ball to Jorge and got it back.

McCarren looked down at his hand. It was still clenched and the nails had imprinted a blood mark in his palm. 1: 13 remained.

The Loyola-Detroit coach was screaming in front of his bench. "Foul him. Foul him."

Gilson used his quickness to avoid Tuttle, the big guard, Carpenter chased him. Gilson avoided him and then realized that Carpenter had herded him toward Tuttle. In time, he changed hands with his dribble. Tuttle reached for the ball and caught an arm instead. The near official blew the whistle. Because Tuttle had been reaching for the ball, it wasn't ruled an intentional foul. It was one and one, rather than a two shot foul.

Gilson, usually a fine free throw shooter, made the first one. The margin moved to four point again. Paul took a deep breath, let it hiss away, and released the second shot. The ball barely cleared the front rim. It wobbled there and rolled away. Jeters grabbed the ball as soon as it dropped below the level of the rim.

"Press them," Turner shouted. "Press them."

One minute and one second remained when Loyola-Detroit crossed the mid court line. Three seconds later, unable to work the ball in close to Jeters, the big guard, Tuttle, put up a desperation shot from twenty-two feet. It hit nothing but net as it fell through.

The lead was two.

Jorge passed the ball over the baseline to Gilson. Paul used the full ten seconds to work the ball to the center court line and across it. The referee was moving beside him, his arm swinging as he counted the seconds. Gilson tossed the ball to Jorge and got it back. He dribbled behind the foul circle and to his left. He pulled up just inside the time line and stood there, bouncing the ball slowly. The point guard, Carpenter, lunged at him. Paul stepped around him and passed the ball to Jimmy Stefano. Jimmy faked a move down the baseline and turned and dribbled toward the mid court line.

No time to look at the clock. It was running in Jimmy's head. Thirty-nine seconds, thirty-eight. The small forward, Touchette, came in low, clawing at the ball. His shoulder rammed into Stefano. The whistle blew. The official held up one finger on each hand. One and one again.

McCarren was in front of his bench, yelling for the intentional foul. The official looked at McCarren and shook his head.

McCarren gave Jorge the signal to call the timeout. He didn't want to use the timeout. It gave Loyola-Detroit time to talk over their options and to plan their strategy for the final part of the game.

That was the risk. On the other hand, he wanted a breather for his players. He'd seen that Jimmy Stefano was tired. McCarren wanted him to take a few deep breaths before he stepped to the free throw line and took the first foul shot. He had to make that one or he wouldn't have a chance to make the second one.

Jimmy Stefano look at the clock. He'd been close. Thirty-seven seconds remained. He'd been off by one second. That was better. It gave the Friars even less time.

Mitchell Winters rinsed his mouth with water from the bottle that was passed to him. He spat it in a bucket. He stared at the scoreboard clock. He wasn't certain he could last another thirty-seven seconds.

Houston Tarr stood with an arm around Theold Brown's shoulders. He comforted him. At least they'd played. At least they'd been in the game.

Theold Brown wanted to cry. One whole side of him felt numb. He wasn't sure which was worse, the pain that came with the injury or the numbness from the shot Sarg had given him.

Jimmy Stefano tried to wipe his mind blank. He didn't want to think about the foul shots. He didn't want the pressure to sit on his shoulders.

The Killer leaned over Jimmy. "Both of these, baby. Got to have these."

"Relax," McCarren said. "Save your energy."

Turner leaned over Jimmy. His voice was hardly more than a whisper. "Close your eyes. See the first one drop through."

Jimmy closed his eyes. He could see the ball, leave his hands. It rolled over the rim and dropped in. He opened his eyes and grinned at Coach Turner.

"Listen up," McCarren said. "Here's how we play it. Jimmy makes both shots we're ahead by four. They get the ball and we play them loose. Just enough pressure to delay them, to make them spend time getting the ball into shooting range. No fouls. No fouls. If they make the shot we're still ahead by two. We don't want them to get a foul shot as well."

"If Jimmy makes one?" Turner said.

"The same. Only this time we make damned sure that there's no foul. A basket and a foul shot and we're tied."

The buzzer sounded. The teams headed back to the court. Turner sat next to McCarren. Their eyes met. Each of them realized they hadn't mentioned the third possibility. Jimmy might miss the first free throw. If that happened, if Loyola-Detroit got the rebound from that missed shot, then there was plenty of time for Loyola-Detroit to work for a good shot. If they made that shot the game would be tied and the pressure would be on the Mountaineers.

Thirty-seven seconds. The clock would not start until after Jimmy made the free throws and the ball was inbounded by the Friars. Or until Jimmy missed a free throw and the ball was rebounded.

Jimmy stood behind the foul circle and waited until the official offered him the ball before he stepped forward and put his toes against the free throw line. He took the ball and bounced it once. He put it up and saw the shot the way it had been in his mind. It barely cleared the front edge of the rim and went in.

Jimmy backed away from the line and turned and looked at the scoreboard. The point registered. The Mountaineers led by three points.

The Killer clapped his hands. "One more time, baby."

The official received the ball. He looked at the players and saw that they were in the rebounding positions down the lane. He offered the ball to Jimmy. Stefano stepped forward and planted his feet. One bounce. He shot. The second foul shot went through without touching the rim.

Up by four.

Tuttle, the shooting guard, scooped the ball and stepped out of bounds with it. Carpenter ran from side to side, trying to free himself. Neither Jorge nor Paul bothered to front Tuttle. They were hawking Carpenter. When the pass was made Jorge almost got to it. At the last moment, afraid that a foul might be called, he backed away.

"Yours," he yelled to Gilson. He stepped away and put himself between Tuttle and any possible pass from Carpenter. Paul played Carpenter close and forced him to work to reach mid court. It took eight seconds to get the ball over the center court line.

Twenty-nine seconds.

Carpenter stopped suddenly. He threw a long pass toward the basket. Jeters pushed away from Mitchell Winters and went for the ball. He caught it one step from the basket. In the air, soaring, he gripped the ball in one hand and slammed it through the basket.

The Mountaineer lead was two.

The Loyola-Detroit defense went into their version of the helter-skelter half-court trap. Jorge passed the ball in to Gilson. Gilson avoided a hand and dribbled behind his back, curling away from Carpenter. He crossed the center court line using all his quickness, and faked a pass to Jorge. Carpenter backed away. Paul saw Stefano breaking toward him from the left corner. He flipped the ball to him and got it back before Carpenter could step between them.

Paul turned and dribbled toward the Killer. Tufts was with him, just inside the center court line. He moved around the foul circle. Jorge had dropped into the right hand corner. Paul saw him break toward center court. The point guard, Tuttle, moved with him. Paul continued his dribble. He turned in toward the lane. At that moment Mitchell Winters, using almost the last of his energy, crossed the lane as if waiting for a pass. Jeters followed him under the basket and to the left side. Jimmy Stefano started it, running the baseline and stopped and sprinted for the left corner of the court.

Ten seconds. Eight seconds.

The clock ran in Gilson's head. He moved into the lane. For a time he almost stopped his dribble. That was when he saw the clear lane to the basket open to him.

Six seconds.

He said, "Oh, shit," and put on his final burst of speed. He heard Jeters shout something. Jeters was out of position and Mitchell Winters had stepped around him and screened him away.

Five seconds.

Paul drove the lane untouched. It's a fucking layup drill, Paul thought as he reached the basket, left his feet and rolled the ball off his fingertips and over the basket rim and in.

Up by four. Only four seconds remained on the clock. Paul turned and looked. Right on the head.

Loyola-Detroit was well schooled. An inbound pass and a long pass to get the ball across the center court line. Two seconds remained when Carpenter tried a shot from twenty-six feet. The basketball hit the backboard, the side of the rim and was rebounded by the Killer.

Tufts headed for the Killer to commit the foul. The Killer passed the ball to Gilson. Paul turned toward the center court line and raced away from Carpenter. He'd just crossed the mid court line when he was fouled by three players at the same time. The buzzer sounded. The game was over. The official didn't call the foul. He signaled that the game was over and walked away.

Paul clutched the ball and looked around. McCarren ran to him and grabbed him and hugged him. "That was the perfect shot," McCarren shouted. "Just perfect."

Loyola-Detroit players staggered from the court and sat on their bench, some openly crying, others with their heads covered by towels.

The Killer danced, his legs pumping, his hands held high. "This is it. This is the dance."

Jorge stood in the jump circle at center court. His head was back. He stared at the lights. Tears ran down his face. His lips moved but sound didn't come out.

Mitchell Winters sat on the court near the basket. He was exactly where he'd been when the buzzer sounded. His head was down.

Jimmy Stefano stood beside him. "Mitch, Mitch, you all right?"

Mitchell lifted his head. He blinked at Jimmy. "I hurt all over."

Mitchell wouldn't allow himself to be carried. Jimmy Stefano took one arm and the Killer the other and they led Mitchell through the passageway. Sarg ran ahead of then and unlocked the dressing room door.

Mitchell's body shook. "Cold," he said.

Sarg covered him with a blanket. "You'd better hurry unless you want to miss the award ceremony."

The Killer shook his head. "I want to be sure he's all-right."

Mitchell clutched the blanket to him and stretched out on the examining table. "Change the bandage. I want to be with the team when we get the trophy."

"No. You're going to the hospital. There's an ambulance on the way." Sarg leaned over Mitchell and peeled the tape and the bloody bandage from Mitchell's nose.

Jimmy sucked in his breath. He said, "Jesus, Mitch," and started to cry.

Mitchell blinked at him. "Is it that bad?"

"It's beautiful, my man," the Killer said. "It looks like a hamburger patty that ain't been cooked yet."

"Help me get him in the shower." Sarg peeled the uniform top over Mitchell's head.

Jimmy, choking back sobs, untied his basketball shoes and rolled the socks down.

Sarg lifted a metal folding chair and carried it into the shower. The Killer and Jimmy braced Mitchell between them and followed.

Sarg turned on the shower and adjusted the temperature. Mitchell sat under the warm spray.

"Check with you later," Jimmy said.

The Killer reached a hand under the spray and patted Mitchell's back. "You rest, my man."

After the award ceremony on court, when they returned to the dressing room, the chair was still under the shower. Sarg and Mitchell were gone.

The late dinner at the private room in the hotel was subdued. Even when the two cases of beer were brought in in a tub of ice, the mood didn't improve. Only later, when word was sent to McCarren that there was a message for him at the desk, when he returned and said, "That was Sarg. He says Mitchell is fine," did the real celebration begin.

McCarren drank a beer with the players. The talk around him was loud and animated. The hard play of the game was forgotten. Only the pleasure of the championship win remained.

McCarren stood. "Coach Turner and I are going to Memorial Hospital to see how Mitchell is. I want to be sure he can fly home with us tomorrow."

The Killer crossed to him. "Can I go with you, Coach?"

McCarren shook his head. "We probably won't be able to see him. The visit is really to talk to the doctors."

"All right, Coach, but if you see him …"

"Bet your life on it. I'll give him your best."

The Killer put a hand on McCarren's shoulder. "Some night, huh?"

"It's still sinking in," McCarren said. He started away and stopped. "Robert, let's save the rest of the celebration until we get back to North Carolina. No partying."

"My word on it."

"Get some rest."

"If I calm down enough."

McCarren and Jack Turner left. The players remained in the private dining room until they finished all the beer. Then they took the elevator to the floor where their rooms were.

❧ ❧ ❧

Robert and Jorge couldn't sleep. Several times they knocked on the door to the room McCarren shared with Jack Turner. There was no answer. They hadn't returned from the hospital yet.

Robert said, "Screw it. He said no partying. He didn't say we had to stay in the hotel. Right?"

Jorge nodded.

The Killer dumped his athletic travel bag on the carpet and found his warm-ups and his jogging shoes. He dressed in his jogging outfit. "How about one last run with the Killer?"

"A victory jog?"

"That's it."

After they were dressed, they moved up and down the hall and checked the rooms. Theold was asleep. He awoke before the Killer could back from the room. He sat on the edge of the bed and rubbed his back.

"Maybe you're not up to it," Jorge said.

"I can't feel any worse." Theold began dressing.

Jimmy Stefano was watching television. He hit the off switch. "Too bad we don't have the trophy to carry with us."

The championship trophy was being engraved and they'd receive it the following day before they left Albuquerque. The watches and rings would be shipped to them later.

Within a matter of minutes, the twelve of them entered the elevator and reached the lobby. Heads turned when they trooped through, past the desk and to the street.

"Now." Jorge and Robert led them. The other players paired up in a file behind them. The pace was sluggish at first. The tired muscles were stiff. After a mile or so, they were warm and perspiring. Robert stepped up the tempo.

The file remained orderly. There almost a military precision.

People stopped on the sidewalks and gawked at them. Many of them were returning to their hotels after dinner and drinks after the game. The green warmups identified the team. There were shouts and hellos and one woman stepped in the Killer's path and hugged him.

Cars slowed on the street. Horns were honked. A traffic snarl developed at one intersection. Windows rolled down and arms waved. Girlish voices poured toward them.

Jorge blew the girls kisses.

Three miles or so from the hotel, about the time the Killer was thinking about turning back, two Albuquerque police cruisers stopped them.

"What the hell...?" One of the young policemen stepped from the car and took a look at them. "You're the Mountaineers. What do you think you're doing"

"We couldn't sleep," the Killer said.

"So we thought we'd take a victory jog." Jorge said.

"I saw that game. If anyone deserves it, you boys do." The young policeman walked to the other cruiser and leaned on the window. When he returned he said, "We'll escort you."

The cruisers bracketed them, one leading and one following behind them, lights flashing as the team continued their jog. The crowds on the sidewalk grew, watching them pass.

"Who are you crazies?" one man in the crowd shouted at them.

"We're the Mountaineers," the Killer answered.

And then the entire team echoed his reply in a unified, joyful cry of triumph.

"We're The Mountaineers!"

Printed in Great Britain
by Amazon

85607983R00223